Publisher
Crime Time
7a King Henry's Walk
Islington
London N1 4NX
Fax: 020 7249 5940
e-mail: editor@crimetime.co.uk
Website:www.crimetime.co.uk

Distribution
Turnaround

Printing
Omnia, Glasgow

Editor
Barry Forshaw

Associate Editor
Judith Gray

Production editor
Paul Brazier

Film editor
Michael Carlson

TV & music editor
Charles Waring

Advertising
Philomena Muinzer
Tel: 0208 964 9106
Fax: 0208 881 5088

Subscriptions
£20 for 4 issues to
Crime Time Subscriptions,
18 Coleswood Road, Harpenden,
Herts AL5 1EQ
www.crimetime.co.uk

CRIME TIME ON THE WEB
Looking for that particular
review or feature? Visit our website on www.crimetime.co.uk –
up-dated weekly, and easier
than looking in your cherished
back issues!

2001 4

THE DESK

The theme of this issue of CT is US v. UK. So what does that mean? We're all aware of the politicians who make capital from the latent and not so latent xenophobia of many Brits, and there are the Americans who will tell you that they are made to feel a certain cultural inferiority by people in this country. (Just ask CT's Michael Carlson, a colonial who has re-settled on these shores.) But, of course, this doesn't apply to *Crime Time* readers, does it? After all, most of us enjoy the best in the genre from both sides of the Atlantic, don't we? Well, this issue is a chance to test your prejudices, as we set the best of British against US gold.

The theme for CT 25 is sex. We did, in fact, do a sex and violence issue back in the days when we had a magazine rather than a paperback format, but it struck me that we had rather squandered those themes, and I thought there was more than enough reason to revisit those twin shibboleths of our moral guardians – look out for a violence issue not too far down the line.

Mark Timlin's recent column on the abrasive style of long-time CT reviewer Gerald Houghton has a certain poignancy. After Mark had written the column, Gerald died unexpectedly (and at a tragically young age). Of course, there are some writers who will not shed a tear for this most unflinching of crime critics (certainly, as editor, I took more flak from outraged writers for his reviews than for those of any other reviewer, but I think Mark spoke for many when he said that Gerald was the person he turned to first). Gerald will be missed – but we have several reviewers on the staff who will cast a similarly cold eye over the genre.

Mike Ashley fans will be remarking on the absence of his *Collecting Crime* column for yet another issue – Mike has a strange idea that his own efforts as an editor of crime anthologies require some attention, an idea I can't seem to disabuse him of. Nevertheless, he'll be back next issue with an erotically-themed column. And now I've got to start editing all this erotica... a dirty job, but some-one's got to do it.

Barry Forshaw

OVER-VIOLENT, OVER-WRITTEN AND OVER HERE:

The Narrowing Divide in American and British Crime Fiction

Michael Carlson

Six years ago, in this very magazine, I wrote a brief piece prompted by the swirl of controversy around P. D. James' proclamation, on late-night BBC World Service radio, that modern crime fiction, set in "the worst inner city area" was devoid of "moral choice" because it provided the reader with no contrast between "good and evil". James' words sparked a tempest in a baroness' teapot. As I said at the time: "It did seem strange to be having this row fifty years after Raymond Chandler wrote his famous essay praising Dashiell Hammett for getting murder out of the parlour." I also pointed out that James' jeremiad recalled George Orwell's essay *The Decline Of English Murder* written more than half a century earlier, which lamented the arrival of commonplace violence in British crime fiction, a decline he attributed to 'Yank mags', the American pulp magazines which came to this country after crossing the Atlantic as ship's ballast.

But that was then and here we are still fascinated by the whole USA v UK thing. It was the topic of a major panel at last summer's Crime Scene. Recently, when *Shots* magazine announced its intention of concentrating on British fiction, I went back through the reviews section (which, admittedly, I had edited) and pointed out that the term 'American' was used by many of the reviewers as a sort of all-purpose and unthinking pejorative, much the way British film reviewers use the word 'Hollywood'. P. D. James' argument recalled previous centuries' critical debate over which topics were fit and proper for serious literature. As popular literature reached larger and larger audiences, and as 'serious' literature began to consider some of that audience as worthy topics for fiction, this debate can now be seen in terms of class. James' own venture into the Holland Park class war reinforced, unwittingly, the basic and most obvious difference between British and American crime fiction, the one which is still encompassed by reference to 'cosy' or 'parlour' mysteries in Britain and 'hardboiled' fiction in America. Though many would argue, correctly, that Britain has moved on from the cosy days, one need only see the British term 'tec' used to describe crime fiction to realise that its parameters are still limited. The 'tec' plays a specific role from a specific place in society. And society is a place of moral values, which need to be passed down from the top to the lumpen proletariat.

The classic whodunit was, in essence, less concerned with the solving of a puzzle than a reaffirmation of that existing social order. The British, more concerned than most people with keeping everything in its place, found this especially satisfying. In this world, crime is an aberration within an otherwise placid and pleasant society. When the crime is solved, usually by an amateur from the upper reaches of that society, superior in his work to the mere professionals, the world returns to its green and pleasant normality. Order is restored and God Save the Queen. It was the movement away from this paradigm that so bothered James. Granted, her hero is himself a professional, but like so many of the policemen in Britain, he bears all the affectations of the upper-class amateur (Dalgleish's poetry, Morse's opera). DCI Peter Wimsey, as it were. And, worst of all, she just won't let it rest! In an interview in the *Financial Times* this March, the Baroness opined it "very curious that these critics, usually young men, think the middle classes are not capable of wickedness..." She worried about her poet detective, ideally suited for the role of observer, losing his soul to such wickedness. And she confirmed that although she could "imagine a corrupt policeman... I like to generate some order out of the dis-

order... some kind of justice in my books."

If British detective fiction has been slow to move away from this model, the recognition that this order, if not a fantasy, has been crumbling, has been a staple of the best British spy fiction. What, after all, is the message of Len Deighton's Harry Palmer? In John Le Carré, the decline of England's green and pleasant order was expressed in its stylistic peak. Novels like *The Honourable Schoolboy* portrayed the unreality of deep seated class structure which underpinned every assumption behind the country's spy activity. The assumptions are proved flawed, if not false, in prose as intricately layered as the structure itself. In America, the sense of a pre-ordained class structure was contrary to all the myths of opportunity and advancement. The American upper class was at the same time ignored and aspirational. The willingness of the country to let money talk in terms of status meant society was in flux. Thus, in America, the early parlour style mysteries were basically puzzles, but little more, and soon gave way to a style of detective fiction more involved with the people who actually committed crimes. It accepted that society was corrupt, often ugly, and featured violence as an everyday means to an end. Crimes might or might not be solved. When solved, the guilty might or might not get punished. The rich, powerful or connected were more likely to get away with things. Even if they didn't, nothing changed. Society didn't revert to some sort of benign order, it continued on in its corruption. This was expressed in prose that, at its best, reflected the harshness of that world, for example, in the straightforward rhythms of Hammett, or in the cynical and disarmingly lush metaphors of Chandler, presenting an irony which has always made him a favourite in Britain. It is significant, and I believe no coincidence, that the two major stylistic innovators in crime writing in the past quarter century, George V. Higgins and James Ellroy, both deal directly with the corruption behind the world of power.

The debate, if not rages, at least stutters on, in the best upper-class fashion, revealing perhaps more about our own mis-, pre- and non-immaculate conceptions than anything earthshaking about good fiction. Which after all should both transcend borders and illuminate what is within them. Still, that basic divide between Britain and America does persist along those same definitions. This remains true even though more and more writers adopt styles from the other side of the pond. Of course Orwell's essay was prompted not so much by the Yank mags themselves, but by James Hadley Chase's appropriation of their style. Chase's reworking of William Faulkner's *Sanctuary* as *No Orchids for Miss Blandish* frightened Orwell to the core. Murders, he felt, should conform to the three Ps: be committed by the professional classes (whom I would argue are the only ones with a hint of upward mobility), with poison, and for reasons of passion (the spirit which works against that mobility). Passion was so far from the provenance of the stiff-upper-lipped Englishman that murder would seem a reasonable response to it (see *What Makes the British Hardman Hard?* elsewhere in this issue). The move to a more American attitude which James decried may have been less the result of literary influence and more a reaction to Britain's subjection to sixteen years of Thatcherism. The return to 'Victorian values' was an assault on the post-war attempt to reorder British society to extend some equality to all classes. Its free market was itself based on an American-style myth of aspirationalism, but without the accompanying promise of upward mobility which drives those markets. Like so many ideas imported from the States, once it has been watered down, made more 'civilised' or 'palatable', it has also had its essence removed. On the political level, the continuation of the same ethos by New Labour has produced a society in which everything, literally, is for sale, but only to certain people. It becomes harder and harder to portray its social order as benign.

The best reaction to those changes has come from British writers seeking out an old fashioned order amidst the crumbling fabric of society. For Inspector Rebus, the antithesis of Morse, or for John Harvey's Resnick, the changes for the worse in society are reflected by similar changes within their police departments, forcing them to try to adapt to a whole new attitude of policing, and also in their personal lives, forcing them to focus on the place of the individual in a less caring society. Writers trying to plop the American style dick into these sceptred isles have had less success. Their prose style often seems derivative in the extreme, and the attempt to turn Walthamstow High Street into Mulholland Drive is doomed even before the Victoria Line train gets there. Similarly, in America there have been significant moves toward a more British style. Not that it ever disappeared. As mentioned above, the parlour mystery in America was always more self-consciously a puzzle, even when it strove to imitate the British class structure with faux-artisto heroes. Ellery Queen, the seemingly misplaced American lord whose father is a police inspector, may be the best example of that. The recent renaissance of women writers, particularly featuring women detectives (or forensic examiners or whatever) have turned the genre upside down, often postulating a society which is, indeed, perfectable. Order triumphs over chaos, ceramic mugs hold endless cups of 'steaming' tea or coffee, and pets solve crimes which humans can't. Bridget Jones, Private Eye? Meanwhile the hardboiled school faces the twin cul-de-sacs of wish-fulfilment sensitive lifestyle writing (detective echoes author's tastes in everything from beer to cable TV channels) and Chandler ad absurdum prose ("his face crinkled like a chiffon-pink French fry swimming in a deep-fryer full of ebony oil"), self-parody as florid as General Sternwood's greenhouse. Perhaps the hardboiled hero is out of place in a world whose villains sit in huge offices with computerised switchboards which put you on hold with muzak playing. In a country where you can steal a presidency, what effect can the lonely PI have? Would Philip Marlowe be demonstrating against corporate control? Could you have a politically correct Sam Spade? Mothers Against Drunk Driving would make it impossible for him to down more than a single shot of bourbon.

The whole US v UK argument may be redundant if we are now living in a post-hardboiled America. On both sides of the Atlantic, the most telling phenomenon may be the relentless rise of the historical mystery. By heading for the past, one can guarantee a visit to a society in which some sort of order is maintained, and one in which the decline of contemporary order is not a factor. At the same time, the continuing popularity of true crime books and serial killer fictions suggests that, rather than a concern with either the ordered or corrupt society, growing numbers of readers may be titillated by signs of chaos within their cultures and be more concerned with using their reading to escape from it into a more peaceful and distant, almost fantasy, setting. But hasn't that always been the case? Violent hardboiled fiction provided a cathartic escapism from a violent culture. Today, television news uses shock and scare tactics to attract viewers and keep them indoors watching more TV, and serves as the visual equivalent of the film noir of Chandler and Orwell's era. But film noir was a minority pursuit, and TV news is in everybody's face. The appeal of escapism may be a given, but in the past Britain had no culture of violence from which escape was needed. So, in a sense, P. D. James may have been right, albeit for the wrong reasons. Society has changed, and fiction follows. Trying to maintain the traditional distinction between British cosy and American hardboiled becomes less and less sensible as the societies grow more and more similar. Britain may not yet embrace fatal violence the way America does, but it is moving that way. The murders of drug dealers and the ambushing of burglars have a distinctly American ring to them. Even royal handmaidens use cricket bats and knives to dispatch their lovers, and plead innocence on the grounds of Oprah-style abuse.

Come back to the castle's mean corridors, Baroness James, all is forgiven.

US OR THEM?

US vs UK Crime Writing

Eddie Duggan

The American author Edgar Allan Poe (1809-1849) more or less invented the crime genre, inasmuch as he established the main literary devices and themes in a handful of short stories published between 1841 and 1845. While there may be scope for some debate – some critics might argue that the roots of crime writing are European and can be found in the *Mémoires* (1828) attributed to Eugène Vidocq, first director of the French detective agency *Le Sûreté*, or in William Godwin's *Caleb Williams* (1794), or in passages in Voltaire's *Zadig* (1747), or in the seventeenth-century pamphlets later collected as *The Newgate Calendar*; while others may try to push the origins of crime writing back to biblical origins, citing Daniel stories such as Bel and the Dragon or Susanna and the Elders as the first detective stories – it is generally accepted that Poe's three Dupin stories, together with *The Goldbug* and *Thou Art the Man*, constitute a significant milestone in the history of the form. Poe's *The Murders in the Rue Morgue* (1841) establishes the conventions of the locked room mystery. *The Mystery of Marie Roget* (1842) produces a detective with the mental faculty to solve a mystery from known facts, without the need to leave his armchair. *The Goldbug*

(1843) is concerned with ciphers and code breaking. *Thou Art the Man* (1844) sets up the basic devices of the least-likely-suspect story, while *The Purloined Letter* (1845) deals with the theme of concealment-as-display.

What is interesting is the fact that Poe chose to set the stories featuring the amateur sleuth Auguste Dupin in Paris, rather than in his native America. It may be because Paris was the location of the detective agency *Le Sûreté,* established in 1812, and, as such, appeared to offer a more appropriate setting for Poe's tales of ratiocination than an American location. The influence of Poe's work can be seen in subsequent developments, most notably in Arthur Conan Doyle's Sherlock Holmes, introduced in *A Study in Scarlet* in the 1887 edition of *Beeton's Christmas Annual.* Doyle (1859-1930) apparently based the character of Holmes somewhat on Dr Joseph Bell, under whom he studied medicine at Edinburgh University, drawing in particular upon Bell's skill in making inferences (not 'deductions') about patients from careful observation. As Julian Symons put it (*Portrait of an Artist: Conan Doyle*, 1979): "As a new case was brought into the room he would say: 'This man is a left-handed cobbler', and then explain: 'You'll observe, gentlemen, the worn places on the corduroy breeches where a cobbler rests his lapstone? The right-hand side, you'll note, is far more worn than the left. He uses his left hand for hammering the leather.'" Doyle also appears to draw upon the conventions established in Poe's Dupin stories, as well as on Emile Gaboriau's Inspector Lecoq. Sherlock Holmes, consulting detective, as a 'professional amateur' is something of a compromise between the amateur, Dupin, and the professional, Lecoq. Doyle also took the device of the 'idiot friend as narrator' from Poe, so Dr Watson, the story-telling sidekick to the world's most famous fictional detective, is based upon Dupin's anonymous narrating companion who, like Watson (and, presumably, at least one of Dr Bell's students) is frequently amazed as 'deductions' based upon careful observation are explained.

While Doyle's Sherlock Holmes stories are laced with a good deal of hokum – for example, the Indian swamp adder in *The Speckled Band*, Holmes's ability to tell a man's age from an analysis of his handwriting in *The Reigate Puzzle*, his ability to tell a cyclist's direction of travel from an examination of the tyre tracks in *The Adventure of the Priory School*, or his knowledge of the Japanese system of wrestling known as 'baritsu' which, as he reveals in *The Empty House*, saved him from death at the hands of Moriarty – they served to establish the series form, as opposed to the serial. The fifty-six Holmes stories appeared as self-contained episodes in *The Strand* magazine between 1891 and 1927. It is surprising to think that Doyle, whom we associate with the nineteenth century, was contemporary with the American hardboiled school, which emerged from the so-called 'pulp' magazines in the 1920s. While prohibition, gang-

sterism, all-pervading corruption and the Depression provided the conditions which produced the so-called 'hardboiled school' in American popular fiction, by the late 1920s Doyle (who had tried to kill off Holmes in a struggle with Moriarty at the Reichenbach Falls in 1893 but resurrected him in 1903) was away with the fairies as he devoted more of his energy to spiritualism.

The period between the 1914-1918 war and the war of 1939-1945 is known, as far as crime writing is concerned, as 'The Golden Age', a usage coined by critic Howard Haycraft. Why the term should be applied to an era which produced sleuths in the shape of little old ladies, affected Belgians and mannered toffs is indicative of an age in which crime fiction is more of a game than a literary genre, formalised to the extent that some exponents on both side of the Atlantic drew up 'rules', apparently without any sense of irony. Ronald Knox (1888-1957) drafted 'ten commandments' in the form of *A Detective Story Decalogue* (1929), which not only set out the rules of fair play that would allow the reader an reasonable chance of solving the mystery, but also codified the era's key ideological aspects pertaining to criminality. For example: "The criminal must be someone mentioned in the early part of the story, but must not be anyone whose thoughts the reader has been allowed to follow", and "The detective must not himself commit the crime", and, bizarrely, "No Chinaman must figure in the story". At the same time, the American author S. S. Van Dine drew up *Twenty Rules for Writing Detective Stories*, a credo along similar lines to Knox's dicta.

Agatha Christie (1890-1976), high

priestess of the Golden Age, usually adhered to the spirit if not the letter of the rules of fair play, though there are a couple of notable exceptions in which she was deemed to have unfairly tricked the reader. Christie's forte was the least likely suspect, and her plots were built upon an edifice of carefully placed clues for the reader to spot. The typical setting was the English country house, which provided the ideal setting in which to place a restricted group of characters, one of whom would be revealed to be the perpetrator of the foul deed. Christie's debut novel, *The Mysterious Affair at Styles* (1920), introduced Hercule Poirot, a retired Belgian detective who made a career of providing least-likely-suspect solutions to Christie's plots. Poirot is something of an oddity, inasmuch as he is a short, limping foreigner with a head shaped like an egg, and with as many eccentricities as a dog has fleas. Christie gave Poirot a Watson in the form of Captain Hastings. This figure was a variation on a type: the eccentric, who is also familiar in the form of the affected toff. Margery Allingham (1899-1982) called hers Albert Campion, while Dorothy L. Sayers' (1893-1957) affected toff was dubbed Lord Peter Wimsey. While this type of fiction is still immensely popular, many find it unpickupable due to its insufferable smugness. The relationship of this form of crime writing to the establishment is acknowledged in the fact that both Christie and Sayers were honoured with the title of dame.

Perhaps the least pleasant aspects of the 'country house' (or 'cosy', as it is called in North America) are amplified when this most stereotypically English form is exported. Perhaps the most insufferable and smug of all the 'cosy' detectives is S. S. Van Dine's Philo Vance, an American version of the affected toff. (Van Dine is a pseudonym of the art critic Willard Huntingdon Wright, 1888-1939). While the American humorist Ogden Nash took a gentle dig at the character with the phrase 'Philo Vance needs a kick in the pance', Dashiell Hammett was more direct in his criticism of Van Dine. Reviewing the first Vance novel, *The Benson Murder Case*, for the *Saturday Review of Literature* in 1927, Hammett thought: "This Philo Vance is in the Sherlock Holmes tradition and his conversational manner is that of a high school girl who has been studying the foreign words and phrases in the back of her dictionary. He is a bore when he discusses art and philosophy, but when he switches to criminal psychology he is delightful. There is a theory that anyone who talks enough on any subject must, if only by chance, finally say something not altogether incorrect. Vance disproves this theory; he manages always, and usually ridiculously, to be wrong. His exposition of the technique employed by a gentleman shooting another gentleman who sits six feet in front of him deserves a place in a *How to Be a Detective by Mail* course."

British crime writers – Christie, Sayers, Marsh, et al. – sought to delineate an ordered world in which the criminal aberration was no more than a pleasing puzzle, an intellectual diversion for the genteel reader. Americans strove to produce something similar, until the quintessentially American form, hardboiled crime fiction, evolved in the pages of the pulp magazines, most notably *Black Mask*. Hardboiled writing typically offers the figure of the loner, an isolated individual at odds with society and the urban landscape in which he is located, engaged in some sort of conflict. Carroll John Daly (1889-1958) has the distinction of creating the first hardboiled hero, the nameless narrator of *The False Burton Combs* in *Black Mask* in 1922. Daly went on to become one of *Black Mask's* most popular authors, with stories featuring tough detective-style protagonists like Terry Mack and Race Williams in *Black Mask* and Stan 'Satan' Hall in *Detective Fiction Weekly*. Daly was not most accomplished stylist writing for *Black Mask*. William F. Nolan put it bluntly in his study of the magazine: "[Daly's] writing was impossibly crude, the plotting laboured and ridiculous, and Race Williams emerged as a swaggering illiterate with the emotional stability of a gun-crazed vigilante" (Nolan, *The Black Mask Boys* 1985).

More accomplished was former detective turned pulpster, Dashiell Hammett (1894-1961). Hammett set the standard for hardboiled writing; even today, blurb writers seek to heap accolades on contemporary crime writers by declaring them 'the new Hammett'. Raymond Chandler (1888-1959) acknowledged Hammett's contribution in his celebrated essay, *The Simple Art of Murder* (1944). Contrasting Hammett's realism with the mannerism of the country-house genre, Chandler asserted: "Hammett gave murder back to the kind of people that commit it for reasons, not just to provide a corpse; and with the means at hand, not with hand-wrought duelling pistols, curare and tropical fish. He put these people down on paper as they are, and he made them talk and think in the language they customarily used [...] He had style, but his audience didn't know it because it was in a language not

supposed to be capable of such refinements." Hammett's influence reaches down through the years. Chandler's own Philip Marlowe, although steeped in sentiment, is deeply indebted to Hammett's Sam Spade, while Hammett's nameless detective, The Continental Op, provides the model for Bill Pronzini's Nameless Detective.

Although the hardboiled genre is as undisputedly American as jazz, British writers have sought to take on some aspects of the form. Whether the wise-cracking tough guy sounds as convincing behind the wheel of a Cortina Mk I while cruising the streets of a London suburb may be a matter of opinion, although several critics have found the British interpretation of this form of popular literature to be particularly distasteful. In his 1944 essay, *Raffles and Miss Blandish*, George Orwell expressed dismay at the popularity of James Hadley Chase's 1939 novel *No Orchids for Miss Blandish* and the fact it bore the influence of American language and morality, and offered 'no gentlemen and no taboos'. A generation later, Richard Hoggart condemned the influence of American popular culture in the form of milk bars and music, as well as magazines, in his 1958 critique of popular culture, *The Uses of Literacy*. However, hardboiled crime writing has developed a particularly British strain. One of the most engaging examples of contemporary British hardboiled writing can be found in Mark Timlin's (b. 1944) Nick Sharman stories. Set in south London's Tulse Hill, ex-cop Sharman operates as a private investigator, who is both geographically and ideologically a far cry from Chandler's Marlowe. The Sharman stories were adapted for a short television series, shown on ITV in 1996.

A darker British writer is the late Derek Raymond (pseudonym of Robin Cook, 1931-1995), whose uncompromising 'Factory' novels, featuring a nameless detective sergeant, will not be to every taste. While Julian Symons found them 'repulsive and preposterous', if one does not expect an adherence to some police procedural decalogue, Raymond's *oeuvre* is perhaps the most disturbing of any British crime writer. More humorous than Raymond, though similarly not to every taste, is Irvine Welsh, whose *Filth* provides a darkly comic crime novel. *Filth* tells the story of Detective Sergeant Bruce Robertson's relationship problems, his job problems, and his health problems, the latter caused by a tape worm. There are plenty of other contemporary British writers who are producing interesting work (Nicholas Blincoe and Denise Danks among them) but space constraints do not allow further discussion.

The best current American writers include George Pelecanos (b. 1957), whose series character, Nick Stefanos, has appeared in three novels as well as occasional cameo appearances in the so-called *Washington Quartet*, four linked novels spanning the period from the 1930s to the present. Popular music and relationships provide the themes around which Pelecanos weaves his plots, with a garnish of booze, recreational chemicals and violence. James Ellroy (b. 1948) has sought to repopulate Chandler's LA with his own cast of characters, such as Lloyd Hopkins in the *LA Noir* trilogy, and yet more corrupt cops in the so-called *LA Quartet*, spanning the 1940s and 1950s. The quartet concludes with *White Jazz*, a novel wrought from language as innovative for the contemporary reader as the clipped economy of the first wave of hardboiled writing must have been for readers in the 1920s. Ellroy himself appears to be haunted by a single event in his childhood – his mother's murder – to the extent that he sought to investigate the murder himself, in his emblematically entitled work of non-fiction, *My Dark Places*. There are of course other interesting contemporary American writers (e.g. Walter Mosley, Joe Lansdale, et al.) but no space to discuss them here. The difference between the American writers and British authors we have deliberated upon is that the American writing appears to be able to move between the past and the present, while the work of their British counterparts is set very much in the here-and-now. For Woody Haut, "Pelecanos uses the past to explain the present", while in "Ellroy's world [...] the past has cursed the present" (*Neon Noir*, 1999).

While the origins of crime fiction may be American, and its most significant development – hardboiled writing – is also American, the strength of the form on both sides of the Atlantic is that it continues to develop and explore a range of issues. For the American authors discussed above, these tend to relate to post-war American masculinity, whether cast from the obsessions of the tortured psyche of the child of a murder victim, now grown to adulthood, or of the cultural interstices of ethnicity, gender and class straddled by a third generation immigrant. The British exponents of the form considered above also explore the theme of masculinity albeit in differing ways, all of which provide the sensitive reader with ample food for thought, and the fan of contemporary crime writing with plenty of page-turning reading.

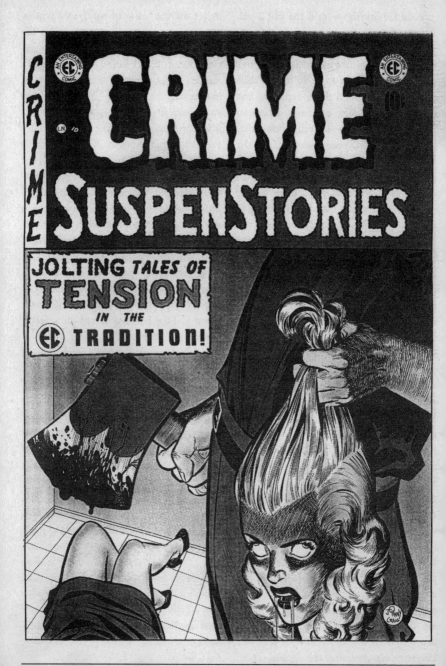

THE GREAT EC CRIME COVERS

Barry Forshaw

As a child, I was beguiled by most of the superhero comics that were common currency of the day, and I was perfectly happy for my universe to be that of Superman and Batman. (As editor of CT, I'm glad to see the latter figure remains popular with CT readers: he is, after all, *pace* Sherlock Holmes, The World's Greatest Detective). Then, one day, I was handed an EC comic – and at a stroke I realised how narrow had been the parameters of the comics I'd read. The first line that took my eye read: "The old man sat amidst unremoved human excrement, moaning a woman's name…" What followed was a tale rich in unsettling characterisation, plotted with a masterly skill and drawn with a sophistication that left most other comics standing. It was to be a while before I realised that the writer of most of these EC *contes cruelles* was Al Feldstein (with plotting aid from the publisher, William M. Gaines). EC comics clearly aimed their material at a more sophisticated reader, and it's hardly surprising that their unflinching treatment of violence soon had them banned in both the United States and this country. The *Crime*

SuspensStories (note the dropped 'e') line was a particular gem of the company, and we plan to bring you the occasional cover in an attempt to recreate the splendours of those days. The underwater strangulation/drowning was drawn by Al Feldstein, originally an illustrator, but later too valuable as writer and editor to exercise this function. The severed head/axe cover was drawn by the mainstay of *Crime SuspensStories* (and sometime editor) Johnny Craig. This notorious cover was cited by the Kefauver committee in the US Senate in the nannyish drive to destroy crime and horror comics. When publisher Bill Gaines was confronted about the lack of taste displayed in the cover, he unwisely tried to suggest that because the severed neck is not visible on either the torso or the head, there is some taste displayed here – at least, taste appropriate for a crime comic. Needless to say, this reasoning cut no ice whatsoever, and soon the glorious days of the title with its highly ingenious yarns (and their distinguishing O'Henry-style twist endings) were no more. But we intend to visit them occasionally in these pages.

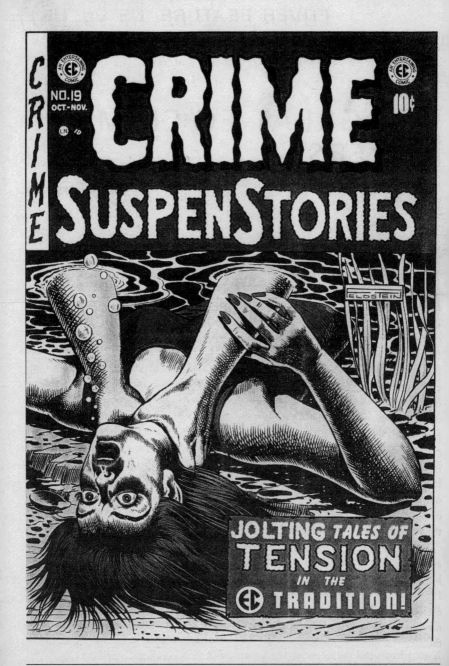

US V UK

Generalisations are easy, but they are also sloppy. And they can be horribly destructive. One of the worst at the moment is that British crime writing is dull, repetitive and 'middle class', whereas novels from America are packed with zing and energy, social realism and excitement. As a British crime writer, all I can say to that is a delicate, middle-class 'bollocks'.

Natasha Cooper

Realistic American crime writing will always be more dramatic than realistic British crime writing in the sense that crime in America is more dramatic: American police are routinely armed; American citizens own guns; some states use the death penalty. With lives at stake, tension rises and so do thrills. So few householders are armed in Great Britain that when one shoots an intruder, it is such a rare event that the outcry echoes for years. Fewer guns do not, however, mean less crime. As we all know, there is a frightening amount of physical and emotional brutality in the UK and therefore a continuing need for crime writers to make sense of the victims' suffering and to deal with the fears it arouses in all of us.

Any sub-genre will begin to seem stale and repetitive when it has been over-used, but that is not confined to any one country. I find myself impatient now with new novels about child abuse, wherever they originate. My irritation has nothing to do with the reality of what abusive adults do to children, which must appal everyone who knows anything about it, but because it has lost its force in fiction. Familiarity breeds not contempt but compassion-fatigue – and with it a dilution of the kind of shock necessary to give that oh-so-desirable energy to crime fiction. A certain degree of unfamiliarity helps to energise readers, which may be another reason why American crime writing appeals so much here and British writing there. (Were that not the case, it would be hard to understand the number of English village mysteries full of unlikely aristocrats that are still coming out of the States.) As so often in the writing game, there is a tightrope to be walked. If the world you offer readers is too like their own, you risk boring them witless. Who wants to read about the life they're already living – unless what you have to say provides startling insights or clues to getting more out of it? On the other hand, if your fictional world is too far removed from readers' experience and interests you risk alienating them.

Lindsey Davis is one of the experts at dancing along this particular high wire. Her version of ancient Rome is the product of much knowledge and careful research. It is also full of dilatory builders, money troubles, tedious employers and all the rest of the familiar burdens that let readers identify with Falco while enjoying the strangeness of another time. Davis' choice of the first century AD also makes a portrayal of the class system much less provocative than it seems in so many novels set in contemporary Britain. Those who inveigh against middle-class novels appear to believe that they do not address the realities of life. But there is no less reality about crime for those who have jobs, pensions and comfortable houses, and no less suffering either. Middle-class victims bleed like any other and a middle-class murderer is as guilty as one who has been living on benefit or drug-dealing in a sink estate. It would be insulting and ridiculous to suggest that there are no middle-class criminals. Violence is violence wherever it occurs, just as conning money out of individuals, companies or the state is theft, whether it is perpetrated by small-time cowboy builders or on a huge scale by financial service fraudsters.

There are, of course, moral and social injustices that are outside the remit of the law. And most of the really interesting novels, middle-class or otherwise, British or American, address them in one way or another. Paul Johnston's way of tackling the questions of class, justice and political exploitation is particularly interesting. He has chosen the late 2020s as the setting for his grimly brilliant dystopian novels. His class system is rigid but based on rules that are gratifyingly different from those we know. In his latest, *The House of Dust*, he takes Quintilian Dalrymple from the

independent city state of Edinburgh to New Oxford, anchoring the ghastly future to what we know with references to real events and ideas from the last few decades. In this chilling novel, he shows how the good intentions of intelligent thinkers can, when imposed by force, be as monstrously destructive as the selfish greed of organised crime gangs, and that the only bulwark against such damage is the courage and determination of free individuals. These are big themes, tackled in a refreshingly unpompous way.

Stephen Booth is a writer who addresses his concerns from almost the opposite pole. His second novel, *Dancing with the Virgins*, is rooted in tradition and deals with the agony of the countryside. With farmers facing ruin and despair as their incomes fall way below subsistence level, something has to give: their integrity, their spirit, or their lives. In this novel all three are at risk, against a backdrop of some of the most beautiful scenery in the British Isles. The plot is darkened still further by Booth's take on the way city folk misunderstand and abuse both the land and the individuals who work it. Davis, Johnston and Booth are only three of the large number of British writers who look at crime – and therefore the whole of life – from unexpected angles and so offer readers a new way of seeing their own lives. Some terrific work is coming out of the US, but so it is from the UK. There is a challenge – to use the world readers know in ways that are fresh enough to arouse curiosity, intelligent enough to provoke new ideas, and dramatic enough to generate real excitement – but there doesn't have to be a competition, chauvinistic or the reverse.

bfi

NFT

CRIME SCENE 2001

12-15 July
Criminal Fiction and Film Exposed

The annual festival of crime film and
literature this year includes:
● A special focus on Agatha Christie
● A whole host of crimewriters including
Jake Arnott, Iain Sinclair, Martina Cole,
John Connolly, Lindsey Davis.
● Live events and panel discussions
www.bfi.org.uk/crimescene

Sponsored by

Media partners

LBC
1152AM

NEWS
DIRECT 97.3

●●●
National Film Theatre South Bank Waterloo London SE1   Box Office: 020 7928 3232

US vs. UK: NOTES FROM UNDERGROUND

Carol Anne Davis

"We're producing a US versus UK issue. Any thoughts?" asked the editor of *Crime Time*.

"I was on the British versus American noir panel at Dead on Deansgate. I could look out my notes for you," I said.

"Just send me a thousand words on the subject by May," he replied then promptly stopped answering his phone.

Three hair-tearing days and one visit to the skip later I had to admit that I'd lost the aforesaid notes so this article is a desperate feat of invention and memory.

American versus British noir. What can you say? It's a panel title coined by a conference organiser in ten seconds – but one that ensures the panellists spend the next week in therapy. Even finding a definition for noir makes most writers leave home or hook themselves up to an absinthe drip. Luckily I found a brilliant book on the subject – *Noir Fiction* by Paul Duncan – and happily quoted from it throughout panel hour. The entire hour was about worldwide noir as we very quickly concluded that it was too hard to find clear differences between dark novels from the United Kingdom and dark novels from the United States. Hell, it was early on a Sunday morning, plus our chairperson had smoked sixty cigarettes the night before and was in danger of coughing up a lung. The consensus was that American noir was similar to British noir and that American cosies were similar to British cosies. In other words, nationality was secondary to whether you lived life on the urban road or in the village street. That's probably why Paul's impressively detailed book is subtitled 'Dark Highways' rather than 'Leafy Lanes'.

Paul's chapter headings on the subject read like a description of a writer's life: Depression, Paranoia, Apathy. You just hope he'll do a follow-up with chapters such as *Help, My Book's Been Edited b y A Dyslexic Embryo* and *Where's My Royalties? The Postman Hasn't Rung Twice*. Paul says that noir requires emotional commitment from the reader. Personally, I'd settle for a tenner. The French coined the term *roman noir* ('black novel') and the English took up the theme in the eighteenth century with Gothic texts. The Russians, notably Dostoyevsky, started writing their tales of angst in the same time period. I'm not sure when our American friends joined in. Women haven't featured significantly in either American or British noir. Apparently we lack the sustained anger and frustration. This is strange because most of us want to kill the advertiser each time we see a menstruating woman skating past in a white mini-dress. Dorothy Parker is one of the rare American female names associated with dark writing, though her noir poems about suicide and desertion often have a distinctly comic edge. Mary Shelley is probably the best known British female Gothic novelist. She wrote *Frankenstein* in a very few hours as part of a bet to write the scariest story. Today's romantic writers do the exact same thing.

Of the British male writers, Gerald Kersh (1911-1968) struggled for years but eventually became highly paid. He wrote about the hell of living and working in Soho. Those of us who go there to buy a dirty mag think it's okay. Kersh dared to write part of his narrative from the murderer's point of view, a brave departure then – and still a rarity in our modern police procedural days. Across the pond, Cornell Woolrich was both smiled upon for his overblown prose and respected for his ability to ensnare the reader's emotions. He wrote about obsessive love and loss and predestination, and did so whilst living in a hotel room. Knowing his luck, it was probably the Bates Motel. Today's noir writers continue to illuminate the shadowy corners of many lives. My first two novels *Shrouded* and *Safe As Houses* showed how killers are formed during abused childhoods. The third, *Noise Abatement*, looked at how unwanted sound can lead people to murderous rage. Some critics said that they were too disturbing for the average reader – yet real life is more disturbing than prose. Another modern novelist who dares to speak out against abuse – especially paedophilia – is the American lawyer Andrew Vacchs. Again, critics argue that he should tone down his material but he has already done so. What he hears in the courtroom is much, much worse than the abuses he commits to the printed page.

So why aren't more people writing such human-darkness exploring tracts? Derek Raymond summed it up best when he said that writers have become fixated on one of the novel's ingredients, that of the need to tell a story. He added that most had forgotten the other main reason – to tell the truth.

Carol Anne Davis latest book is the true crime *Women Who Kill: Profiles of Female Serial Killers* (Allison & Busby). Her website can be found at http://www.tellitlikeitis.demon.co.uk.

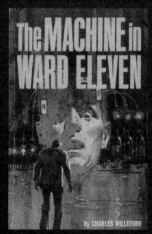

US GOLD

CHARLES WILLEFORD: SOME THOUGHTS

Peter Walker

Peter Walker has not written an article on Charles Willeford, he tells us; these thoughts are (apparently) based on a complete misunderstanding of Wittgenstein's methodology. Still, a good piece on Willeford, nevertheless...

1. With Mr Bush and his fellow astronauts in the White House (complete with computers that don't have the letter 'w'), it is hard to argue with Charles Willeford's statement that he "had a hunch that madness was a predominant theme and normal condition for Americans living in the second half of this century". This was written in 1963 about his paranoid classic, *The Machine in Ward Eleven*. This is about to be republished by No Exit and is, in fact, a collection of loosely interlinked short stories. The title story is brilliant. I wrote the blurb for the cover and said Willeford has a kind of 'Chekhov-

ian wistfulness' in the way he writes. I was thinking of Chekhov's classic *Ward 6*. Partly I was trying to make a case for associating Willeford with Chekhov in order to make a claim for just how good a writer Willeford is. You may agree or disagree with me. Anyway, *The Machine in Ward Eleven* includes the following question: "How many American males had consciously directed every effort to achieving the absolute bottom of the pile, burrowing their way deliberately to the exact centre of the bottom of humanity? If I could only get down there, really down, all the way down, without any side help, here was a unique and terrible aspiration. How? How? An intelligent man could mediate for years on this fascinating challenge". It seems to me that Willeford stayed true to this idea in one way or another throughout all of his writing.

2. Paul Duncan in his *Noir Fiction: Dark Highways* says that Willeford's theme "is the sexually obsessive man, the competitive man, the intelligent man who must prove himself better than others. This is a man who cannot live quietly with another human being. He must control, defeat, destroy the other. This done, the man cannot help but move on to the next challenger." I couldn't have put it better myself. One particularly good example of this – well, a personal favourite anyway – is Richard Hudson, the car salesman from *The Woman Chaser*. Car salesmen, for some reason, get a particularly bad press in Willeford's books. *The Woman Chaser* also includes a brilliant précis for a film called *The Man Who Got Away*. Apart from Paul's writing, including a piece in *Crime Time 9*, there are two very good critical works which include Willeford. Both are by Woody Haut, *Pulp Culture* and *Neon Rain*.

3. One of the scary things about Willeford's writing is how real his nutters are. Willeford does a really good psycho. Look at the list: Russell Haxby (*High Priest of California*), Richard Hudson (*The Woman Chaser*), James Figueras (*The Burnt Orange Heresy*), Freddie Frenger (*Miami Blues*) and Troy Louden (*Sideswipe*). All are complex characters: ordinary and scary, complex and prone to superficial rages, appealing and lethal. All are seen without burdensome moral comment. All

are the guy next door. It's like walking into a room full of Ripley's. Take Pop Sinkiewicz in *Sideswipe*. Having retired to Florida, he ends up in prison following a bizarre set of circumstances. There he meets Troy who patiently explains, "I'm what they call a sociopath. It means I can tell the difference between right and wrong but I just don't give a fuck."

4. Willeford said in an interview (quoted in various places) that "A good half of the men you deal with in the army are psychopaths. There's a pretty hefty overlap between the military population and the prison population, so I knew plenty of guys like Junior in *Miami Blues* and Troy in *Sideswipe*. Like some of these other tankers [i.e. tank crew] I knew used to swap bottles of liquor with infantrymen in exchange for prisoners, and then they'd shoot 'em for fun. I used to say 'Goddammit, will you stop shooting those prisoners!' and they would just shrug and say 'Hey, they'd shoot *us* if they caught us!'. Which was true – they used to shot any tankers they captured. So that sort of behaviour became normal to them, and I used to wonder 'What's gonna happen when these guys go back into civilian life?' You can't just turn it off and go to work in a 7-11. If you're good with weapons or something in the army, you're naturally gonna do something with weapons when you get out, whether it's being a cop or a criminal. These guys learnt to do all sorts of things in the army which just weren't considered *normal* in civilian life."

5. I think Willeford is a great writer because he tells his story without us realising he is doing so. He became criti-

cally acclaimed in his lifetime and had the respect of his peers. He was just breaking into the big time when he died. His novels are imperfect but all the time they showed great improvement. The fact that he wrote for the pulps – and his books were cheap – shouldn't hide this fact. There was nothing minor about them. With Willeford, what you see is what you get.

6. There's a Willeford website at www.dennismcmillan.com/charles willefo. This includes, amongst other things, information about Don Herron's *Willeford* (ISBN 0 939767 26 0, 470 pages). It is described as the "first extensive critical appreciation of the life and writing of Charles Willeford (1919-1988), author of *Miami Blues*, *The Burnt Orange Heresy* and *Cockfighter*. From his early Depression-era experiences as a teenage hobo, through his twenty-year enlistment in the army and air force (including his role as a tank commander with Patton's Third Army, fighting in the Battle of the Bulge), his years of struggle in the paperback original jungle, to a final triumph with his series of crime novels about Miami homicide inspector Hoke Moseley, this books tells his story. Don Herron provides the fascinating background to all of Willeford's nooks, from *Proletarian Laughter* (1948) through the fifth Hoke Moseley novel, left unfinished at the time of his death. The stories behind *High Priest of California, Pick-Up, Wild Wives, Lust is a Woman, The Hombre from Sonora* and *Off the Wall* are detailed here for the first time. Herron includes much previously unknown information on 'lost' books such as *The Whip Hand*, and on the unpublished novels that Willeford turned to for the sub-

stance of the Hoke Moseley series. Lesser-known literary facts of Willeford's forty-year career are also chronicled, from his assistant editorship of Alfred Hitchcock's *Mystery Magazine*, to a twenty-year stint as mystery reviewer for the *Miami Herald*. Willeford's other artistic endeavours are treated in depth, including his acting career, starting with stage plays in the late 1940s and culminating in a major part in his movie *Cockfighter*, directed by Monte Hellman and starring Warren Oates and Harry Dean Stanton. Herron features the most complete bibliography of Willeford's work ever assembled, as well as his longest interview – over one hundred pages of a never before published conversation with the author of *Miami Blues*. The site also includes details of a collection of Willeford's other writings, reviews and so on which looks pretty good.

7. Compiling a Willeford bibliography was harder than I anticipated, partly because different books appear with different names and some books are actually parts of other books.

Proletarian Laughter (1948). There were only a thousand copies printed. It apparently contains a preface by the author and seven prose 'schematics' interlaced with the poems. I say 'apparently' because there appears to be no chance of ever seeing it.

High Priest of California (1953). This was Willeford's first published novel.

Pick-Up (1955). This is Willeford straying into Goddis territory. It has a lot in common with Charles Bukowski and an amazing ending, of sorts, which makes you go,

"You what?"

High Priest of California and *Wild Wives* (1956). Published as a 'double header', mine is the totally weird Re/Search edition complete with pictures, introductions and original cover reproductions. *Wild Wives* (Willeford's original title was *Until I Am Dead* – actually a better title – why do they do that?) tells the story of Jacob C. Blake, PI. It starts with the time-honoured tradition of the girl walking into the office. She produces a gun and than squirts him with water. He's angry and says you ought to be spanked. "Without a single word she leaned over the desk, reached behind her and pulled up her plaid skirt exposing pin panties and a firm, beautifully rounded bottom. 'Go ahead', she said calmly. 'Spank me. I deserve it'." There's a photo as well. Added to this, my edition includes a script for a play of *High Priest of California*.

Honey Gal (1958). Again impossible to get hold of. The original title was *The Black Mass of Brother Springer*. The publisher didn't like that one, asked for another and *Nigger Lover* was substituted. Not surprisingly that didn't make it. (It was published in 1989 by Black Lizard as *The Black Mass of Brother Springer*, Willeford's original title restored.)

Lust is a Woman (1958). Willeford's title was *Made in Miami*.

The Woman Chaser (1960). The original title was *The Man Who Got Away* but it is also known as *The Director*.

The Whip (1961). One of the 'lost books'.

Understudy for Love (1961). The original title was *The Understudy: A Novel of Men and Women*.

No Experience Necessary (1962). The original title was *Nothing Under the Sun*. Willeford disclaimed this book due to some editorial tampering but he apparently salvaged part of it by using it, with only a slight rewriting, as the Pop Sinkiewicz half of *Sideswipe*.

The Machine in Ward Eleven (1963). A collection of interlinked short stories.

The Burnt Orange Heresy (1971). This is possibly the best Willeford.

Cockfighter (1972). The film version of this was permanently banned in the UK for cruelty to animals.

The Hombre from Sonora (1971). Published under the pseudonym Will Charles and described as an 'existential western'.

A Guide for the Undehemorrhoided (1977). A short account of Willeford's haemorrhoid operation. He published 1,000 copies privately. You can only speculate as to why.

Off the Wall (1980). An account, strangely, of the Son of Sam case, telling the story of Craig Glassman, the deputy sheriff who captured David Berkowitz. This one sounds really weird.

Miami Blues (1984). The first of the crime novels featuring Hoke Moseley. Willeford's original title was *Kiss Your Ass Good-Bye*.

New Hope for the Dead (1985). The second Hoke Moseley.

Sideswipe (1987). The third Hoke Moseley novel.

Kiss Your Ass Good-Bye (1987). A self-contained fragment from Willeford's long novel *The Shark-Infested Custard*, finished by early 1975, but rejected by

everyone who saw it as 'too depressing' to publish.

The Way We Die Now (1988). The fourth Hoke Moseley novel.

The Shark-Infested Custard (1993). The long novel deemed 'too depressing' to publish when offered around in the mid 1970s, in print at last.

Writing and Other Blood Sports (2000). A collection of the author's reflections of writing, writers and related facts of life mentioned above.

The autobiographical books are:

Something About a Soldier (1986). Willeford's account of his time in the army.

I Was Looking for a Street (1988). Covers Willeford's childhood and the period when he went on the road as a teenager during the Depression before joining the army.

There is also talk about various 'lost' Willeford books. Main amongst these is the 'legendary' *Belhaven,* the fifth unfinished Hoke book. There's a lot of talk about this from time to time but no plans to publish it.

8. And finally... Nothing exists. Willeford died in 1988. A funny and incisive critic of the American Dream. One of literature's giants.

DONNA LEON

Barry Forshaw

Her Brunetti books may be thoroughly Italianate, but Donna Leon is American – albeit the ultimate ex-pat in her Venetian retreat. But she still belongs under the US Gold sobriquet...

The elegant Durrants Hotel (round the corner from the Wallace Collection) in London has been the home away from home for many a visiting foreign writer and always maintains its sedate character. Coming into the lobby, one finds a mini Italy. The staff are bustling about in a cheerful mood and talking fluent Italian to a guest who has made them all feel they are in Venice. The reason? Donna Leon is in town, and the creator of the highly individual Inspector Brunetti series has agreed to do a tour for the latest book, A Sea of Troubles (Heinemann). Leon has charmed the staff at Durrants, as effortlessly as she charms her interviewers. Having said that, some might find her a touch fierce: she's an unreconstructed academic who has always known exactly what she wants and has successfully achieved it. Not for her Orwell's remark that we all look at ourselves *sometimes and regard ourselves as failures; she has always wanted just one thing – and she's got it. But what?*

Happiness. I haven't sought power, I haven't sought influence, and I haven't tried to write the great American novel. I'm living in Venice, which is exactly where I want to be, and when I go on book tours such as this, I make a point of meeting up with old friends. I also have a thing that many authors don't pursue: anonymity. And that's just fine by me.

But surely even the most well ordered of lives has its frustrations?

I try to keep at bay everything of that nature. Negative people, for instance – I just don't want to know. And by cutting all my ties and moving abroad, I've done just that.

Is this why Brunetti is one of the few literary coppers with a relatively placid private life?

Yes – I'm sure that's true. I write the kind of book that I would like to read. Although I don't write like Henry James, even though I read him more than I read detective stories.

So she isn't on the point of dumping Brunetti in the Grand Canal?

Definitely not. As long as my various publishers (with whom I'm inordinately happy) are happy to go on printing the books, I'm happy to go on writing them. There will be no culling of Guido Brunetti – although I suppose one shouldn't talk about culling in Britain right now…

YOU PLAY THE BLACK AND THE RED COMES UP

by Eric Knight (aka Richard Hallas)

Woody Haut

W̲hen it comes to citing novels that evoke 1930s California, *You Play the Black and the Red Comes Up* often goes unmentioned. Written under the name Richard Hallas, and marketed as a 'hard-boiled novel' in the style of James M. Cain, Knight's book was first published by McBride in 1938, and republished by Dell in 1951, Gregg Press (Boston) in 1980, and by Black Lizard and Carnegie-Mellon Press, Princeton in 1986. What surprises many is that this 130-page first-person narrative

was written by an Englishman who crossed continents as well as genres, authoring, in addition to *You Play the Black*, lachrymose fiction like *Lassie, Come Home* and *The Flying Yorkshireman*. Sadly, *You Play the Black* would be Knight's only hardboiler, prompting one to wonder how Knight, who lived in LA for just two years, could be feted for writing the bathetic *Lassie*, but remain virtually ignored for writing what amounts to a genre classic. According to California historian Kevin Starr, *You Play the Black* is the "most sociologically explicit of the hardboiled California novels", with a "crackpot utopian subplot". Indeed, it's a quirky fast-paced novel that reads like a cross between Horace McCoy's *They Shoot Horses, Don't They* and Thomas Pynchon's *The Crying of Lot 49*. Its protagonist, Dick, an Oklahoma-born Marine AWOL, hops a freight in Texas bound for southern California only to find life on the west coast a perpetual gamble, and people noticeably different: "Instantaneously and automatically, at the very moment they cross the mountains into California, they go insane." With eccentric characters and abrupt plot turns – each chapter represents a different bet and a possible means of cheating fate – the novel is a veritable catalogue of southern California culture, depicting in the process movie people, hoboes, amusement park workers, homosexuals, followers of Aimee Simple McPherson's Four Square Gospel, advocates of Townsend's Ham & Eggs programme and Upton Sinclair's End Poverty in California campaign, Palos Verde socialites and members of various ethnic communities.

At the time, LA was well known for its eccentrics. This was a period in which, out of 1,833 churches in Los Angeles, only a thousand belonged to orthodox religions. Says the sexually ambiguous movie director Genter regarding the era's various fringe movements, "I kept thinking that the goofier the plan the more quickly people seem to fall for it in California." And, "These people were so slaphappy they couldn't tell the difference between Thursday and a fan dancer." Dick gladly joins the fray, embroiling himself in the Ecanaanomic Party – a mishmash of McPherson's

church, Sinclair's party and Townsend's programme. Along the way the protagonist falls in love with Sheila, an unbalanced and secretly Mexican socialite, only for his former girlfriend to inform him that she's pregnant. Seeking a remedy to his predicament, Dick decides to kill her. But the woman is a born survivor. When he tries to drown her off the coast of Catalina, he discovers that she's an expert swimmer. Even the arsenic he administers has no effect. Then, at the Long Beach amusement park where he works, Dick loosens a bolt on the chute, only for it to fly off and kill an unsuspecting Sheila. Dick is arrested and convicted for a crime that he has barely committed. Genter visits him in prison, tells him the world is merely a movie, and that he is responsible for Sheila's death, for he gave Dick the idea that he should kill his former girlfriend. The director commits suicide, leaving a note exonerating his friend. Released from prison, Dick's conscience proves too much for him, but when he confesses his crimes, the police simply laugh at him. Fed up, Dick leaves town. Having hopped the same freight that brought him to LA, he concludes that "California was just a dream". But in the desert, he realises how attached he is to southern California and its bizarre inhabitants. At the risk of misfortune and nightmare, he decides to return.

Thanks to the success of *Lassie, Come Home*, one is able to piece together Knight's biography. Born in Leeds in 1897, Eric Mowbary Knight was the third son of Frederick Harrison and Hilda Creasser Knight. When his father, a wholesale jeweller, died in the Boer War, leaving his family penniless, Hilda went to St Petersburg as governess to the children of Princess Xenia, and later to America, while Knight was raised by relatives in Yorkshire. He began work at twelve, as a bobbin doffer in a Leeds mill. Over the next three years he worked in an engine works, a sawmill, and a glass factory. In 1912, aged fifteen, he joined his mother and brothers in Philadelphia, where he became a copy boy for the *Philadelphia Press*. He attended the Boston Museum of Fine Arts and the National Academy of Design. Come World War One, he joined the Canadian Light Infantry, and served as a signaller. Both brothers, having enlisted in the Pennsylvania 110th Artillery, were killed in France in 1918. Knight's mother died shortly afterwards.

After becoming an artillery captain in the US Army Reserve, Knight reported for several newspapers in Connecticut, New York and Pennsylvania, and, between 1926 and 1934, was drama and movie critic for the *Philadelphia Public Ledger* and the *Town Crier* magazine. He sold his first short story, *The Two-Fifty Hat*, to *Liberty* in 1930, and began contributing to popular magazines like *Cosmopolitan*, *Esquire*, *MacLean's*, and the *Saturday Evening Post*. In July 1917, he married Dorothy Hall of Boston. The couple had three daughters, but divorced in 1932. Knight then married writer Jere Brylawski. Two years later, Knight's first novel, *Invitation to Life*, appeared, after which he moved to Hollywood to work as a scriptwriter. Though the studio did not renew his contract, Knight, having designed and built a house in southern California, published in 1936 his second novel, *Song on Your Bugles*, which might well have been subtitled 'a portrait of an artist as a young Yorkshireman'. The following year, the Knights moved east, to a farm in Croton-on-Hudson. His first real success came with the publication of a novella, *The Flying Yorkshireman*, in a 1938 anthology. During the late 1930s he travelled back to Yorkshire, where observing the unemployed inspired his novel *The Happy Land* (1940), aka *Now Pray We For Our Country*, a critical but hardly a popular success, which details the disintegration of a mining family under the pressures of unemployment. Impoverished Yorkshire was also the setting for his most famous book, the aforementioned *Lassie, Come Home* (1940), which was a Junior Literary Guild Selection, first appearing in a shorter version in the *Saturday Evening Post* in December 1938, the same year as *You Play the Black*.

At the outbreak of World War Two, Knight volunteered his services to the British Ministry of Information. He would write one more novel, *This Above All*, set in the Battle of Britain and acclaimed as "the first great novel to come out of the Second World War". It was an immediate bestseller in the United States and in England and, with a few changes requested by the Hays Office of movie censors, was made into a 1942 movie starring Joan Fontaine and Tyrone Power. A tragic love story set during the Battle of Britain, it explores the ambivalence of its working-class hero toward English society. It was a Book of the Month Club Main Selection, and within the year had sold over 35,000 copies in Great Britain alone. After working on the Ministry of Information's film *World of Plenty*, Knight lectured and delivered radio talks on America for British audiences. In 1942, he returned to the United States, became an American citizen and was commissioned as a captain in the Special Services Division. He contributed to war information films and worked on the military pocket guides to several countries. In January 1943 Knight was promoted to major. Sent to Cairo, his transport plane crashed in Dutch Guyana, and Knight was killed. Posthumously awarded the Legion of Merit, Knight would secure a place in doggy heaven with the release, a few months later, of *Lassie, Come Home* starring Elizabeth Taylor and Roddy McDowell.

Despite, or maybe because of, *Lassie's* success, few reviewers took kindly to Knight's hardboiled novel. In his influential essay, *The Boys in the Back Room*, highbrow critic Edmund Wilson calls *You Play the Black* a "clever pastiche of Cain [...] indicative of the degree to which this kind of writing has finally become formularised that it should have been possible for a visiting Englishman [...] to tell a story in the Hemingway-Cain vernacular almost without a slip." Believing that all California hardboilers lacked literary weight, Wilson quotes Knight's protagonist, who, at the end of the novel, says, "I could remember everything about California, but I couldn't feel it. I tried to get my mind to remember something that it could feel, too, but it was no use. It was all gone. All of it. The pink stucco houses and the palm trees and the stores built like cats and dogs and frogs and ice-cream freezers and the neon lights round everything." If that's lightweight writing, let's have more of it. But Wilson really meant the region, as represented by the quote, lacked reality. Of course, it's that very lack of reality that makes Califor-

nia and Knight's writing – the work of an outsider – so attractive. Wilson goes on to say that Knight's novel is simply a "devil's parody of a movie", which contains everything excluded by "Catholic censorship: sex, debauchery, unpunished crime, sacrilege against the Church", which Knight lets loose "with a gusto of pent-up ferocity that the reader cannot but share... What a pity that it is impossible for such a writer to create and produce his own pictures!"

Certainly, Knight would have liked to have forged a career writing for the studios. During his short tenure in Hollywood, he did, in fact, write a number of unproduced original screenplays. They had titles like *The Hypothetical Murderer*, *The Bandit Governor*, *A Future in Hollywood* and *The Magnificent Liar*. While his film reviews discussed a variety of related subjects, including his dislike of poorly written dialogue, his favourite actors, and the arbitrary decisions made by the Pennsylvania movie censors, he also occasionally lectured on film history. But other than his uncredited contribution to the documentary *Prelude to War* (1943) – on why the US should enter WW2 – his only real connection would be the screen adaptations made from his books.

Wilson wasn't the only critic to pan Knight's novel. Most classified it as an imitation hardboiled novel. Another wrote, "James Thurber himself couldn't have done a better parody... After it is all over you feel sort of disgusted with yourself for having strung along with him." Perhaps there were so many parodies around that it was all too easy to ascribe that label to anything that looked as though it was written in that style. Yet how could critics have missed the novel's more salient points? For not only does Knights' novel stand the test of time, but its evocation of the 1930s is the equal of anything written by McCoy or Nathaniel West. What's more, Knight's novel appeared a year before West's *Day of the Locust* and McCoy's *No Pockets In a Shroud* (though five years after *They Shoot Horses, Don't They*). However, David Feinberg, in his introduction to the Black Lizard edition of Knight's novel, maintains that critics disliked the book simply because the author was an Englishman who dared to write a hardboiled novel. This might well have been the case, yet when Wilson's essay appeared in 1940, that other notorious English writer of hardboiled fiction, the middle-class public-school refugee Raymond Chandler, had already published *The Big Sleep* (1939) and *Farewell, My Lovely* (1940). Perhaps critics dismissed Knight's work, but were willing to accept Chandler's, because the former appeared out of nowhere, had no body of hardboiled work behind him, and had not served an apprenticeship writing for pulps like *Black Mask*. What's more, Knight's book was neither a whodunit nor a detective novel, but was anthropological and political in scope. While eschewing Chandler's wisecracking artificiality and cynicism, *You Play the Black* contains a playfulness noticeably absent in the work of Cain and McCoy.

It could be that critics, on the eve of World War Two, were, if not xenophobic, reluctant to entertain the notion that a foreigner could write a hardboiled critique of America. For here was someone apparently masquerading as an American – never mind that Knight had been living in America for some thirty years – who had the nerve to write about the culture. With his morally anarchic manner, Knight, rather than relegate cultural information to mere background material, turns it into the very subject of his novel. Though mocking in his depiction, Knight, still hanging on to his working-class perspective, replaces the genre's usual cynicism with a sense of what is possible. Englishman he might have been, but Knight illustrates, as Hammett had nine years earlier in *Red Harvest*, that hardboilers can be an effective means of criticism. No lightweight imitation, *You Play the Black* is the strongest and most individual of statements. Had he lived longer, Knight might well have written other hardboiled novels. Certainly there is one more such novel from the same period in the Knight archives at Yale. Entitled *Rose Without Warning*, it concerns a young girl's climb from marathon dance halls to stardom. Unfortunately, it would go unpublished.

So successful was Knight that his portrait was painted by the famous American artist Andrew Wyeth. Standing against a mountain range, Knight wears a blue shirt and a pencil moustache. With brown hair, chiselled face, and penetrating gaze, he looks like an emaciated Errol Flynn. The portrait is preserved for the masses on a website devoted not to noir fiction, but – you guessed it – to collies, at the end of which there is a picture of a hand-carved sculpture that Knight did of his favourite canine. The dog bears an uncanny resemblance to a petrified sheep. A short biography accompanies the two images. While it cites Knight's fiction, *You Play the Black* is conspicuous by its absence.

NOT ALL BLACK AND WHITE: WALTER MOSLEY

Mark Campbell

Walter Mosley is a crime writer. Or is he? Ducking and diving the established genre rules, he's always managed to be one step away from what you'd expect. Literary but never pretentious, issue-based yet never less than entertaining, his novels veer from the philosophical short stories of Always Outnumbered, Always Outgunned to the quasi-science fictional Blue Light. And somewhere in between you'll find Easy Rawlins, hero of six acclaimed novels that boldly take crime fiction to places it's never been before.

Why did you chose the crime genre to tell your stories?

The first book I ever wrote, *Gone Fishin'*, wasn't a crime book. There's a serious crime that happens, but you wouldn't call it a crime novel. There's no policing and no catching of the criminal, or even almost catching. But no-one wanted to publish it. I sent it out in 1989, and at that time in America the number of black writers in mainstream publishing was really small, and so their notion of what black people could do was also very small. But even though I had written a story about black characters, the main characters were male, so that was another strike against it. There were women, but it was mainly about these men. The other thing is that there were no white people in it, and so it wasn't really talking about racism or race. It was just talking about these young men's lives coming of age in the Deep South, living the way black people did then. And nobody was interested in publishing it.

So then I wrote about the same people in a crime novel and the publishers said, "Ah! A novelty! This is something we can sell for a while." Now I enjoyed writing it very much, I'm very into the genre so it didn't insult me or make me feel bad. And of course the idea was to get publishers to keep on publishing me, so I had to keep on writing in that genre. And that was okay, because it was the same story, the same characters...

Does is bother you that publishing is so genre-led?

Well, publishing is – what can you say? But it does bother me, yes. The argument is really a political one – and it's not about race, it's about capitalism. If you start writing a comic novel about, say, a nurse, and you write three or four and they're very successful, and they sell a couple of million copies or something, and then all of a sudden you write a very serious, surrealist tome, the publisher is going to say "No". Now that's wrong, because you're a writer, you're an artist. So basically, what I did was I ignored that. I wrote my mysteries, then I wrote *RL's Dream*, which is certainly no crime book, then *Blue Light*, which is definitely not. And I don't care; I don't pay any atten-

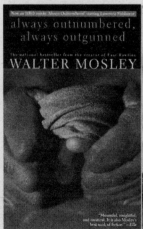
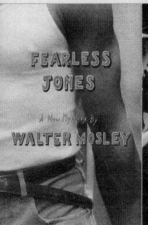
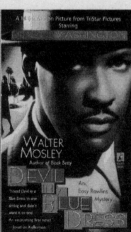

tion to the publishers, whatever they say.

Did it occur to you to use a pseudonym?
Er, no. Because it's me writing, and it's my career as a writer that's important. It's a business to me in as much as I expect to get paid, but it's also my art and because of that whatever I write must have my name on it.

What's the racial makeup of publishers in America? Were you having to face a largely white clique?
There are no mainstream black publishers, although there are a couple of black people in publishing. But I don't want to make it just black and white – there are also some Dominicans, Puerto Ricans, Latin Americans, Mexicans, South East Asians. But I mean, largely it's just white people! Although I think it's beginning to change, and I've had a lot to do with it because I started a publishing institute at City College, a college mainly made up of people of colour, and we're getting into the publishing world. But it's a difficult thing. I published *Gone Fishin'* with a small black publisher called Black Classic Press. So there is certainly racism in publishing.

Presumably it's not deliberate...
It's not deliberate – but all the people know about it. I tell them – like I'm telling you, like I tell everybody in America – so they know it. But they start to come up with excuses, and the excuses are racist. Someone will tell me, "Well, it's hard to get a talented black man or woman to work for us because they can get a job anywhere." And I say, "Listen, you got five people working for you and they're all from Harvard – you mean they can't get jobs in other places?" And they go, "Oh

well, that's not the same thing." So I say, "Oh I see..." I mean, what are you going to say to them?

I've read that Easy Rawlins is President Clinton's favourite character – is there any truth in that?
Yeah, he loves Easy.

Does that make you happy?
Sure, why not? I mean, I haven't been happy with everything in his presidency, but my criticisms of his presidency are actually my criticisms of the people who vote in America. People in America, probably not unlike people in England, have lost a sense of their democratic rights and have become kind of lost in this popularity contest among a very small group of people who could even *be* President. You have to be white, male, Christian, married, straight, no deformities, between thirty-five and sixty, belong to the Republican or Democratic party...

Have a perfect family...
You know, when you figure out everything a President has to be, it's like one percent of the country at any particular moment could be President. Now taking that notion into account, you have to say, "God, that's not democracy." But that's our decision – we could vote a first generation Vietnamese woman in as President, you know. And we don't.

Could it happen in your lifetime?
Listen, I hope so. A lot of people don't have any faith in the youth. It's funny, but I have a great deal of faith in them. Their cynicism actually makes them less venal than their parents' generation, my generation.

Less venal?

Yeah. They're more likely to get into a fight on the street and less likely to start a war. [Laughs] I like that. When you really look at it, that's better.

You mean they've got a passion for what they believe in.

Right, but the passion is personal. The *New York Times Magazine* the other day said that 57% of the youth dream about being famous. There's been some criticism of that, but on the other hand, I was giving a talk the other day on MTV and I said, "Listen, I think that everybody in this room should consider running for office. Let's stop thinking about other people making the rules – we should all have our moment of value and fame and worth and power." They say JFK had an IQ of 103 and Madonna 144, you know what I'm saying? Maybe she'd make a better president.

Let's turn to your childhood. Fill me in on the details...

I was born in Los Angeles and lived there till I was about twelve. Then my parents moved to West Los Angeles, to a nicer neighbourhood, more middle class. I lived there till I was eighteen or nineteen, left, and ended up in Vermont. I went to college, dropped out, went to college, got a degree, dropped out again, moved around, lived in Massachusetts, lived in New York, became a computer programmer for many years, and decided one day to try my hand at writing.

You worked as a computer programmer?

Yeah, for insurance companies, Mobil Oil, banks – back in the early '80s.

So what swung it for the writing?

I just started writing and I liked it. I had no intention or expectation of becoming wealthy.

When did you think writing might be a job for life?

Every time I published a book, I said, "Hey, I'm going to do this now until I have to get a job again." But I haven't had to since, so it's been good.

Do you imagine the audience you're writing for?

Gee, that's a hard question to answer. I mean, certainly there's an audience I'm writing to, and they're relatives of mine, a little bit older than me, from the Deep South. I'm always thinking about the audience in the sense that I want to relate to them and entertain them, and maybe get a little knowledge in there if I can. At least, what I think is knowledge.

With Socrates Fortlow, it seems you're saying this is the character – he just happens to be black.

Right.

Could you see him working so well as a white character?

I think it would work quite well with a white character actually. There are certain issues of race that he has that someone white would experience more as class. But it's pretty much the same thing, you know.

And there's humour there too, with Socrates' two-legged dog. Have you ever wanted to write an all-out comic novel?

Well, you know my next book, called *Fearless,* is a comic mystery. I like writing things that are funny – I enjoy it. And also I'm writing a series of short, short stories about two black characters, one a dead man who's been resurrected and one an angel trying to convince him to go back into death, both living in New York and having a series of dialogues. And many of the dialogues are quite funny.

Who are your literary influences?

I think my primary literary influence is from my family. My father loved to tell stories, and the men and women on my mother's side of the family loved to tell stories too. Then after that I like Camus, Marquez and Michael Moorcock. There's a lot of people that I like reading.

Do you enjoy publicising your books?

Do you mean being on tour?

Yeah.

Well, it gets tiring after a while, but I enjoy meeting people and doing readings.

So this is it for life now? You're settled?

Boy, it would be great if one could say that about oneself, wouldn't it? You can never tell. The lifetime of most successful novelists is about ten years. And after that, people forget who they are. I've been doing it for ten years now…

You can buck the trend.

Yeah, people do. I hope I do. But it's hard.

Final thought: what would you say to someone starting out as a writer?

The reason you should do anything is because you love doing it. If someone were going out with somebody who was really beautiful, they'd say, "Look at who I'm with." Well that's fine, but do they actually like being with them? That's the question. And I think that's a hard question to answer when people start worrying about making money and becoming famous, that kind of stuff. But I think they really need to concentrate on that.

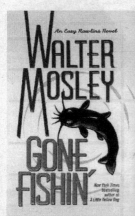

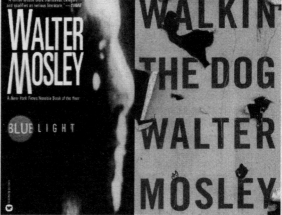

THE HOUSE OF DEATH
PAUL DOHERTY

A magnificent new murder-mystery series featuring Alexander the Great

It is 334 BC and the young Alexander waits with his troops by the Hellespont, poised to attack the empire of the great Persian king, Darius III.
To win the approval of the gods for his enterprise he makes many offerings, yet the smoke does not rise, the sacrifices are tainted. Worse, his guides are being brutally murdered, Persian spies are in the camp, and Alexander's generals have their own secrets.

Into this turmoil comes Telamon, a physician, and boyhood friend of Alexander. As the climax builds and Alexander throws off his nervous fears, winning a brilliant and bloody triumph over the Persians, Telamon at last succeeds in uncovering their enemies.

Paul Doherty is the internationally renowned author of many historical novels. He studied history at Liverpool and Oxford universities, and gained a doctorate at Oxford. He is now headmaster of a London school, and lives near Epping Forest.

- First in a new series of historical mysteries featuring Alexander the Great
- Paul Doherty has published many hugely successful historical novels and murder mysteries
- Follows the enormous success of the historical mysteries of Steven Saylor and Elizabeth Peters

House of Death
Paul Doherty
28 June 2001 • hardback • £16.99
1 84119 302 X • **CONSTABLE**

GREG RUCKA MEETS BATMAN

Judi Rohrig

There's some heavyweight sleuthing been going on in a place called Gotham City, and it's not accompanied by any Blam! Twack! Pow! drifting out from television sets while Mom and Dad sit around shaking their heads at flashing psychedelic images. Nor is it the sludgy, dark, oil-dripping pan that filmmaker Tim Burton held out to Batman aficionados in shadowy movie houses.

Here at the beginning of the twenty-first century, Gotham City has become a place where men scratch for clues and rack their well-trained brains to figure out crimes. No X-ray vision. No glowing Kryptonite. The Batman – cape still firmly in place – now sits behind his computer or dabbles in his lab and contemplates his findings. Just like a 'real' detective. And the mad scientist bringing Batman back to the basics, back to scratch-his-head investigation, back to loyal fans, just happens to have four mystery and suspense novels under his belt. His name is Greg Rucka.

Creator of the innovative bodyguard series that pits one Atticus Kodiak and company against abortion zealots (both pro and con), narcissistic, possessive parents in a custody battle, a professional killer hired by the tobacco companies, and a lover with a big secret (*Keeper, Finder, Smoker, Shooting at Midnight*), and a fifth one on its way (*Critical Space*), Greg Rucka has also noticeably and successfully tackled the graphic novel world with Antarctic crime-solving in *Whiteout*, and the Eisner award-winning *Whiteout: Melt*.

But a little more than a year ago, Greg Rucka was asked to step into the world of the Dark Knight, the Caped Crusader.

The Batman

And what he did with his offerings in last year's group effort – DC Comics' No Man's Land and No Man's Land the novel – led DC to a measure not short of locking Rucka in a room while he hands out new Batman the Detective stories along with a six-issue run about Helena Bertinelli, aka The Huntress, in the just completed Cry For Blood.

Rucka had already gone deep, demonically blending together the flavours of hard-boiled Dashiel Hammett with Frank Miller, tossing in a little Dennis LeHane, John D. MacDonald and Dennis O'Neill; then stirring around fedoras and dangerous babes with crusaders' capes, buxom crime-fighters, sicko clowns and two-faced former attorneys. And what he's figured out about the Dark Knight... hey, it's nothing short of amazing! Don't believe me? Just listen to a conversation I had with him.

When you were first offered Batman, what had you envisioned for that particular character?

When it first appeared that I would get a chance to work with the character, I had all these visions of taking Bruce Wayne back into Gotham City and into the 1970s. He was living in that big penthouse – if you've read *Strange Apparitions* – and there was this big piece of me that wanted to bring him back to his roots in that sense, to put him back down on the ground. That's something I'm inclined to do with every superhero character I encounter. "Okay, let's get rid of all the trappings and let's put them down on street level and watch them interact." That had been my gut instinct, my first desire. I wanted to work through Wayne as much as Batman. I got about twenty minutes into really working on that idea when Denny O'Neill said, "We're doing *No Man's Land* next year." Which basically meant: any ideas you have must bow in the face of this overall one. Which was a disappointment! In many respects *No Man's Land* serves much the same purpose for me – taking Bruce and moving him into Gotham, putting him down in the street. So it was sort of the best of both worlds.

Are you getting any chance to do any of what you wanted now?

Not in the same way. But I'm not so inclined to do it as I was two years ago, mostly because the events of *No Man's Land* influenced it, changed it. That's one part. The other problem is that it is a Batman book. Batman has to appear in costume. And that's really vexing. There's a couple where I've written scripts and looked at them and thought, "How am I going to get Batman..." I can get Bruce Wayne into it, but to justify a costume change is something like hitting the story with a hammer, trying to find a way to force him in. There actually are two stories coming up where I had that problem. I think it's worked out in both cases, but that's proved difficult.

Do you feel as though, if you had a few more pages, it might be less of a challenge?

Needing to fit Batman in a costume has less to do with space than with the kind of story I want to do, I am becoming more and more interested watching Bruce Wayne interacting with Gotham, because Bruce Wayne is garbage – he's bullshit. It's just the mask that Batman's wearing most frequently – there's something to me very fascinating with that because he kind of turns it into a spy story, or undercover Batman, when he's wandering around Gotham trying to influence things as Bruce Wayne, trying to preserve his identity as Bruce Wayne. That's his major link. Batman doesn't talk to anybody, really, about anything except 'the work'. You never see Batman sitting around in a restaurant, chatting with his friends. But for Bruce to know what's going on in the city around him, he's got to get out there and meet the people and talk to them. And that's sort of antithetical to his image.

Where does the detective fit in here, or how are you envisioning Batman/Bruce – who gets to play the detective? Both? Are you saying that Bruce gets to collect the clues?

The principle that I'm writing from is that it's all Batman, all the time, and that Bruce Wayne is just a costume that he wears from nine in the morning until five at night. And since it's all Batman, all the time, he's always on the case – I mean, he is pathologically committed to his holy war, which is to fight crime in all of its guises and all of its forms. He's always in the mode. When he's on a specific case then he's more focused, but anything that he does, whether he's dressed as Bruce Wayne or not, is directed to the goal of solving the crime. So everything he does is in one way or another feeding his ability to do that. He's sort of like Holmes, just sitting in Baker Street, smoking endless pipes and reading everything in the world. And in much the same way, Batman is a sort of idiot savant: he knows very little about those things that are not related to what he does. He can tell you chemical compositions of various gunpowders from around the world, but he could not very easily tell you the chemical composition of something that isn't relevant.

Holmes is the best example. Watson has a bit where he describes Holmes when he's trying to figure him out and he realises, my God, this guy has an encyclopaedic knowledge! He beats cadavers to learn what post-mortem trauma looks like! But if you ask him what the birth process is

like between a mother and a baby, he can't tell you, even though that would seem to Watson to be fundamental medical knowledge. Batman's the same way: how babies come into the world really doesn't interest him – it's how you violently terminate a life, that's what he needs to know everything about.

Because it's pertinent to solving the crime.

Exactly.

At what point did you make these discoveries about Batman? Because it seems to me that in No Man's Land, the novel, you really got very deeply inside Bruce and the Batman, especially in those sections where Batman has to be Bruce again, where you could feel the real discomfort and pain of that. How much did you let Bruce and Batman actually talk to you?

I think Batman is such an archetype – I think my conception of him, roughly, was almost sui generis, you know, from the first time I encountered the character at fifteen or fourteen, and when I really got into the character. I'm not talking about my first experience, which would be out of the Adam West TV show. That presented it in a very specific way, where I knew it was Batman and I knew it was Robin. But I was very young. Even watching that, I understood there was something else going on, but the camp in the show overrode it. When I first encountered – and I use this word advisedly – a 'serious' Batman, it would have been in Frank Miller's *Dark Knight Returns* and *The Year On*. The second you see that character in those stories you *know* that character, because he is such an archetype – he is recognised as the grim loner. That's one of the reasons why the character is so enduring.

I've been at a couple of conventions where Devin Grayson's told the story when people ask, "How'd you get into comics?" And the story is consistently that she got home from work one day, was flipping channels, and saw an episode of *Batman and Robin: Animated*. In the episode, the moment she saw it, it was Batman driving the Batmobile with Robin in the passenger seat, and Robin leans back and puts his feet up on the dashboard and drops his hands behind his neck. And Devin said, "At that instant I knew everything about those characters. I understood their relationship. I knew who they were." That's their power.

Bruce is more difficult. Bruce has required a fair amount of thought for me. As a writer in comics, which is very fan-influenced, a lot of people have different takes on Bruce. And then there's an editorial take on Bruce, incidentally, which we are supposed to abide by. The editorial take on Bruce is that he is incompetent, pretty much – he's not supposed to be able to do anything. Which I find very difficult, because that's going too far in the other direction. But Bruce has taken some serious thought for me. And he goes to the fundamental questions.

You know when the first Batman movie came out, the Michael Keaton one, I remember reading all this stuff in the media about, "Oh he's crazy! The Joker is his mirror image!" And all this stuff in an attempt to psychoanalyse the character of the Batman – that pathology is dark and corrupt in some way. And I know it's not. In my heart, I know it's not. He *is* screwed up. Nobody is going to convincingly argue

to me that Batman is a healthy individual. But he's not a malfunctioning human being to such an extent that he needs to be removed from society, which is an argument I've heard. Just in talking about it, you can tell that I've given this far too much thought. I've strayed from the question, but I'm not sure I know what the best answer is. The more I work with the characters, the more I understand them, and the more I consider them. I don't worry about Batman. Batman I think right now is in very good hands. He's healthy. I think he's safe. But it's the characters around him that I'm concerned about more.

Like Jim Gordon?

Oh, absolutely. I think that Gordon really needs to be cared for. I think Alfred could use some TLC. Though Alfred is in really good hands right now – Chuck Dixon's using him in Robin, where he's using him quite well. As such, Alfred is kind of off limits to Batman writers because Alfred is over in *Robin*. But the cops... And in particular Gordon, and especially what we did to him in the end of *No Man's Land*. The guy needs a break! Those are the relationships that need more attention.

It really, really goes to what Batman is, to a great extent. Everybody thinks they've got a unique and killer understanding. And I think frankly that Batman really ain't that complicated. He's an archetype, and everybody recognises him. He's had sixty-odd years of pretty much non-stop attention.

(The above is a product of our reciprocal relationship with Ed Gorman's Mystery Scene in the US)

US GOLD

THE AMERICAN EYE: JAY RUSSELL

Russell's Marty Burns is one of the best in the current breed of US private eyes. Here's the lowdown:

Marty Burns first rocketed to fame as a child star in that classic 1960s sitcom *Salt & Pepper*. Who could forget his impish grin and suggestively raised eyebrow as he asked the weekly question, "Hot enough for you?" to an adoring nation. After some tough years when the parts wouldn't come (and he earned his living as a real life private eye!) Marty climbed back to the TV summit in the Fox detective drama *Burning Bright* where he stars as – who else? – Marty Burns! He remains impish and suggestive, though he does now seem to have a problem with getting that eyebrow up.

The following lively feature was originally commissioned for *BooBubble Today*, the web magazine of BooBubble.com. Sadly, the BooBubble burst and the interview never saw print. Until now.

Twenty Questions with Marty Burns

Is Marty Burns your real name?
If I were making one up, I'd certainly invent something better.

What was it like being a child star in the 1960s?
Probably not too different from being one today. Except people kept mistaking me for Danny Bonaduce.

Are children exploited in Hollywood?
Everyone is exploited in Hollywood. That's the whole point of the goddamn place. If you can't exploit people you might as well sell insurance and live in New Jersey.

What's your sign?
Yield. With No Parking Anytime rising.

What's the very best thing about being a big star?
If you tell them the name of someone famous who you slept with, the cops in LA don't write the ticket when they catch you

speeding. Also you can have more than ten items in your cart in the express lane at the supermarket and no one gives you a dirty look.

What *is* the name of someone famous who you slept with?

Show me a badge and I'll tell you.

Is it true that you worked as a real-life detective?

Detective is a little grandiose for the kind of penny-ante work I did. The streets I walked down weren't mean so much as grumpy. I didn't always get my man, but I *always* got my retainer in cash.

Who's your favourite Beatle?

Pete Best. I really identify.

If you could have dinner with anyone in all of history, who would you choose?

Pete Best.

If you didn't already play you on television, who would you cast in the role?

Pete Best. Kidding. Anyone but Adam San-

dler. Or Martin Lawrence.

Is television rotting the minds of our children?

We're rotting the minds of our children. Television just provides the ambience.

What's your favourite food?

The hot pastrami sandwiches at Johnny's in Culver City.

Who is the great love of your life?

Johnny in Culver City.

What's the best thing you ever did?

Decide not to take that part in *Shakes the Clown*.

What's the worst thing you ever did?

Decide to take that part in *Bazooka Beach Massacre*.

Where do you sit politically?

At the intersection of George W. Bush and Franklin D. Roosevelt. It's just up the street from a really good International House of Pancakes.

Can you tell us a secret?

JFK was really a suicide.

How would you describe yourself in a personals ad?

Clueless seeks same. No Scientologists.

What's next for Marty Burns?

Lunch. At Johnny's in Culver City.

Thank you Marty Burns.

You're wel... wait a minute, that was only nineteen questions.

Okay, smartass. Who the hell ever told you you could act?

What? Why you, I oughta... Hey, come back here with that micropho.....

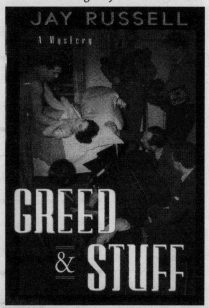

Greed & Stuff, Marty Burns' latest adventure through the depths and degradations of Hollywood, is available from St Martin's Press for a measly $23.95.

WAGON MEN: CHARLES SHAFER

Racking your brain, trying to think up a new crime fiction character? Tell you what, the next time you're watching your favorite cop show on TV and the hero detectives are poking around a crime scene, take a look in the background. You'll see a couple of uniform men leaning against the wall, maybe have their hats tipped back, chewing on a toothpick, something like that. That's the paddy wagon crew, and more importantly two of the most colorful cops you're ever going to meet. Hard to believe? Okay, but just imagine yourself riding around in a truck all day – or night – sifting dead bodies out of fires, fishing floaters out of rivers, bagging shooting victims, scraping up the aftermath of traffic accidents. Wouldn't be long before you'd be colorful, too. And dead bodies is only one of many jobs wagon crews are responsible for. They also transport prisoners, and act as an ambulance when a real one isn't available. Which can be often in Chicago.

I knew one wagon man who claimed six babies were named for him because over the years he and his partner had acted as doctor and nurse for their delivery. Starting to get the idea? Kinda thought so. Here's more. After having to deal with the tragedies of life day in and day out you might think wagon men would become stone cold, withdrawn. Just the opposite. Wagon men love to tell jokes only they'll never laugh at yours. Well, maybe amongst each other they might, but not so you would notice. It's as if they have their own private union and the rest of humanity exists solely as fodder for their fun. For example, I was a rookie cop one sweltering July afternoon and got a call to assist a wagon crew at a third-floor office. Arriving in a flash, I rushed up the stairs with my gun at the ready only to find two old-time coppers lounging in the hallway. One guy gives me a tired look, and says, "Uh, need to get in that room, kid, and it's locked. How's about we boost you through the transom? Soon as you get the door open, me'n Joe here, we'll take over." Happy to prove my worth, I shinnied up the door and dropped inside. Then caught this awful odor. Like nothing I'd ever smelled before. Gagging, I turned to investigate. Right behind me, perched in a desk chair, was a three-day-old stiff, cooking in the heat. Eyes glazed over, staring at nothing. Flies buzzing around its mouth and nose, having a feast. I ran for the door but couldn't get it open. My friendly wagon man hollered from the opposite side, "Damn, don't know why, but this thing won't budge. Hey, open some windows in there, breeze the place out. Meanwhile we'll work on the lock."

By this time I realised they had the door braced shut. In agony and out of options, I raced around flinging open windows and stuck my head outside. I actually considered jumping. Might have too, had I not been three stories up. When the wagon crew finally came strolling in, I thought my ordeal was over. Wrong again. I had to help get Mr Dead Guy from the chair and onto a stretcher for the trip down to ground level. Meaning to get my misery over, I grabbed a limp arm. Only trouble, I was now the only one standing, because the wagon crew were rolling on the floor, roaring, pointing fingers at this dummy rookie with four layers of dead skin bunched up in his hand. I know, gruesome, but you have to laugh. That or go goofy.

By the way. Wagon men will tell you folks always wait until they're at least on the third floor before dropping dead, especially those at 250 pounds or more. To wagon men it's all a conspiracy so they'll have to tote deadweight down three flights of stairs. If you should become a rookie cop and have to assist a wagon crew in such a task, don't let them talk you into taking the low end. Awful body fluids sometime slide out, and with your hands occupied, you won't be able to defend yourself. Rule of thumb: never trust a wagon man. Ever.

War Story Department

One of CPD's great legends unfolded one Spring morning up on the Northside. Secreted back in a dark alley, an Eighteenth District wagon crew was popped awake by their dispatcher, who said, "Eighteen-Seventy, go to Division and the river. You got a floater." Joe and Vic get over there, and sure enough, find a body bobbing along in the gentle current. Joe said, "Hey, man. Tell Mr Aquanaut ain't no swimming allowed around here."

"Think, Joe," Vic said. "By the time we get through fishing this guy out, it'll pretty near be supper time."

"Oh, man. I'll never make it that long without my Budweiser."

Vic picked up a handful of stones, and was soon pelting this unfortunate soul who had the audacity to drown on Vic and Joe's beat. Joe picked up his own stones and joined in. In no time the water splashed, then churned, and the floater started drifting. That's when Vic said, "Got me an idea." He lumbered back to the paddy wagon and grabbed the noose used to catch wild dogs. (Another of their fun jobs.) Returning, he poked the floater with the noose's wooden handle, shoving it outward into the river. "Perfect," Vic said, and went to the paddy wagon, boasting into the radio, "Eighteen-seventy, Squad. You was right about that floater, but it's on the Thirteenth District side of the river. Better give them a call."

The Thirteenth District wagon crew caught on as soon as they arrived. Wasn't difficult with the original wagon crew on the opposite bank, waving and laughing. Not to be outdone, they pushed the body back across the river, into Eighteenth District territory. Back and forth that body went for days, and with wagon crews from all three watches and both districts involved. In the end the Coast Guard had to be called to do the dirty work.

Fiction? Could be, but I myself don't doubt that story for a minute because remember, we're talking about wagon men.

ROBERT CRAIS:
AN INTERVIEW IN TWO PARTS

Michael Carlson

Part One:
Demolition Angel:
Imagining What You Do Not Know

I spoke to Robert Crais for the second time in six months immediately after he'd been interviewed on stage by John Williams as part of Crime Scene 2000 and had then given a reading from Demolition Angel, his first novel outside the Elvis Cole series, and one that stars Carol Sharkey of the LAPD Bomb Squad. We adjourned to the conservatory of a pub near the South Bank, with John Connolly along to ask the intelligent questions on behalf of The Irish Times. *I have borrowed from some of the answers to their questions to fill out answers to my own.*

Demolition Angel *is your first non-Elvis Cole novel…*
I want to keep expanding, trying new things. *LA Requiem* was different from the previous Elvis novels. I'd written eight of them, and I wanted to write in the third person for a change, have a main character

who was a woman, and do something that was a flat-out suspense thriller. Writing *Requiem* was a sea-change for me; it made

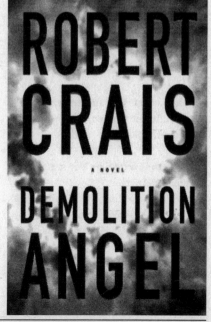

me want to do other things I'd never done. Like have a woman's POV. I think I write women respectfully and well. I'd done a lot of writing female characters when I worked on *Cagney and Lacey*.

In LA Requiem, *you introduced a detective named Samantha Nolan. Did she serve as a prototype for Carol Starkey?*
Well, there was an important difference. Sam's strong traits, her aggressiveness, which make her a good cop, come from her inside strength. Starkey manifests the same characteristics on the outside, but inside she's been so damaged that for her these things are armour plating.

It's interesting that Carol is bomb-damaged, as it were, psychologically, and the male lead is physically disabled too.
That *is* interesting, but it wasn't conscious. Sometimes these things just happen!

Are there elements of Cagney or Lacey in Carol Starkey? Sometimes I think she may be the kind of character they'd have been if it weren't television.
No, that wouldn't be appropriate. They're totally different women, from each other and from Carol.

You've been working on the screenplay of Demolition Angel...
It's the hardest writing I've ever had to do. At first they wanted one of those two or three million dollar guys, but I said who better than me – it'll be a piece of cake, and Larry Mark, who you know [see below], said OK. What's hard is you have to take 640 pages of manuscript with maybe 150 scenes, and cut that to 120 pages with

maybe forty scenes. You start thinking you wrote it correctly the first time! It took me three months and boy was it hard! But they were happy with the result. Still, I have no interest in being a screenwriter... Books are better!

Have you optioned any of the Elvis books?
Well, I get offers but I've turned them down. They're mostly wanted for TV, and I know the medium too well. It can't help the books, really it can only be destructive, especially to the characters.

Strong female leads seem to be in the zeitgeist for male writers now. Michael Connelly and Robert Parker, for example.
No serious novelist wants to write the same thing over and over again. Isn't writing all about imagining what you do not know?

Part Two:
LA Requiem :
Los Angeles Is Where You Go To Make Your Dreams Come True

When I'd spoken with Crais in Los Angeles, it was February, the sun was shining, and it was warmer than London in July. He looked like a grad student on Spring break, tanned and fit, hair close-cropped, wearing a cut-off Air Force Academy sweatshirt. He entered the restaurant smiling broadly, and for good reason: the paperback of LA Requiem had just cracked the New York Times *bestseller list. LA Requiem was Crais' eighth novel starring Elvis Cole, an offbeat detective who specialises in wearing loud shirts and cracking wise. He may appear counter-cultural, but his detective work is surprisingly mainstream; he harbours far fewer of the* 'hippie' instincts evinced by, say, Moses Wine. Cole's character has deepened novel by novel, and LA Requiem marks another such advance. It also marks the emergence of Cole's silent sidekick, Joe Pike, into a more major, more human role. It's the best Elvis novel yet.

I'd been given extra ammunition for the interview: at a fund-raiser the previous night I'd discovered that a TV writer I know (we studied with the same film teacher) has been one of Crais' best friends ever since their days of working together on Cagney and Lacey. So I started by discussing the way it's a small world, and how everyone in LA seems to come from someplace else. Crais did too. He grew up in Cajun country. He began selling short stories while still studying mechanical engineering at Louisiana State University. His first sales were mostly to the burgeoning original anthology science fiction market in the early 1970s.

At that point there were only two or three mystery magazines but SF had this huge market. They needed material, and that encouraged me, so I came out to LA.

With the idea of writing for TV?
Well, I was a fan, and I had this fantasy of making a living by writing for TV and writing SF stories (which didn't pay much) on the side. I grew up loving series like *Star Trek*, *The Man From UNCLE*, that sort of stuff. I admit it – I was a Trekkie.

[A strange idea pops into my mind]. It sounds like you were influenced by Harlan Ellison.
Where'd you get that from? Yes, I think he's a genius, he writes about real people from real places, like Painesville, Ohio. His book *The Glass Teat* sort of demystified him for me, but I'd been reading him for a long time. I was doing a lot of rereading.

One of my favourites as a teen was *The Maltese Falcon* – I hadn't read it in years, but the Mystery Guild was including it in their list of the ten best ever written, and wanted me to write the intro – and it blew me out! I was amazed at how well it held up but still had a dated quality.

How did you get from Hammett to TV writing?
Basically by writing spec scripts. I had zero idea of what a script even looked like. I knew no one. So I went to a second-hand bookstore and bought some scripts – they were probably stolen from studios – for $2.50 each, and I ran them through my typewriter. Now these were the days before videotape, but we didn't even have a TV. I'd go in department stores and watch for free. *Baretta* with Bobby Blake, and *Bye Bye Black Sheep* with Robert Conrad were my favourite shows. So I walked into the Writer's Guild one day and bought a list of agents. I got lucky; I found a legit guy who read my spec scripts, submitted one, and it sold, and once it sold everything else happened. I like to say on *Baretta* I wrote for the bird. I did five stories and three teleplays for *Baretta* and then went to Universal as a story-editor for *Quincy, ME*. I was the baby writer, the youngest on the lot. I worked on the second season of *Hill Street Blues* and then went to *Cagney and Lacey*.

Once I got going I worked exclusively in TV for nine years, on *LA Law* and *Miami Vice*. TV *consumes* you, especially when you're a staff writer. It requires *all* your energy. I wrote maybe three or four stories in my spare time, and two book manuscripts that were among the worst books ever written by mortal man. But I wanted to write books. TV was getting increasingly less satisfying. I didn't like the working environment. Our team on *Cagney* was writing great stuff, but in the nature of the beast, with input from so many other directions, I found the results dispiriting. My desire to go my own way got stronger, and finally I'd had enough. I either had to go to the mental hospital or go write a book! So I went cold turkey. I rented a cabin and stayed there three months and wrote *The Monkey's Raincoat*.

What was the hardest part of that decision?
Leaving the money behind. I had no idea if I'd be able to write a coherent novel and then if it was any good it'd be stuck as a cheesy category genre novel, with no support. But I was immediately entranced by the character of Elvis Cole. Despite the setting, Elvis is a southern thing, really. Of course, I'm a southern boy, we had our painting of Elvis at home, but when I sat down to write I went through a list of names and this one would indicate to the reader that the character would be different. Actually it may have turned off more people than it attracted!

Thinking it was a gimmick?
Well, either thinking a) it was stupid, or b) that I was actually writing about Elvis Presley as a private eye, and being disappointed.

Of course the real Elvis was an honorary DEA agent, courtesy of President Nixon!
And he's still alive!

Elvis Cole is also much more of a cop than he seems on the outside.
Well I come from a family of cops and I share their values. I must have cops in the blood. But readers seemed to like Elvis and

the word of mouth seemed to sell the series.

Yet you bought back LA Requiem *from your publishers...*
Yes, and Doubleday and Ballantine positioned it properly in the marketplace and supported it.

Is there a problem marketing later novels in a series?
Well, most people believe you have to start with the first book and read sequentially, but I didn't read the Dave Robicheaux books in order – I think *Black Cherry* was the first I encountered – but I don't believe I enjoyed them any less. *LA Requiem* is getting a *huge* number of first-time readers and the result is that the Elvis backlist is blowing out of the stores.

It's a great title.
And not only here in LA! For me as a writer it was very important. I'd written seven pretty much straightforward novels. I broke POV for the first time in the sixth, and I wanted to do other stuff. One of the things *Requiem* is about is cross-genre writing: it's part detective novel, part police procedural, and part suspense novel. I wanted to write a Joe Pike story, and I didn't know how. Joe is so internalised he barely speaks. I didn't know the details of his scenes explaining his past, but I knew *why* he was what he was. I was uncertain at times. I thought my readers might be uncomfortable – "I want Elvis' POV, I want Joe Pike to stay mythic, not real", that sort of thing. But I don't feel the ghost of Raymond Chandler stalking me with a .45 making me write it one way. And the reader responses have been most appreciative.

Chandler's ghost may not be stalking you, but Los Angeles certainly is!

I love LA – it's a magical place. I grew up with Chandler and Ross MacDonald.

I think LA is all things to all people, a community of islands linked by freeways. It's a place where you go to make dreams come true. People go there because there's something edgy about it; that edginess crackles in the air, it hangs over everything. It can be a place of desperation. I think *LA Requiem* ends reaffirming the American Dream, LA style. The place of dreams is also a place of dashed dreams.

But the bottom line is you really like Elvis Cole.
Toward the end of *Demolition Angel* I began to miss Elvis and Joe. You know, Joe's scenes in *LA Requiem* were amazing to me. Right now I'm outlining the next Elvis Cole book, and I'm chomping at the bit to write it. I love him. I've spent thirteen years with these guys, and they're great guys, it makes it fun to write!

[Bob has to rush off to a meeting with the executive who bought *Demolition Angel* for Columbia Tri-Star.]

He's the guy who produced *Jerry Maguire.*

Oh, you're seeing Larry Mark? He was at that reception yesterday too – another product of the same film teacher!
You guys are everywhere, London and LA!

And in the end, so was Robert Crais.

The Elvis Cole Novels
Monkey's Raincoat (1987)
Stalking the Angel (1989)
Lullaby Town (1992) (Elvis goes
    Hollywood!)
Free Fall (1993)
Voodoo River (1995) (Elvis in the Bayou!
    Introduces Lucy Chenier)
Sunset Express (1996)
Indigo Slam (1997) (Elvis v Russian Mafia)
LA Requiem (1999)

Orion published the last two, and also
    published *Demolition Angel* (2000)

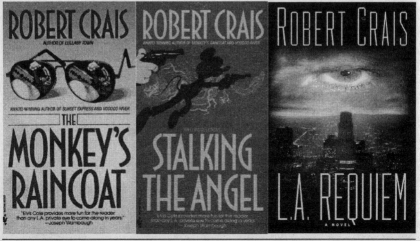

hugger mugger

Robert B. Parker

Spenser is back and embroiled in a deceptively dangerous and multi-layered case: someone has been killing racehorses at stables across the south, and the Boston P.I. travels to Georgia to protect the two-year old destined to become the next Secretariat.

When Spenser is approached by Walter Clive, president of the Three Fillies Stables, to find out who is threatening his horse Hugger Mugger, he can hardly say no: he's been doing pro bono work for so long his cupboards are just about bare.

Disregarding the resentment of the local Georgia law enforcement, Spenser takes the case. Though Clive has hired a separate security firm, he wants someone with Spenser's experience to supervise the operation. Despite the veneer of civility, Spenser encounters tensions beneath the surface southern gentility. The case takes an even more deadly turn when the attacker claims a human victim, and Spenser must revise his impressions of the Three Fillies organization – and watch his own back as well

ISBN: 1901982939
£5.99
Paperback 324pp

BLOOD WASHES BLOOD

A True Story of Love, Murder and

Redemption Under the Sicilian Sun

Frank Viviano

In the beginning, before the mystery, there is the killing. Two gunshots at a deserted crossroads. A highwayman in the robes of a monk. A face that he recognizes in the dusk.

There is his name, my name, scrawled into the death registry of Maria Santissima delle Grazie, a country church in western Sicily: *Francesco Paolo Viviano, son of Gaetano, was buried this day.* There is the raw fact that edges into fable, a bandit ancestor with a red sash tied around his waist, the birth throes of the sinister empire known as the Mafia.

There is the elemental drama, a betrayal and murder that my immigrant grandfather hides for more than eighty years, until a November morning in Detroit five months before his own death, when he whispers another name to me: 'Domenico Valenti.'

From Blood Washes Blood *(Century/Random House)*

That whisper in 1992 sent me to Terrasini, Sicily. To the village where my namesake was born, raised and murdered, after a life that encompassed two failed revolutions and made him a celebrated bandit – a Mediterranean Robin Hood, who travelled and robbed by night in the robes of a friar. Sicilians called him *lu*

Monacu, 'the Monk'. *Blood Washes Blood* is a seven-year journey in search of the Monk. It is meant, first and foremost, to offer a compelling tale, a saga of 'ordinary' people caught up in sweeping events – in History with a capital H – and prevailing over them. I have my grandparents to thank for that: *Blood Washes Blood* is their memoir, the dramatic narrative of betrayal, escape and self-redemption that was their most important legacy to me. It speaks to the universal immigrant experience, in Britain or America – whether its starting point lies in Sicily during the Risorgimento, Ireland in the potato famine, the Eastern European *stetl* wracked by pogroms, or south China during the Taiping Rebellion. But it is also very much a detective narrative, set in the deeply evocative landscape of western Sicily and aimed at solving a murder that occurred more than a century ago. The search revolves around that murder's central questions: why was my namesake killed? Who was Domenico Valenti, his presumed assassin? Why did my grandfather conceal this murder for eight decades? Why did he reopen it in the final months of his life?

When I began searching for the Monk and his killer, I knew virtually none of the story's key details, and not much more about its setting. I had been to Sicily several times between 1980 and 1995; it would be impossible for a reporter covering worldwide organised crime to avoid Sicily. But my professional trips took me to the sites of contemporary front-page crimes and trials. It was only after my grandfather's last enigmatic words to me that I spent more than one night in Terrasini, the village of his and my other grandparents'

birth, looking for answers to the book's central questions. As those questions are pursued in *Blood Washes Blood*, the lives of my grandparents, the Monk and Valenti are gradually reassembled. At crucial junctures, they are entwined with my own experiences on the road – most notably, a nightmarish 1992 episode in the ruins of Yugoslavia, in which I was taken captive by renegade militia. With two decades of experience as a foreign correspondent, much of it on the trail of killers and their victims, I was confident that I had the skills to solve the mystery of the Monk. Instead, I found myself in a labyrinth of other, interlocked mysteries, where everything – names, identities, motives – fell under the same enigmatic veil as my grandfather's last words. Eventually, the mysteries were solved, one-by-one, until they merged in a single story with an astonishing climax. What I had never imagined, when I arrived in Terrasini, is that the story had an author, and his text was me.

The drama behind this story is peopled by a remarkable cast, drawn from the fierce embrace of a Sicilian childhood and the shadows of our family mystery. In addition to the Monk, my grandfather and myself, they include:

❖ **Antonina Randazzo**

the Monk's first wife, his comrade in the revolution of 1848 and on the mountain roads. Utterly forgotten 120 years after her death, Antonina's unexpected rediscovery in a faded nineteenth century document carries the book into Sicily's clandestine parallel universe – the realm of its bandits, folklore and ancient resentments, where the truth about my family's past lies hidden.

❖ **Domenico Valenti**

the chieftain of a powerful clan in western Sicily, and one of the founders in the 1870s of a new organisation that will later be called the Mafia.

❖ **Henri d'Orleans**

duc d'Aumale, the son of a deposed king of France, a Bourbon grandee who owns an enormous swath of countryside around Terrasini. The Monk and his sons are this exiled duke's vassals.

❖ **Gaetano Viviano**

'The Falcon', eldest son of the Monk, and his successor as a celebrated bandit. Ruthless and brutal, he unwittingly alters our family history in a violent confrontation with my grandfather.

❖ **Angelina Tocco**

my paternal grandmother, a weaver of fables and a high priestess of Sicily's parallel universe. She is Frank Viviano's wife for sixty-seven years after their daredevil 1917 elopement to Canada.

❖ **Caterina Cammarata**

my maternal grandmother, is domesticity incarnate, a woman who measures her days in the nursing of babies and preparation of meals. Yet she too has a secret life, and it proves a key to the larger mystery of *Blood Washes Blood*.

❖ **Pietro Palazzolo**

'The Damned', my grandfather's boyhood friend in Sicily, he murders thirty-one of his neighbours, one by one, in a maelstrom of vengeance. It is justified, in Sicilian eyes, by the ancient proverb that 'blood washes blood'.

❖ **Michele Cortese (Mike)**

my closest friend in Terrasini and a returned immigrant from New York. He

was my chief guide to the *sistema del potere* – the underworld power structure that rules Sicily.

As it happens, the most important influences on my work are British rather than American. For many years, I earned a living as a travel writer, as well as a newspaper journalist, and I devoured every word published written by Norman Lewis, Eric Newby and Bruce Chatwin. Lewis most kindly read and commented on this manuscript; he was once married to a Sicilian, who was herself a daughter of the 'parallel universe' that is investigated in *Blood Washes Blood*. In the realm of the crime narrative, inspiration came from both sides of the Atlantic – from the brilliant Eric Ambler for his absolute control of plot, from Graham Greene and James Elroy for their ability to set a scene. A debt to all of these writers (and many more, as a long, solitary career on the road occasions a great deal of reading) is present in everything I put on paper, including newspaper and magazine articles. I feel very strongly that journalism must recover the attention to 'story' – to plot, character development and sharp description – that once marked it, but nearly disappeared in the modern obsession with brief, fact-filled dispatches that were rid of all drama. In the future, it seems to me, readers will turn to Internet news synopses for such facts, and the role of journalists must return to that of dramatic narrators and portrait-painters.

My own working habits tend toward periods of frenzied productivity – I've written as much as twenty-five double-spaced pages in a single eight-hour burst – interspersed with a day or two of utter exhaustion in which I write nothing at all. This is almost certainly a hangover from three decades as a foreign correspondent, principally covering wars. When the news is breaking, I'm obliged to file stories as quickly as I can get them into my laptop. The exhaustion is inevitable, and crashes down as soon as the flow of news and professional adrenaline eases. I've done some of my best work in Shanghai, Moscow, Belgrade, Berlin and Palermo, cities where extreme tension lies just below the surface of what appears to be 'ordinary' life. It's my conviction, and the heart of *Blood Washes Blood*, that there is no such thing as 'ordinary' life; that in the closets of apparently conventional family histories, hidden skeletons almost always rattle. To return once again to other writers, this is a consistent theme in Graham Greene, Eric Ambler and John Le Carré. A debt to them may prove far more explicit in my next book. I'm entertaining the idea of a sortie into fiction: a serious post-Cold War thriller, set in the Caucasus and the Balkans, that draws directly upon real characters and my own real experiences covering civil war and international organised crime, but frees my imagination from the constraints of dry, documented fact. If I succeed, the result will be 'truer' in spirit and implication than anything I've written in a newspaper.

Biographical Information

Frank Viviano is the senior at-large foreign correspondent of the San Francisco *Chronicle*, based in Europe, and the former Asian correspondent of San Francisco-based Pacific News Service. He is the author of seven books, including the critically acclaimed *Dispatches from the Pacific Century* (Addison-Wesley, 1993). He collaborated with Magnum photographer Nikos Economopoulos on *In the Balkans* (Abrams, 1995). As an overseas reporter, Viviano has covered events ranging from the fall of Ferdinand Marcos in the Philippines and the Tiananmen Square crackdown in China, to the collapse of the Soviet Union, the Gulf War, civil wars in Central America, Kosovo, Croatia and Bosnia, and the criminal underworld in Italy, Eastern Europe, Russia and Germany. His articles have appeared in more than two hundred newspapers and magazines in America, Europe and the Far East.

The only two-time recipient of the World Affairs Council's Thomas More Storke Award for Achievements in International Reporting (1986 and 1989), he holds a doctorate in history from the University of Michigan. In 1985, he was honoured as journalist of the year by the Media Alliance, the nation's leading organisation of freelancers. In 1993, a consortium of independent newspapers named him American Writer of the Year. In 1998, he was selected as journalist of the year by the Northern California Society of Professional Journalists.

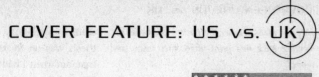

US GOLD

DONALD E. WESTLAKE

Lee Server

Unavailable for thirty years or so but never forgotten by discriminating readers, the novels of Tucker Coe concerned a tough but emotionally shattered and disgraced ex-cop named Mitch Tobin. Tobin has screwed up his life big time, cashiered from the NYPD after a sleazy adultery ended up costing his partner his life. Now all the man wants to do is to be alone with his misery, his only purpose in life a self-imposed, Kafkaesque assignment to build a wall in his tiny backyard. But the world keeps dragging him back. In a series of five novels – *Kinds of Love, Kinds of Death; Murder Among Children; Wax Apple; A Jade In Aries; Don't Lie to Me* – published between 1966 and 1972, Tucker Coe detailed the turbulent life of this unusual mystery fiction protagonist. The books have been cult favorites for decades but only now are they returning to print. They follow the recent return of another distinctive byline from the 1960s and 1970s – Richard Stark, author of the sublime criminal adventures of the man known only as Parker, with two new works released and a third on its way. Both these authors are, of course, the creation of a more corporeal writer – a one-man conglomerate as the book jackets used to say – the legendary Donald E. Westlake. We spoke recently about the return of Tobin and Parker, and about other things, too – pen names and loaded words, hotel room mirrors, fan mail from prisoners and busting heads.

Are you pleased to see the Tucker Coe books are coming back into print after thirty years and more?

I had really, until very recently, thought that this was a thing I had done, a long time ago, and it was gone. It was a garden I once cultivated and it had gone back to the wild. There was never much interest in Coe. He got very good reviews. He didn't get a lot of reviews. But very good reviews. Only sporadic paperback interest. Not much foreign interest. And then it ended. And now, all of a sudden, thirty years later, here he is again. And I just got a fax from my agent in Britain saying there is a publisher there who wants to do Tucker Coe all of a sudden. It's going to take me a long while to figure out why this is his moment.

How did the Mitch Tobin series take shape?

In the early years, in the 1960s, I was trying out different things, different ways of writing, different stunts. I wanted to do something that was slowed down, steeped in emotion. About three or four years before I had done a novel called *361*, which I thought of as my Peter Rabe novel.

The Gold Medal crime novelist?

Yeah. A paperback writer in the 1950s and 1960s. In his best books what he was absolutely wonderful at – the only one I know who was better than Hammett at this – was giving you the emotion without saying it. Everything is surface, really stressed emotion that you're painfully aware of but he never says anything. This was wild, this was wonderful. I met him many years later, briefly, in San Francisco, and I was not surprised to hear that he had

studied psychology, and that his master's thesis was on frustration! Anyway, I did that, and then I had also started doing the Richard Starks. And again this was the dampening down of emotion, almost novel as a movie, just what you see and what you hear.

But there's a world of difference between the powerful effects of Hammett and Rabe – and I'll add Richard Stark – and all those so-called cinematic writers whose stuff reads like a functional screenplay.

It's down to the language. You're choosing words that aren't loaded with emotion but are loaded in other ways. So it seems that it's just objective, but the words have spin on them. This is what Hammett is doing, and Rabe. I remember a sentence of Rabe's in one of the books – there's a guy, a low-level crook, and a more important crook took his girlfriend away. He's in a parked car and he sees the two of them walk by. And the sentence was: "He was so perfect at this now he could smile." And the word 'perfect' seems as though it's objective, but it isn't. That's great. He gives us everything without seeming to. It's the choice of words. And I'll tell you somebody else who did it in a slightly different way was Nabakov.

So you'd perfected this style. You were consciously trying to start on fresh ground with the Tucker Coe series?

I didn't know about a series when it started. I never thought of any of them as a series. I wanted to do something, yes, that was different, slower, admitted emotion. When the character of Mitch Tobin came along, entered my head, I said, "All right, this is interesting, here is a guy who's trying to be what I have in the other books, but he can't." He's driven by his repressed emotions, by this other stuff. And while most crime-solvers in these books are interested in the crime and the other characters, this guy was mostly interested in himself. You know, his attitude is, "Okay, this guy killed him... now leave me alone!" And that was an idea that appealed to my contrary side.

And so I did the first one. And I showed it to Lee Wright, my editor at Random House. She was a great editor, my first editor, and she had a lot of opinions and theories. For instance, she thought you could never use the word 'dead' in a title. 'Death', yes, 'slaughter', but not 'dead'. And it was determined – I'm not sure now how – that the Mitch Tobin novel would have a pen name. And Lee Wright had a pet theory that a successful, a memorable pen name would be an unusual first name and a normal last name. That would trigger a memory in people. The only example I can remember now was the science fiction writer Cordwainer Smith. So at that time in the backfield of the New York Giants the two running backs were Tucker Frederickson and Ernie Koy. So I said, "Okay, how about Tucker Koy". And she said, "I don't know why, but that sounds obscene." Ha! And somewhere around there I thought of a second book that would involve him and I said, "And it's going to be a series." Well, even then, I saw the problem with it was there was no way it was going to be a long series. He was a character who would be working through his problems. It couldn't go on forever. By the end of the fourth book I could feel there was a real strain. I felt, either he gets

over it and becomes healthy and he's just another private eye, and I can't use him. Or he wallows in his pathology and he becomes a kvetch and I can't use him. So I knew the fifth book was the last one. This was the end and he was going out. I didn't want to do a Holmes over the falls with him, but for me this was the end. So at the end of the book he goes to sleep. And that's it. A long sleep.

But you saw that as a conclusion, not as an open ending?
Whichever way he goes, and it's up to him, I don't know whether he gets better or worse... but whichever way he goes, he's not a guy I can use any more. The great thing about Parker and Dortmunder is that they are not impelled to change. But Mitch Tobin reacts to the cases and they bother him and they alter him.

Mitch Tobin's world has fallen apart, he's traumatized. He's having pretty much what we'd now reduce to calling a mid-life crisis.
Oh yeah. And his fucked-up relationship with his patient wife. Oh yeah, that's right.

You generally show an aversion to outright autobiographical writing, but I wonder if you look back and see any personal impetus for the series and the character.
Well, I was under forty when I wrote all of those. But actually, now that you ask, well there were changes in my life from the beginning of that series to the end. I had a marriage come to an end and I met the woman I'm married to now. But...

It wasn't conscious, anyway...

Quite seriously, I believe that writers should not know what they're doing. It's okay to know what you've *done*. But you can't know what you're doing and successfully do it. Some years ago, Larry Block was living on the road. He was between marriages. Sixteen months driving around in a station wagon, all over the country, and staying in motels. And he continued to work. He said what he learned afterwards was that in every motel in America the space where you could put your typewriter faced a mirror. And he said you can't work if you can watch yourself working. So he spent sixteen months putting towels over mirrors. You have to be unobserved while you're working.

So at least while you were writing about Tobin obsessively building a wall in his garden you only saw it as his problem, not yours.

That's right!

Did the editor or publisher ever have any reservations about a traumatized or neurotic cop/detective hero? Anyone say, "Don, what's with this guy and his wall?"

No! Every once in a while, at the desk, I think of something and say, "Is this too much on the money? Too goddamn obvious?" And sometimes you say, "No, it doesn't matter if it's obvious. It's right." And I do remember thinking, he's building this wall, Jesus, this is heavily symbolic. But it's so heavily symbolic it isn't even symbolic any more. It's right. And I kept it in. But I remember fretting over it, thinking, Can't I do something subtle? Ha!

In Tobin's self-imposed isolation – his silent turmoil and that wall he's building – I thought I caught a bit of metaphoric resonance about the writer's life. Stuck in the house, piling up the pages, alone and at the same time all churned up with the drama of the story in your head.

Yeah. I don't know how far you can carry it! But you're reminding me of what my writing practices were at the time I wrote those books, which have changed completely. From the mid-sixties until about 1973, I was working ten p.m. to four a.m. Then I'd go to bed and get up at noon. Then up in the afternoon doing whatever and then at night go to work. I had young kids, everyone went to bed. And the later it got into the night the greater my sense of being alone, in the only lit room anywhere, just me. I had this sense of being in a basket at the bottom of the dirigible. So... yeah! There was a relationship between me and Tobin there.

Did you feel the need to research the background, hang out with cops?

Never for a book. The first time I did a screenplay, *Cops and Robbers*, the producers wanted the cooperation of the New York Police Department, so they wanted me to hang out with them, get on their good side and request their expertise. So I had a lot of conversations and did a prowl car tour on the upper West Side. I went on these domestic dispute calls and all sorts of things. Only when there was a real threat of violence did they say, "You stay in the car." And I said, "You bet!" And that was very interesting. And I learned about the particular tribalism of the cops. They really are instinctively and automatically in their own group and you are not. Even if you're the brother of a cop but you don't wear the uniform, you're seen as an outsider.

In addition to Tucker Coe, there's been another resurrection, and a more active one, with the return of Richard Stark.

Really astonishing to me. The first twelve of those were paperback originals and they could not have been more disposable if they were today's newspaper. Nobody expected, ever, to see any of those things a year later. You were paid, they were published, and everybody goes home. That was it. When the movie *Payback* came out last year, and the book was reprinted, you had to think, this ain't bad for a thirty-five-cent paperback original from forty years ago. And I mean, when they were written there was no *excessive care* taken, let me tell you! The care I took was strictly for me, because I enjoyed what I was doing, no one else was that concerned.

Did you feel the need to reread the original Starks when you were bringing him back to life?

Yeah, for specific reasons. I'm at work on a Parker novel now. I realised that there were two characters from the past who had to come into this book, and they were from about the tenth book – a Gold Medal. So I had to reread it so I would know what it was that Parker knew. And – it sounds immodest – but I thought, you know, this is pretty good! Ha! And, honestly, I really remembered virtually nothing about the book. And so I'm going along saying, "Now what the hell is going to happen? Oh, is that what that was? I see." And then, also, I could see a moment about two-thirds of the way through where I could see where the writer didn't know what the hell he was doing, but kept going! Wait a minute, you're vamping

here! You should have thrown these pages away if they're not working!

What's different about writing the new Parkers from the ones nearly forty years ago?

The one difference that I'm aware of – and I'm sorry for it, and there's nothing I can do about it that I can think of – is that I'm not as carefree about it. Back then it was a pen name that nobody connected with me. I was this anonymous guy in the middle of the night spewing out this stuff pretty fast. And I can't quite get there again. For good or for ill I know that the book is going to get noticed a little bit. So I can't quite shoot from the hip as I could before.

Do they take longer to write?

Yeah! Ha! But they all do now. I'm not as fast as I was in the 1960s and 1970s. It's like they say, when you first fall in love you want to do it all the time! It gradually calms down...

I imagine the Richard Stark readership is probably more self-conscious now than in the Gold Medal days.

Yes. When *Comeback* came out I got a bunch of letters, responses from fans, collectors of the series who were happy about it. And that's tapered off. But, yeah, it's a different time, different circumstances for these books than when they came out as cheap little paperbacks. There are two kinds of readers that I used to hear from, letters that I used to get that I don't get now. The first is that I was getting letters from prisoners. And that was kind of nice. They wanted to talk shop with Richard Stark. Tell me things, capers they did that didn't go off so well. Great stuff.

Hilarious, some of it. And then the other kinds of letters I used to get were from city black guys. They wrote to tell me they just loved Parker. Now the books had few black characters in them, they're not racist but they're not politically correct either. The only thing I came up with was that they essentially lived in a society that rejected them and they loved this guy that had rejected society. He lived outside and he didn't give a shit what society thought about him. Anyway, I'm not getting those letters now.

You've told me you tried to return to Parker several times through the years since his early retirement and each time you abandoned him. Now Richard Stark is back in the saddle. Three books into his comeback do you have any new theories about why you stopped and why you could start again?

Why did Parker go away? I have thought about it. And where did Parker come from? When I arrived in New York I didn't know anybody, I had no connections, I hadn't been to any of the right schools, had no important friends in the literary world. I was on my own. And I think Parker came out of that sense of being outside and of wanting to bust into a world that didn't know me, didn't invite me in. By the time Parker went away from me it was fourteen years later, I'm making a decent living as a writer, movies have been made from my books and one of them a classic – *Point Blank*. It's hard to keep your 'outsider' hat on. And I think that's why he went away when he did. God knows I tried to bring him back and it never worked. And I think I know why he came back finally. You know, there's a thing at the Writer's Guild, they're at the barricades fighting about ageism – discrimination against writers over the age of forty or fifty. They're over the hill to many producers. And there's a lot of that sort of thing going around. Make way for the new kids on the block. And I think Parker came back because in a way I had the feeling of becoming an outsider again. Oh yeah, I'm the old guy? I'm still better than you are! That kind of feeling. I think Richard Stark came out of retirement to beat some more heads!

(Thanks to Mystery Scene*)*

US GOLD

ANOTHER 'LOST' GENIUS –
The Mario Balzic Novels of K. C. Constantine

Peter Walker

"Aww, Jeez, Mario…." If I can start on a personal note: agree with me, disagree with me, think I'm mad, but I want to make this point. I get attached to characters, especially when there is a series in which you can build a bit of history with them. You get involved. Watch them grow and grow old. You read a book and know the past events they are describing. I can not, for example, read a book in a series out of sequence. Dave Robicheaux, Dave Brandstetter, Isaac Sidel, Jacob Asch, Steve Carella – I'd miss them all. Maybe I'm not making my point very well but there is one character who for me is so real I can – almost – have conversations with him: Mario Balzic. Put it another way: I'd argue that K. C. Constantine's series about Rocksburg's Chief of Police Mario Balzic is one of the best this genre – or any other genre – has to offer. Like Jerome Charyn, Constantine is an all too neglected writer of genius. He easily compares with other so-called serious writers.

I was going to give you all the benefit of my investigations into Mr Constantine, whose well-known dislike of publicity means he's a fairly elusive person. In the end, however, I wondered what the point of this would be. My guess is that to read and know his books would give you a fairly good basis to infer the rest – if you wanted to – and if Mr Constantine wants to maintain a separate 'real' and 'fictional' persona, then who am I to argue? He 'interviews' himself in one of his books, and there is a lot of biographical information there. There's stuff on the Internet including a *Sunday Night CBS Profile* which is pretty interesting. Constantine appears in a kind of cameo in *Bottom Liner Blues* as N. M. Myushkin, the 'Mad Russian' novelist, who'd published nine critically acclaimed novels but made no money from them. Constantine describes Myushkin as "short, thick, wide, with large, veiny hands, wrists, and forearms. He was wearing a white T-shirt and gray shorts and running shoes with no socks." Make of that what you will. I was also going to include all sorts of wonderful bits of information about Mario and Rocksburg but, hey, who am I kidding. Go out and get the books.

The interview took place via email and Mr Constantine prefaced his answers with this: "Herewith your thoughtful questions and my answers. I was trying to compress my answers as much as possible so I hope I don't come off too smug or glib, which is always a possibility when I'm trying to pack as much information as I can into small space."

A lot of writers won't let their characters grow old (e.g. Spencer, Robicheaux) whereas with Mario it's intrinsic to the books – any comments on this?
When I started the Rocksburg series, I'd never read enough series fiction to know whether characters aged or not. All I'd read was Spillane's Mike Hammer books. I didn't start reading Simenon until after I'd begun the Rocksburg series, and I was looking at other things in his work. I guess I must have decided that since time, economics, politics, etc., move on, it would be incongruous to comment on those changes while my main character was staying the same. I really don't think I gave it much thought. I had read Eric Hoffer's *The Ordeal of Change*, and I think any psychologist worth his degrees will agree with Hoffer's contention that change, whether good or bad, is definitely stressful if not painful. For example, John Czarowicz might not have committed the murders in

Grievance if the Social Security statutes then in force had allowed him to receive his full retirement benefit without limiting his earnings. Shortly after *Grievance* was published, a law was passed abolishing those limits. From Social Security's inception, there never had been a limit on unearned income, i.e. stock dividends, bond interest, mineral royalties, etc., which meant that a person who made, say, $100,000 a year in such un-earnings was paid his full retirement benefit, while a person earning, say, $20,000 a year painting houses or driving a truck, would have lost a dollar in benefits for every two dollars he earned over a certain amount if he was between sixty-two and sixty-five, and lost a dollar for every three dollars he earned over a certain amount if he was over sixty-five. It was a grossly iniquitous law, and one well repealed. I don't think it's possible to write about such changes while your main character remains forever forty-six.

There is a very specific criticism of the social/ economic/political situation in the States. Why is this so important to you?
It's important because in the mass news media the line that used to separate news, advertising and editorials gets fuzzier by the day. Local television news is a bad joke, and local newspapers are almost as lame. In *Cranks and Shadows* Balzic sought out a young reporter who told him in detail why, given the mindset of his bosses, it was impossible for him to do anything approaching investigative journalism. The ominous thing for a representative democracy – or for what proclaims to be one – is that in the

mainstream news media there aren't very many investigative journalists. If you don't subscribe to the *NY Times*, the *Washington Post*, *Rolling Stone*, or *Mother Jones*, your choices run out fairly quickly, but those subscriptions add up real fast. Some of the best investigative journalists work for papers and magazines that focus on business, but, the *Wall Street Journal* aside, their circulation isn't very great either. So even though I'm always recommending the reports and essays of Lewis Lapham, Neal Postman, William Grieder, Donald Barlett, and James Steele to anybody who'll listen, whenever I'm in my cellar, I think what the hell, it's my book, let me get my two cents' worth in.

You've named Eric Hoffer amongst others as a literary influence – could you say something about this and other writers who have influenced you?

Hoffer's just a great writer, that's all. You can't open *The True Believer* or *The Ordeal of Change* without knowing you're reading some of the best stuff ever written. Hoffer had the uncommon curiosity to look at the obvious, the mundane, the stuff everybody else seemed to look at but not see, and to write about it with such clarity that, while you may not always agree with him, there's never much doubt what he's trying to say. The other great influence on my writing is Flannery O'Conner. I speak of her as though she's still alive, because of course to me she is. She took some of the most complicated human problems and presented them in the most simple vernacular. Until I'd read her, I didn't know you could do that. Of course I'd read Mark Twain and Ring Lardner and most of the

other great students of American dialects, but none seems to have touched me in the way she has. And it's not because I agree with her theology – I don't. I don't pretend to be a Christian, much less a Roman Catholic like she was. It's a tribute to her remarkable ability that I never doubt the authenticity of her characters – all because of her skill at getting into their minds in their diction. Because of who and what I write about, I'm sure Ms O'Conner would be appalled if she were alive and learned that I was trying to emulate her. But no matter what she might think of my stuff, I can never overstate my debt to her.

Are you a 'crime writer' or a writer who writes about crime? How do you view the genre?

All I know is that after the first four books I decided that my subject was not the solution of particular crimes so much as it was the economic decline of south-western Pennsylvania because I guess I'm never going to get over having been born in the middle of the Great Depression. First coal mining went to hell in the 1950s and 1960s, and then steel making went the same way in the 1970s and 1980s. These two industries didn't just vanish by themselves in this part of America; their demise was aided and abetted by a combination of highly questionable political, management and union decisions. Some of those decisions bordered on the criminal, but they weren't indictable even though their consequences were horrendous. There are whole towns on welfare, not just individuals, towns whose tax-bases have been so depleted by the closing of mines and mills that they can't even collect garbage or provide street lights without disbursements from the general state treasury. I keep waiting for some ambitious politician to talk about these towns in the same way they talk about individual welfare fraud: how the town would collectively drive up to the welfare office in a white Cadillac convertible with all its illegitimate offspring in tow, but no politician, no matter how ambitiously he wants to get elected to provide welfare for 'only the truly needy' has sunk that low – not yet.

Furthermore, the crimes that fascinate me have less to do with bodies in the street than with how grossly and purposely iniquitous tax laws are written. For example, a few years ago Pennsylvania politicians offered voters in ten southwestern counties a referendum on whether we wanted our tax dollars used to build sports stadiums. The vote was overwhelmingly no in all ten counties, in one county by ten to one, and even in the closest vote it was six to four against. The same state politicians – who had previously revised the welfare law so harshly that parts of it have been struck down as unconstitutional – within a year after that referendum voted to increase the state debt by $545 million to build two sports stadiums and a convention centre in Pittsburgh, and they did so while telling the grotesque lie that no tax money would be used to retire this debt. And who reported, exhorted, editorialised and publicised this travesty of corporate welfare in the name of urban renewal, social progress and city pride? *The Pittsburgh Post-Gazette*, circulation some 500,000 plus, who once admitted in a three-inch story way back when they first started beating the drum for new stadiums that the publishers were part-

owners of the Pittsburgh Pirates baseball team, one of two teams that would benefit from the building of these stadiums.

I don't think I'm writing in any genre, which, I suppose, makes me something less than fully professional. I think those genre labels get pinned on books mostly so retailers can know what part of the store to stock the shelves in, and what part of the store fans can go to without wading through a lot of stuff that doesn't interest them. I just write about what interests me and hope that I'm writing about it in a way that informs and entertains readers. Of course I'm aware that a lot of people are pissed off because my plots are insufficiently puzzling. I don't care. Crime puzzles don't interest me. For example, in *Grievance* the puzzle for me wasn't whether or how Rugs would catch the killer, but how Rugs would work the most notorious case of his career while his mother's behaviour grew uglier day by day and while he was falling in love with Franny Perfetti. Maybe I should write a disclaimer for all my books: "For those seeking crime puzzles, seek elsewhere."

How is the series going to develop with Rugs?
See all of the above.

So there it is. Fortunately both Blood Mud *and* Grievance *are now available from No Exit Press but do yourself a favour: get the rest of them.*

MIKE RIPLEY

Lights, Camera, Angel will be the tenth — tenth, for God's sake! — in the *Angel* series, which began in 1988. I suppose it's an object lesson in an author being unable to kill off a series hero, or maybe just a sign of an author who can't do anything else. The plot sees Angel landing a job as a driver to a

Canadian film star currently shooting a Chinese-funded, modern-day vampire movie set in New York, at Pinewood Studios. Confused? You will be, especially as the movie in question, called *Daybreak*, is based on a script written some years ago by American crime writer Walter Satterthwait and – guess who? – Mike Ripley. In the book, the scriptwriter is a composite character called Walter Wilkes Booth and he makes several cameo appearances.

Researching it was a dream. Pierce Brosnan invited me to Pinewood to see the last few days of the shoot of *The World Is Not Enough*. I had known his mum and stepfather for some years, and indeed his stepdad used to be a driver in the film industry, looking after Stanley Baker among others. Spookily, Pierce and I are almost exactly the same age (and there the similarities end) and we worked out that we both saw *Goldfinger* as kids at almost exactly the same time. I remember thinking, "Gosh, I wish I could write that", whilst Pierce thought, "I can *be* that", and on reflection I think he got the better deal. Anyway, I got treated like royalty on the set – even got to play sink-the-model-nuclear-submarine – and one of the highlights was over lunch in the cafeteria, with Hugh Grant and Liz Hurley on the next table whispering loudly: "Who's that with Pierce?" I started writing it the minute I got home. Or, to be honest, once I had a plot to go with it. In an *Angel* book the characters in Angel's world are set up and waiting for something to happen and it would be mad to change that. I usually remember to include a plot about halfway through, but basically they are not whodunits, they are *how does he get out of this?* stories. Or, occasionally, *how the hell did he get into this?*

Writing series fiction with the same basic cast of characters is limiting, but there's no doubt it's fun, and when you're doing comedy the fun element is crucial. The literary establishment is very snooty about series characters, but Evelyn Waugh always advised new writers not to kill off good characters as it was such a bore to invent new ones. And there is a challenge in that you can't – and certainly shouldn't – assume that a reader has read any of your previous books. Therefore you have to think up new ways of introducing your characters every time. The problem with a lot of situation comedy is that the situation is either not very strong to start with or is explained once and then forgotten. In superior comedy writing, say *Only Fools and Horses*, you never forget the market-trader background to Del Boy's family which explains the characters and their actions. Not that I wouldn't like to do something else. I would like to write a book that really scared people, as there is only the thinnest of lines between a laugh and a scream, but I guess I'm stuck with being funny – or trying to be – and the longer that goes on the more difficult it is to take things seriously.

When I started writing, I was working in London and commuting from wildest Essex with Jonathan Gash, a neighbour, of *Lovejoy* fame. On the train one day, I was rereading Margery Allingham's *Tiger in the Smoke* and raving about what a brilliant snapshot, almost a photograph, of London it was for 1951 and how somebody should use the crime novel to do a similar snapshot of London in 1987. (The era of greed is good, worries about where the next

BMW was coming from and, of course, THATCHER!) Jonathan Gash simply looked at me and said: "Well, get off your arse and do it". So I did. I wrote the first page of *Just Another Angel*, took it out of the typewriter and read it. Rightly deciding it was pretentious rubbish, I tore it up and rewrote it for laughs. About three-quarters of the way through, I put a plot in it – one ripped off (but acknowledged) from Alexander Dumas – and it was immediately accepted by Collins and published in 1988. My editor there was the legendary Elizabeth Walter, who had been Agatha Christie's last editor, and the first thing she ever said to me was, "How many more can you do?" When I said maybe three, before I ran out of jokes, she said that eight was the usual number to allow me to give up the day job – as long as I didn't have children. It didn't exactly work out that way, but Elizabeth's confidence in her authors was a source of great strength to me and many other writers in her stable.

Influences? I would have to say Len Deighton was the key one. At university a tutor marked one of my economic history essays with the words, "More Keynes, less Deighton please", and I was very proud of that. In the late Sixties, John Le Carré was torturing our souls (brilliantly) and riding the crest of the spy fiction wave, but I always went for Deighton because either he or his heroes always had tongue firmly in cheek. Deighton was cool. It was the same with crime fiction. I always preferred Margery Allingham, Edmund Crispin and Michael Innes to the more serious British mystery writers, because they had a sense of fun. With Americans, the wisecracks seemed to come more naturally and were far less mannered, so Chandler must be listed as a great influence, certainly the earliest, but also Rex Stout and the Nero Wolfe stories.

And my writing peers? Well, I'd be very flattered to be made a peer of some of the crime writers of today. Of my generation, I would consider Minette Walters, Ian Rankin and Michael Dibdin as world class

MIKE RIPLEY

bootlegged angel

'The outrageous rip-roarious Mr Ripley is an abiding delight ...'
COLIN DEXTER

novelists who just happen to do crime, but they are all far better writers than what I am. And there are loads of writers I read for pleasure and not because I have to as a critic. Reginald Hill, Rodney Wingfield, James Lee Burke, James Ellroy, Carl Hiaasen, Elmore Leonard and some, like Margaret Maron, the late Sarah Caudwell, Walter Satterthwait, Justin Scott, Andrew Vachss and Colin Dexter, who became good friends. Of the younger crowd putting some fresh blood into the scene, I am very impressed with the likes of Christopher Brookmyre, Denise Mina, John Connolly and Nicholas Blincoe, and the earlier work of Colin Bateman and Jeremy Cameron. As a reviewer for ten years now, I am conscious of getting tram-lined into reading just crime as I see about 250 new crime novels every year. I have to make a conscious effort to read outside the genre, which makes it very rewarding when I manage it. The novelist I most admire is probably Gore Vidal, and I've read everything he has written, including his three detective stories written as Edgar Box. As a historian by training and now an archaeologist by profession, I'm very sceptical about historical novels (and especially historical crime novels!) but I do make a bee-line for Allan Massie and Ross Leckie, and I just loved Julian Rathbone's *The Last English King* and *Kings of Albion*.

But there's always vintage crime fiction to 'discover'. In the last couple of years I have reread the Lionel Davidson canon (surely one the most intelligent thriller writers ever), tracked down a couple of P. M. Hubbard books I had not read and come, late in the day, to realise how good John Bingham was and William McIlvaney

is. There, back to crime fiction again, which probably makes me sound like a real saddo, but I do love the genre because it is so all-embracing. Last year I selected, with Harry Keating, the Top 100 crime titles of the twentieth century for *The Times* and we tried to match a book to every year. For 1981 we ended up with Sarah Caudwell's *Thus Was Adonis Murdered* and Thomas Harris' *Red Dragon*. Professor Hilary Tamar and Dr Hannibal Lecter in the same breath. Brilliant! In what other genre could you find such a contrast? That great critic Julian Symons – and we got on very well together despite the fact that he hated my books, and told me so! – used to say: "Crime writers write too much". Maybe I read too much, but I've found that fans are very well read indeed and most crime writers are very badly read. Even worse, I know crime writers who never watch movies and boast that they don't own a television. That makes me despair, because the last two generations of mystery readers (and hopefully the next as well) are coming to the genre through film and video or TV. Think of the quality of the writing in *The Usual Suspects* or *Seven* or in *NYPD Blue*, *The Cops* or *The Sopranos*. To ignore writing like that is foolish and it amazes me that there is not a Crime Writers' Association award for film or television. There again, nothing the Crime Writers' Association does should surprise me. As the only crime fiction critic of a national newspaper (for ten years) never to be asked on to the judging panel of the CWA Dagger Awards, I suppose I should know my place!

As to the mechanics of writing, well, I suppose they're odd because I make them so. I really do find writing a bore and I sit there praying for the phone to ring or the postman to call and where are the Mormons when you really need them? I never start a book until I have the opening *and closing* lines in my head. Those are the interesting bits. The 256 pages in between can be a chore. I will have a structure in my head – I think of it as a mental storyboard – with various references such as set-piece scenes, plot points, technical bits (like how to steal a light aircraft or jacknife an articulated lorry) and jokes. The jokes are important. They may be one-liners or conversations or sometimes key words or facts I've picked up in some pub or another. I usually carry a policeman's notebook with me and jot down just one or two words per page to remind me of something. When I start a book, I rip out the pages and blu-tak them around my office, ripping them down when I use them. When they've all gone, it's time to finish the damn thing. I suppose I'm quite a fast writer, but I'm nowhere near as fast as some I know. I don't rewrite much, if anything because I hate it. I would rather stare at a blank page for a day and then get it right rather than slap down any old rubbish and go back to pick the bones out of it. I suppose that's my journalistic background, which certainly helps. My best ever stint was

18,000 words in a sixteen hour period to finish a book ahead of deadline (something I've always tried to do). I was quite proud of that – and not one word had to be changed – but I wouldn't recommend it; certainly not to a non-smoker. I think Benson & Hedges got the advance for that one.

I can normally do an *Angel* in four months. When I wrote for television, I once did an episode of *Lovejoy* in three days, and last year I did a film script for a competition in four days. It didn't win. But of course I was *thinking* about them for

'The outrageous rip-roarious Mr Ripley is an abiding delight...' **COLIN DEXTER**

months beforehand. I really would like to get back into scriptwriting although I've seen TV writers desperate to get into print with a novel, and I know novelists who moved into TV and are totally depressed when their scripts get changed or are not made. And we all know novelists who are publicly appalled at what TV has done to their personal creations, though few of them send the cheques back. I follow Colin Dexter's philosophy: "Books is books, telly is telly". (Though he probably said it more grammatically than that.) Take the money and run, don't whine about it. For most crime writers, unless you're on the bestseller list, it's the only way of making any decent money. It used to be said that getting on the telly would increase your paperback sales tenfold, however bad the TV adaptation was. I'm not sure that's true any more, actually, and we can all think of cases where increased book sales have *not* followed a television series. But publishers get very excited at the first whiff of a TV version and it helps to get a book into places like W. H. Smith. Now I come to mention it, I don't think any of my books have ever been sold in Smith's and I was told that one paperback – *Angel City* – was rejected because it had hypodermic needles on the cover. I don't think they bothered to check that it was about the illegal dumping of hospital waste, not drug-taking.

The TV rights to *Angel* were sold back in 1990 just after the second book came out. For a while it looked as if Carlton were going to do it, but they did Mark Timlin's Sharman books instead. Since then the rights have been re-sold several times and are currently with the BBC, but the wheels of television grind exceeding slow until one of the suits in broadcasting says, "Go!", and then all hell breaks loose. I used to be asked *ad nauseam* who I would like to see playing Angel on the box and my stock answer was: somebody young, unknown, cheap and grateful. I was told, by a producer, that this was not a good thing to say and that I should go for a big star to impress the suits. At one meeting, when asked the awful question, I said: "Well, if Kenneth Branagh's busy..." and three – *three* – of the people round the table produced mobile phones and said, "Do you want me to check?" I guess they had his agent on speed-dial.

Do I write for myself or my readers? Good question. I suppose all writers write for themselves to some degree and I rationalise it by writing comedy. In essence I'm a failed stand-up comedian who wants to make people laugh by telling them about things which make me laugh. Basically I'm in the entertainment business, presenting a character who gets away with murder, is cheekily irresponsible and says things we all could have but only think of too late when the moment has passed. There is, of course, a moral edge to *Angel* though it might go unseen. He never allows the baddies to prosper – unless he does – and usually some sort of justice gets done. But there are loose ends – just like in life. The books rarely end with everything neatly tied-up. For myself, I have experimented with various plot structures just to see if I could do it. *Angel Hunt*, for example, has three circular plots that eventually overlap into a conclusion. *Angels in Arms* is a straight-line, almost a western plot, with the good guys riding to the rescue like the

US cavalry – hence the number of references to westerns. (Actually, the last third of the book is *The Wild Bunch* without the blood if you read it carefully!) In *That Angel Look*, I played about with the time frame and had triple-flashbacks, very much like *The Usual Suspects*. I have tried to cover what I suppose you could call social issues in the books: the stock market and the big bang in the city ten years ago, animal liberationists, the homeless, the fashion business, bootlegging and drug smuggling. One book, *Angel City*, got rave reviews from the *Telegraph* for being funny, *Tribune* for raising awareness of the homeless and *Gay Times* for being sympathetic to young gays. I was quite proud of that, though my best ever review was, "had me rolling on the floor with laughter" – in *Taxi Globe*.

Places which get the creative juices going? Above all it has to be London, where the bulk of the Angel stories are set. I worked there for twenty years, though I've never lived closer than seventy-five miles away, which is fine by me. Every time I visit, I usually spot something or hear something that ends up in a book. The other cities that have inspired me, though I've never used them directly in my fiction, are Chicago and San Francisco, both exciting, humming, places. I love New Orleans too, but as the jazz trumpeter I almost certainly was in another life, not as a writer. Oddly enough, though, I have never really been classed as a 'London' writer and I never get asked to contribute to conferences or anthologies on 'London noir' writing. I suppose it's because I'm not noir enough. Reg Hill once described me as flying the flag for the new British hard-boiled school, but I'm soft-boiled really. Bit like an egg.

The future? Well, it was a bit of a blow last year when the *Daily Telegraph* suddenly decided not to review crime fiction on a regular basis any more and I was 'let go' after eleven years and over 500 books reviewed. However, the *Birmingham Post* asked me to take over the monthly Crime File column from the late F. E. 'Bill' Pardoe in January and that's going really well. And I've just agreed to do another *Angel* novel for Constable/Robinson for, we hope, March 2002. I haven't got a title yet but it will involve Angel in an archaeological dig. Everyone I've said that to has made some sort of crack about sharpened trowels being really useful weapons. I have to point out that the *Time Team* mob might use trowels for the cameras, but real archaeologists start with bulldozers: eighteen tons moving at fifteen miles an hour, and they can be hotwired...

Bibliography

Just Another Angel (1988)
Angel Touch (1989)
Angel Hunt (1990)
Angels in Arms (1991)
Angel City (1994)
Angel Confidential (1995)
Family of Angels (1996)
That Angel Look (1997)
Bootlegged Angel (1999)
Lights, Camera, Angel! (2001)

Lights, Camera, Angel! Is published by Constable Robinson

NO EXIT PRESS

ROBBERS

Christopher Cook

Two aimless Texas drifters, Ray Bob and Eddie, find themselves on the run after an impulsive act of violence escalates into more. They are joined by Della, a young working class woman who's had to leave town when a casual pick-up in a hotel bar has unexpected and lethal consequences. The trio are pursued by Rule Hooks, a Texas Ranger who follows his own lonely code, and breaks it.

In this fast-moving southern noir that marries poetry to action, the story flows over terrain from the Texas hill country through coastal swamps into the lush East Texas riverbottoms as each flawed character seeks his own secret redemption. *Robbers* is a literary thriller of the first water.

ISBN: 1901982963 £10.00 Paperback 400pp

NO EXIT PRESS

available from bookshops
or ring 020 7430 1021
www.noexit.co.uk

A DAY IN THE LIFE OF
MARGARET MURPHY

A friend observed recently that my stories seem to need darkness for their creation. They have a point: plots, characters, scenes and scenarios seem to shimmer in the shadow margins, like tantalising peripheral glimpses of the Pleiades. Chapters are drafted in longhand on lined paper, and redrafted and crafted on a computer. I do most of my writing on a 486 I bought almost ten years ago; absurdly, I'm rather fond of it. The monitor occasionally flickers and blurs, fading in and out, causing me no end of anxiety in the process, but for now, it's functioning.

I never was much good in the morning, but now I have the luxury of being able to admit it to myself. So, it's a slow emergence. Of course, if I have to interview someone for research, or attend a court hearing, it means an early start, and I can do it – just don't ask me to do it too often. Other days, I'm at my computer by

10.00am. It hasn't been easy to structure my day since I gave up teaching two years ago: for seventeen years I had been regimented by the bell, and one or two Pavlovian responses have been difficult to eradicate – if anyone rings at the door around lunchtime, I drool like a puppy. It's great not having to get up at six-thirty in the morning. So great that initially I had trouble motivating myself to get out of bed at a reasonable hour and start work – and keep at it even though there was nobody watching and appraising my performance. Of course, in the long term, agents, editors and ultimately, with a little luck, the reading public will all judge the final result, but that can seem a long way off when your struggling with the next chapter, or the next scene, or even that bloody paragraph that stubbornly refuses to be written.

If I need to send emails – and being bookings secretary of Murder Squad, a consortium of crime writers, I usually do – I have to use the Pentium PC in the next room. That can take anything up to two hours. I make coffee, let it go cold, plough through the messages, send replies, post off copies of the Murder Squad brochure to interested parties and tell myself I'll get down to some proper work in a few minutes. Sometimes the snail mail gets in the way, though; I find I can't just ignore it, even leaving it till later is a problem. I usually deal with it on the day it arrives, otherwise it eats into my soul, destroying the muse, preventing me from working. I do a lot of reviews, so I can legitimately take a break to read a chapter or two in the middle of the day, and still call it work. It doesn't quite stop me feeling guilty (I was brought up a Catholic – years of therapy would be needed to achieve totally guilt-free self-indulgence), it does take the edge off, though. In between, I might continue the quest for a builder to sort out the flooding problem we've had in the garage for nearly a year now. Of course, they say it should never have been built there in the first place. "It's a sump. Look at the run-off from the garden." At this point, they usually gaze regretfully at the marshy patch that used to pass for a lawn. "And that's clay soil, that is..." The builders have suggested a variety of remedies: a) pulling down the garage and starting again with raised foundations; b) putting in land drains (since the garden is barely larger than a pocket hanky, this seems less than feasible); c) digging up the garage floor and re-laying it on a slope, so that at least the water will run out. This, the cheapest estimate, will cost more than we spend on petrol for a year. I decide to think about it. Meanwhile the car sulks on the drive, reminding me that it isn't used to being left out in all weathers.

I feel fortunate that I am able to make a living from writing, but there's not a lot of slack, and every little helps, so I tutor creative writing students for the Open College of the Arts, and Monday to Thursday, for a couple of hours a day, I teach dyslexic children. I feel fiercely protective of them: some of these children have had every ounce of confidence knocked out of them; sometimes they can be difficult, resisting the slog of trying to make sense of a code they can't seem to crack, but they can also be a joy, and I'm proud of every step forward they make. Perversely, I can also resent the interruption to my working day. It *is* two hours, after all, and I was just getting into my writing, wasn't I? Sometimes I almost convince myself. Despite my selfish mutterings, I usually enjoy their company, and it is a small part of the day when I am focused on someone else's problems, rather than my own. And when I'm in a more rational frame of mind, I accept that my best creative time is between seven in the evening and midnight. Just as well, because three-thirty to seven is written off by teaching and then sorting out dinner. Murf is a great chef's assistant, but he prefers being bossed about in the kitchen to taking charge. I think he sees himself as an updated Johnny Craddock. He's fond of quoting that infamous blooper, "I hope your doughnuts all turn out like Fanny's..."

I'm not particularly house proud, but I trained as a biologist, and having grown the nasty little buggers on neatly labelled plates of agar, I know about bacteria, their unpleasant lurking habits and their opportunistic ability to grow at an exponential rate, given the right substrate and a little warmth. So, while the furniture may be allowed to gather dust, I set time aside to keep the bathroom and kitchen clean. Seven to ten pm is prime writing time, and the two hours to midnight are useful for daydreaming, finding answers to plots, letting characters come alive in my imagination, and seeing just what they're capable of. I'm working more and more from what could loosely be termed a synopsis, which according to Chambers is 'a summary or outline, especially of a book'. Summary, it ain't and outline...¿ No, it couldn't really be called an outline, either, given that it may have a one-line suggestion for a subplot next to an entire scene, with dialogue – descriptions and all. I'm going to have to think of a new word for this rapid neural

firing – perhaps *synapsis*, instead of synopsis¿ Whatever you'd call it, this method suits the way my brain works. It's not haphazard exactly: I end up with a structure that, though flexible, does contain the main features of the narrative and plot. Working with dyslexics has taught me that the brain doesn't favour linear thought – especially in creative mode – ideas float into the mind like soap bubbles, and they're just as ephemeral – there's no point in trying to grasp them: they'll vanish with barely a trace. It's best to sketch them fast before they disappear.

I like research, and I read a lot around the subject: books, newspaper articles, the Internet, it doesn't matter what the source is, I read, take notes, allowing the facts to ferment before doing the creative stuff. For *Dying Embers*, I did a lot more face-to-face work, talking to homeless people, finding out about police procedure. I even persuaded the manager of the Liverpool *Big Issue* to talk to me, to get the overview. Until I made the switch from book research to interviews, I would have said I was naturally shy, and it wasn't an easy transition. But I am also doggedly determined: I needed to know things, and I intended to get the best information I could. I was surprised to find it does get easier and more enjoyable, and creatively, dealing with real people is far more stimulating than referring to case books and newspaper archives. Generally, I invite my source out for a meal. It's a pleasant way of researching the background, but also time-consuming. Before they will accept an invitation, I have to convince them that I am really a writer, and not a crank with a prurient interest in homelessness, or drug abuse or mortuary procedure, or whatever. It took a *long* time to gain entry to a mortuary, and this was another example of a situation in which the personalities were as illuminating as seeing the setting and taking notes on procedural detail. The two technicians I met were very experienced. The woman had a bad back from lifting heavy corpses (never cadavers), and both were to some extent hardened by what they had seen. They remembered cases, but never faces, and they spoke with a distance and dispassion that could result only from years of dealing with death and its attendant human misery. Not that they were without humour. Before they gave me the guided tour, they made me promise not to use the terms 'gurney' for trolley, or 'morgue' for post mortem room (it's not as snappy, but a promise is a promise), and *never*, under *any* circumstances was I to substitute 'autopsy' for the perfectly serviceable *post mortem*. Then the chief technician, a woman, asked me if I'd been a teacher. "Yes," I said. "How did you know?"

"You look like a teacher," she said.

"What does a teacher look like?" I wondered.

"You."

One up to Val Ramsbotham.

'Walking the beat' is another important aspect of my research. My novels are set mainly in the north-west, and I like to get a strong sense of place. *Dying Embers* features Adèle, a homeless woman; this meant searching ruined cobbled back streets of towns and cities to find disused warehouses, peering into dark doorways, trying to find ways in to old buildings, experiencing how frightening these places can be.

The pace of life is dictated by the build-up to the launch. So far, my novels have all been published in September or October; this seemed the right time – a hangover from teaching, which has the autumn fixed as the real start of the year, but it's put me in competition with the big thriller writers, as well as crime authors of the kind of stature that make me feel Lilliputian by comparison. It does nothing for an author's delicate self-esteem to phone her publisher the week before publication of her new novel and get an ansaphone message to the effect that the publicist is on tour with Colin Dexter, but if she has any messages or queries about Colin Dexter, she can leave them after the tone. The autumn publication of *Dying Embers* was particularly busy: Murder Squad had readings and bookshop events up and down the country, my publishers set up radio interviews, local press wanted to do profiles or features, and in between, I was working on the programming committee for Dead on Deansgate, sending out invitations for my launch party, sorting out the catering (I did it all myself in the end), and a week or two after publication, jetting off to Zimbabwe for five days for the British Council, to present workshops and readings to Zimbabwean writers and to address a special education conference.

While I'm checking proofs on the new title, I'm writing the next and may be researching and jotting down ideas for the synopsis of the one after. So, it's a midnight finish, on a good day; I unwind with a book, or a programme I've taped earlier in the evening. I've given up trying to see Murf off to work. I mean, what sane person *would* get up at five-thirty in the morning if they didn't have to? It's a chaotic life, but it's never – ever – dull.

GERALD KERSH

Paul Duncan

Kershed: Whatever Happened to Gerald Kersh?

Over the past ten years I have been reading, researching and writing about Gerald Kersh so that one day he would get back into print, and perhaps garner some of the acclaim and recognition that he rightly deserves. At last, it looks as though that is about to happen. In the UK Harvill Press have just published *Fowlers End* with a new introduction by Michael Moorcock, and in the US i-books are to publish *Night and the City* this summer, with an introduction by me. And best of all, editor Barry Forshaw has allowed me a couple of thousand words this issue to explain the wondrous world of Gerald Kersh. In Barry's words, "All CT readers should be reading him!" And who am I to disagree?

Gerald Kersh was a prolific and successful writer of fantastically nightmarish short stories and novels. However, in 1949, after his luxurious Barbados mansion burnt down without insurance, his wife Lee left him and took all his money. On top of this, Kersh was suffering from over-

work, nervous breakdowns and recurrent malaria and dysentery. In New York, his friends rallied to help the best they could and one in particular, Flossie Sochis, gave up her job and paid for his bills with her savings until they ran out. Kersh went to England to convalesce, and was nursed by Flossie and journalist Freda Court. Officially a Canadian resident, in 1950 Kersh was forced to move to Canada to protect his tax position. This is an extract from a biography of Gerald Kersh, presently without a publisher, which explains how Kersh came to write one of his best short stories *Whatever Happened to Corporal Cuckoo?*

On the evening of October 10th, Kersh boarded an overseas plane at Luton airport, bound for Vancouver on a journey that would take him two days. Watching him climb the steps, Freda Court and Flossie could see that Kersh was already in the preliminary stages of the malarial fever. They returned to Freda's Stoke Newington house where they spent a sleepless night worrying about him.

The following day, whilst Kersh was

still airborne, Flossie received an urgent cable from lawyer Levin: on September 28th 1950, Senator Morritt had attached Kersh's income in conjunction with Lee's divorce and alimony action. In plain English, that meant that by law Kersh could not draw any funds or advances from his agents or publishers. Kersh had no private bank accounts and no savings, so how was he to live in Vancouver?

When Kersh arrived in Vancouver on October 12th 1950, he was very sick, had fifteen cents in his pocket, and was depressed by news of the attachment. He pawned his gold ring for $20, only for the pawnbroker to tip off the newspapers that Kersh was in town. Sick as he was, shivering with chills, boiling with fever, he found himself besieged with reporters for whom he had to put on a good show.

Kersh tried to continue working – it was not in his nature to sit still and do nothing. He persuaded Marie Anthony to act as his secretary in the evenings. She was an ex-actress, who worked mornings as a coffee shop waitress, afternoons as a doctor's receptionist, and evenings as an author – her novel *A Lion Roared in Trafalgar Square* was due to be published in England early in 1951. She worked on Kersh's Vancouver novel, tentatively entitled *The Good, the True and the Beautiful*.

In an effort to sell Kersh's short stories in Canada, Flossie air-mailed him manuscripts from London, and cabled some magazine editors in Toronto, but with no success. Unfortunately, the newspapers in Vancouver and nearby Victoria had no budget for buying Kersh's stories. So Kersh tried to survive in his box of a hotel room. He was trapped in a place he did not know

or have any feeling for. He was alone. His friends in New York were a quarter of the world away. Flossie and his family were on the other side of the world. Soon Flossie would get in a tin can and float, ever so slowly, towards him.

Drifting in and out of consciousness, a story of memories began to form in his mind. He remembered a room whose walls were made of steel, and the gentle rocking motion of the Queen Mary. She slid out of Greenock on July 6th 1945, bound for New York, holding inside her ribs of steel fourteen thousand souls: mostly men, although there were a few ladies and a dog. Dogs were not allowed on board but the young American officer who had saved it, lifting it from atop barbed wire where it had been trapped for days, would not go home without it, and neither would his men. Throughout the trip, this bag of bones was fed by men from all the companies so that, by the time they docked, the German Shepherd was fit, renewed, playful, alive to the world. It was a symbol that these soldiers were leaving the war behind them and embracing their life ahead.

Kersh was resplendent in his crisp uniform and sharp beard. He was on official business as a war correspondent, intent on making his way across America to the Pacific coast on a lecture tour for the Ministry of Information. Having been warned that no alcohol was allowed on board the Queen Mary, Kersh had taken the precaution of smuggling several bottles under his garments. He offered an officer a taste, and found he immediately had many new friends from the other ranks. After the bottles had been jettisoned through a porthole, Kersh was lucky enough to make the acquaintance of Charles Bennett, a Hollywood screenwriter (who had previously worked with Mr Hitchcock, and was presently working for Mr DeMille) on his way home after doing his duty for the Ministry of Information, and even luckier to procure from him a bottle of ginger ale containing Scotch. Kersh was a quick study, and this bottle remained hidden from all ranks.

The five-day voyage was a long trip for Kersh, because during it he found plenty of time for reflection and introspection. That past year, he had seen too much of death and the evil that men do. Carl Olsson was Kersh's best friend and, in June, Kersh watched him die of cancer. Carl was a journalist who specialised in reporting the front-line experiences of sailors, soldiers and airmen. In fact, his reports followed the same format as Kersh's short stories: an introduction giving the background information, followed by the character narrating the story to be told. As his name may imply, Carl was originally from Sweden. He was making a lot of money in the manufacture of glycerine by an artificial process when he went, aged sixteen, to fight in the Great War as a trooper in a cavalry regiment, before being transferred to a special branch of the Engineers that dealt with 'counter-measures.' He never spoke of his experiences at Passchendaele.

One night on another battlefield Carl became hopelessly lost in No Man's Land, and found himself in a bunker underneath six high-explosive projectors at the moment of their ignition. The world exploded and fell upon him. He woke in the South of France, weeping, a nun stroking his head, comforting him. When the doctors examined Carl, they pronounced him shell-shocked, found he had a terrible dread of confined spaces as a result of his premature burial, and his lungs had been badly damaged from the gassing. They gave him six months to live. Carl fought back death and, through the force of his will, made himself better. If he knew there was something to fight, he would draw upon his inner resources and defeat the enemy.

So when Carl went down with shingles in 1945, having stretched his six months of life to twenty-five years, everyone sent him funny letters and get-well presents, because no-one dies from shingles, do they? And then he went into hospital with a dose of pleurisy. He was convinced he would be out in no time, because the doctors did not tell him he had cancer – they thought it kinder to leave his mind at peace. Kersh told his friend the truth, reasoning that Carl had been a fighter all his life, and would prefer to go down fighting. Carl lasted three weeks more. The day before he died, as Kersh was leaving, he said, "I'll be with you the day after tomorrow." Carl replied, with a grim smile, "I shouldn't hurry if I were you," and they shook hands.

Kersh knew that death could never be accepted. Death must be fought.

Before he left for New York, Kersh had seen reel upon reel of film footage of the concentration camps: Belsen, Dachau, Buchenwald, Ebbensee and others. The film was being assembled and edited by Sergei Nolbandov for the Ministry of Information – Kersh was to write the narration. On the screen, Kersh saw fat, well-fed German soldiers dressed in warm clothes and women guards in their silk stockings with their hair neatly set or permanently waved. The dead – 10,000 found dead and 13,000 who died in the days after the liberation – were strewn across the camp like weeds. Occasionally, they were piled up. The Germans had let the prisoners die of starvation, dysentery or typhus or, if they were lucky, were tortured to death or shot. The dormitories were full of naked bodies – alive or dead, it was hard to tell them apart. One person was alive, in a bed with two dead people, too weak to escape the grip of death. Skin and bone, with waxen, shiny skin, these people were allowed to waste away. The thinking behind this was that dead, a starved body is much lighter to carry and takes longer to decay, doesn't create such a stink. Kersh watched as the Germans, men and women alike, were made to carry the bodies to a mass grave. (Could some of these people have been his relatives? Two of them had been taken away on one of the death trains.) The Germans found it distasteful to touch the skin of the dead. The bodies filled pit after pit. The liberated people washed themselves of the filth. The local people looked on, dumbfounded, practised looks of innocence on their faces. The English soldiers razed the camp to the ground. Only a sign marked the spot where the evil had been done.

This is what Kersh feared. That people will forget what they have seen with their own eyes. That people will deny that it ever occurred.

Gerald Kersh / Fowlers End

That people will attribute such behaviour to a disease of some sort which breaks out occasionally and can be controlled through drugs or psychology. Kersh knew that it was worse than that. That this ability to be cruel, to disassociate ourselves from the horrible things we are capable of, exists within us all. We are all capable of killing and torturing, and worse, turning a blind eye to the people doing it. We cannot change our nature.

Kersh secured some hot water and freshened himself up with a wash and a shave. He timed the strokes of his blade with the ebb and flow of the ship. Stripped to the waist, he saw what he saw every day of the week: an axe-scar in centre of his forehead, a knife-scar on his left wrist, a small tooth-scar on knuckles of his right hand. The scars had not been acquired on the battlefields of Europe but on the proving grounds of Soho, in the lounge bars of the seedier side of London. One of the innumerable people who hated the sight of Kersh tried to do him in with a hatchet. Kersh side-stepped, thus saving his own life, but suffered a small gash on the head and a bit of concussion. In retaliation, Kersh threw a marble-top table at his assailant and knocked him out. But the guy had his revenge. It seems the blow disturbed a trigeminal nerve in Kersh's head which sent pitchforks of pain through Kersh's brain, keeping him awake nights.

Over time, Kersh had accepted these imperfections as part of himself and no longer noticed them – he would absent-mindedly finger his scars when talking. Kersh saw that the soldiers on the ship showed their scars to each other. They were signs of brave or foolish deeds. They were signs that they had escaped death, and the more scars the better. Each scar had its own story, and the telling of these stories affirmed that life had won again. Good over evil. Life over death.

In a hotel room in Vancouver, Kersh returned to consciousness. The memories had coalesced into one coherent story about an immortal soldier, a soldier who had been blown up, speared, cut and shot innumerable times, yet he healed up almost immediately. He had cheated death, but what for? It would be a story about human nature and how it never changes. And so, Kersh wrote the story, calling it *Whatever Happened to Corporal Cuckoo?*

As Kersh wrote the story, he couldn't help laughing. He called the French immortal soldier Lecoq, and had the children call him Le Cocu, which means a man whose wife has been unfaithful to him. Anglicised to Cuckoo, the Frenchman wandered the earth looking for wars to fight. With each war would come another wound or two, so that Corporal Cuckoo began to resemble the battlefields he fought upon. Thinking of Cuckoo's wounds reminded Kersh of his recurrent malaria. He began to feel that he would have the malaria for the rest of his life, like the headache. It was something he had to live with, something to be fought with mind and body. There would always be wars, and always soldiers with the strength of will to fight them.

If only each battle didn't leave him so weak...

Soon after Flossie arrived in New York, Kersh cabled her that he'd sold his *Corporal Cuckoo* story to the Montreal Standard. This sale was through the good graces of their staff writer Jacqueline Sirois, a young cousin of Lee's whom Flossie had met in New York. The money Kersh received was just enough to bail him out of his Vancouver hotel and pay for a plane ticket to the East. He got his visa on November 7th (as luck would have it, the recently published interviews and pictures of him in the Vancouver newspapers helped to identify him to the US consul and expedite his visa) and on the 11th touched down in Pennsylvania, where the plan was for him to live with Flossie's parents.

Kersh was so ill, he had to be stretchered off the aeroplane.

After more than a year of treatment by the doctors at the University of Pennsylvania, Kersh was pronounced fit and well. Dr Fitz-Hugh reported that Kersh's body had spontaneously healed the malarial abscesses in his liver. "It is what religious men call a miracle," he said. Kersh had risen from the dead yet again.

Paul Duncan can be contacted at kershed@aol.com

To get the regular Kershed newsletter e-mailed to you free of charge, just send an e-mail to kershed@aol.com and I'll put you on the mailing list

Kersh Website:
http://harlanellison.com/kersh

Kersh Chat Room:
http://clubs.yahoo.com/clubs/geraldkersh

CONSPIRACY THEORIES

The Essential Conspiracy Theories

by Robin Ramsay

Do you think the X-Files is fiction? If so, you must be one of those deluded fools who think Elvis is dead, and believe that the US actually went to the moon, and don't know that the ruling elites did a deal with the extra-terrestrials after the Roswell crash in 1947...

Boy, it really is getting strange out there. At one time, you could blame the world's troubles on the Masons or the Illuminati, or the Jews, or One Worlders, or the Great Communist Conspiracy. Now, in addition to the usual suspects, we also have the alien-US elite conspiracy, or the alien shape-shifting reptile conspiracy to worry about – and there are books to prove it as well!

Conspiracy Theories? They are all in here – but not just lined up to be ridiculed and dismissed. OK, there is some of that, but the author also tries to sort out the handful of wheat from the choking clouds of intellectual chaff. For among the nonsensical Conspiracy Theory rubbish currently proliferating on the Internet, there are important nuggets of real research about real conspiracies waiting to be mined.

This book has done the mining for you. Fully sourced and referenced, this is both a serious examination of Conspiracy Theories and the Conspiracy Theory phenomenon, and a guide to further explorations of the subject.

ISBN 1903047307 £3.99

CHARLES SPENCER

Like an old lag up before the bench, I can only claim in mitigation that my circumstances drove me to crime.

My night job is as theatre critic of the *Daily Telegraph*, and like all critics, I suspect, I sometimes feel that my trade is grotesquely parasitic. Sitting in constant judgement of other people's artistic endeavours is a curious, indeed unnatural, way of earning a living. I felt a strong need to try to craft something myself, especially since the time I spent on Britain's theatrical trade newspaper, *The Stage*, had provided me with a subject matter I desperately wanted to write about. 'Serious theatre' still receives serious coverage in the press, but there is an almost forgotten side of showbiz that still struggles gamely on in the face of almost total 'highbrow' indifference. I refer of course to light entertainment, that fascinating nether-world of working men's clubs, talent contests, striptease joints, tribute bands, end-of-the-pier shows and stand-up comedians who owe a greater debt to Max Miller than to Bertolt Brecht.

Uniquely in Britain, *The Stage* provides detailed coverage of this neglected scene, and I thought it would provide a fine basis for a comic novel. I was keenly aware though that most contemporary novels consist of a beginning, a muddle (NB muddle is not a typo) and an end, and I thought I could provide my first fiction, *I Nearly Died*, with a stronger structure by giving it a thrillerish, whodunit element. In short I fell into that most despised of genres, the comic crime novel. I've now written three of them. The latest, *Under the Influence* (Allison & Busby, £16.99) finds my hero, a boozy showbiz hack called Will Benson, on the trail of a missing Vermeer and meeting up with close friends from his adolescence whom he hasn't met in years. There's still a strong light entertainment bias, including a hypnotism show, a heavy metal gig and a strange obsession with the Wombles, but I hope *Under the Influence* is also a deeper, and a sadder, book than its predecessors. It's a novel about lost ideals, lost love, and the possibility of redemption, about the value of friendship and the pain of betrayal, and, although I hope it's still funny, I have tried to make it moving too. I'd be thrilled if readers of *Crime Time* gave it a whirl.

NO EXIT PRESS

Straight From The Fridge Dad

A DICTIONARY OF HIPSTER SLANG

by Max Décharné

Much of the slang popularly associated with the hippie generation of the sixties actually dates back before WW2, hijacked in the main from jazz and blues street expressions, mostly relating to drugs, sex and drinking. Why talk when you can beat your chops, why eat when you can line your flue and why snore when you can call some hogs? You're not drunk – you're just plumb full of stagger-juice and your skin isn't pasty, it's just cafe sunburn. Need a black coffee? That's a shot of java, nix on the moo juice. Containing thousands of examples of hipster slang drawn from pulp novels, classic noir and exploitation films, blues, country and rock'n'roll lyrics and other related sources from the 1920s to the 1960's, Straight From The Fridge Dad lays down the righteous jive, perfect for all you hipsters, B-girls, weedheads, moochers, shroud-tailors, bandrats, top studs, gassers, snowbirds, trigger-men, grifters and long gone daddies.
ISBN: 1842430009 Price: £9.99 Hardback 224pp

PEPPY PLOTTING BY PETER GUTTERIDGE

F oiled Again *is the fifth in the Nick Madrid/Bridget Frost series. It's a weird one. I wanted to satirise sports sponsorship, and the sport I know best – because I took it up competitively for a few years in my thirties – is fencing.*

I once spent a weekend in New York with the British fencing squad (as a freelance journalist, not a fencer) for a tournament with the US fencing team. I was trying to break into the *Sunday Times* magazine, which paid thousands of pounds for an article, and I had told them that fencing was just about the only sport at which Britain regularly beat the US (true). The deal was that I should pay my own way for the weekend but that the magazine would take a feature from me and cover my expenses if Britain won. Inevitably, we lost, but I had a great weekend anyway – and now that particular competition is the starting point for this book. I also wanted to write something about the British fascists in the 1930s *and* have Nick go back to his northern roots. Now the Blackshirts were really big in the thirties in the north-west, where Nick is from. And their leader, Oswald Mosley, fenced for Britain at the same time that he was fermenting racial hatred. So I had a sort of link – fencing/Nick in the north-west/Blackshirts – but how to get a plot and make it work in a first person narrative set in the present day was a bit of a challenge. The words 'dinner' and 'dog's' came constantly to my mind.

The stuff I love has nothing to do with the kind of stuff I write: Conan Doyle, Raymond Chandler, Elmore Leonard, James Ellroy. If I could have written Joseph Heller's *Catch-22 or Something Happened...* well, I'd presumably be Joseph Heller. Actually, my greatest influence has been the Road movies of Bob Hope and Bing Crosby – those two characters are the real models for Nick and Bridget. The problem I have at the moment is that as the crime critic for *The Observer* I'm reading a lot more crime than ever before, and I'm trying desperately not to be influenced by it. Fortunately nobody else is doing exactly

what I'm doing, but I have to be careful with Carl Hiaasen – I love his work but I know my stuff can be seen as wannabe-Carl.

I spent my twenties trying to write The Great Novel. I bummed around doing all kinds of jobs – from kitchen porter to bookkeeper – and spent a year in California working on the major opus. The result was pretty much unpublishable, although I did use some of it in my last novel, *The Once and Future Con*, about the Arthurian legends. I wrote three other novels after that which I do look on with affection – and I think all are publishable. The first of them was a pastiche Sherlock Holmes adventure narrated by a Victorian adventurer called Anthony Thinblood, and with it I learned about continuity. In writing the late sections I kept forgetting that early on I'd had Holmes sever Thinblood's right hand in a duel. At the climax of the novel Thinblood and the heroine escape from a Venetian palace on the Grand Canal in the middle of the night (it's that kind of book) and Thinblood rows them to safety in a rowing boat. My editor (it was nearly published) sent me a card saying; "Wouldn't the villains find them in the morning, Thinblood rowing in circles?"

I never miss the usual suspects – Elmore Leonard, Hiaasen, Ellroy, Rankin, Reg Hill, McDermid – and my mates (but not just because they're mates but because they're good) such as Denise Danks, Alison Joseph and Danuta Reah. I've got in the habit of buying Grisham on audiotape – I think because I heard *The Partner* on a long car journey and was so impressed by the plotting, which I thought exceedingly clever. I do read other crime – and I'm very depressed by Chris Brookmyre and that new guy Barney Hoskins (the one with the hairdresser serial killer) because they're so bloody funny. I keep up with a lot of writers outside the crime field. My all time favourite is the US writer Thomas Pynchon. I think *Gravity's Rainbow* is the greatest novel ever written and I try to put a little homage to Pynchon in every novel of mine.

I love the work of George P. Pelecanos but I'm always disappointed when the novels end in an explicitly described bloodbath. Ellroy's violence is almost comic-book, it's so over the top. Violence has been done – there's no easy way to describe the blood and gore without falling into cliché. I remember how chilling Ian Rankin's *Black and Blue* was when near the start he described – in a very economical way – some thug taking out of his holdall a drill and a couple of other domestic appliances. The thug has some guy taped to a chair and just the threat of violence with everyday appliances was really powerful. Having said that, Colin Harrison's last novel (*Afterburn*?) had some less economical but nevertheless virtuoso, limb-loss violence which really got to me. I felt sorry for Boris Starling when I read *Messiah*. Having started off with a lot of blood and gore with the first murder he had nowhere to go with all the others except to splash still more blood around the place. In my stuff, I try to have brief episodes of realistic violence – but on the whole it tends to be Nick Madrid on the receiving end of some malign animal's spite. The exploding toad in *No Laughing Matter* is either my high or my low point, depending on your view of toads.

I think I'm alone in all crime fiction in having a protagonist who is lousy in bed (though Nick is getting better). So I tend to go into detail about the practicalities of sex to get the laughs – in *Once and Future Con* Nick and his first love get stuck when they finally have sex (it's called the honeymoon disease and it can really happen). Jokingly is, I think, the only way to look at sex. (Or am I saying that because women have always laughed at me??)

Elmore Leonard writes his novels virtually as screenplays – not deliberately so that they will be filmed (although most of them have been) but because that's his training. I'm a bit of a film buff – I took a degree in film studies in my thirties, used to programme an arthouse cinema and have been a reviewer and feature writer about film. (I'm currently going bankrupt replacing my video collection with DVDs.) My experiences interviewing movie stars informed a lot of the Hollywood stuff in my first book, *No Laughing Matter*. I remember once interviewing Jeff Bridges in the back of the limo taking him to Gatwick at the end of his promotional visit for some movie – I think it was *Fabulous Baker Boys*. We got to the airport and his plane was going to be delayed for two hours. He invited me into the first class lounge with him because he didn't want to be on his own. Problem was what to talk about – obviously the big movie star wasn't going to confide personal stuff to me. He asked about me out of politeness so I burbled on... and on. By the end of the two hours it was: "So what was the name of your auntie's cat again, Peter?"

To be honest I start out each novel thinking it will make a great movie then shoot myself in the foot because I get carried away by fiction's potential – by which I mean you don't need to worry about a budget. So *No Laughing Matter* is set in three different countries and *Two to Tango* is set in the Andes. I even blow the budget on the ones I set in this country by sending my characters off to foreign climes for the final part.

Writing a series as I do, the main characters are already in place. Usually the female character Nick is going to get involved with comes next. Plotting happens pretty early on. In crime fiction it is nearly always important because of the nature of the genre, but I'll read Bill James, for example, more for Harpur and Iles' relationship and the pleasure of the other characters than for the plots. Same with Elmore Leonard. I do struggle with plots so I was amused when the *Times Crime Supplement* said "peppy plotting is Guttridge's stock-in-trade". Peppy plotting eh? Here I am with vaulting literary ambitions and I end up a tongue-twister.

I don't write for myself in the sense of writing indulgently but because humour is so subjective I have to write what I think is funny and hope readers will feel the same. (They don't always, of course. I know people who hate the books. Some critic on the *Jersey Post* hated *Two to Tango* so much he gave away the identity of the killer at the end of his review. It's very easy for writers to take childish revenge for that sort of thing, though. His name attached to a ludicrous character...) As with most writers, I can only write about things that interest me. Fortunately, over the years I've had a great number of enthusiasms so I'm not short of settings for a while yet.

I live in one of a cluster of about half a dozen houses in the middle of the country in Sussex. I work in a converted cowshed and sometimes days go by without me seeing another soul, especially in winter. I quite like that, although it means that when I do see or phone people I just babble on. Most writers need solitude to write. I like writing in cafes or bars too. I wrote a lot of *Two to Tango* on a laptop on the 7.13am train to London which I took every day for a few months whilst I was working on a project for the BBC. The rest I wrote lying on a sunbed beside a hotel swimming pool and/or sitting in a beach shack in Goa, where I went for three weeks to do the yoga. Writers should definitely be of the world, otherwise what the hell are they going to write about?

I'm an atheist who would like to find spiritual meaning in something. So I usually end up taking the piss out of religions – in *Once and Future Con* I play around with the idea of competing Messiahs turning up at the start of the new millennium, each with slogans: "Gethsemane – this time we fight!" and so on. I think crime writers need to have a moral perspective so they can make sense themselves of some of the terrible events they describe.

I want to write a non-series book set in Hollywood in the early forties among the British actors there – I've just done a short story for a historical crime anthology edited by Maxim Jacubowski set then. But I'll probably be doing another Nick and Bridget book that will probably be about undersea treasure hunting and modern day pirates.

GEOFFREY ARCHER

When I was in my teens I was very taken with the novels of Nevil Shute, who wrote *A Town Like Alice* and *On the Beach*, both made into films. He had a brisk, colourful style and used technical information in an easily digestible way. I always remember thinking they were the type of books I'd like to write one day. I actually started thinking seriously of trying to write thrillers when *Day of the Jackal* came out. Frederick Forsyth's story was straight out of the front pages, and as a newsman that was the only genre of book I could imagine doing. Then my ITN colleague Gerald Seymour wrote *Harry's Game* which was also a terrific read. When Gerald left ITN to write full time, I thought this is what I too would like to do. However, it took me another twenty years of pounding the news beat while writing novels in my spare time before the books took off sufficiently to make it possible.

The first novel I wrote was never published and I look back on it more with pain than affection. I started the book in 1976, a story set in Beirut, where I'd been to report on the civil war. I'd witnessed some mind-warping scenes in a dramatically beautiful country and felt desperately frustrated by the impossibility of encompassing it all in two-minute news items. Paradoxically I decided the only way I could tell the *real* story of what it was like to be in a city being turned into a Swiss cheese by bullets was to write about it in a work of fiction. The book had a strong opening chapter, but I hadn't thought the story through. Over a couple of years I battled on with the book, working on my days off from News at Ten, then ran out of puff. I was about half way. A year later I decided to have another go and managed to devise a second half to the story. The end result was a bit of a curate's egg. I did several grinding rewrites on a typewriter, then submitted it to an agent who offered it to some publishers. They suggested a further rewrite, which I grudgingly did, but it still didn't get bought. So I gave up, writing off the years of effort as a salutary learning experience. After a year or two to recover, I decided to start all over again with a new story. This was to be my first published novel, *Sky Dancer*. No. That first work really wasn't publishable. I did manage to cannibalise part of it, however, for my third book *Eagle Trap*, some of which was set in Lebanon.

Oddly enough, I don't read very many thrillers or crime books. I've enjoyed Ian Rankin's Rebus character recently and loved *Monstrum* by Donald James. Some of the works of Iain Banks have gripped me pretty tightly and Lionel Davidson is another great thriller writer. I don't go for the Tom Clancy/Patrick Robinson stuff, despite my first three books having been somewhat in that genre. I enjoy quite a lot of women's fiction – Anita Shreve is a writer I admire. I find female characters rather more interesting than male ones.

Sex is one of the most difficult elements of a story to get right. With my last book *Fire Hawk* I opted for being more explicit than in my earlier works. My younger readers (under fifty) seemed to like it, but I had one letter from an older reader who thought I'd been gratuitous. He said the sex had spoiled an "otherwise excellent thriller". We've been through a period when explicit sex has been fashionable. Perhaps the pendulum is swinging back. In my new book *The Lucifer Network* the sex is more restrained.

I need routine if I'm to have any chance of countering the 'anything but' syndrome. I spend a few months researching a story and the main characters, and will prepare as detailed an outline as I can, which I discuss with my editor at Random House. Then I start to write. I try to do office hours, starting at 9.30am and working through to mid afternoon, with a short break for lunch. In the afternoons I do something else – maybe go to the gym,

read or catch up on admin and domestic matters. Then quite often I'll work for another couple of hours in the early evening. The shortest time it's taken me to do the actual writing of a book is six months, the longest a couple of years when I was doing it part time.

Of course a novel can consist almost entirely of character interaction, but for my sort of books plot is of primary importance. Adventure fiction without a strong action story doesn't make sense. Characters are immensely important too of course. I've always tried to have a strong female figure in my books as well as a believable and sympathetic male protagonist. In *The Lucifer Network* I'm again featuring secret agent Sam Packer who first appeared in *Fire Hawk*.

The new book, *The Lucifer Network*, is the second featuring SIS agent Sam Packer who first appeared in *Fire Hawk*. The story is set mostly in a Europe where an upsurge of refugees from the Balkans has provoked dangerous rumblings from right-wing extremists. It begins in Zambia, where the death of a gun-runner gives Packer his first clue that something cataclysmic could be about to happen. He learns that a terrorist gang has been armed with a frighteningly powerful weapon. His problem is to identify the gang, its nationality and its target before mass murder is committed. The search for the truth brings him into a tortuous relationship with the gun-runner's daughter, and also sees him embarking on a perilous espionage mission by submarine. There's a third Sam Packer story currently being written, much of which is set in Burma. To be published in 2002, God willing.

MICHAEL INNES

Michael Innes was a writer who created a highly individualistic strain in his work by synthesising two key elements in his personality: the professorial element and a pronounced Celtic side. The latter

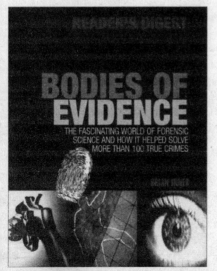

frequently surfaces in his quirky thrillers starring his alter ego Sir John Appleby (an idealised surrogate for the author in much the way that Bond was for Ian Fleming). His books were always stylishly written – under his own name of J. I. M. Stewart, he wrote acclaimed biographies of Conrad and Hardy – and more than many of his contemporaries, Innes maintained a consistently high quality throughout an almost over-prolific output.

The Author

Born in Edinburgh, John Innes Mackintosh Stewart was educated at Oriel College, Oxford. After graduation he went to Vienna, to study Freudian psychoanalysis for a year. His first book, an edition of Florio's translation of *Montaigne*, got him a lectureship at the University of Leeds. In later years he taught at the universities of Adelaide, Belfast and Oxford. Under his pseudonym, Michael Innes, he wrote a highly successful series of mystery stories. His most famous character is Inspector John Appleby, who inspired a penchant for donnish detective fiction that lasts to this day. His other well-known character is Honeybath, the painter and rather reluctant detective, who first appeared in *The Mysterious Commission* in 1975. Stewart's last novel, *Appleby and the Ospreys*, appeared in 1986.

"A master – he constructs a plot that twists and turns like an electric eel: it gives you shock upon shock and you cannot let go" – *Times Literary Supplement*

"Mr Innes can write any other detective novelist out of sight. His books will stand reading again and again" – *Time and Tide*

Innes created one of the most famous and enduring detectives of all time, who inspired a lasting vogue for donnish detective fiction.

The stories are often witty and whimsical, rich in literary references and quotations. Innes' books are recommended within Waterstones' *Guide to Crime Fiction* as "urbanely well written and probably the best example of an important strand in British Crime Fiction."

Titles Available (published by House of Stratus)

The Inspector Appleby Series

The Ampersand Papers
Appleby and Honeybath
Appleby and the Ospreys
Appleby at Allington
The Appleby File
Appleby on Ararat
Appleby Plays Chicken
Appleby Talking
Appleby Talks Again
Appleby's Answer
Appleby's End
A's Other Story
An Awkward Lie

The Bloody Wood
Carson's Conspiracy
A Connoisseur's Case
The Daffodil Affair
Death at the Chase
Death at the President's
    Lodging
A Family Affair
The Gay Phoenix
Hamlet, Revenge
Hare Sitting Up
Honeybath's Haven
Lament for a Maker

The Long Farewell The
    Mysterious Commission
A Night of Errors
The Open House
Operation Pax
A Private View
The Secret Vanguard
Sheiks and Adders
Silence Observed
Stop Press
There Came Both Mist and
    Snow
The Weight of the Evidence

Other titles

A Change of Heir
Christmas at Candleshoe
From London Far
Old Hall, New Hall

Going it Alone
The Journeying Boy
Lord Mullion's Secret
What Happened at
    Hazlewood

The Man from the Sea
Money from Holme
The New Sonia Wayward

Cream of the Crop

The Journeying Boy (1 84232 740 2)

Humphrey Paxton, the son of one of Britain's leading atomic boffins, has taken to carrying a shotgun to "shoot plotters and blackmailers and spies". His new tutor, the plodding Mr Thewless, suggests that Humphrey might be overdoing it somewhat. But when a man is found shot dead at a cinema, Mr Thewless is plunged into a nightmare world of lies, kidnapping and murder – and grave matters of national security.

The Man from the Sea (1 84232 744 5)

When a man swims to shore from a freighter off the Scottish coast, he interrupts a midnight rendezvous between Richard Cranston and Lady Blair. Richard sees an obscure opportunity to regain his honour with the Blair family after he hears the swimmer's incredible tale of espionage, treason and looming death. But this mysterious man is not all he seems, and Richard is propelled into life-threatening danger.

A Family Affair (1 84232 733 X)

Over a period of twenty years, a series of highly elaborate art hoaxes have been perpetrated at carefully time intervals, and in each case the victim has a very good reason for keeping quiet. Inspector Appleby's interest is kindled by an amusing dinner-party anecdote – when he enlists the help of his wife and son, the ensuing investigation is truly a family affair. The scenes shift swiftly between glorious stately homes and the not-so-glorious art gallery of the irrepressibly dubious Hildebert Braunkopf.

Appleby and Honeybath (1 84232 718 6)

Every English mansion has a locked room, and Grinton Hall is no exception – the library has hidden doors and passages... and a corpse. But when the corpse goes missing, Sir John Appleby and Charles Honeybath have an even more perplexing case on their hands – just how did it disappear when the doors and windows were securely locked? A bevy of helpful house-guests offer endless assistance, but the two detectives suspect that they are concealing vital information. Could the treasures on the library shelves be so valuable that someone would murder for them?

"Expect vintage ingenuity, well-tempered jokes, unruffled prose. You'll be undisappointed" – *The Times*

The Appleby File (1 84232 717 8)

There are fifteen stories in this compelling collection, including: *Poltergeist* – when Appleby's wife tells him that her aunt is experiencing trouble with a Poltergeist, he is amused but dismissive, until he discovers that several priceless artefacts have been smashed as a result; *A Question of Confidence* – when Bobby Appleby's friend, Brian Button, is caught up in a scandalous murder in Oxford, Bobby's famous detective father is their first port of call; *The Ascham* – an abandoned car on a narrow lane intrigues Appleby and his wife, but even more intriguing is the medieval castle they stumble upon.

Appleby on Ararat (1 84232 715 1)

Inspector Appleby is stranded on a very strange island, with a rather odd bunch of people – too many men, too few women (and one of them too attractive) cause a deal of trouble. But that is nothing compared to later developments, including the body afloat in the water, and the attack by local inhabitants.

"Every sentence he writes has flavour, every incident flamboyance" – *Times Literary Supplement*

REG GADNEY

Strange Police tells the story of a criminal syndicate formed to steal the Elgin Marbles from the British Museum and return them to Greece. The British government, security services and the CIA are implicated in the plot. So is the central character, Alan Rosslyn. Beyond price, the Elgin Marbles constitute, arguably, the single greatest collective work of art in the world. The Greeks have argued with good reason and great passion for their return to Athens. With less passion than the Greeks, the British have argued that they should stay put in London. Meanwhile, I would be surprised if anyone reading this who is

British has seen the Elgin Marbles more times than they have visited Madame Tussaud's. So whether the British actually love them and consider them as more than treasure trove and thus genuinely deserve to keep them is doubtful.

There are two unpublished novels. *The Jutland Summer* and *Love is Murder*. I imagine the latter remains not worthy of the light of day. The former is set against the background of the Battle of Jutland. I might, conceivably, return to it one day. But I am wary of so-called period fiction but the themes of the story – the violence and hopelessness of naval warfare in

World War I and secret incest – still interest me.

I wouldn't presume to speak for anyone else. But as far as my own stories are concerned, I find it powerful and effective to leave as much as reasonably possible to the reader's imagination. It's usually fairly clear when an account of violence is gratuitous, that is to say, uncalled for, without any credible motive, or there simply to titillate. Nonetheless, if a violent crime or a violent criminal has a central part in the book, then it would be odd to avoid the nature and circumstances of the violent acts that take place. In other words, the issue of violence should not be avoided, particularly when it's vexed. With regard to the erotic – here again, I can't speak for anyone else. As far as I'm concerned, my reply to your question about violence generally applies.

Generally, I prefer to take about nine months thinking about the idea of a book. I try to write the first draft without interruption as fast as possible. Then I go to four or five subsequent drafts and that's when the book, as it were, gets written. I'd say I am my editor. Editing and rearranging and revising is what I do mostly. The physical process of writing is not one I especially enjoy as such.

I am fond of Athens in the heat as well as London in the early hours, but I am sucker for deserted London streets in the rain or mist or snow. London's law courts, railway stations and networks of disused tunnels and empty churches also intrigue me. I am not at home with the vaunted and so-called energetic spirit and clutter of American cities.

I could never write bearing a potential reader in mind. I have no idea who the reader will be. If I knew, I'd write him or her a private letter instead. In so far as I avoid writing letters, that really would be something. So I suppose I write for someone who may be me. A me I don't know. It's different when I'm working on TV adaptations such as the one I did of Minette Walters' *The Sculptress* – I tried to honour her intentions. And I was pleased to see the Minette Walters phenomenon really took off after that show!

I find ceremonies, prize events, writers reading in shops doing the funny voices, opening fetes and car boot sales altogether embarrassing and pretty third rate and pointless entertainment. If you mean should a writer accept some state reward or honour, say a title of some sort, then I do tend to think the less of those who do. You simply cannot accept a title from some government or royal committee whose membership is secret and say you do not consider yourself above everyone else. I like that old saying, either Italian or Chinese: higher monkeys sit in tree, more clearly we see monkeys' bums. Think of writers, architects and film wallahs sitting in the House of Lords and you'll get the point.

I'm over half way through the first draft of my next book. Its provisional title, *The Damage Report*, is one that I got from a chance remark made to me by a well-known libel lawyer. Libel, however, is not its theme. To say more would, I think, be like trying to describe a baby in the womb. Touch wood – so far it's alive and well and kicking.

Strange Police *is published by Faber*

BEST OF BRITISH

DENISE DANKS' CRYSTAL BALL

How often does a crime novel read like science fiction?

On 18th January, 2001, *The Times* published a story that had appeared in *New Scientist* about an Australian inventor, Dominic Choy, who had applied to patent his design for a virtual reality sex doll – a "lifelike flexible mannequin covered with imitation skin". It would be powered by tiny motors to respond to a user's touch – or to signals from a partner delivered via an Internet connection. Fans of Denise Danks' Georgina Powers crime series, will by now be having a strange feeling of déjà vu.

In her third novel, *Frame Grabber*, published by Constable in 1992 – almost ten years ago – and due to be reissued by Orion next year, Denise invented an almost identical virtual reality suit and headset. It too "would allow partners to 'see' each other and could be programmed so that partners enter a virtual world and have a sexual experience with a virtual human or another real human linked via the system to the same world".

Just like Danks' machine, Choy's software will allow the user to select whom they wish to interact with – he suggests, a film or pop star. Of course, Danks' imagination conjured up an altogether more frightening scenario. As *The Literary Review* said at the time, *Frame Grabber* was " a health warning for all couch potatoes". Danks herself told *Crime Time* that she felt vindicated by Mr Choy's enterprise. "The crime fans liked *Frame Grabber* but some po-faced people in the virtual reality industry were never happy with what I wrote. They only ever saw it as a military or gaming application. They liked to ignore the third big software market, the market that in fact sets the business model for the Internet – sex. That's the game most people like to play, isn't it? Still, in a world where this morning is old hat, it's nice to know that *Frame Grabber* hasn't dated. I might send Mr Choy my book, tell him to bump up his business insurance for when he gets sued because someone pressed the wrong button."

FROM VERTIGO TO LES DIABOLIQUES: BOILEAU-NARCEJAC

John Kennedy Melling

We must first understand that the partnership of Boileau and Narcejac wrote not only crime and detective novels. They wrote pastiches, very useful reference books on the genre, stories for children, plays, contributed to some of their film versions – in similar mould to the American Ellery Queen collaborations. Secondly, they also wrote as individuals both before and after their meeting. Let us first look at their respective lives.

Thomas Boileau was born on April 29th 1906 in Paris, at 60 rue de Dunkerque in the ninth arrondissement, son of an executive in a maritime agency. He went to school there between the ages of seven and thirteen, and started voraciously reading crime fiction, from Nick Carter to Fantomas. He graduated to the Commercial School in 1919, and took his first job in a factory in 1923, staying until 1932 (apart from his military service in 1927). His first published work came in 1930, and in November 1932 the same journal, *Lectures Pour Tout* published his first police novel *Two Men on the Trail*. The next year he gave up employment to become a full-time author. Two *romans policiers* appeared in 1934, one published by *Le Masque*, the second a feuilleton in the first journal. 1935 saw the publication of a remarkable story in the weekly *Ric et Rac – Six Crimes Without a Killer* – a locked room mystery with six murders in locked rooms with no traces left for the investigators, written in the first

person. In 1938 he received the Grand Prix d'Aventure for *Le Repos de Bacchus*. The following year he married Josephine Baudin and they lived in the rue Viollet-le-Duc, behind the Circus Medrano, until 1982. He was called up again in 1939, and was a prisoner of war until 1942 with Jean-Paul Sartre as a fellow prisoner. He carried on writing novels and made contact with Thomas Narcejac by post in 1947.

Thomas Narcejac (whose real name was Pierre Ayraud) was born July 3rd 1908 at Rochefort-sur-Mer in the Rue Gambetta and studied from 1914 to 1919, while his father was called up. He first read Arsène Lupin in 1916, the year he lost his left eye from a friend's carelessness with a gun. He graduated very well, had an operation for

cancer which made him give up sports, and entered college at Santerres, where the family moved. He obtained his bachelor's degree in Philosophy in 1926, his L-es-L degree in 1930, became a professor at Vannes, married, and lived there till 1937. He won further degrees in 1931 and 1932. His first daughter was born in 1933, his second two years later. In 1937 he became professor in literature and philosophy in Troyes; his final Chair was at Nantes where he remained till his retirement in 1967. His first published crime fiction appeared in *Le Masque* series in 1946, his novels continued until 1979, his pastiches from 1946 to 1959, his critical works from 1947 to 1975. We shall look at some of these later.

The Collaboration

The first joint fictional effort (*L'ombre et la Proie*) appeared in three bi-monthly feuilletons in the prestigious *Revue des Deux-Mondes* from June 1951 to January 1952. Thereafter one or more novels, stories and plays appeared annually until 1993, and one last book in 1997. Boileau died at Beaulieu-sur-Mer on January 19th 1989. Some were pastiches of Arsène Lupin, for example the 1973 *Le Secret d'Eunerville* and the 1975 *Le Second Visage d'Arsène Lupin*. Among their most famous titles was the early *Celle Qui N'Etait Plus* (*She Who is No More*) or *Les Diaboliques* from 1952. It was filmed without their participation in 1954 by Henri-Georges Clouzot, with Simone Signoret, Vera Clouzot, Paul Meurisse and

Charles Vanel. The book has Fernand Ravinel and his mistress Lucienne Magard killing his wife Mireille – but her body vanishes and she comes back alive. Fernand commits suicide, and the two women cash in the insurance he had contracted with Mireille.

Two years later *Sueurs Froides* (*Cold Sweat*) was published by Denoel, and achieved world fame as Hitchcock's *Vertigo* in 1959: again, this was produced without their collaboration – the adaptation and dialogue were by the playwrights Alec Coppel (*I Killed the Count*) and Samuel Taylor (*Sabrina Fair*) and it stared James Stewart and Kim Novak. The original story varies considerably from the film, as we

Panther Crimeband

Boileau & Narcejac
The Victims

might expect; in the book Roger Flavieres strangles Madeleine and waits for the police, while Paul Gevigne, the plotting husband, is killed – an aspect which Hitchcock did consider incorporating in the film. The book was republished as *D'Entre les Morts* and my copy naturally refers on the cover to Hitchcock's masterpiece.

Eight other books were filmed or televised by others, including *Les Magiciennes* by Serge Friedman in 1959 from the 1957 book, published again by the influential Denoel. Some of the films on which they did collaborate, like *Les Yeux Sans Visage* (1959 with Pierre Brasseur and Alida Valli) and *Pleins Feux Sur Assassin* (1960 with Pierre Brasseur, Pascale Audret and Jean-Louis Trintignant) were directed by George Franju who died in 1987, ten years after Clouzot. One of the interesting television productions was *Le Train Bleu S'Arret Treize Fois* (*The Blue Train Stops Thirteen Times*). Tele Monte-Carlo wanted a feature that would attract the north to the sunnier south of France, to be filmed in Cannes and Monte-Ccarlo. From this came the fresh idea of the famous Blue Train (the scene of an Agatha Christie book), to be directed by Friedmann, Michel Drach, and Yannick Andre. Friedmann we have mentioned. Drach was to direct an episode in the Maigret series on August 3rd 1968. Andre directed three episodes on the Inspector Leclerc Series in 1962, forty episodes of the *L'Abonne de la Ligne* series in 1964, three episodes of the later 1981 *Thèophraste Longuet* series, and nine episodes of the 1970 series *Le Service des Affaires Classées*, so their credentials were good. The thirteen Blue Train episodes and stops were Paris, Dijon (with Raymond Pellegrin), Lyon (with Jean-Louis Trintignant), Marseilles, Toulon, Saint-Raphael, Cannes, Antibes, Nice, Beaulieu, Monte-Carlo (with Odile Versois and Lila Kedrova), Monaco, Menton (with Jean Servais): the episodes were transmitted on Fridays, save for Monaco on Sunday, between October 8th 1965 and May 13th 1966, scripted by B-N.

Non-Fiction

Apart from many stories in famous crime magazines, Boileau was a reviewer in *The Saint* Magazine from 1955 to 1968. Narcejac's many critical pieces included *Le Cas Simenon*, published by Presses de la Cité in 1950, and he also wrote the book *Une Machine a Lire: Le Roman Policier*, published by Denoel in 1975. Together they wrote *Le*

JAMES STEWART
KIM NOVAK
IN ALFRED HITCHCOCK'S
MASTERPIECE

VERTIGO

Vertigo | Boileau & Narcejac

Roman Policier in 1994, published by Press Universitaire Française, and *Le Roman Policier* published by the same company in 1975 as no. 1623 in the *Que Sais-Je?* series. In 1993 this volume was reissued under the same number and title by Andre Vanoncini, who devoted two pages to our subject. They are also favourably mentioned in volume 2025 in this series, on *Le Roman d'Espionage* by Gabriel Veraldi, as the first-named authors in the Denoel list.

Awards

After Boileau won the Grand Prix du Roman d'Aventure in 1938, it was won in 1948 by Narcejac for *Le Mort est du Voyage*. 1965's *Et Mon Tout Est un Homme* gained them the Grand Prix de l'Humour Noir. The 1973 *Le Secret d'Eunerville* won them the 1974 Prix Mystère de la Critique. The 1988 title *Le Contrat* secured them the Prix Trente Millions d'Amis, and in 1990 they won the Paul Feval Prize for *Le Soleil dans la Main*. Yet it has been said that, like Simenon, they are not taken seriously by the intelligentsia!

Conclusion

Boileau left Paris in 1982 for his winter home of Beaulieu-sur-Mer and died there in 1989. Narcejac retired in September 1967, remarried in Nice on December 22nd (to Renée Dellery, another professor), and died on June 7th 1998. Between them or alone they wrote nearly two hundred books, and many articles and short stories. Their work encompassed all the traditional elements of place, character, plot, family strife, doubles, denouement, their own differing forms of psychology, and even occasionally a series detective. Famous actors and actresses appeared in their films and television plays. Apart from those already mentioned there were Jean Marais (again), François Perrier, Micheline Presle, Jeanne Moreau, Lino Ventura, Eva Bartok, Gert Frobe, Juliette Greco, Annie Girardot, Danielle Darrieu, Elsa Martinelli, and Isabelle Adjani, the last in the 1996 remake of *Diabolique*.

When I was in Nice researching for this article I first contacted the Tourist Information Office who quickly put me in touch with the Municipal Archives. They put the telephone down in less than sixty seconds! I contacted the famous newspaper *Nice-Martin*, whose librarian Allan Salpin proved a mine of knowledge and co-operation. Narcejac in his last years suffered from increasing eye trouble, so writing became difficult. When interviewed about his books for children he said he used to regularly write four pages a day, but at eighty he became lazy and wrote, three, two or even one! His wife was a great help with correspondence. They were very surprised to see their prize-winning book *Et Mon Tout Est un Homme* was a film in New York titled *Body Parts*, and *Champ Clos*, their 1988 book set on an island facing Nice, was a German production film with Jacqueline Presle. He was nearly ninety when he died at their home in Rue Giuglia, where they had lived for thirty years. I realised this road was only a few minutes' walk from my own hotel, the Westminster-Concorde, on the 'Prom'. I walked up the Rue Giuglia to see if a nameplate might be still there, but I found no trace.

DISCUSSION FORUM: THE GOLD DAGGERS

Those outside the crime genre (ie those who neither write nor read it) have been moved to say: "You never seem to be happy unless you're whinging about something, do you? If it isn't the fact that crime books are not covered by literary editors, then the book stores never stock the ones that people want, there too many crime books published etc., etc.well, are you ever happy?" Maybe these disinterested observers have a point. But, actually, it's probably true that admirers and practitioners of any genre chew away at their favourite hobbyhorses (if that's not a mixed metaphor) – this is human nature, after all, isn't it?

A considerable amount of discussion has been centred recently on the Macallan Gold Dagger Award. And the consensus seems to be this: the award should be in May – or at least not in December. If a shortlist were announced at the London Book Fair, with a six-week period provided where bookshops can sell the Gold Dagger shortlist (and maybe the others), it's felt that Borders/Books Etc., Waterstone's, Ottakars and maybe even W. H. Smith would support it. After all, the CWA would be happy, as would Macallan, the authors and publishers, with (hopefully) increased publicity and sales. Along with this, there's a strongly expressed view that the award should be moved back to an evening rather than a lunchtime event in May – although this is one of the more controversial ideas, as many visitors to the awards ceremony do not live in London and would find it hard to get home from an evening event.

And how about making books published in the previous calendar year admissible? This would leave the whole summer to push and sell the winners (probably in paperback), free of the competition of the Booker, the Whitbread and Christmas. The regulars at *Crime Time* have pronounced views on this, and while it may not result in quite as much blood spilled as the battles between hard-boiled and Home Counties enthusiasts, it's caused a lively debate.

But we'd like to know what you think. Any strong views on any the points raised here? Let us know.

NO EXIT PRESS

ALL THE EMPTY PLACES
by Mark Timlin

It's the oldest story in the world: Boy meets Girl, boy loses girl, boy gets girl. But when the boy is Nick Sharman, and the girl has a violent ex-jailbird as an old boyfriend, who promises extreme retribution on anyone who gets involved with her, it's never going to be that simple...and both Sharman...and the girl are looking at a lot of trouble.

What with a bent brief planning an audacious multi-million pound robbery with a bunch of heavy duty thugs in tow, a beautiful sister who is a fast track CID officer, and enough ordnance to stock the Woolwich Arsenal, the scene is set for a savage and bloody confrontation under the streets of the City of London which ends literally explosively, with only one man standing. And guess who that is.

The latest Sharman shows there is life in the old dog yet, if only just.

Price: £5.99 ISBN: 1 84243 004 1

Mark Timlin has written 15 previous Sharman novels, the most recent being Quick before They Catch Us (available from No Exit – 1901982866). He lives in east London, has a Rolex and drives flash old American cars.

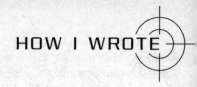

TOP CRIME SCRIBES
TELL US HOW...

From Agatha Christie to Ruth Rendell
Susan Rowland
Palgrave, £13.99, 0 333 68463 X

Upon finishing this book I realised that my true subject is pleasure. These six authors are not only important to me as an individual, they continue to draw in millions of readers. Strikingly, there has been an inverse relationship between their enormous popularity and critical attention. Their comparative neglect has been an additional spur to *From Agatha Christie to Ruth Rendell*. As well as inspiring the reading public, Agatha Christie, Dorothy L. Sayers, Margery Allingham, Ngaio Marsh, P. D. James and Ruth Rendell/Barbara Vine have all made definitive contributions to the crime and detecting form. Christie, Sayers, Allingham and Marsh constitute the 'Four Queens' of the so-called 'golden age genre'. A distinction needs to be made between the earlier authors and P. D. James and Ruth Rendell. The modern writers engage in a literary debate with the earlier form in order to scrutinise its limits and to develop the representation of crime in literary realism. As the critical neglect of

all six authors is astonishing, I offer *From Agatha Christie to Ruth Rendell* as a much needed antidote!

All six writers maintain their reputations because their novels are not only widely read, they are repeatedly re-read. This suggests that the reader is engaged

From Agatha
Christie to
Ruth Rendell
Susan Rowland

CRIME
FILES

General Editor: Clive Bloom

not so much by the 'closure', the 'whodunit', but the 'process', the *means* by which the criminal is finally identified out of many suspicious possibilities. If the pleasure of these novels does not rely upon the final pinpointing of the criminal, then it must also be found in their stories of social and self-discovery. This is not to deny the very real differences between these authors in social and political terms. I decided to pursue a dual strategy of thinking about the genre as a whole and thinking about individual artistic visions. Unsurprisingly, these novelists are interested in social attitudes to crime, but they express their analyses in stories ranging from social comedy to tragic realism. Whereas Sayers and Christie are both comic in humorous terms, they are also comic in the sense of the 'divine comedy', writing a universe in which a detective has a mythical function to restore order. By complete contrast, P. D. James, fond of associating her work with Sayers in particular, is a writer of bleak tragedies. For her, secular modernity is irredeemable, even by the sensitive policing of Adam Dalgliesh.

Again, I realised that the popular linking of Ruth Rendell with P. D. James is highly misleading. Rendell is a Gothic and utopian writer. Her innovations, including the evolution of a whole new writing persona in Barbara Vine, are dedicated to seeking out the liberal possibilities in crime and detecting genres. If class is a source of social stability for Christie, Sayers, Allingham and Marsh, then for Rendell its irrationality *provokes* crime. *From Agatha Christie to Ruth Rendell* looks at genres, authors and individual novels. I consider such issues as feminism, the Gothic and

psychoanalysis in relation to these powerful women writers. P. D. James and Ruth Rendell were kind enough to let me interview them and the results are included. I hope that my book provokes further and heated debate!

How I Came to Write *Unfinished Business*
Carol Smith

The idea for my first novel, *Darkening Echoes*, came to me out of the blue. I'd long been seeking inspiration, aware that I needed a strong, original voice before I even started plotting. Too many wannabes fail to break through because they imitate rather than create. It's there if you dig deep enough and nobody ever suggested it was easy. I knew this all too well; I was an agent. And also how tough and competitive it is – certainly not a calling for the faint-hearted. And then, by luck, I had to go into hospital where I found myself one of five strangers in a six-bed ward. It was that empty bed that sparked off the idea, my opening for a psychological thriller. Eat your heart out, Alfred Hitchcock! The book came out in 1995. I have produced one every year since.

The key was the random grouping. I love looking into small lives. Jane Austen and J. B. Priestley, along with Patricia Highsmith, have long been my heroes and, lacking their genius, I have to work hard at my craft. I set my second novel in the block I live in, my third in a holiday resort. Four was relatively easy – my own extended family – but what on earth could I do for the fifth? I was fast running out of ideas. Until a colleague saved the day. "Everyone at some time works in an office," she said. And excluding farmers, teachers, vets, ballet dancers, firemen, nannies, soldiers, astronauts, taxi drivers and so on, she was right. I had worked in offices since my teens; there is nothing in the world I know better. And so *Unfinished Business* was conceived; even the title came off pat. For years I ran a business with a tightly-knit team that made a perfect blueprint for the book. The friendships, rivalry and petty hassles, all were grist to my mill. Not the actual people (I am not quite that naïve), but a close approximation set in the actual mews. I changed the names and the nature of the business and settled down to do some relevant killing. And now came the spooky part. My feisty main character is a golden career girl, doted on by everyone she meets. She dies on page one at the hands of an unknown killer but we see her in flashback as the wonderful creature she was. Spirited, talented, universally loved, a veritable Diana of popularity and charm. The morning I switched on the breakfast news and heard of the death of Jill Dando I could scarcely believe it. At that stage, only my publisher had seen sample material. Life was beginning to imitate my art. I wrote the book while the police investigation proceeded and reality followed invention with dizzying speed. Yet I always managed to stay several chapters ahead and my story has a killer and a definite resolution. Though only days after I finally delivered, a Dando suspect was arrested.

Unfinished Business was published in August, so now I am scratching my head for a new idea. Preferably something far away from the headlines, but these days you just never know.

How I Wrote...
Molly Brown

A Sense of Focus is loosely based on a case that made the news a few years back. A married couple were charged with the murder of their illegally adopted child, and the woman's defence was that she had been as much a victim of her husband's abuse as the child. *Angel's Day* was based on a television news report about some clubs in Soho that were ripping off tourists by luring them in with promises of a show that never materialised (because the club didn't have an entertainment licence), then charging them astronomical prices for non-alcoholic drinks (because they didn't have a liquor licence either). And it was all perfectly legal because the clubs were not actually providing anything for which they were not licensed.

The Vengeance of Grandmother Wu was inspired by some accounts of demonic possession as reported by nineteenth century Western missionaries in China, combined with a drawing I once saw in a shop window in Soho, of an absolutely drop dead gorgeous ancient Chinese warrior. I got the idea for *Doing Things Differently* from the book, *Wild Swans* by Jung Chang, which is about the lives of three generations of her family in China. Suicide as a form of protest is a recurring theme throughout the book. When Jung Chang's grandmother, a former concubine, was going to marry an elderly widowed doctor, the doctor's children objected so strongly to the marriage that at a family gathering, one of the doctor's sons took out a gun and shot himself in front of everybody, including his own wife and children. To me, the interesting thing is that the woman he perceived as such a threat to his family was standing right there, but he didn't shoot her – he shot himself instead. And the 'shame' of the act fell not upon the man who had killed himself, but upon his father, because the father was seen as having caused his son's death by becoming involved with an unsuitable woman. Later on, under Mao, suicide was considered a highly effective means of protest because everyone was supposed to be happy under the new regime and every time someone killed himself it was a great source of embarrassment for the government. What I tried to do in *Doing Things Differently* was to take that idea to its illogical conclusion: a society where all conflicts are resolved by emotional blackmail.

Molly Brown's latest book is Bad Timing and Other Stories *(Big Engine)*

Too Close to the Sun
Russell Andrews

The idea for *Icarus* came from Academy Award winning screenwriter William Goldman. He told me that he knew a personal trainer/physical therapist who was dating quite a few women. When talking to clients, the trainer would discuss these women intimately, but refer to them only by their nicknames, so as to protect their real identities. He said it was a kind of 'trainer's code'. My first reaction was: what a great idea there must be lurking inside there for a thriller. And that was the initial premise of *Icarus*: what if a physical therapist is murdered. One person believes that the killer is one of the therapists five girlfriends – but that person doesn't know any of the women's real names, only their nicknames. And the only thing he knows about their lives is what he's picked up in casual conversation with the therapist. It seemed like a good starting point. And then things got complicated. The next thing to figure out: who is the person searching for the killer? What kind of man is he, what does he do, etc. etc. And then: what is his connection to the murdered therapist? What drives him in his search? And finally: where does the suspense come in? Is our hero being threatened himself? If so, by whom? And why? The first thing was to try to define our hero. I wanted to keep certain elements from *Gideon*, my first thriller, particularly the Hitchcockian concept of an innocent man being caught up in something beyond his control; something he doesn't understand. So I wanted an ordinary, everyday kind of hero. No cops. No spies. I wanted someone who'd be somewhat of a stranger to a world of violence and deception. I've always been fascinated by the restaurant business. It's got the right touch of glamour and celebrity combined with hard work and a certain mystery as far as what really goes on behind the scenes. So, voilà, the lead character, Jack Keller, became a successful restaurateur.

The second step: for Jack to have a connection to the therapist, he'd have to be injured. The therapist would have to be someone who could take away Jack's pain. This concept became intertwined with all the rest of the creative steps until things fell into place. Eventually, I had Jack's past, I had his link to the therapist, now named Kid Demeter, and I had the threat I needed. The more I thought, the more I liked the idea of everything tying together.

Suddenly, Jack's past became a direct link to the violence and fear he was experiencing in the present. The murders that were occurring were tied to murders in the past. As it should be in a novel of this sort, my lead wasn't just someone trying to solve a crime. He was someone who was at the very centre of that crime. The next to last step was deciding who the killer would be. With everything else in place, it wasn't all that difficult a decision. I think I came up with someone who wouldn't be obvious – but who would be believable. And, of course, scary. The final step was the title. I liked the idea of a 'Russell Andrews-type title' – a one-word, mythologically-oriented title. I gave the lead character, Jack Keller, one of my own fears – a fear of heights. As that fear became more and more central to the book, *Icarus* seemed to be a natural name for it. And the concept of using the image of Icarus, the boy who flew too high and fell to his death, further tied things together, both thematically and from a plot standpoint. Writing *Icarus* was the most fun I've ever had working on a book. The research was fascinating and entertaining. I spent a few days working in one of New York's top restaurants – 11 Madison Park – so I could really get a feel for how that business worked. I spoke to doctors and physical therapists (and worked with a couple of physical therapists) to really understand the bond between patient and someone who can relieve pain. Most fun of all, I spent a lot of time in Kid Demeter's world – the downtown clubs, the lap-dancing clubs and the after-hours all-night illegal clubs that are all over Manhattan. Every one of the women suspects in the book is based on

someone I met doing my research. To finish off the process, I'd like to say that I slaved and sweated in a dark and dank attic. But that would be a total lie. When I needed to make the big push to finish the second half of the book, I retreated to a 250-year-old cottage in the middle of Sicily with only my computer to keep me company. No one could disturb me there and I did slave away for six weeks. But I also ate extremely well, which seemed fitting for a book with a restaurant background.

Icarus *is published by Little, Brown.*

Getting Going
David Ralph Martin

I didn't start off with the idea of writing a series – in fact all I had to begin with was half an uncommissioned manuscript and no idea how to finish it. Then Tom Crabtree, a friend of mine down here in Bridport, Dorset, knowing I had something to do with writing for television, asked me to look over a comic novel he'd written about an 'Agony Uncle' on an upmarket woman's magazine. At the time, Tom Crabtree wrote a column called 'On the Couch' for *Cosmopolitan*. I thought his book had a good chance – it was stylish and funny and he'd got the tone right – so I tried to help him out with the story. In return I asked him if he wouldn't mind if I sent up half a book to the same editor, Caroline Upcher, who was then working for William Heinemann. To cut it short, she gave me enough encouragement to finish the first book, and my agent got me a contract to do another one. Over time, it occurred to me that one of the minor characters in *I'm Coming to Get You*, a victim, had enough life in her to play the part of the avenger in the second book, *Arm and a Leg*. At the end of that, another character's end was unresolved, so, at the prompting of Thomas Wilson, another editor at Heinemann, I used that character's end to start off *Dead Man's Slaughter*. This procedure worked, I think, because I was already using the same protagonists and the same locale – a detective sergeant, a detective constable and a staff nurse, all working in Bristol – to investigate what became, as it often does in real life, an ever-growing circle of crime, punishment and retribution.

More simply, like Topsy, 'it just growed'.

How I Wrote *My Best Friend*

Laura Wilson

Like my two previous books, *My Best Friend* did not begin with anything as noble and writerly as plot or character, but with objects. In 1995, in the course of writing a non-fiction book for children about life during the Blitz, I had to visit a TV and film prop hire company in order to get some stuff for a photo shoot. I spent an entire morning wandering around a huge repository of period artefacts from kitchen ranges, taxidermy and cash registers to crappy little things like beer mats and used lipsticks. The bizarre juxtaposition of all these scraps of the past made them far more fascinating than if I'd seen them neatly ranked and labelled in a museum, and I couldn't get them out of my mind for months afterwards. I used to sit on the bus playing a sort of Kim's Game and making lists of all the items I could remember in my notebook. I suppose I could have just

got a life, but writing about them seemed easier, somehow...

However, I didn't find a use for them until 1998, when we spent most of the winter camping out in a freezing holiday cottage while our house was being renovated. I don't know if it was the disruption or the privations (spending entire days hopping around in a sleeping bag to keep warm, being attacked by the farmer's geese every time I went outside, a clean pair of knickers acquiring the status of a major sartorial event...) but I felt as if I was marking time until I got home. The only good thing that could be said about the cottage was that it contained early editions of all of Enid Blyton's *Famous Five* books. Enid Blyton had topped my parents' *index librorum prohibitorum* and I had somehow managed to get through my entire childhood and adolescence without reading anything she'd written. As my feelings of lethargy increased, I spent entire guilty afternoons sitting with my back pressed against the single, feeble radiator, in the company of Julian, Dick, Anne, George and Timmy the dog.

Somehow, these two things merged and out of them came the central character of *My Best Friend*, Gerald Haxton, a lonely misfit who works for a prop-hire company, and his mother, a famous children's writer. I had met the perfect physical template for Gerald for about five minutes a few years earlier, and must have made a mental note for future reference, because he came straight back. However, I had no idea what the character sounded like, and that was a big problem because I always write in the first person. At first, I kept hearing E. L. Wisty, Peter Cook's man in the shabby mac. This was hopeless because I wanted a serious character, but I didn't know what to do about it. I dithered, hoping inspiration would strike, until one day I turned on Radio Four halfway though a programme about obsessive people, and there was Gerald, talking about how he'd seen *The Poseidon Adventure* 943 times, and how he always ate the same food afterwards: a tuna sandwich on brown bread, followed by a banana. I grabbed my notebook and pencil and took down, verbatim, every single thing he said so that I could get the cadences and phraseology, and after that I'd got him so thoroughly that he never really went away (as my partner remarked only last week, "God, you're getting boring...")

My Best Friend *is published by Orion.*

Writing *Homage*
Julian Rathbone

By the author of the bestselling *The Last English King*

Two years ago it felt as if money was being shovelled at me off the back of a lorry. Royalties(!!!) from *The Last English King*, renewed film options (ditto), commissions to write film scripts, and, less glamorous, private pension plan pays tax-free lump sum! "Let's go to California", said the Significant One, "we might not be able to afford it next year." "We will if we save it", says I. "Don't be stupid", says she... so off we went, with two offspring too. San Diego, Tijuana, La Jolla (home of Raymond Chandler), Los Angeles, up the coast to Monterey, inland to Yosemite and Lake Tajo, Napa Valley, San Francisco – it was all perfect, the only hitch was we left our Summer of Love tape in the hire car, and no prizes for guessing what had been playing from it as we crossed the Golden Gate Bridge.

Well, you have to use an experience like that. How to get round the ignorance of someone who had only been in California for three weeks? Make the hero an English PI brought over to help a friend. More difficult was contriving a plot that used every place we went to – the first draft was a mess, a barely disguised travelogue, so I cut Yosemite and Lake Tajo and tidied it up into *Homage*. Homage to what? "The American Way of Life", says one of the characters. Well, not exactly, but buy it, read it, and you'll see.

Homage is published by Allison & Busby.

Grave Concerns
Rebecca Tope

Grave Concerns is the second book featuring Drew Slocombe, undertaker. In *Dark Undertakings* he was working for a traditional funeral director, and the mystery concerned a cremation. In the second book, Drew has set up on his own, specialising in natural burials. I worked for seven years in the office of a Sussex undertaker, during which time I was asked perhaps ten times for details of 'alternative' funerals. The response, as still happens routinely, tended to be discouraging. Yes, in theory you're allowed to be buried in a field or woodland or your own garden, but the knee-jerk reaction is almost always to try to talk people out of anything so inconvenient. On a bad day, we would tell people the Council wouldn't stand for it, and fob them off with spurious regulations. The truth is that there are scarcely any laws to impede such a burial – and the correct advice is to steer very clear of the Council, who will almost always wade in with a million groundless objections.

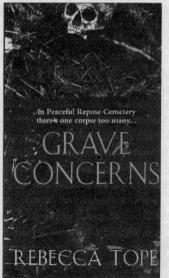

In Peaceful Repose Cemetery there's one corpse too many...

GRAVE CONCERNS

REBECCA TOPE

Before long, I found myself in a rather invidious position, torn between employer and customer, despite my boss' relatively open mind on the subject. Natural burials can be done very cheaply, without the services of an undertaker at all. The conflict of interest isn't hard to detect, I'm sure. So I dreamed of doing it differently. I am only too aware of the enormous power of the status quo, particularly in matters associated with death. It is a very rare individual who will persist in going against the tide, and the subtle (and not so subtle, sometimes) pressure to conform is enough to deter the vast majority from taking the whole thing into their own hands. There are articles in the broadsheets three or four times a year, paying lip service to more ecological and personal methods of disposal, but nothing to suggest a genuine sea change. I decided to add my two penn'orth, hoping to show what was possible, in an entertaining way. Initial reactions to the book have been very gratifying. Two or three readers have told me they've already changed their funeral plans, from cremation to burial in one of the 'green' cemeteries. I've linked my website to the Natural Death Centre, in the hope that some readers will make practical enquiries. But *Grave Concerns* is primarily a murder mystery, not a polemic. It was fun to write, and I hope it'll be fun to read. Drew is becoming a popular protagonist – and he's due for another appearance in a third title, *The Sting of Death*, sometime soon.

The Drew Slocomb books are published by Piatkus.

IAN RANKIN: IT'S THE WRITE TIME TO GET OUT THERE

In January, BT's innovative getoutthere.bt.com, a site created by BT to enable young people to showcase their creative work, will launch a new zone for young writers. getoutthere.bt.com has been running for a year and has been helping budding musicians and film directors get their big break. Celebrities that have dedicated their time to judging music tracks and shorts films uploaded to the site include Radio 1's Mary Anne Hobbs and the critically acclaimed Christopher Eccleston.

Budding authors are invited to upload poetry, novels, short stories, scripts and journalistic pieces to the site where their work will be judged by some of the world's most seasoned novelists. Judges will include Ed McBain (*Cop Hater*), Jenny Colgan (*Amanda's Wedding*), Jake Arnott (*The Long Firm*) and Ian Rankin (*The Falls*). Upload your work to the site and you could achieve the ultimate goal every writer dreams of – getting your work published. BT has teamed up with book publishers HarperCollins and Curtis Brown, the UK's largest literary agency, to make this happen. And it doesn't stop there. Every month the uploader voted number one in the writing zone charts will win a laptop computer with runners-up winning books from the HarperCollin's website.

April's judge was Ian Rankin, author of crime novels such as *Knots and Crosses* and *Set in Darkness*. Those lucky enough to have their literary masterpieces read by this distinguished novelist and judged the best with have the opportunity to meet the man himself over lunch. And look out for successful husband and wife writing duo Josie Lloyd and Emlyn Rees, authors of *Come Together* and *Come Again*, who have written an interactive short story specially for getoutthere.bt.com.

BETTER THAN THE SURGERY
PAUL CARSON

Barry Forshaw

Medical thrillers are clogging bookshop shelves almost as much these days as the legal variety, and it takes something special to rise above the uninspiring throng. Paul Carson's Final Duty (Heinemann) demonstrates that he is an author who may be content to utilise familiar concepts, but does it with skill and intelligence. Speaking to Carson (in London to promote the book) is a civilised experience: this is a writer who makes no claims for his own literary skills, but clearly takes pride in producing adroit and engaging thrillers. Final Duty has Doctor Jack Hunter moving from his native Dublin to a new job at a top Chicago hospital, hoping it will initiate the career break he is hoping for. But the hospital's collusion with powerful drug companies (shades of Le Carré's current concerns) frustrate his groundbreaking research in cardiology. And then his boss is shot dead...

Presumably Carson's own experience as a doctor based in South Dublin was essential background for the book?

Oh, inevitably, but I'm keen to keep the research in the background – the plot is the thing. That's always foregrounded.

What is the appeal of the doctor hero in thriller?

I think people generally like medical men. They feel they are working at the coalface, and (scandals notwithstanding) public confidence in the profession hasn't been dented too badly. Don't forget that Harold Shipman, for instance, was a man on his own – it's not so easy to do what he did in most practices.

Is his hero a surrogate of the author?

To some degree. I lead a nomadic existence. Certainly, the parochialism of Ireland is something that (as Joyce says) one needs to get away from, even if one ultimately returns.

How did he come up of the concept of *Final Duty?*

Actually, from a news snippet that I encountered. Apparently, a pharmaceutical company had used holocaust inmates for research, and we know about the Swiss government's collusion with prominent doctors involved in the camps. But although these are serious themes, I try to keep the entertainment element paramount.

Is John Buchan an influence on his picaresque narrative?

Peripherally, perhaps. But I try to make sure that the Chicago settings are as authentic as possible. I spent time there with a psychiatrist friend.

How useful was Carson's experience editing the magazine *Irish Doctor?*

Useful, yes, but it really was a separate endeavour to what I'm doing now. I had written books on health, but what I'm doing as a novelist is what really energises me. Hopefully, I've found a place in a niche market, and I'll be happy if I can just sustain that.

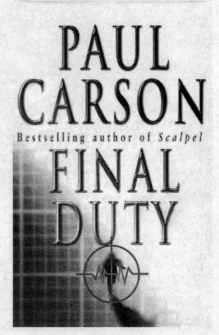

PAUL CARSON

Bestselling author of *Scalpel*

FINAL DUTY

EMPATHY WITH THE DEVIL
EMMANUEL CARRÈRE

What drives someone to batter his wife to death,

shoot his son and daughter, then have lunch with

his parents before killing them too?

One Frenchman spent seven years finding out

Sunday January 14, 2001

A little over eight years ago, on Saturday 9 January 1993, Jean-Claude Romand murdered his wife, his two children, his father and his mother. Seven months later he received a letter. "Monsieur," it began, "my proposal may well offend you... I am a writer, the author to date of seven books. Ever since reading about your case in the newspapers I have been haunted by the tragedy of which you were the agent and sole survivor. I would like to try to understand as much as possible of what happened and to make a book out of it... I am not approaching you out of some unhealthy curiosity or a taste for the sensational. What you have done is not in my eyes the deed of a common criminal, or that of a madman, either, but the action of someone pushed to the limit by over-

The **Adversary**

EMMANUEL CARRÈRE

A TRUE STORY OF
MONSTROUS DECEPTION

whelming forces, and it is these terrible forces I would like to show at work."

So began a period of seven years in which the writer Emmanuel Carrère continued to be haunted by Romand's crime. He wasn't sure what drew him to it, and that was what made the book that eventually became The Adversary so hard to write. The question of what was pushing him 'to want to tell such a monstrous story' was one which frequently troubled him and made him very uneasy. In any case, he received no reply from Romand, so he translated his obsession into a novel, Class Trip, an eerie tale of a nervous child and his overactive, or perhaps all too correct, imagination. The plot is nothing like Romand's story, and yet, says Carrère, Class Trip and The Adversary are 'blood relations'. Class Trip was a huge critical and popular success, and two years later, long after Carrère thought he had got Romand out of his system, the prisoner sent him a letter. Purely by chance, Romand had read Class Trip, and had recognised his own childhood in it. The writer and the murderer embarked on a long correspondence.

Carrère lives in the ninth arrondissement of Paris, between the bourgeois delights of the Grands Boulevards and the seamy trendiness of Pigalle and the Moulin Rouge. He lives in a spare, sunlit apartment and appears to be, at first sight, the wrong person. Expecting a tortured forty-two year old, I am greeted by a sprightly student lookalike, a straight, boyish, floppy-fringed man who speaks in a fast stream of extraordinary articulacy. The reason you might expect someone else is that The Adversary is not just an account of

a murder in the 'true crime' genre. Carrère had initially planned to write it like that, to construct his own In Cold Blood out of this minor news item. But he found that to 'erase' himself from the narrative as Truman Capote had done was 'dishonest'. He had to deal with his obsession with the murder, and give an account, as he puts it, "of my relationship to this story – my impressions, my hypotheses, my doubts, my anxieties". In order to be truly honest, in other words, he had to implicate himself.

Jean-Claude Romand started lying in his second year of medical school. Or perhaps it was earlier than that, though 'lying' is not what he would have called it. He grew up in a family that placed a great deal of emphasis on honesty, and yet white lies were common currency – emotions were dangerous, and harsh truths might hurt. But at medical school something more serious was set in motion. He was dumped by his girlfriend, Florence, and, depressed, he failed to turn up for his end-of-year exams. He had the whole summer to admit this, but he said the exams had gone well. And when the results were posted up, he told his parents and friends that he had passed. None of the other students noticed this wasn't true. For the next twelve years he enrolled in the second year over and over again, while reading the same books his friends were studying and pretending to graduate alongside them. Academically, he could proceed no further, but again, no one suspected anything. At some point, love-sick over Florence, he told people he had cancer. She came back to him immediately, but none of his doctor friends thought to inquire further about his illness. Later, the couple were married, Florence passed her thesis in pharmacology, and Romand invented for himself a high-flying job.

They had two children, and moved, along with some of their university friends, to a town near the border with Switzerland. Romand had to be there because he was, he said, a research scientist at the World Health Organisation (WHO) in Geneva. In fact he spent his days alone in his car, reading books and magazines, and spent nights in hotels when he thought it was appropriate to be away on business. He did go to the WHO sometimes, and roamed the ground floor, where he took money out of the cashpoints, posted his letters and booked holidays through the WHO travel agent. He never ventured upstairs to the offices, but he stole stationery and bits and pieces of WHO-branded equipment. He even got hold of a photograph of the building, which he gave to his parents to put on their wall, marking it with a red 'X' to indicate where his office was. But what, you may wonder, did the Romand family live off? This is where his lies turned to petty crime. He told people that due to his privileged professional position he could invest their money in high-interest accounts. His parents and his uncle Claude gave him their savings, amounting to tens of thousands of francs. Then came Florence's parents: a retirement bonus of 400,000 francs plus a million francs from the sale of their house. Florence's uncle was diagnosed with cancer, and Romand said he was developing a miracle cure that was at an experimental stage and naturally very expensive. He procured for him several doses of a Fr15,000 placebo.

Years later, Romand began an affair and persuaded his mistress to give him Fr900,000. No one ever saw their cash again. Florence's father wanted some to buy a car: he died of a fall two weeks later, when Romand was alone in the house with him (Romand was not charged with his murder, and when it came up at the trial, he insisted it was an accident). Corinne, his mistress, asked him for her money back, and there was nothing he could do. The truth was closing in on him. A week later all his family were dead. "'I think that he wanted to be found out," Carrère suggests during our interview. "I think he felt trapped, and that it would have been a great relief to him to be discovered. At each stage the consequences became greater. At the beginning it was a little lie, then his wife might have asked for a divorce; later, because of his dodgy financial dealings, he might have had a brief stint in prison. But nothing more than that. And it never happened. His luck was his terrible misfortune."

First Corinne wanted her money. Then someone from the board of his children's school tried to get hold of Romand at work and found no trace of him. A woman whose husband worked at the WHO asked Florence if she was taking her children to the office Christmas party, of which Florence, understandably, knew nothing. For ten years, Romand's wife never called him at work or looked at the statements of their joint bank account. And yet, in the end, all it took was a few phone calls to reveal the truth. "But," says Carrère, "He thought it was preferable that his family should die than that they should suffer from the knowledge of the truth about him." Romand bought some jerry cans of petrol and some barbiturates for himself. He went to a gun shop and purchased a stun wand, two tear-gas canisters, a box of cartridges and a silencer for a .22 calibre rifle. Then, trying to convince himself that these were presents for his father, he had them gift-wrapped.

In the early morning of 9 January 1993, Romand battered his wife with a rolling pin, washed it and put it away. He covered her with a duvet and told the children she was asleep. He poured bowls of Coco Pops for Caroline and Antoine, and, after watching a video of *The Three Little Pigs* with them, he took them upstairs, one by one, and shot them. Then he drove to his parents' house, and after lunch he shot them too. His mother was the only one shot in the front – she saw her son murder her. That evening, Romand went up to Paris to see Corinne. He pretended they were going for dinner with a distinguished doctor, took her to the forest of Fontainebleau and tried to kill her in the car. She looked into his eyes and pleaded with him until he stopped. He drove home and spent the next day shut in with the bodies of his dead family. That night, just in time to be rescued by the rubbish collectors, he swallowed the barbiturates and set fire to the house. Emmanuel Carrère sets up his involvement with Romand's story in such a way that it is tempting to think he imagines himself as the murderer's double. "On the morning of Saturday January 9, 1993," the book begins, "while Jean-Claude Romand was killing his wife and children, I was with mine in a parent-teacher meeting at the school attended by

Gabriel, our eldest son. He was five years old, the same age as Antoine Romand. Then we went to have lunch with my parents, as Jean-Claude Romand did with his, whom he killed after the meal." Nothing more is made of this synchronicity, but later, following in the murderer's footsteps by means of hand-drawn maps Romand has sent him, Carrère says he feels "a painful sympathy" for Romand and his harboured secrets.

Almost immediately afterwards he writes that he is "ashamed", "ashamed in front of my children", and he begins to think that writing about the story might in itself be a crime. To the question of what drew him to the case, he replies that what got to him was that "the lie wasn't covering up anything else. We all know stories about people who lead double lives, but here there was no double life – hiding behind the lie was nothing but a total void. And I found echoes of that emptiness in my own life... I don't go to an office, no one knows exactly what I do – I am the only witness to my life, which was the case with Romand. I spend days on my own staring at the ceiling, and he spent his days alone in his car. And I'd say that in that respect there was some kind of identification – I wanted to know what went through his head all those empty days he spent in his car." Some might say that this form of identification was quite a leap of logic. One man spent empty days and ended up writing a number of books. The other's empty days added up to multiple murder. And yet the only allegiance Carrère will admit to is this emptiness, and even then, at another point in our conversation, he strongly rejects the idea of any identification with the murderer. "There was no identification on my part," Carrère insists, "but I think there might have been some kind of empathy."

What, I ask him, would he say was the difference between identification and empathy? "Well," Carrère replies, "I didn't put myself in his position. That's why to have written it in the first person from his point of view – and I've been asked if I considered this – would have been in the realm of obscenity. Part of the story is that this man never really had access to himself, in a way, and to say, I know the truth about you, to say "I" on his behalf, would have been not only a literary crime but also a moral crime."

Carrère is very clear on this point. It was essential that *The Adversary* should never become a collaborative effort between writer and murderer. He went to see Romand in prison when he had finished the book and gave him a set of proofs – on one condition: "I could not let him change anything – not even if he'd told me his car was green instead of blue – even the smallest factual change would convert it into his version, and that for me was completely impossible." And yet, Romand had his own expectations of what the book would do for him. In a letter to Carrère he wrote: "A writer's approach to this tragedy can transcend other, more reductive visions", such as those of psychiatrists or lawyers. I ask Carrère what he made of that. "I think it was because a writer is disengaged from the task of judging him. I felt the responsibility he was attributing to me as a very heavy one – it was as if there was, on the one hand, the justice of men, from which

he could no longer expect anything, and on the other hand divine justice, in which he believes and from which he therefore expects everything. And I thought that he imagined me in a strange position between the two."

At one point Carrère surprises me by referring to Romand as 'a figure of evil'. In the book he doesn't come across as someone who would believe in such absolutes, and yet when I press him on the subject he replies that he believes 'deeply' in Evil. But, I argue, Romand seemed, from his behaviour, to be psychotic. Does Carrère really think someone suffering from a clinical condition can be accused of being evil? "Yes, I think psychosis is absolute evil. That's not a moral condemnation – psychosis is hell on earth." And from this it seems clear that Carrère's sympathy, empathy, identification – whatever you may wish to call it – has evaporated. In his uncertain guilt and shame, Carrère had waited a year after he finished the book before publishing it. And when it was eventually published, he says, he felt relieved. The book was a success (it is now being made into a film starring Daniel Auteuil), and he was released from a 'double-bind'. A relationship that had been two-way became three-way: himself, Romand, and the readers. It meant something to others, he was not alone; and now he is separate from Jean-Claude Romand, no longer his double or his shadow. Emmanuel Carrère, at least, has been freed.

The Adversary *is published by Bloomsbury at £14.99*

AUTHORS IN LONDON

Barry Forshaw

Talking to two young authors in the capital recently might lead one to think there's a new breed of thriller writer at work in the genre: young, ambitious, articulate and briskly aware of the direction they wish their careers to take. Matthew Reilly (whose helter-skelter

THE INTERNATIONAL BESTSELLER

SOME DOORS ARE MEANT TO REMAIN UNOPENED

TEMPLE

MATTHEW REILLY

thriller *Temple* is published by Pan) and Brad Meltzer (whose *The First Counsel* is a Hodder & Stoughton title) share the same vigorous and engaging manner. Reilly is particularly concerned with pace and visceral excitement, and he seems unworried by the sacrifices in characterisation that such demands entail. Certainly *Temple* is great fun: an Indiana Jones-style ride, delivered with gusto. *Ice Station* had marked Reilly out has this kind of writer, and the pace of his novels seems to be reflected in the whirlwind publicity tour his publisher has demanded. He's unfazed by this – Reilly regards himself primarily as a purveyor of entertainment, and it's no surprise to learn that his book has been optioned for the movies: it has cinematic possibilities in no uncertain terms. He's pleased with the response that his tale has received among readers, and is well aware that a narrative set between the past and the present runs the risk of one narrative overwhelming other. Reilly is canny enough to know that he'll never be Joseph Conrad, but he's more than happy to be a popular entertainer with a large audience.

Matthew Reilly

himself) says this is a simple one to answer: in the real world, we see lawyers frequently managing to spring clients who are patently guilty of certain crimes (the inevitable American sportsmen come to mind) whereas in books, the profession can be presented as Knight Errant figures, in a world in which real justice is seen to be done. It is, says Meltzer, for this reason that we're happy to accept the convention. Not that he is happy with all books in which the profession is centre stage – he's aware that more bad writing is appearing in books by and about lawyers than in just about any in the genre. But not in his own work: he's an ambitious writer who is determined that each new book should be quite unlike its predecessor.

Brad Meltzer has more complex aims; *The First Counsel* is signally different from his first novel, the much-acclaimed *The Tenth Justice*. This is a fast-moving narrative involving a romance between a White House lawyer and the First Daughter, and the mayhem that ensues. Meltzer was, he says, careful to ensure that the presidential offspring of his novel would be a generic First Daughter – she is not Chelsea Clinton. But the book functions on more levels than simply that of a thriller: he was concerned, he points out, with dealing with issues of friendship and betrayal, a recurrent theme in his work. Meltzer works hard on his own friendships, and it's hardly surprising that issues like this assume centre stage in his books. He writes about lawyers: why do we like to read about lawyers, when we all appear to dislike them so much? Meltzer (in the profession

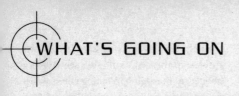

CRIME TIME NEWS

James Sallis

The much-acclaimed biography of crime writer Chester Himes by James Sallis (a major crime writer in his own right) continues to glean reviews, nearly a year after its UK and US issue. Two weeks ago, there were major full-length reviews in the New York Times, LA Times and Chicago Tribune, and Sallis appeared on a number of radio shows: New York and Company in NYC, Steve Nester's Poets of the Tabloid Murder, National Public Radio's Public Interest and Fresh Air. Sallis will be speaking about Chester Himes at the LA Times Festival of Books next month. Parleying such lengthy interest into his own fiction, the sixth – and last – of Sallis' Lew Griffin series has been turned in and is due both in the US and UK this Autumn. It's entitled *Ghost of a Flea* (after the William Blake painting) and has, apparently, the dense texture of its predecessors.

Julia Wallis Martin

Julia Wallis Martin's *The Long Close Call* has been commissioned as a two part drama by United Anglia. It will be produced by Keith Thompson (*Prime Suspect, Oliver Twist*) and directed by Renny Rye (*Lipstick on my Collar, Singing Detective, Cold Lazarus, Jake's Progress, Oliver Twist*).

Lawrence Block

After much to-ing and fro-ing in Hollywood, an actor has been signed to play ace crime writer Lawrence Block's resourceful protagonist, Keller. The eponymous film will star Jeff Bridges. "We've got him at just the right point in his career, with a new gravitas from such films as *The Big Lebowski* banishing those middle years. And better still," says Block, "I've been asked to write the screenplay!" British director Martin Bell will be at the helm.

Campbell Armstrong

Quirky crime writer Campbell Armstrong has a new novel coming out from HarperCollins, a kind of thriller set in Glasgow – change of direction, change of publisher (thank Gawd, says Campbell). *The Bad Fire*, by name. In Glasgow mythology, 'the bad fire' is where little kids go when they are very bad... viz, hell. The Scotsman is publishing three extracts close to publication.

Leslie Forbes

Forbes' second novel, *Fish, Blood & Bone* (published by Weidenfeld & Nicolson), has been nominated for the Orange Prize (now in a long list of eighteen, along with

Margaret Atwood and Amy Tan). Forbes says she's delighted to be rubbing shoulders (on the list, anyway) with such writers. The film option for her first novel, *Bombay Ice*, has just been bought by Bollywood/Hollywood indie producer, Mark Burton – producer of Sundance winner film *The Terrorist* (which Michael Ondaatje loved). FilmFour is putting up the first stage development money. Forbes met Burton, and discovered he has taken travelling theatre productions from America all over India and also worked in theatre in London for four years in the 1980s. A good man all round.

Cooper Makes Way for James

After a year as a popular chairman of the CWA, Natasha Cooper will be stepping down at the AGM giving her much need-

ed time to spend on her own writing. Her successor is the indefatigable Russell James, who also writes for *Crime Time*. Cooper appeared on Saturday Review (Radio 4), reviewing (with others): Seamus Heaney's new collection, *Electric Light* (Faber), Peter Whelan's new play *A Russian in the Woods*, Jean-Pierre Sinapi's new film *Uneasy Riders,* ITV's series *Time of Our Lives*, and discussing the implications of Jeremy Bowen's series *Son of God.* Along with several other crime writers (eg Ian Rankin, H. R. F. Keating, Janet Laurence, Simon Brett), Cooper was at the Queen's party for the British Book Trade at Buckingham Palace.

The Unusual Suspects

All six of the Crime Writer's Cartel, The Unusual Suspects, spoke at Corpus Christi College, Oxford on 3 April for the British Council's international conference on the teaching of literature (with university representatives from places as diverse as Austria, Madras, South Africa and Japan). The Suspects discussed how British crime and thriller writing explores images of modern Britain, and how it can encourage foreign readers of English – largely through the 'what happens next' use of suspenseful plotting. The Suspects show how modern British crime and thriller writing is a direct descendant of classic storytelling: *Bleak House* is a crime novel, for example, as is *Edwin Drood*; many of Ian McEwan's books could be considered thrillers or crime novels, as could some of Graham Greene's, Kazuo Ishiguro's and Margaret Atwood's. Umberto Eco and Italo Calvino deconstructed the form to discuss history and semiotics, and Iris Murdoch used it to discuss philosophy.

Cath Staincliffe

The fourth Sal Kilkenny mystery by Cath Staincliffe, *Stone Cold Red Hot* (Allison & Busby) was launched at Waterstone's Deansgate. A capacity crowd turned out to meet author Cath Staincliffe who read from the book, and a stimulating discussion ensued with lively debate among the audience as to how violent (or not) are the confrontations that Sal faces. Cath was interviewed by Jenni Murray on BBC Radio 4 Woman's Hour and also joined in a discussion on criticism and writing (whether it is cruel to be kind) with Jane Holland, who has been described as a critical Rottweiler – Cath played the good cop. She has recently completed the fifth book in the series called *Towers of Silence*, as well as her first stand-alone psychological thriller *Cry Me a River*. In addition to her writing, Cath has been involved in many varied Murder Squad events in the last year: everything from literary festivals and crime conventions (Murder Squad received rave reviews from both Crime Scene 2000 and Dead on Deansgate for their 'crime collage', which consisted of themed readings from their work) to workshops with prisoners and creating crime stories with A-level students based on scene of the crime evidence. Cath is currently weighing up whether to begin the next Sal Kilkenny book, write a second stand-alone thriller, or to work on short stories, which she really enjoyed doing for the Murder Squad's anthology.

Judith Cutler

Cutler's got a new detective at work for her: one W. G. Grace, who's opening the batting with the *Strand* magazine. Will he make it to a full length? Cutler would love him to.

Gary Lovisi

Lovisi has a western and a crime story coming out in two major new anthologies. He's been working on a new book that's a survey and price guide to all sleazy digest paperbacks of the 1950s. *The Sexy Digests* will be 100 pages with over 350 covers shown. A new issue of *Hardboiled* will be out soon, a 200-page trade paperback with a striking colour cover by Rick Hudson. Later this year, *Classic Pulp Fiction Crime* will be out with stories by a lot of the great old-timers.

Agatha Christie

Fans of Agatha Christie can look forward to a new – and perhaps controversial – adaptation of *Murder on the Orient Express*. The new feature, a Kraft Premier Movie, will air as a CBS Sunday Movie in the US and will air in the UK later in the year. *Murder on the Orient Express* is a contemporary adaptation of the classic 1934 Christie novel and stars Alfred Molina as Hercule Poirot. Also featured are Meredith Baxter, Leslie Caron and Peter Strauss. Interestingly, this particular production brings the Belgian detective into the present day. Though generally suspicious of the advantages of twenty-first century technology – it is no substitute for the 'little grey cells' – Poirot does occasionally make use of modern gadgetry to help in his investigations, including a palm-top computer. Also new to this production are revelations of Poirot's love life! Some will recall his admiration of a certain Countess Vera Rossakoff...

Val McDermid

Val McDermid has been awarded the Los Angeles Times Book Prize in the Mystery/Thriller category for *A Place of Execution*. This is the first time in the twenty-one year history of the prize that there has been a separate category for crime fiction. The other shortlisted authors were James Lee Burke, Michael Dibdin, George P. Pelecanos and Peter Robinson. Val told a packed auditorium at Royce Hall on the UCLA campus that she was 'gobsmacked' to have won the $1,000 award, and remarked that the quality of the books on the shortlist sent out a message that some of the best contemporary fiction writing around was being produced in the mystery genre.

Martin Edwards

Martin Edwards is to celebrate ten years since the publication of his first short story with a collection of his complete short crime fiction. The book is called *Where Do You Find Your Ideas? And Other Crime Stories* and boasts a characteristically entertaining foreword by Reginald Hill. The title comes from one of the twenty-seven stories contained in this bumper volume and also provides the theme of the book – each story carries a fresh introduction by the author explaining how he came to write it. The stories include various Harry Devlin cases, as well as historical mysteries, two Sherlockian pastiches, and a number of one-off stories of psychological suspense. The book will give readers an idea of the range of Martin's writing, as well as one or two clues as to future directions his work may take. The book is to be published in July by Countyvise Press, who published the CWA anthology *Northern Blood 3* to considerable acclaim a couple of years ago. New paperback editions of *I Remember You* and *Yesterday's Papers* have been published by New English Library in April and May. Meanwhile his non-fiction book on the law of equal opportunities was recently published by Tolley's, who have already commissioned a second edition. And he's still hard at work on a non-series crime novel.

Carol Anne Davis

True crime books attract far more attention than realistic crime fiction. That's what Carol Anne Davis, author of *Women Who Kill: Profiles of Female Serial Killers* has found – by publication day her publisher, Allison & Busby, had sold three quarters of the first print run of the book. Their American distributor has made it their lead title and there's also interest in translation rights, including Japan. Carol's already been interviewed by a newspaper that has a million-plus circulation and has also been interviewed by several magazines. *Women Who Kill* went on sale in Britain on April 2nd and will be on sale in the States from June.

Hilary Bonner

Hilary Bonner's latest novel *A Kind of Wild Justice* highlights two of the hottest legal issues around at the moment – the explosive problem of DNA proving guilt retrospectively and the controversy over whether or not the ancient law of double jeopardy should finally be overturned. Hilary knew it was extremely topical but still couldn't quite believe it when Jack Straw announced a review of the double jeopardy law and then the body of James Hanratty was exhumed for DNA tests – right on publication time. "My friends accused me of fixing it", she says. "It has certainly drawn a lot of attention to the book." Hilary Bonner launched *A Kind of Wild Justice* at a champagne party in London before rushing back to the West Country for the CWA conference in Torquay, of which she has been co-organiser. In between, she stopped off at Plymouth to guest on the quiz show Westcountry Challenge. She says, "I had been carrying publication date, April 5th, and the dates of the conference, April 6th, 7th and 8th, around in my head for weeks before it suddenly dawned on me that they were right on top of each other. Then Westcountry TV invited me to take part in their quiz show, along with fervent promises to wave my book at the cameras, and being a writer quite prepared to sell my grandmother for TV publicity, naturally I said yes, but the logistics were horrific." *A Kind of Wild Justice* (large format paperback published by Heinemann at £10) tells the story of what happens when it is discovered through a chance DNA test that a man tried and acquitted twenty years previously of a brutal murder was in fact guilty after all. It is set principally on Dartmoor, not far from the Torquay conference venue at The Grand Hotel, where, appropriately enough, Agatha Christie spent her honeymoon. Events at the sellout conference included an Agatha Christie walk through Torquay with Christie expert Professor B. J. Rahn, and a cruise up the River Dart past Dame Agatha's home. Actor Edward Woodward was the guest speaker at the Saturday night gala dinner.

John Baker

John Baker has accepted a two book deal with Hodder and they are keen to make the next his breakthrough book. *The Chinese Girl* was selected as the Ottakars Crime Book of the Month for May (the month when the Orion paperback is published). The next Sam Turner mystery will be published by Orion in August. It is entitled *Shooting in the Dark* and centres around a death threat to a blind woman and her sister. It is about sight and seeing, how easy it is to miss seeing the wood for the trees, and the way that we are often intent on seeing what we want to see rather than what is plainly there before us. The novel pits Sam and Geordie against an intelligent and ruthless adversary. In the pipeline is a sequel to *The Chinese Girl*, again set in Hull. It will be entitled *White Skin Man* and will deal with the themes of racial prejudice and intolerance. A hard-hitting political novel with no apologies. After that？

Yet another Sam Turner novel, perhaps taking Sam out of the country for a while before returning for a watery denouement in York. Then John says he would like to write a stand-alone with a first-person narrative voice: political, concerned with sleaze and corruption in the British government. No police or detectives, just an everyday tale of politicians lining their pockets. And perhaps the odd one or two being troubled by conscience.

Murder Squad –
Crime Fiction to Die For

The Murder Squad is John Baker, Chaz Brenchley, Ann Cleeves, Martin Edwards, Margaret Murphy, Stuart Pawson and Cath Staincliffe.

It's been a hectic six months for Murder Squad. Soundings Audio commissioned an article on Murder Squad, to be linked with a promotional offer of Squaddies audio tapes, and articles have also appeared in Crime Time, Sherlock Holmes the Detective magazine, as well as the Crime Writers' Association's own newsletter, Red Herrings. This article, entitled Beating the Midlist Blues, won the 2000 Leo Harris Award. Enquiries continue to flood in, and it seems the University of the Third Age has got wind of their readings, because they've had several bookings from that quarter just recently. The Squad has done well over 60 events in the last year, in places as far flung as Gateshead and Kent. As well as readings

and discussions at bookshops and appearances at national crime fiction conventions, Murder Squad has starred at literary festivals in Knutsford, Huddersfield, Durham, Harrogate, Halton Lea, Hull and Chester. They have worked in prisons, schools, libraries and the wider community, meeting people who know their books and also introducing new readers to the genre. The idea of setting up the group has captured the imagination of readers, writers and publishers alike and they are travelling further and further afield. Worcester and Crowborough are on the cards for the Autumn, so do keep an eye on their events page – they could be coming to your area soon! Their next exciting new development will be the publication of the *Murder Squad Anthology* by Flambard Press. *Murder Squad* is a collection of stories that will give you an idea of the range of their work and will include pieces about your favourite series characters as well as new and innovative fiction from the Squad. The book will be out in the Autumn and will make an excellent Christmas gift.

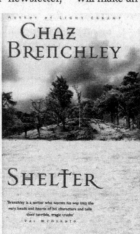

Chaz Brenchley

Chaz's most recent publication is *Shelter* (New English Library). It's in the nature of major change, one that you can't see coming: if you're ready, you adjust by degrees in a slow curve, which is a more comfortable experience but much less exciting. Late last year Chaz spent a couple of weeks in Taiwan, as a guest of the government:

he only went because he didn't want to be the kind of person who turns down trips like that. Chaz says that he had an amazing time there – never felt so alien or so welcome, both at once – and now he can't keep away and is going back under his own steam. he is also planning a novel (a contemporary crime thriller with cyberpunk grammar, Patricia Highsmith meets William Gibson on ground that's foreign to both) and thinking about a major project, while trying desperately to finish his current book and write a proposal for the next.

Ann Cleeves

October's the big month for Ann this year. It will see the Pan paperback edition of *The Crow Trap* and the new Macmillan hardback *The Sleeping and the Dead*. Despite her move, the new book is still set in Northumberland. In the middle of a drought a body is discovered in a dried up reservoir. It is the body of a teenage boy and it has been there for thirty years. Hannah relives her memories of her relationship with the boy, while trying to cope with the independence of her own teenage daughter. Then there is another murder and the police believe that the incidents are connected. Hannah, who knew both victims must be a suspect... Ann has enjoyed all the Murder Squad gigs but the highlights must be the Brought to Book events in Sedgefield and Halifax. Sedgefield was special because young people did the acting; there was a real buzz in the audience. In Halifax, all the readers' groups in Calderdale seemed to be taking part – more like a pub quiz than a traditional library event. She has recently been made an associate of Opening the Book,

the reader development organisation, so it'll all be useful experience. The work as reader-in-residence in two prisons will continue until July, but soon she'll be leading training sessions for library staff too. Left Coast Crime in Alaska was fabulous because it gave authors a chance to get out into the wilderness. Ann had a placement in Gustavus, a small settlement in Glacier Bay. The scenery was mind-blowing and the people hospitable. She ran workshops in a school, a library and a prison, but still had time to see the country – saw a moose (and ate it). The only unpleasant experience was flying out in a very small plane in a gale. Now it's back to Yorkshire and the new book – a first person narrative which will be set in Morocco and Newbiggin.

Margaret Murphy

Margaret's agent offered her new novel to a number of publishers: feedback was very good, but the whole process took so long – six months from finishing the book to the final result – that she was seriously frightened. She lost sleep. As if in sympathy, her computer had a complete nervous breakdown and she lost all my files. Thankfully, Margaret does her creative writing on a venerable 486 that is too old and wise to succumb to such nonsense, so her writing continued, only in a greater state of angst. Margaret has been offered an excellent two-book deal by Hodder – and they're keen for her to make the breakthrough. Publication will probably be in the spring of next year (they're wrangling over the title, so there's no point in giving it here), but you will be able to get *Dying Embers* in Pan paperback in September 2001.

Stuart Pawson

The next book, *Chill Factor*, is a little longer than the previous ones, and because he wasn't working to a deadline it fell behind schedule. This, plus a change of publisher, meant that Stuart didn't have a book released in 2000, which spoilt his book-a-year sequence since he started writing. Allison and Busby are publishing *Chill Factor*, which is scheduled for October 2001. It's a Charlie Priest story, and the poor bloke faces another diverse catalogue of traumas with his usual humour until he finally gets his man. "And woman?" you ask. Read it and find out. After a rather unfocused year 2000, Stuart's aim for this year is to write two books. The first is number eight in the Charlie Priest series (working title: *Laughing Boy*) and then a stand-alone spy thriller. Other ambitions for the year are to have a go at the American market and to climb two hills (Suilven and Stac Polly) on the West Coast of Scotland before he grows too decrepit. Stuart will also be updating the Meanstreets website, so any comments about this will be gratefully received. They are thrilled to have been invited to make a return visit to the St Hilda's conference at Oxford, in August, so dash out and book your place. It's an exciting time for Murder Squad, too, with a couple of similar organisations being formed, which hopefully will lead to some friendly rivalry and joint ventures.

Black Plaques to Celebrate Fictional Murders

Digital publishers House of Stratus are planning a new scheme to celebrate fictional UK murder and crime. The company, which owns the rights to most of Britain's classic crime writers, plans to place black plaques around the UK as an extension of English Heritage's blue plaque scheme. Research by the company has shown that people are as intrigued to find out where fictional characters lived as they are real-life historical celebrities. Likewise, people's natural morbid curiosity means they're equally fascinated by fictitious crime scenes as by the real thing. House of Stratus has bought the rights to a host of crime writers who set the agenda for the genre in the twentieth century. These include R. Austin Freeman, the first crime author to introduce inverted narrative and forensics into crime fiction; Edgar Wallace, an immensely popular author from the 'Impossible Crime School' whose novels were made into no less than fifteen feature films; and G. K. Chesterton, whose Father Brown stories inspired Ellery Queen and Agatha Christie.

House of Stratus Commercial Director, Tim Forrester, takes up the story:

"We're planning to begin in Belgravia where Lady Ashbrook was murdered in cold blood in the drawing room of her townhouse in *A Coat of Varnish* by C. P. Snow. Dependent on the scheme's reception, we shall roll it out nationally with one unveiling every two months – Oxford's St Anthony's College being a good example – the location for the shooting of Dr Umpleby in *Death at President's Lodging* by Michael Innes. The scheme will be developed into a crime map of Britain so you can find out what dirty deeds were done down the road – all fictitious, of course."

HENRY CECIL

Biography

Judge Henry Cecil Leon was born in Norwood Green Rectory near London in 1902. In 1923 he was called to the Bar and between 1949 to 1967 he served as a county court judge. He developed his writing skills while serving with the British Army during the Second World War, telling stories to officers to keep their minds off alcohol while sailing on 'dry' ships. These formed the basis of his first collection, *Full Circle*, published in 1948. Thereafter the law and official functions provided the main source for many of his stories and plays. Cecil had an extraordinary ability to examine the law in both a humorous and a more serious, analytical way, providing a series of thought provoking works. The titles being published by House of Stratus include some of his best-known work, many of which have been filmed, notably *Brothers in Law* and *Alibi for a Judge.* Though his books deal with the legal system many have more than an element of the mystery/thriller genre about them.

Cecil was a hugely influential writer – providing stimulus for both those taking up a law profession and writers themselves e.g. John Mortimer (Rumpole): Hitchcock, too, was an admirer, and planned to film *No Bail For the Judge* with Audrey Hepburn

According to the Evidence
ISBN 1-84232-048-3

Alec Morland is on trial for murder. He has tried to remedy the ineffectiveness of the law by taking matters into his own hands. Unfortunately for him, his alleged crime was not committed in immediate defence of others or of himself. In this fascinating murder trial you will not find out until the very end just how the law will interpret his actions. Will his defence be accepted or does a different fate await him?

The Asking Price ISBN 1-84232-044-0

Ronald Holbrook is a fifty-seven year old bachelor who has lived in the same house for twenty years. Jane Doughty, the daughter of his next-door neighbours, is seventeen. She suddenly decides she is in love with Ronald and wants to marry him. Everyone is amused at first but then events take a disturbingly sinister turn and Ronald finds himself enmeshed in a potentially tragic situation.

Hunt the Slipper
ISBN 1-84232-055-6

Harriet and Graham have been happily married for twenty year. One day Graham fails to return home and Harriet begins to realise she has been abandoned. This feeling is strengthened when she starts to receive monthly payments from an untraceable source. After five years on her own Harriet begins to see another man and divorces Graham on the grounds of his desertion. Then one evening Harriet returns home to find Graham sitting in a chair, casually reading a book. Her initial relief turns to anger and then to fear when she realises, that if Graham's story is true, she may never trust his sanity again. This complex comedy thriller will grip your attention to the very last page.

Natural Causes ISBN 1-84232-058-0

When megalomaniac proprietor of the Clarion Newspapers Ltd, Alexander Bean is humiliated in court by judge Mr Justice Beverly, he swears revenge. He engages the services of Sidney York to find a way to blackmail the judge. The situation gets out of hand when Sidney dies in a mysterious accident. The judge and his family fall under suspicion. Thus Alexander Bean becomes involved in a story that runs out of control for all those involved until it reaches its final unexpected conclusion.

No Bail For the Judge
ISBN 1-84232-059-9

A dour and highly respected High Court Judge finds himself on trial for the murder of a prostitute. He has no recollection of the events leading up to the murder so believes he may be guilty. His daughter, however, is convinced of his innocence, so she enlists the help of a petty thief to help solve the complex mystery. Hitchcock always wanted to film this novel.

Tell You What I'll Do
ISBN 1-84232-065-3

Harry Woodstock is a lazy but amiable criminal who would rather live by fraud than by working .He is very comfortable in Albany Prison, Isle of Wight where a clergyman visits him in an attempt to reform his character. When he is out of prison he stays with a friend in Albany, Piccadilly and tries to avoid a violent criminal who is convinced Harry defrauded him out of £60,000. Understandably, Harry feels safer in prison so, when not dodging his enemy, he spends his time thinking up ways to get himself inside again. His amusing story ends with an ingenious solution for them all.

Unlawful Occasions
ISBN 1-84232-067-X

Mrs Vernay and her husband live in a flat above the Chambers of Brian Culsworth Q.C. in the Temple. One day Mrs Vernay receives a visit from a Mr Sampson and she gets the impression that he is a blackmailer. She then immediately seeks advice from Mr Culsworth in his chambers below. Mr Culsworth's client, a Mr Baker is bringing an action to recover his share on a win on the pools. The story of these people becomes inextricably linked in a brilliant novel of suspense and humour.

The Wanted Man   ISBN 1-84232-068-8
When Norman Partridge moves to Little Bacon, a pretty country village, he proves to be a kind and helpful neighbour and is

liked by everyone. Initially it didn't seem to matter that no one knew anything about his past or how he managed to live so comfortably without having to work. Six months before, John Gladstone, a wealthy bank-robber had escaped from custody. Gradually, however Partridge's neighbours begin to ask themselves questions. Was it mere coincidence that Norman Partridge had the build and features of the escaped convict? While some villagers are suspicious but reluctant to report their concerns to the police, others decide to take matters into their own hands…

Titles available in re-issue (House of Stratus)

EDGAR WALLACE

Born in 1875, the illegitimate son of an actress, Richard Horatio Edgar Wallace was adopted by a Billingsgate fish-porter and grew up in the poorer streets of London. He wrote more than 170 books, mostly thrillers, but also plays and countless newspaper articles. In the late 1890s he served in the Royal West Kent Regiment and the Medical Staff Corps. As a war correspondent for The Daily Mail in South Africa he sent back reports that led Kitchener to ban him as a correspondent until the First World War. One of Britain's most prolific writers, Wallace earned well but lost fortunes due to his extravagant lifestyle and obsessive gambling. He died in Hollywood in 1932 on his way to work on the screenplay of King Kong.

Key Info

King of the modern thriller, classic Wallace novels feature sinister criminal acts, numerous plot twists and plenty of shadowy killers and secret passageways.

In his heyday Wallace sold five million books in a year, one out of every four books sold in the whole market.

Unsophisticated page-turners, the often gripping narratives have been hugely influential and more of his books have been made in to films than any other twentieth century writer.

Cream of the Crop

The Rule of the New Pin
(1 84232 666 X)

Jesse Trassner is more than careful with his money. He is rich and he does not trust banks. His nephew Rex Lander enjoys high living but is all too often short of funds. After going out to avoid meeting an acquaintance from his past, Trassner is found locked inside a vault. He is dead. This is no static mystery but a gripping tale

Titles in Print

Admirable Carfew
Angel of Terror
Avenger
Barbara On Her Own
Big Foot
Black Abbott
Bones
Bones in London
Bones of the River
Clue of the New Pin
Clue of the Silver Key
Clue of the Twisted
   Candle
Coat of Arms
Council of Justice
Crimson Circle
Daffodil Mystery
Dark Eyes of London
Daughters of the Night
Debt Discharged
Devil Man

Door With Seven Locks
Duke in the Suburbs
Face in the Night
Feathered Serpent
Flying Squad
Forger
Four Just Men
Four Square Jane
Fourth Plague
Frightened Lady
Good Evans
Hand of Power
Iron Grip
Joker
Just Men of Cordova
Keepers of the King's
   Peace
Law of the Four Just
   Men
Lone House Mystery
Man Who Bought
   London

Man Who Knew
Man Who Was Nobody
Mind of Mr J. G. Reeder
More Educated Evans
Mr J. G. Reeder Returns
Mr Justice Maxwell
Red Aces
Room 13
Sanders
Sanders of the River
Sinister Man
Square Emerald
Three Just Men
Three Oak Mystery
Traitor's Gate
When the Gangs Came
   to London
When the World
   Stopped

(Publisher: House of Stratus)

of adventure involving memorable characters in locations ranging from Yeh Lin's London restaurant to Ursula Ardfern's Hertfordshire cottage.

When Gangs Come to London (1 84232 711 9)

Tough, ruthless gangsters from Chicago descend on London and for two weeks their violent campaign of murder and intimidation holds the city in a crushing grip of fear. Scotland Yard has never seen such an onslaught. When a lull ensues, Captain Jiggs Allermain of the Chicago Detective Bureau suspects the rival gangs of forming an uneasy alliance. Suddenly a shot rings through the House of Commons – unleashing an outburst of terror even more bloody.

The Frightened Lady (1 84232 686 4)

Everyone tried to conceal the truth but the Frightened Lady is unable to hide her fear. Chief Inspector Tanner quickly realises that many things about the household of Lord and Lady Lebanon are not easily explained. Why are two American 'toughs' employed as footmen? Why is Lady Lebanon so unwilling to answer any questions? What he does know is that the only obviously innocent person is utterly consumed with terror. Here is Inspector Tanner's first real clue.

The Crimson Circle (1 84232 761 6)

When James Beardmore receives a letter demanding £100,000 he refuses to pay – even though it is his last warning. It is his son Jack who finds him dead. Can the amazing powers of Derrick Yale, combined with the methodical patience of Inspector Parr, discover the secret of the Crimson Circle? Who is its all-powerful head and who is the stranger who lies in wait? Twice in a lifetime a ruthless criminal faces the executioner.

The Forger (1 84232 682 1)

Forged notes have started to appear everywhere. Mr Cheyne Wells of Harley Street has been given one. So has Porter. Peter Clifton is rich, but no one is quite certain how he acquired his money – not even his new wife, the beautiful Jane Leith. One night someone puts a ladder to Jane's window and enters her room. It is not her jewels they are after. Inspector Rouper and Superintendent Bourke are both involved in trying to solve this thrilling mystery.

The Man Who Was Nobody (1 84232 697 X)

Bearing a letter from her employer, Marjorie Stedman, confidential secretary and niece of Solomon Stedman, enters the drawing room of Alma Trebizond, actress and wife of Sir James Tynewood. Tynewood is unpleasantly drunk. When a second delivery is required Marjorie travels again to Tynewood Chase. Left alone by Doctor Fordham, she hears a shot. When she opens the door she discovers Sir James lying in a pool of blood. The man holding the revolver is someone Marjorie has seen before.

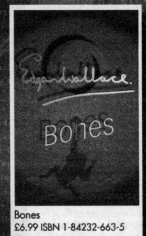

DESMOND BAGLEY

The Author

Celebrated for his action-packed stories and attention to detail, thriller writer Desmond Bagley was born in the Lake District and spent his early working life in the aircraft industry. His adventurous spirit took him on an exciting road trip to South Africa, where he settled as a freelance journalist and film critic. The first novel, *Golden Keel*, was a classic thriller based on a true story and achieved instant success. His fast-moving thrillers were written against international settings reflecting his extensive travels. He went on to write a further fifteen gripping stories, which have all been translated into more than 20 languages. Bagley's books markedly fell from favour, but the new House of Stratus re-issues may cause a revival of interest.

The Bahama Crisis ISBN 1842320041

The Mangans, having fought on the losing side of the American War of Independence, sail to the Bahamas, where they settle and prosper. Several generations later, Tom Mangan is the affluent proprietor of a number of luxury hotels, whose future looks even brighter with the injection of fifty million dollars provided by a well-heeled Texan family. The day Mangan clinches the deal with his friend, Bill Cunningham, should be the happiest day of his life, but a family tragedy followed by a series of misfortunes and disasters eventually leads him to suspect a conspiracy to ruin him, or, perhaps, something even more horrifying.

The Enemy ISBN 184232005X

Financial consultant, Malcolm Jaggard, begins a desperate investigation when

Titles available

Bahama Crisis	The Golden Keel	The Tightrope Men
The Enemy	Landslide	The Vivero Letter
Flyaway	Night of Terror	Windfall
The Freedom Trap	Running Blind	Wyatt's Hurricane
High Citadel	The Snow Tiger	*(House of Stratus:*
Juggernaut	The Spoilers	*reissues 2000)*

flourishing industrialist and former Russian scientist, George Ashton, the father of Jaggard's fiancée, mysteriously disappears following a vicious acid attack on his daughter. Ashton is traced from his home in Buckinghamshire to the wintry forests of Sweden, in a compelling tale about rivalries between intelligence groups and shocking experiments in genetic engineering.

Flyaway ISBN 1842320106

When Max Stafford, head of Stafford Security Consultants, is brutally beaten up in his own office, and Paul Billson disappears in North Africa, the race is on to discover the secret of the famous 1930s aircraft, *Flyaway*.

The Freedom Trap ISBN 1842320505

An agent of the British Government is sent on a new and deadly assignment – to snare The Scarperers (a notorious gang of criminals who organise gaol-breaking for long-term prisoners) and Slade, a notorious Russian double agent whom they have recently liberated. The trail leads him to Malta, where he comes face-to-face with these ruthless killers and must outwit them to save his own life.

High Citadel ISBN 1842320122

Isolated in the biting cold of the Andes, after their plane has been hijacked and forced to crash-land, Tim O'Hara's passengers are fighting for their lives. While one group of survivors, lead by O'Hara, attempt to cross the peaks along a deadly, snow-covered pass, the other is working to stall the armed group of soldiers who plan to kill them all once they have managed to cross a torrential river. Ingenious ideas are

put into action in a dramatic attempt to prolong their survival until help arrives.

Juggernaut ISBN 1842320130

It is longer than a football pitch, weighs 550 tons, and moves at an average of five miles per hour. Its job – and that of company troubleshooter, Neil Mannix – is to move a giant transformer across Nyala, an oil-rich African state. When Nyala erupts into civil war, Mannix finds himself, and the juggernaut, at the centre of the conflict. Can Mannix deliver the transformer to its destination or will warring factions finally halt its progress and destroy it?

Landslide ISBN 1842320149

Geologist, Bob Boyd, who works in British Columbia timber country, has no memory of his past following a terrible accident, which only he survived. Hired by the powerful Matterson Corporation to survey land before they build a great new dam, he begins to uncover the shaky foundations of the Matterson family and becomes a fly in their ointment. Matters are complicated when he falls in love with Claire Trinavant, the last link to a forgotten family whose name strikes a mysteriously resonant chord.

Night of Error ISBN 1842320157

The only discernable bond in the relationship of brothers Mark and Mike Trevelyan is their fascination with the sea and its secrets. When Mike hears of his brother's death, during an expedition to a remote Pacific atoll, the circumstances are suspicious enough to force him to investigate, and when he is the victim of a series of violent attacks, his search for the truth becomes even more desperate. Mike has only two clues – a notebook in code and a lump of rock – enough to trigger off a hazardous expedition and a violent confrontation far from civilisation.

Running Blind ISBN 1842320165

It all begins with a simple errand – a package to deliver. But for Alan Stewart, standing on a deserted road in Iceland with a murdered man at his feet, the mission looks far from simple. Set amongst some of the most dramatic scenery in the world, Stewart and his girlfriend, Erin, are faced with treacherous natural obstacles and deadly threats, as they battle to carry out the mission. The contents of the package are a surprise for the reader as much as for Stewart in a finale of formidable energy.

> 'In this sort of literate, exciting, knowledgeable adventure, Mr Bagley is incomparable'   *Sunday Times*

The Snow Tiger ISBN 1842320173

A small mining community in New Zealand is devastated when 'the snow tiger' (an avalanche) rips apart their entire township in a matter of minutes, killing fifty-four people. In the course of the ensuing enquiry, the antagonisms and fears of the community are laid bare, and a ruthless battle, for control of a multi-million pound international mining group, is exposed. The tension in the courtroom mounts as each survivor gives his graphic account of the terrifying sequence of events.

The Spoilers ISBN 1842320513

When film tycoon, Sir Robert Hellier, loses his daughter to heroin, he declares war on the drug peddlers. London drug specialist, Nicholas Warren, is called in to organise an expedition to the Middle East, in an attempt to track down the big-time dope runners, inveigle themselves into their confidence and make them an offer they can't refuse. No expense is spared in the plans for their capture, but with a hundred million dollars worth of heroin at stake, the 'spoilers' must use methods as ruthless as their prey.

The Tightrope Men ISBN 1842320181

Giles Denison's life is turned upside down when he awakes to find himself in a luxurious hotel in Oslo and, peering into the bathroom mirror, discovers the face of another man! He has been kidnapped from his flat in London and transformed into famous Finnish scientist, Dr Harold Feltham Meyrick. Compelled to adjust to his new persona (including meeting his daughter) and to play out the role assigned to him by his captors, he embarks on a dangerous escapade from Norway to Finland and across the border into Soviet Russia.

Windfall ISBN 1842320203

Jan Willem Hendryk's legacy amounts to a staggering £40 million – £34 million to go to an agricultural college in Kenya's Rift Valley, and the remaining £6 million to be divided equally between his only surviving descendants: Dirk, a South African, and Henry, a young drop-out living in California. But a number of suspicious circumstances emerge, including a clause in the will stating that Dirk must spend one month of every year in Kenya. What seems at first a simple matter of greed gradually assumes sinister proportions.

JAMES HADLEY CHASE

James Hadley Chase was born in London and initially worked as a book wholesaler. He was heavily influenced by American crime and gangster writers and his own books fall within that genre, with many of them based in the US. Chase developed a number of series characters, with several books dedicated to each. All are fast moving tales of murder, intrigue, blackmail and espionage. Characters include ex-commando Brick-Top Corrigan, Californian private eye Vic Malloy, former CIA agent Mark Girland, and millionaire Don Miclem. Hailed as "the thriller maestro of the generation", Chase died in 1985, and was a major influence on modern day writers such as James Elroy and Carl Hiaassen

Cream of the Crop

The Fast Buck (1 84232 102 1)

International jewel thief, Paul Hater, knows a secret that everyone wants to know – and will go to any lengths to uncover. How long can he remain silent? When Hater is arrested in possession of a stolen necklace, the police use every possible means to persuade him to reveal the location of the rest of the collection. He remains silent and so begins his twenty-year prison sentence. Having exhausted all their leads, the International Detective Agency, acting on behalf of the insurers, must patiently await Hater's release before they can hope to find out more. But just as his day of release approaches, Hater is kidnapped by a ruthless international gang determined to force the secret from him and prepared to go to any lengths to do so.

Goldfish Have No Hiding Place (1 84232 103 X)

Eastlake is the kind of place where 'nice' people live – nice, well-off, civilised people. People who know all about each other and where everyone knows everyone else's business – rather like living in a goldfish bowl. So when scanners are set up in the self-service shop in an attempt to catch petty shoplifters, it comes as rather a surprise when some dark secrets begin to emerge. A perfect opportunity for blackmailers.

Have a Change of Scene (1 84232 106 4)

Larry Carr is a diamond expert in need of a break. So when his psychiatrist suggests he has a change of scene, he jumps at the opportunity to move to Luceville, a struggling industrial town, and become a social worker. This, he thinks, will give him all the rest he needs… until he runs into Rhea Morgan, a ruthless, vicious thief who also happens to be extremely attractive. He falls headlong into the criminal world and embarks upon a thrilling, rapid and dastardly adventure in true Hadley Chase style.

Hit and Run (1 84232 108 0)

Lucille Aitkin was the kind of woman who

Bibliography

An Ace Up My Sleeve

An Ear to the Ground

The Fast Buck

Goldfish Have No Hiding
     Place

The Guilty Are Afraid

Hand Me a Fig Leaf

Have a Change of Scene

Have this One on Me

Hit and Run

Hit Them Where it Hurts

Just a Matter of Time

Knock Knock Who's
     There?

Like a Hole in the Head

Make the Corpse Walk

More Deadly than the
     Male

My Laugh Comes Last

Not My Thing

So What Happens to Me?

Tell it to the Birds

The Whiff of Money

You Have Yourself a Deal

You're Dead Without
     Money

(All reissued by House of Stratus)

encouraged men to run around after her and most men were more than happy to do so – so why did she suddenly want to learn to drive rather than being chauffer-driven in style? And why was Chester Scott's Cadillac covered with bloodstains on the *wrong* side? And at the same time, why was patrol officer O'Brien run over on a deserted beach road when he should have been on duty on the highway? It seems that somebody knows how these events are connected, and whoever it is seems intent on blackmail.

Knock Knock Who's There?
(1 84232 111 0)

Johnny Bianda is a man with a dream. He wants to own a boat off the coast of Florida and he only needs $186,000 to buy it. He steals the money from his firm, knowing that one day they'll notice and one day they'll kill him for it – after all, it is the Mafia. But for Johnny Bianda, the risk is worth taking and he knows it will be at least a year before they catch up with him. Unfortunately for Bianda, the knock on his door comes sooner than he thinks.

More Deadly Than the Male
(1 84232 114 5)

George Fraser is a lonely man, and a bored man. But he has exciting dreams. In his dreams, he lives in a thrilling world of gangsters, guns, fast cars and beautiful women. And of course, in his dreams, he is the toughest gangster of them all. George Fraser prefers his dream world to his real, ordinary life so he begins to boast about it, pretending that he is, in fact, a hardened and ruthless gangster. But George Fraser boasts to the wrong people and suddenly his dream world becomes all too real.

My Laugh Comes Last (1 84232 115 2)

Farrell Brannigan, President of the National Californian Bank, is an extremely successful man. So when he builds another bank in an up-and-coming town on the Pacific coast, he is given worldwide publicity, and this new bank is hailed as 'the safest bank in the world'. But Brannigan's success came at a price and he made many enemies on his way up the ladder. It seems that one of them is now set on revenge and determined to destroy both the bank and Brannigan himself.

The Whiff of Money (1 84232 118 8)

Secret Agent Mark Kirkland has been given the task of locating and retrieving three pornographic films. His mission must remain top secret as the films, rather embarrassingly, feature the daughter of the future president of the United States. His quest leads him to the depths of Bavaria where he finds Soviet agent, Malik, and sidekick Lu Silk also rather interested in the whereabouts of the films. Who will find them first? And once found, who's to say they won't immediately disappear again?

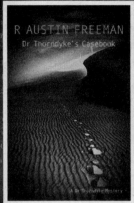

STEVE AYLETT

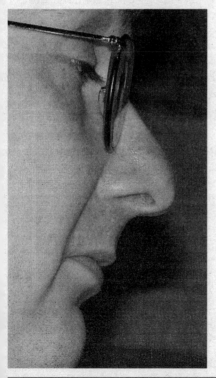

Steve Aylett was born in Bromley, England, in 1967. He left school at seventeen and worked in a book warehouse, and later in trade and law publishing – here he invented the concept of 'fractal litigation', whereby the flapping of a butterfly's wings on one side of the world results in a massive compensation claim on the other. His first book *The Crime Studio*, published in 1994, was generally regarded as a 'cry for help'. This was followed by *Bigot Hall, Slaughtermatic, The Inflatable Volunteer, Toxicology* and *Atom*. He is published by Orion in the UK and Four Walls Eight Windows in the US, and was nominated for the 1998 Philip K. Dick Award (*Slaughtermatic*). His toured 'Shroud' show, during which he silently impersonated the Shroud of Turin, caused rage and impatience in clubland in the early 1990s. His stories have appeared in the bestselling *Disco Biscuits* anthologies (Sceptre). He lives in Brighton, England.

"It's less insulting to the reader to say

something in a few words, like 'progress accelerates downhill', than to spend an entire book saying that. I still just write the kind of books I'd like to read, that I'd like to find out there, and luckily enough people share that taste to be into them. I don't like zany. I often feel people don't see past all the fireworks to what I'm talking about. Maybe sometime I'll do something with all the fireworks stripped out, no jokes, for the hard-of-reading – so they'll see what's always been there from the beginning.

"Placing your head inside the reaction out there will certainly rot your brain, it's a displacement of energy. People may read one of my things and think it's all a particular way, for good or ill. But there's *Slaughtermatic*, which is fairly conventional old-time satire which nobody else does these days, then there's *The Inflatable Volunteer* which has no satire and is this big splurge of funny poetics. And later there's stuff that's unlike any of that because I've hardly started yet. So I have to disregard all this. My head stays here. I certainly don't think in words. I'm not sure that anyone does. Does anyone really think in sentences, like in films when you see someone thinking and you hear a voice-over? I don't anyway. I see stuff visually, as shapes, colours, textures and mechanisms sort of hanging there in space. If there's a hole in someone's argument I visually see a hole in it, in the armature and mass of the thing. I'll see the shape of a whole book that way before it's written, and so far, the books have all ended up the way I saw them originally.

"If a saxophone became fossilized, how would anyone know it had never been an animal? Rain sounds the same everywhere."

Bibliography

The Crime Studio (first published 1994), Orion (UK)

Bigot Hall (first published 1995), Orion (UK)

Slaughtermatic (1998), Four Walls Eight Windows (US), Orion (UK)

The Inflatable Volunteer (1999), Orion (UK)

Toxicology (stories) (1999), Four Walls Eight Windows

Atom (2000), Four Walls Eight Windows (US), Orion (UK)

BULLETS

Adrian Muller

John Harvey

Fans of the author will be delighted to hear that, since completing his highly acclaimed Resnick series, he is planning to return to crime fiction with a stand alone novel. *In a True Light* will be published by William Heinemann in October. The book focuses on an ex-convict who is trying to trace the whereabouts of the daughter he never knew.

Don't Adjust Your Television Set

US fans of crime drama have had the chance to see some curious adaptations on telly. First came *The Sign of Four* starring 1980s throwback Matt 'Max Headroom' Frewer as Sherlock Holmes. More recently Poirot fans had to contend with Alfred Molina as the Belgian detective in a modern version of *Murder on the Orient Express*. Not only did viewers get to see Hercule tinker with a laptop, there was also a hint of romance. What would Captain Hastings say to that?!

John Le Carré

To mark John Le Carré's seventieth birthday, Hodder & Stoughton are republishing a number of the author's novels in uniform new editions with an introduction by Le Carré himself.

More Sherlock

Published this July is *Starring Sherlock Holmes* by David Stuart Davies, editor of *Sherlock Holmes – the Detective Magazine*. This illustrated guide to film, stage, radio and television portrayals features an unprecedented collection of stills, posters and behind-the-scenes shots. Priced £29, *Starring Sherlock Holmes* comes with an introduction by Ian Richardson and two alternative front jackets, one featuring Basil Rathbone, the other Jeremy Brett.

The CWA's Debut Dagger Crime Writing Competition

Fancy yourself as the next Lindsey Davis or Ian Rankin? The why not enter the Crime Writers' Association's annual crime writing competition? Only unpublished writers can enter. There are no guarantees, but the first two winners were published by HarperCollins and Orion. Two short-listed entrants were also published as a result of their work being seen by editors. You have until 14th August to produce the opening pages (up to 3,000 words) of your crime novel and a 500 word outline of its plot. Crime includes anything from historical mysteries and period whodunits to thrillers. There is an entry fee of £10. For more details or an entry form visit the CWA website at www.thecwa.co.uk, send an e-mail to debut.dagger@thecwa.co.uk or send an SAE to New Writing Competition, PO Box 62, Okehampton, EX20 2YQ England.

MYSTERY WRITERS OF AMERICA'S
EDGAR AWARDS

Best Novel:

The Bottoms – Joe R. Lansdale (Mysterious Press)

Nominated:

A Place of Execution – Val McDermid (St Martin's Minotaur)

A Dangerous Road – Kris Nelscott (St Martin's Minotaur)

Red Light – T. Jefferson Parker (Hyperion)

The Whole Truth – Nancy Pickard (Pocket Books)

Best First Novel by an American Author:

A Conspiracy of Paper – David Liss (Random House)

Nominated:

The Ice Harvest – Scott Phillips (Ballantine Books)

Death of a Red Heroine – Qiu Xiaolong (Soho Press)

Crow in Stolen Colors – Marcia Simpson (Poisoned Pen Press, Berkley Prime Crime)

Raveling – Peter Moore Smith (Little, Brown)

Best Paperback Original:

The Black Maria – Mark Graham (Avon)

Nominated:

Murder on St Mark's Place – Victoria Thompson (Berkley)

Killing Kin – Chassie West (Avon)

The Kidnapping of Rosie Dawn – Eric Wright (Perseverance Press/John Daniel & Co.)

Pursuit and Persuasion – Sally S. Wright (Multnomah)

Best Fact Crime:

Black Mass: The Irish Mob, the FBI, and a Devil's Deal – Dick Lehr & Gerard O'Neill (Public Affairs/Perseus Books)

Nominated:

The Seekers: A Bounty Hunter's Story – Joshua Armstrong & Anthony Bruno (HarperCollins)

Portraits of Guilt: The Woman Who Profiles the Faces of America's Deadliest Criminals – Jeanne Boylan (Pocket Books/Simon & Schuster)

Author Unknown: On the Trail of Anonymous – Don Foster (Henry Holt)

Moonlight: Abraham Lincoln and the Almanac Trial – John Evangelist Walsh (St Martin's Press)

Best Critical/Biographical Work:

Conundrums for the Long Week-End: England, Dorothy L. Sayers, and Lord Peter Wimsey – Robert Kuhn McGregor with Ethan Lewis (The Kent State University Press)

Nominated:

The Doctor and the Detective: A Biography of Sir Arthur Conan Doyle – Martin Booth (Thomas Dunne Books/St Martin's Minotaur)

Women of Mystery: The Lives and Works of Notable Women Crime Novelists – Martha Hailey Dubose with additional essays by Margaret Caldwell Thomas (Thomas Dunne Books/St Martin's Minotaur)

The Red-Hot Typewriter: The Life and Times

of John D. MacDonald – Hugh Merrill
(Thomas Dunne Books/St Martin's
Minotaur)

Best Short Story:
Missing in Action – Peter Robinson (*Ellery
Queen Mystery Magazine*, November
2000)
Nominated:
Delta Double-Deal – Noreen Ayres (*The
Night Awakens*, MWA anthology edited
by Mary Higgins Clark)
A Candle for Christmas – Reginald Hill
(*EQMM*, January 2000)
Twelve of the Little Buggers – Mat Coward
(*EQMM*, January 2000)
Spinning – Kristine Kathryn Rusch
(*EQMM*, July 2000)

Best Young Adult:
Counterfeit Son – Elaine Marie Alphin
(Harcourt Inc.)
Nominated:
Silent to the Bone – E. L. Konigsberg

(Atheneum Books for Young Readers)
The Body of Christopher Creed – Carol
Plum-Ucci (Harcourt Inc.)
Locked Inside – Nancy Werlin (Delacorte
Press)

Best Children's:
Dovey Coe – Frances O'Roark Dowell
(Atheneum)
Nominated:
Trouble at Fort La Pointe – Kathleen Ernst
(American Girl)
*Sammy Keyes and the Curse of Mustache
Mary* – Wendelin Van Draanen (Knopf)
Walking to the Bus Rider Blues – Harriette
Gillem Robinet (Atheneum)
Ghosts in the Gallery – Barbara Brooks
Wallace (Atheneum)

Special Edgar Award:
Mildred Wirt Benson, the original Carolyn
Keene, author of the Nancy Drew mystery
series

NEW BRITISH CRIME TITLES:
(author, title (series), publisher, price)

June

Jane Adams, *Like Angels Falling*, Macmillan,
£16.99

Rennie Airth, *The Blood-Dimmed Tide* (John
Madden), Macmillan, £12.99

Ace Atkins, *Crossroad Blues* (Nick Travers),
Robinson, £6.99

Pauline Bell, *Reasonable Death* (DI Mitchell),
Constable, £16.99

Robin Cook, *Shock*, Macmillan, £16.99

Denise Danks, *Soft Target* (Georgina
Powers), Gollancz, £9.99/£16.99

Lindsey Davis, *A Body in the Bathhouse*
(Marcus Didius Falco), Century, £15.99

Paul Doherty, *The House of Death*
(Alexander the Great), Robinson, £16.99

James Ellroy, *The Cold Six Thousand*,
Century, £15.99

Penelope Evans, *First Fruits*, Allison & Busby,
£17.99

Robert M. Eversz, *Killing Paparazzi*,
Macmillan, £9.99

John Fusco, *Paradise Salvage*, Scribner,
£10/£16.99

Jonathan Gash, *Every Last Cent* (Lovejoy),
Macmillan, £16.99

Alan Glynn, *The Dark Fields*, Little, Brown, £10.99

Sue Grafton, *P is for Peril* (Kinsey Millhone), Macmillan, £9.99

Susanna Gregory, *An Order for Death* (Matthew Bartholomew), Little, Brown, £12.99

James Hall, *Kill Switch* (Rafferty & Thorn), HarperCollins, £9.99

Steve Hamilton, *Winter of the Wolf Moon* (Alex McKnight), Orion, £9.99/£16.99

Sylvian Hamilton, *The Pendragon Banner* (Sir Richard Straccan), Orion, £9.99

James Harland, *The Month of the Leopard*, Simon & Schuster, £10

Ellen Hart, *The Merchant of Venus* (Jane Lawless), The Women's Press, £6.99

Alan Jacobson, *The Hunted*, Hodder & Stoughton, £17.99

Anita Janda, *The Secret Diary of Dr Watson* (Holmes & Watson), Allison & Busby, £17.99

Paul Johnston, *The House of Dust* (Quint Dalrymple), Hodder & Stoughton, £17.99

Max Kinnings, *Fixer*, Flame, £10.99

Richard Littlejohn, *Reasonable Force*, HarperCollins, £5.99

Sam Llewellyn, *The Malpas Legacy*, Headline, £9.99/£17.99

Marianne Macdonald, *Blood Lies* (Dido Hoare), Hodder & Stoughton, £17.99

Sharyn McCrumb, *The Song Catcher* (Ballad), Hodder & Stoughton, £17.99

Michael McGarrity, *The Judas Judge* (Kevin Kerney), Robert Hale, £17.99

Gwen Moffatt, *Quicksand*, Constable, £16.99

Peter Moore Smith, *Strange Bliss*, Hutchinson, £10

Natasha Mostert, *The Other Side of Silence*, Hodder & Stoughton, £17.99

Chris Paling, *Newton's Swing*, Vintage, £6.99

Eliot Pattison, *Water Touching Stone*, Century, £10

Daniel Pennac, *Passion Fruit* (Belleville Quarter), Harvill Press, £9.99/£16.99

Danuta Reah, *The Butcher's Birdsong* (Lynne Jordan), HarperCollins, £9.99

Nicholas Rhea, *The Sniper* (Pemberton), Constable, £16.99

Kevin Sampson, *Outlaws*, Jonathan Cape, £10

Andrew Taylor, *Death's Own Door* (Lydmouth), Hodder & Stoughton, £17.99

July

William Aaltonen, *The Feel of Glass* (debut crime novel), Michael Joseph, £9.99

Peter Benjamin, *Terms and Conditions*, Town House, £10

Giles Blunt, *Forty Words for Sorrow* (John Cardinal), HarperCollins, £12.99

Janie Bolitho, *Saving Grace*, Constable, £16.99

T. R. Bowen, *The Black Camel* (John Bewick), Michael Joseph, £5.99

Mark Burnell, *Chameleon*, HarperCollins, £9.99

Robert Crais, tba, Orion, £12.99

Neil Cross, *Nowhere, Forever*, Jonathan Cape, £10

Paul Doherty, *The Slayers of Seth* (Egyptian), Headline, £9.99/£17.99

John Farrow, *Ice Lake* (Emile Cinq Mars), Century, £9.99

Nicci French, *The Unburied* (Grace Schillings), Michael Joseph, £10

Neil Gaiman, *American Gods*, Headline, £10

Elizabeth George, *A Traitor to Memory* (Lynley & Havers), Hodder & Stoughton, £17.99

Maggie Gibson, *Blah Blah Black Sheep*, Gollancz, £9.99

Philip Gooden, *Death of Kings* (Nick Revill), Robinson, £6.99

Anne Granger, *Risking It All* (Fran Varady),

Headline, £17.99

Georgie Hale, *Without Consent*, Hodder & Stoughton, £17.99

Humphrey Hawksley, *Red Spirit*, Headline, £17.99

Lauren Henderson, *Pretty Boy* (Sam Jones), Hutchinson, £10

Quintin Jardine, *Autographs in the Rain* (Bob Skinner), Headline, £9.99/£17.99

Will Kingdom, *Mean Spirit*, Bantam, £9.99

Lury & Gibson, *Dangerous Data*, Bantam, £9.99

Joseph O'Connor, *Inishowen*, Vintage, £6.99

Gill Paul, *Compulsion*, Hodder & Stoughton, £17.99

David Peace, *Nineteen Eighty*, Serpent's Tail, £10/£15.99

Michael Pearce, *The Face in the Cemetery* (Mamur Zapt), HarperCollins, £16.99

Elizabeth Peters, *The Deeds of Disturbance* (Amelia Peabody), Robinson, £6.99

John Sandford, *The Devil's Code*, Pocket Books, £6.99

Kevin Wignall, *People Die* (debut crime novel), Flame, £10

August

Robert Barnard, *The Bones in the Attic* (Charlie Peace), HarperCollins, £16.99

Mark Billingham, *Sleepy Head* (debut crime novel), Little, Brown, £9.99

Lizbie Brown, *Cat's Cradle* (Elizabeth Blair), Hodder & Stoughton, £17.99

Michael Cordy, *Lucifer*, Bantam, £9.99.

Leif Davidsen, *Lime's Photograph*, Harvill Press, £9.99/£15.99

Tim Dorsey, *Orange Crush*, HarperCollins, £5.99

James Humphreys, *Riptide*, Macmillan, £16.99

Greg Iles, *Dead Sleep*, Hodder & Stoughton, £17.99

Faye Kellerman, *The Forgotten*, Headline, £9.99/£17.99

Michael Kimball, *Green Girls*, Headline, £10

Ludlum, Robert & Shelby, Philip, *The Cassandra Compact*, HarperCollins, £16.99

Hannah March, *A Necessary Evil* (Robert Fairfax), Headline, £17.99

Edward Marston, *The Repentant Rake*, Headline, £17.99

Maureen O'Brien, *Revenge*, Little, Brown, £16.99

Kathy Reichs, *Fatal Voyage* (Tempe Brennan), William Heineman, £15.99

Lawrence Sanders, *McNally's Chance* (Archy McNally), Hodder & Stoughton, £17.99

Lisa Scottoline, *The Vendetta Defence*, HarperCollins, £9.99

Gerald Seymour, *The Untouchable*, Bantam, £10.99

Marcel Theroux, *The Paperchase*, Abacus, £10.99

Donald Thomas, *Sherlock Holmes and the Running Noose* (Sherlock Holmes), Macmillan, £16.99

David Wishart, *Last Rites* (Marcus Corvinus), Hodder & Stoughton, £17.99

September

Adam Baron, *Superjack*, Macmillan, £9.99

Sally Beauman, *Rebecca's Tale* (sequel to DuMaurier's *Rebecca*), Little, Brown, £16.99

Ken Bruen, *London Boulevard*, Do-Not Press

Paul Charles, *Hissing of the Silent Lonely Room*, Do-Not Press

Deborah Crombie, *A Finer End*, Macmillan, £16.99

Judith Cutler, *Will Power* (Kate Power), Hodder & Stoughton, £17.99

Linda Davies, *Something Wild*, Headline, £9.99

Jeffrey Deaver, *Shallow Graves* (John

Pellam), Hodder & Stoughton, £17.99

Jeffrey Deaver, *Bloody River Blues* (John Pellam), Hodder & Stoughton, £17.99

Jeffrey Deaver, *Hell's Kitchen* (John Pellam), Hodder & Stoughton, £17.99

Frederick Forsyth, *The Veteran* (short stories), Bantam, £16.99

Martha Grimes, *The Blue Last* (Richard Jury), Headline, £17.99

Joyce Holmes, *Bitter End* (Fizz & Buchanan), Headline, £17.99

Maggie Hudson, *Looking for Mr Big*, HarperCollins, £5.99

James H. Jackson, *The Reaper*, Headline, £17.99

Bill James, *Split* (new series), Do-Not Press

Alan Judd, *Legacy* (Charles Thoroughgood), HarperCollins, £16.99

John Lescroart, *The Indictment*, Headline, £17.99

Frederick Lindsay, *Darkness in My Hand* (Jim Meldrum), Hodder & Stoughton, £17.99

Jenny Maxwell, *Bright Rooms*, Warner, £5.99

Bill Murphy, *Fractions of Zero*, Hodder & Stoughton, £17.99

Margaret Murphy, *Dying Embers*, Macmillan, £5.99

Anne Perry, *Rutland Place* (the Pitts), HarperCollins, £5.99

Anne Perry, *Come Armageddon* (Tathea fantasy sequel), Headline, £17.99

Jerry Raine, *Small Change*, Do-Not Press

Elizabeth Redfern, *The Music of Spheres*, Century, £15.99

Ruth Rendell, *Adam and Eve and Pinch Me*, Hutchinson, £16.99

Simon Shaw, *Selling Grace* (Grace Cornish), HarperCollins, £9.99

Karin Slaughter, *Blindsighted* (debut crime novel), Century, £16.99

Veronica Stallwood, *Oxford Double* (Kate Ivory), Headline, £17.99

Sarah Strohmeyer, *Bubbles Unbound*, Headline, £9.99

Peter Tremayne, *Smoke in the Wind* (Sister Fidelma), Headline, £17.99

Margaret Yorke, *Cause for Concern*, Little, Brown, £16.99

For further information on the above titles, or to order books, contact:

Crime in Store

14 Bedford Street, Covent Garden, London WC2E 9HE

Tel: +44 (0)20 7379 3795, fax: +44 (0)20 7379 8988

Email: CrimeBks@aol.com   Website: http://www.crimeinstore.co.uk

Murder One

71-73 Charing Cross Road, London WC2H 0AA

Tel: +44 (0)20 7734 3483, fax: +44 (0)20 7734 3429

Email: 106562.2021@compuserve.com   Website: http://www.murderone.co.uk

Post Mortem Books

58 Stanford Avenue, Hassocks, Sussex BN6 8JH

Tel: +44 (0)1273 843066, fax: +44 (0)1273 845090

Email: ralph@pmbooks.demon.co.uk   Website:

http://www.postmortembooks.co.uk

TO THE MAX

His own books have earned him the sobriquet King of the Erotic Thriller; he's one of the genre's premier editors...

Mr Maxim Jakubowski

More substantial when it comes to characterisation and mood and as accomplished as the second novel by broadcaster and food expert Leslie Forbes, *Fish, Blood and Bone* (Weidenfeld & Nicolson, £12.99) follows her atmospheric *Bombay Ice*. A forensic photographer inherits a house and garden in London's East End from relatives she never knew she had. When her botanist new neighbour is murdered, the mystery takes the protagonist to Tibet and India on a scientific expedition with curious parallels to a nineteenth-century botanical quest at the time of the mapping of the Himalayas. Meticulously structured and full of the smells and sounds of the Indian sub-continent, this is high-calibre storytelling with a wonderful sense of empathy for foreign cultures and a strong emotional punch.

Fred Willard's *Princess Naughty and the Voodoo Cadillac* (No Exit Press, £6.99) is a rollicking deep American South ride of a novel, and a wonderful follow-up to Willard's debut *Down on Ponce*, which was short-listed for best new crime book of the year. Tough guy Ray Justus loves glam girl gangster Ginger Loudermilk and drives a Cadillac with a curse of death. His partner, Peanut Shoke, lives to kill the Shitass Ronnie Gordon, simpleton and snitch. Meanwhile millionaire Bobby Nelms longs to be a spy while Bill Schiller plans to retire with Nelms' bundle and Maggie Donald trades sex for what she wants, which certainly doesn't include threadbare bagman Dunbarton Oakes. Get the flavour? An engaging gallery of cheerful grotesques on a bloody joyride on the trail of a suitcase of cash and a guilty delight of an amoral crime novel which just sparkles with wit and colour. Alan Watt is another new American writer and his *Diamond Dogs* (Duck Editions, £9.99) displays an assured voice and tone in its complex psychological tale of an alienated young American college football star who turns to crime and his mixed-up relationship with his harsh small-town sheriff father. Despite the tension that sunders them, the father, a rabid Neil Diamond fan, covers up for his son when the FBI come probing and the explosive denouement takes place in that holy of holy of evil and gaudiness, Las

Vegas: it doesn't disappoint. A major new talent. Many of today's best American noir writers owe an important debt to Chester Himes and the first major biography of the much-exiled black writer *Chester Himes: A Life* (Canongate, £20) by James Sallis (himself the author of a series of a crime novels set in New Orleans, featuring black investigator Lew Griffin) is an exemplary stroll through the life and times of a much-troubled activist and innovator, who followed time in prison with recognition in Europe and critical disdain in his home country. Makes you want to read his classic Harlem books all over again.

In their criminal wisdom, Picador are offering readers their money back if they deem *The Ice Harvest* by Scott Phillips (£10) less fun than *Fargo*. As much as I enjoy the Coen Brothers' romp, this is doing this first novel a disservice. True, we are in the American Midwest and snow surrounds the landscape and the lowlife characters, but this venture into white noir is darker, sharper and very much in the league of sombre masters like James M. Cain and Jim Thompson. Truly the real thing and a future classic. It's Christmas Eve in Wichita, Kansas, and the snow falls steadily, casting a bleak shadow over buildings and minds. The streets are deserted, traffic is light and most people have returned home for the festivities while crooked lawyer Charlie Arglist moves and weaves between shady strip clubs and rundown bars on a nine and a half hour mission to get out of town. But Wichita, like hell, is not an easy place to leave behind, when you have scammed the mob and things naturally go wildly wrong. This is a race against time set against a cold gallery of losers and lost ideals, with a most wonderfully ironic twist at the end. Delightfully mean spirited, this is a razor-sharp slice of low-down Americana with a gothic vengeance both gripping and touching and one cannot help feeling an odd sense of compassion for these pitiful criminals doing their U-turns in the snow. Stunning.

Veteran Lawrence Block seldom disappoints, and *Hit List* (Orion, £16.99) is another pleaser, reintroducing us to professional hitman Keller, a cool, competent and uncharismatic killer in the line of duty. His well-organised life is severely disrupted and his principles assaulted when he discovers someone has put a hit on him. A panic attack and a snuffed romance follow, as he almost gets a taste of his own medicine. Ruthless but flawed, Keller is a great invention and his hard-boiled amorality has both poignance and grace in the way that death loses its aura of terror and is just for him a day at the office. Entertaining if worrying. Violence and sudden death come as easily to Nick Sharman, Mark Timlin's south London private eye in *All the Empty Places* (No Exit Press, £14.99), the sixteenth excursion of the laconic detective among our home-grown mean streets. It begins when Sharman falls for a girl with a shady past, but then the path of true love has never been easy for the loveable rogue, and soon he is tangled up in a multimillion pound robbery, heavy-duty thugs and enough ordnance to stock the Woolwich Arsenal. The plot races along like a salsa dancer overdosing on red peppers, and never lets go until the final bullet. A guilty pleasure.

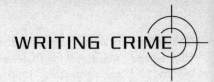
CT prides itself on the number of top crime writers who are happy to write for these pages – and here's Natasha Cooper (aka Clare Layton), regularly to be found as reviewee at the back of CT for her Trish Maguire crime treats, talking about the crime writer's life…

EMOTIONAL REALISM

Natasha Cooper

Every year there are novels that appeal to a whole range of different critics and readers and yet leave me cold, even though I can share the general admiration for the pace or place, plot or prose. When I first started reviewing, I tended to assume that I'd missed some subtlety everyone else saw. Now I know that I resist any novel in which one (or more) of the main characters operates in ways that do not convince me. Rennie Airth's *River of Darkness* is a good example. Wonderfully reviewed by almost everyone, shortlisted for a large number of prizes, bought in huge quantities and loved by thousands of readers on both sides of the Atlantic, the novel sticks in my mind more than many others that I enjoyed more on first reading. There was a lot to admire even then, and much to remember now with real approval. Airth's description of the post-war British countryside, baking in heat, and its terrorised occupants was convincing and beautifully done. Inspector John Madden was an attractive character to lead the police investigation, and the woman doctor who fell in love with him was equally appealing. The murders were suitably horrific but the author did not dwell on them unpleasantly, and so on.

As I read, I found there was a barrier between me and what was happening in the novel. My resistance came partly from the anachronistic behaviour of the woman doctor. I simply could not believe that any woman of her date, type and class, even though she had been married and was now a doctor, would have dealt with a new love affair as the character did in *River of Darkness*. There was also the problem of Madden himself. I could not accept that any man as intelligent and sensitive, and as affected by his First World War service as Madden, would have reacted as he did to the discovery that the killer he was hunting had also fought in the trenches. There would have to have been some powerful emotional conflict, even if it were savagely squashed down in the interests of duty or stiff-upper-lip self-respect. Airth makes the reader privy to Madden's thoughts and yet there were none that made sense of the experiences he had shared with the killer, so I couldn't believe in him.

The latest novel in which my inability to accept a character's motivation and emotions is Julie Parsons' *Eager to Please*. Judging by the quotes on the jacket, her two earlier titles (neither of which I've yet read) were much admired. Jeffrey Deaver describes her as,

"One of those rare authors who can successfully combine psychological insight, literary style and heart-stopping suspense." The *Sunday Independent* review refers to "a dark, compelling and original new voice" and also announces that she "makes Patricia Cornwell read like Thomas the Tank Engine". Clearly I must read *Mary, Mary* and *The Courtship Gift* because I did not respond to the new novel with anything like so much admiration. *Eager to Please* is a pacey enough revenge thriller, and there is some fine descriptive writing in it, but I simply could not swallow the way several of the characters behave. The heroine, for example, is utterly convincing in the first chapter. Paragraph by quick paragraph, this efficiently covers the twelve years of the life sentence she has to serve for the murder of her husband. It tracks the shock of her first introduction to prison life, and the difficulty of learning to live within the system, as well as the long dreary days that have to be endured. Her refusal to admit her guilt is quickly established, as is her eventual yielding to the common-sense view that if she is ever to get out on licence she will have to pretend to have come to terms with guilt. In these pages, she is a hurt, angry, frightened – damaged – woman. And a realistic one.

Her first few weeks out in the world are also convincing, as she fumbles through actions and ideas that would be second nature to everyone who has not been removed from normal life for twelve years. The problems come with the revenge she takes on the man she claims actually did murder her husband. The section of the novel that deals with her campaign is thoroughly entertaining and very readable; but it is built around a woman who bears so little emotional resemblance to the first that it makes no sense of what the reader was told at the beginning. If there had been a convincing explanation of the psychological basis for her transformation, it might have worked. The fact that Rachel Beckett is to some extent an unreliable narrator does not help. Withholding from the reader information necessary to make any sense of what is going on may add to suspense but it doesn't do much for a character's psychological credibility. And it is not only the character of Rachel that does not seem real. Her probation officer, Andrew Bowen, behaves bizarrely in giving her a part-time job looking after his own paralysed wife so that he can have some time off. At first I assumed that he was setting Rachel up for another murder conviction so that he could rid himself of the burden of an unloved wife whose dying is taking too long, which would have provided an intriguing subplot, but no: he just wants a carer – in which case why wait for Rachel? There must have been plenty of people he could have paid to give him a few hours' free time in the pub.

So it goes on, and this lack of emotional realism makes it impossible for me to believe in any of the rest of the novel. It may, of course, be simply that the author was hurried into delivering before she was quite ready. If so, her publishers did her a disservice because this could have been a terrific book. Other people object to invented police procedure or cod science. For me they don't matter much. What does matter is the ways in which fictional police officers or scientists react to what they see, hear, smell and feel. But then I'm more interested in where emotion comes from and what it makes people do than in any number of well-researched facts. I'd never make a trainspotter.

Natasha Cooper

WHAT MAKES THE BRITISH HARDMAN HARD?

Michael Carlson

In honour of our UK v USA debate, our film editor takes a penetrating look at the current cycle of British gangster movies and asks the obvious question...

Only a generation ago, the cinema's epitome of British masculinity wore a dinner jacket, played chemin der fer, and drank martinis 'shaken not stirred'. Today, James Bond has been replaced by his contemporaries, the Krays, as role models for British manhood. Middle-class actors crave roles as East End toughs in a series of ever more preposterous gangster films. If this switch from Sean Connery and Roger Moore to Ross or Gary Kemp is any indication, British masculinity is being stirred, if not shaken, by gangster chic. But beneath all the geezer bluster, lurks deep-seated macho unease at what exactly is doing the stirring. US distributors famously told Harry Salzman they didn't want the first Bond film because they didn't think audiences would believe in a British hero as a womaniser. Forty years later, it seems, for once, the Yanks were right. On the sur-

face, gangland would appear to be a perfect metaphor for a generation raised on show-me-the-money Thatcherism. But Bob Hoskins playing Harold Shand in *The Long Good Friday* was hardly a role model, while Arthur and Terry were figures of fun in *Minder*. Was it really only twenty years ago that close-cropped hairdos and glottal cursing were the mark of football hooligans and neo-nazi yobbos, embarrassing rather than aspirational?

The current stampede of luvvies, footballers, pop stars, and stand-up comics into gangster roles resembles a giant casting call for a remake of *Bugsy Malone* – which was Alan Parker's way of saying all this American gangster bluster and violence was, well, childish. Twenty years later, men want to be called lads and girlie has replaced Greer-y as a behavioural model for young British women. It would be acceptable if all this were *sui generis*, but what's really going on in British cinema is not a rethinking of cream-pie shooting guns, but an endless remake of Quentin Tarantino. If Tarantino hadn't shown that a mix of the stylish language and imagery from decades of gangster movies could transform such unlikely figures as John Travolta, Steve Buscemi, or even himself into action heroes, it's unlikely Britain would have ever spawned any of these 'reservoir lads' films. It was all Nick Hornby could do to reclaim football for middle-class boys a decade after American baby-boomers had indulged their retro fantasies with baseball (spawning such films as *Eight Men Out, Major League* and *Bull Durham*). Peter Medak's *The Krays* began the British movie equivalent of fantasy gangland. In *Lock Stock and Two Smoking Barrels*, Guy Ritchie established his own street cred by letting Vinnie Jones do his mugging on camera. The hooligans' football idol became a minor movie star, a hardman whose authenticity came in a sport where tugging at the shirt is considered tough-guy behaviour: he became the everyman's diamond geezer made good. And down the tunnel after Vinnie came all sorts of shaven-headed singers.

This repositioning of middle-class pop stars as working class tough guys reached an apotheosis of sorts in Simon Monjack's *Two Days, Nine Lives*, which previewed in February, but remains, not surprisingly, unreleased. Even this ostensibly sensitive tale of nine people experiencing forty-eight hours of therapy in a posh drug clinic came loaded with gangster baggage. In fact, a better title might have been *Barrels, Docs, and Crack Smoking Luvvies*. In scenes

later cut from the putative release print, Clive the therapist was shown in his previous career, robbing bingo halls with a shotgun, and shooting a cashier whom he crippled. As played by Ralph Arliss, this left him so traumatised he hasn't been able to change his hair or clothes since the shooting, so he resembles Kevin Keegan guesting in *The Sweeney*. In the scenes that remain, Luke Goss stars as Saul, pop music producer with a drug problem. Hair cropped, designer needle tracks covered with a designer scarf, and spitting lines between clenched teeth, Goss is all head-butting aggression, which in the context of psychotherapy gives 'nutter' a whole new meaning. He expresses rage by quivering like Daffy Duck trying to pronounce 'preposterous'. Aggressive behaviour means a posturing head extended to form a human question mark, like Frank Gorshin playing the Riddler in the Batman TV show. When Goss plays scenes with the adoring Danny (Jonathan Brüün, whose name, complete with two adjoining umlauts, must originate in the same country as Häagen-Dasz), they're like Beavis and Headbutt. If all this seems out of place in a would-be sensitive film, *Two Days* is at least right in suggesting these geezers need therapy.

So why does lad culture want so desperately to appear tough? What do they fear might shatter their fragile macho facade? Why does Luke Goss pronounce Bros as 'bras'? What is it that really makes British hardmen hard? For the answer, we turn to *Sexy Beast*, the most stylish of this current gangster cycle. Because beneath its glossy surface, the kind of style Gore Vidal called "forty commercials looking for a product", *Sexy Beast* is really about a gangster's wish to escape the relentless rage of repressed homosexuality, and be left alone to indulge his feminine nature. For British hardmen, the all-purpose endearment and ultimate insult of choice is 'cunt', equating a man with the passive sexuality of the female organ. Contrast this to any episode of *The Sopranos,* where the equivalent term is 'you fuck' or, affectionately, 'you fat fuck'. The American gangster looks at his colleague as a fellow predator in the sexual jungle, not as an obscure object of desire. After all, where Americans call their male friends 'buddy', 'pal', or 'home-boy', the British lad's term is 'mate', which to everyone else in the world (except Aussies) connotes two creatures of opposite genders getting it on. "This is my mate", should mean Tarzan has found Jane, not Michael Portillo. Again, a generation of Brits plays craven homage to Tarantino. This time, it's the Tarantino who, in the otherwise forgettable *Sleep With Me* delivered a memorable deconstruction of *Top Gun*, read as an allegory in which the gay pilots, led by Ice Man, try to pull Maverick over to 'the gay side', where he can learn exactly what those heat seeking sidewinder missiles finding your flaming red exhaust chute actually symbolise. In *Sexy Beast*, Ray Winstone has already gone over to the gay side, and his former mates are trying to pull him back to the straight side, while revealing their own repressed desires. Repressed? Remember, even Vinnie Jones is best remembered for fondling an opponent's balls.

The film opens with a suntan-oiled body glistening in the Spanish sun, like a Christmas turkey basting in a roasting pan. In his bikini, bedecked in gold jewellery (gangsters quickly adopt female rules of display), we can't tell at first whether Ray Winstone is male or female. We see he's male when he applies ice cubes to his balls, a symbolic scrotum-shrivelling de-manning. His name is Gary Dove. He's a retired gangster, growing, as his name suggests, peaceful and soft. His friends call him Gal. I didn't say this was going to be subtle. As the camera eyes lasciviously the young Spanish pool boy, Gal contemplates his good life, like Joe Orton on a Moroccan vacation eyeing Kenneth Williams. A giant testicle of a boulder flies over his head, landing in the pool, drenching him in an explosion of liquid,. enough to unfreeze anyone's *cojones*.. It's an omen, because big balls Don Logan (Ben Kingsley) soon arrives, intending to pull Gal back to London for a big job. Logan has a permanent hard-on for the world (Logan equals 'log on', geddit?). The epitome of designer tough, after marking his territory (he deliberately misses the loo while pissing), he practices his tough guy faces in the mirror, method actor meets Travis Bickle. We soon learn that Logan and Jackie, the wife of Gal's mate H, were once an item, until Jackie put a finger up his bum during sex. This is wrong, Don tells Gal, and worse, he liked it. Dumped by Don, Jackie then married H, who's presumably unflustered by digital probes (Preparation H is, after all, a popular haemorrhoid remedy). Don't laugh. Remember, the guys who wrote *Sexy Beast* also wrote *Gangster No. 1,* an exercise in models playing gangsters: if we think about what children sometimes call their bodily functions we can only be glad they don't make a sequel called *Gangster No. 2*, which is basically what its reviews should have called it. Don also reveals that Gal's wife Dee Dee used to be a porn actress. This makes sense, since it gives her extensive experience of pretend sex with disinterested men. Married to a porn star, with H for a mate, and far from Britain, Gal is presumably free to indulge in anal stimulation and eyeing pool boys to his fat heart's content.

But this won't do for Don, who is so upset at revealing his inner, so to speak, self, that he breaks his tough guy routine, and flees to the airport. Finally regaining his composure, he gets himself removed from the flight and blackmails the airline into letting him go by claiming a steward touched him up, doing a very convincing impersonation of a homophobe. Returning to Gal, he is killed by Dee Dee, brandishing the inevitable lock stock and phallic smoking barrel. Don is buried in the hole left in the swimming pool by the giant testicle. .Dee Dee's big swinging shotgun dick contradicts the analysis of gangster movies offered in *Love, Honour, and Obey,* arguably the nadir of this British cycle: "Women fuck it up in the end", no double entendres intended. Among an absurd cast of tough guys Jude Law and Rhys Ifans, and molls Sadie Frost and Denise Van Outen, *L, H, & O* featured Kathy Burke dragging gangster Ray Durdis' impotent gangster to sex therapy. Back in *Sexy Beast* Spain, despite Dee Dee's taking care of business, Gal still must return to London. The big caper has been organised by crime lord Teddy Bass in elaborate revenge for being buggered by bank chairman Harry at some Cliveden-style society orgy. Harry is played by James Fox, who's wandered in from a remake of *Performance,* and we all know what that signifies. And the working class crime lord so offended by the upper class' polymorphous perversion is named Teddy Be Ass. I warned you. How do Teddy Be Ass' villains revenge themselves on gay Harry? They assemble, naked, in a Turkish bath. Do I need to draw you a picture? In case I do, they penetrate the backside of the bank with a giant dildo of a power drill. When they break through into the vault, it releases a huge spurt of water. The naked gangsters swim up the tube and grab Harry's jewels. Gal stuffs some earrings for Dee Dee into his bikini, thus providing himself with the family jewels he lacks. Teddy, having raped Harry's vault, then shoots Harry in a needless bit of literal overkill. He drops Gal at a bus stop, paying him a tenner like a used hooker, knowing the secret of his shame is safe with a Gal. It's a buddy movie gone haywire. Having, like Teddy, proved he's NOT homosexual, Gal can now return to Spain, give Dee Dee his jewels and enjoy retirement, accepting his femininity, frolicking on top of Don's body in his pool.

Far-fetched? Director Jonathan Glazer said the eponymous *Sexy Beast* was money, but I think he was having us on. The Guardian's Jonathan Romney, without a hint of irony, described *Sexy Beast* avoiding "the usual gangster geezerisms". He noted that "above one hardman there is another, then another, then another...", then pointed out Ian McShane as Teddy Bass played the ultimate man on top, "with a curiously prissy walk". He suggested Glazer might be "trying to cram too much in". Some of us might suggest that's the whole point.

THE BIG WRAP UP

Michael Carlson *looks at current crime films*

The key words in considering Ridley Scott's adaptation of *Hannibal* are okey-dokey, Hannibal Lecter's new signature phrase, much like Bart Simpson's "eat my shorts". At first glance, it seemed that Lecter had merely opted to disguise himself as Truman Capote, since he was too recognisable when in character as Bryan Cox's type of cold sadistic killer. Then we realise that this is not a disguise, but rather a new personality Scott and Anthony Hopkins have made for the good doctor. Well, not totally new, because they were actually following Thomas Harris' literary lead. Indeed, when I reviewed the book I remarked how Lecter was starting to resemble a sociopathic Roy Strong. The book needed some Lecter-lightening in order to help convince the reader of its denouement (Starling going off with Lecter, albeit under drug-induced hypnosis). In fact, the novel seemed devised simply to get to that point, with a nice trip to Florence and a little human snacking along the way. With the film's ending changed, and, in its way, more effective, the camping of Hannibal Lecter seems more like a way of keeping Hopkins interested, and

less like character development. I'm surprised Timothy McVeigh didn't invite him to his execution. Tellingly, Lecter's best scene comes with his previous victim Mason Verger, the one instance where the 'old' Lecter comes to the fore. (Gary Oldman, by the way, deserved something for his supporting roles in both this and *The Contender*.)

The strongest point of the film is the atmospheric setting in Florence, and the playing by Giancarlo Gianinni of the Italian cop Pazzi, who fatally succumbs to greed (keyed tellingly by his wife's insistence on good tickets for the opera, where Lecter eyes her as if she were a rich fois gras). Which raises another interesting point, because Lecter/Capote begins to take on the aspect of a masked avenger, only killing those who deserve it, or, at least, offend his increasingly effete sensibilities. Perhaps the weakest point of the film is the short shrift given to the internal politics of the FBI, an almost inevitable result of using visual shorthand to indicate Krendler's (Ray Liotta) perfidies. Krendler was actually the book's major villain, and thus his inevitable sauté had an element of ultimate revenge; in the film, again inevitably, it's there as a set-piece finale. Julianne Moore plays Starling as a creature devoid of charm, humour, and indeed humanity – the coldly efficient type of FBI agent Hollywood has given us ever since the FBI starting committing major blunders like Waco. Since Lecter's original attraction to Starling was based on her vulnerability, it's hard to see what the new Lecter sees in the new Starling, unless humourless butch appeals to okey-dokey Truman. It's also hard to wonder why we should care about her. However, this new personality also helps justify Starling's resistance to Lecter. *Lecter III* ends with the possiblity of *Lecter IV* dangling like Pazzi over the Piazza. The idea of a one-handed Lecter escaping the US on a commercial flight, even if apparently not in first class, indicates that without Julianne Moore, the FBI really is feeble.

Another adaptation was Steven Soderbergh's *Traffic*, which makes its transition to the big screen smoothly enough, losing some of the British television product's intensity and adding pace and some flair in the person of Don Cheadle. *Traffic's* major artistic point, the different colouring of different locales, also comes borrowed from TV. Although technically it works better on the big screen, I found it relatively insulting to see first Pakistan and then Mexico portrayed in a shit-brown palette, while the white people get shown in blue light. But race is the real core of *Traffic*. The film's nadir comes when we're shown the ultimate degradation of the pretty blancmange of a senator's daughter, actually giving it up to a black man. If drugs can make you do this, they must be bad. In this film, justice means Mexicans die, blacks go to prison,

and whites enter family therapy. *Traffic* makes a pretence of documentary accuracy about the drug problem, but blunts any idea of accuracy by trying to victimise the consumers of drugs, who are the root of the problem. Confessional therapy and baseball between them will save the world from drugs? Yo no credo, senor! Equally absurd is Michael Douglas' turn as a vigilante. Or the idea that the police would never look at the mobile phone in the dead assassin's pocket and find Catharine Zeta-Jones' number on its callback. Or that the assassin would be so dumb as to skip killing the man who could eliminate all the world's problems. Frankly, *Traffic* seemed a pretty bog-standard exercise, enlivened only by one's vicarious pleasure at watching Michael Douglas' family drag him through hell, and by Don Cheadle's stylish playing. Between this and *Erin Brockovich*, Soderbergh seems to be mapping out a new Oscar-friendly career as a Hollywood liberal, using conservative story-telling techniques to tell liberal morality tales, a sort of hipper Norman Jewison.

There's nothing conservative about the format of *Memento,* a very effective neo-noir film that raises interesting questions about the whole noir genre. It's a movie about story-telling, and about how we shape motivations to give us the results we want, and the fact that director Christopher Nolan never lets his gimmick become gimmicky is a sign that it works. Guy Pearce plays Leonard Shelby, whose dislike of being called Lenny signifies the basic tension of the film: is he an investigator Leonard or a film-noir fall-guy chump Lenny? Aided by a wonderful performance by Joe Pantoliano, Pearce's character changes before our eyes with each new polaroid photo and each new caption, and we participate in those changes, by trying to fit the pieces together. In most film noir, the characters' memories aren't erased every few moments; they simply act like they are. In this one, Shelby tries to play the private eye, but everyone else is playing with memories that are or aren't there, until a brilliant finale flips the tables and gets us back where we started. I liked this one better the more I thought about it, and how often can we say that nowadays?

Certainly not after seeing *Along Came a Spider*. In this Morgan Freeman reprises the role of Alex Cross, the profiler hero of *Kiss the Girls*, but really he's reprising what has fast become the Morgan Freeman role: a weary wise man, who, given the number of times he's given attractive female sidekicks, remains strangely chaste, like the monkish persona he has in *Seven*. In *Spider* he's actually given a scene with a woman who could be his wife, but he spends the scene working on a ship in a bottle, which ought to tell you something about both his inner serenity, his wisdom, and his lack of sexuality. What is it with black male detectives and white female sidekicks? (See Senator's daughter, above, for a clue). It's not quite as frustrating as watching Denzel go platonic on Julia Roberts in *Pelican Brief*, or go unplatonic (but paralysed from the waist down) with Angeline Jolie in *The Bone Collector*. This becomes all the more obvious when Freeman is given as a sidekick bleach blonde Monica Potter, whose face appears to have been surgically altered to give her Julia Roberts' features (plus an upturned nose identical to the ingenue her Secret Service agent is suppos-

edly protecting). Although the film's kidnapper is the one wearing the prosthetic face, you really want to believe that a face as devoid of character and full of flat planes as Potter's must surely harbour something different underneath. And so it does. There's a strange feel to this film. Director Lee Tamahori manages to make most of the supporting cast look like they're playing in front of process screens; Michael Moriarty, Jay O. Sanders and company all seem to have been given the look of waxworks. You know the old adage about great books never making great movies, and mediocre books lending themselves better to classic adaptations. Well, Tamahori and novelist James Patterson prove the inverse is not true. Garbage in, garbage out.

Virtually everything you need to know about *Out of Depth* is revealed in the title, and this is not a submarine picture. Perhaps because it is based on a true story, it is the first British gangster-chic flick to show what happens when 'nice' people get mixed up with hardmen (a lesson a whole generation of British directors, writers, actors, pop stars, soccer players and critics have yet to learn). What's interesting is imagining an American remake already taking shape for this one, because Sean Maguire seems to be doing Matt Damon in *Good Will Hunting*, and Danny Midwinter has watched Michael Rappaport one too many times. Nicholas Ball steals the show, in the same sort of way James Caan did in *The Way of the Gun*, by simply being too focused on his role for the rest of the material. Maguire plays Paul, an East End lad making good in the outside world, whose barmaid mom (Rita Tushingham, as wonderful as ever in a telling role) is abused by local tough guy Phil Cornwell (who's also in the Rappaport sweepstakes – who would've thought he was such an influential actor!). Convinced by drug-dealer pal Midwinter to hire out his revenge to pros, Paul gets dragged into what turns into a murder, and thence into drug smuggling, and watches his straight life go down the toilet. Writer/director Simon Marshall's first feature has an admirable feel of care, and he crafts his scenes carefully. Perhaps too carefully, because there's an element of the mechanical in the way the story moves from point A to point Z, and many characters, and indeed scenes, play as if they are merely devices. For example, Maguire's relationship with his posh girlfriend (Josephine Butler) comes and goes with little visible emotion: she exists to fuel the drug-related plot, and perhaps to supply some rage motivation. But none of her scenes, apart from her first with Tushingham, play with any sense of depth or reality. Marshall's direction can't keep up with the precision of the screenplay, mostly because scenes play too slowly, individuals are given too much space (literally and metaphorically) within group scenes, like theatre rehearsals put on film. Set pieces look too familiar and many shots seem to take their artistic finish from adverts (cars shown disappearing lovingly down a road, lads at a bar drinking and going home). It's a very smoothly finished but rough product, if that's not too contradictory, with enough interest to keep one watching, but not enough to draw one in. Still, there's enough bite in the finish to hold out much promise, and I seriously wouldn't be surprised to see this one show up, à la *Traffic,* on someone else's storyboards on the other side of the pond one day soon.

FILM ON THE PAGE

Michael Carlson reviews the latest books about film

Billy Wilder by Glenn Hopp
    (1 903047 36 6)
Brian De Palma by John Asbrook
    (1 903047 42 9)
Ridley Scott by Brian J. Robb
    (1 903047 56 0)
John Carpenter by Michelle LeBlanc &
    Colin Odell (1 903047 37 4)
The Oscars by John Atkinson
    (1 903047 34 7)
Sergio Leone by Michael Carlson
    (1 903047 41 2)
all from Pocket Essentials at £3.99

There's another batch of titles from Pocket Essentials, and Glenn Hopp's study of Billy Wilder is the pick of the litter. Wilder, of course, directed one of the all-time classic crime movies, *Double Indemnity,* as well as *Sunset Boulevard,* which could be seen as the ultimate in film noir. But what impressed me most about this volume was Hopp's analysis of Wilder's often-overlooked *Kiss Me, Stupid,* which, as he puts it "savours rubbing the audience's face in all the libidinous hustling... Wilder challenges the rigidity of middle-class morality and small-town life, where keeping up appearances can sap one's honesty." There, in a nutshell, is both Wilder and film-noir. It's not just small-town life being challenged (even in *Kiss Me, Stupid,* Dean Martin is a big city guy) but it is small-town mentality against which Wilder works, always in favour of emotional honesty. Although Hopp doesn't consider them in their crime context, Wilder also directed two of the great crime comedies: *Ball of Fire* and *Some Like It Hot,* both of which have their fun with the gangster film. But at heart, he is a satirist of morality, and although his later satires are wonderful (*One Two Three, The Apartment,* and *Ace in the Hole* especially) what makes those two classic films noirs is the absence of satire, and their exposure of the shallowness of cynicism. It's as if Wilder were looking for a specifically American context in which to adapt Lubitsch. In a way, *Stalag 17* may be the refined essence of Wilder, as the honest cynic is battered by a small-town mentality, before his innate wit enables his (and others') survival. Hopp discusses the films succinctly and well, providing enough to spark further thought, and rightly emphasising Wilder's skills as a writer, and more, a collaborative writer. He also comments tellingly that the second half of *Stalag 17* plays like Hitchock. So does much of Brian De Palma's oeuvre, discussed with great gusto by John Ashbrook. He is strongest on the consistencies of De Palma's career, the auteur touches which illuminate even his weakest films. I was particularly taken with his analysis of *Sisters,* which reminded me that it is probably the best David Cronenberg movie ever made by someone not Cronenburg.

Ashbrook has never seen *Get To Know Your Rabbit,* and relies on Richard Luck's analysis. My memory of the film is vague but pleasant, and I do believe it worth noting that 'getting to know your rabbit' had a point when the characters doing the knowing were studying to be 'tap-dancing magicians' and would be pulling said rabbits out of their hats (while doing the bojangles at the same time). The point of the film is that the conjuring school (run by Orson Welles) is by definition absurd. Ditto in *Greetings.* Robert de Niro isn't just using a naked woman as a canvas on which to draw; he is using her to illustrate the JFK assassination 'magic bullet' rather than sleep with her. There's a link between the political and the obsessive psycho-sexual which forms a main thematic concern of much of De Palma's work (even if, as Ashbrook notes) much of that concern seems to be in abusing female characters, often played by actresses with whom he is involved. In fact, Ashbrook's own obsession with misogyny leads to a brief diversion about *Blow-Up* and 'free love', which prompts the following: "It was only when they (ie, liberated women) started falling pregnant or catching diseases that they began to realise that the men were having a *wail* [sic] of a time at their expense." [Italics mine.] Owwwooooh, indeed. So much for the Sixties. Crime movies have been De Palma's biggest successes. I've always thought his remake of *Scarface* was a metaphor for Hollywood in the Seventies, buried under a mountain of cocaine. But *Scarface* was a remake, *The Untouchables* was a remake, and a good portion of his work has been remakes of various

Hitchockian themes. De Palma may well be an old-fashioned studio-type director, more comfortable giving his own slant to material developed for him. When working on more personal projects, the ghost of Hitch never seems far away.

Ashbrook is also good at detailing why De Palma, despite commercial success, has never been recognised as a successful commercial director. It's an interesting contrast to the position of Ridley Scott, who started out as a (literal) commercial director, and then worked his way through various projects until he came to his current niche as probably the most successful of the old-style for-hire directors. Brian Robb's study of Scott concentrates on his successful climb through the business, emphasising the way he has learned to be a player within the industry, and arguably its most bankable director. Robb identifies Scott's strong point as creating worlds, one of the things which makes *Blade Runner* still his best movie. So many of his films are set in a costume world, where design can become a character, where the film, in Robb's words, takes on a reality of its own, and this is where Scott is able to shine. Yet much of Scott's success has come, quite simply, from sticking women in traditional male genre roles (something we can see being continued in *Hannibal*). Robb extracts particularly critical quotes, such as the one which calls *Thelma and Louise* "both extravagant and shallow", or Roger Ebert's linking of *GI Jane* with *T&L* as "similarly shrewd yet feather-brained… Scott may even be able to convince people they're seeing a risky treatment of a controversial issue (but) the moments held up as feminist triumphs are when women imitate the worst of male behaviour." If we look at Julianne Moore's portrayal of Clarisse Starling, far more testosterone-laden than Jodie Foster's, we can see that at work still. Scott is quoted as saying audiences found the ending of *T&L* the antithesis of a Hollywood ending, yet since it reprises the ending of *Butch Cassidy* and allows the characters to live in image while dying in script, we might better see it as an archetypal Hollywood ending, or a modern archetype: that is probably how we ought to see Scott, as a modern archetype.

Michelle LeBlanc and Colin Odell put a convincing case for John Carpenter, auteur, while asking if he is perhaps the last of the "intelligent commercial American filmmakers". The answer to that is that the auteur theory developed to recognise the individual styles within mass-produced collaborative art – yet led to a rash of directors seeking total control of projects and few filmmakers with total control are able to sustain a uniquely personal vision in today's economic climate. That makes Carpenter somewhat unique nowadays, particularly for his persistence in staying within the genres of exploitation; in fact he has often responded to a commercial hit by making a resolutely non-commercial film (e.g. a remake of *The Thing* which the world neither needed nor wanted). I recall vividly the impact *Assault on Precinct 13* made at the London Film Festival, after its run in Edinburgh had given it new life, and I confess a real fondness for Carpenter outside the horror genre (particularly the way-ahead-of-its-time *Big Trouble in Little China*, and the Philip Dick-like SF film, *They Live*). This book is full of similar enthusiasm, and perhaps could do with a bit more serious criticism. Is cheap and cheerful really a way to describe a movie? This is a British term usually used by people ignoring the irony implicit in its usage: it means sub-standard, non-functional, designed to please those with no aesthetic sense, and brightly coloured on the outside. Like a curate's egg, which isn't part good just because parts of it are good – it's a bad judgement to lay on any film! It's also a phrase which has no meaning in the United States, who according to John Atkinson would do better if they paid more attention to British films when they handed the Oscars.

I assume reviewing constitutes fair comment, and thus I don't have to say registered trademark every time I mention the O-word, but that's what Pocket Essentials had to do and it is distracting as hell when you read it. Atkinson basically sees cinema as aspiring to David Lean and Michael Powell, mostly Lean, and really seems to be swimming off Catalina when he gets pre-1940. Lauren Bacall invented the femme fatale? Hollywood writers went in front of Senator McCarthy in 1947? Cinemascope is a 'gimmicky invention'? Defining the 1940s as a decade in which 'The British Are Coming' and including *Casablanca* as part of the evidence lost me somewhere after *Red Shoes* picked up its nomination. If this were a British history of the O-word awards, fine, but as a general history it's not only far too Anglo-centric, it's also very much tilted to the past three decades. This isn't meant harshly. After all, the reading public is most interested in the films they know best. The awards themselves mean nothing, apart from increased box office for films and larger fees for their makers. They are best used merely as some sort of gauge of the way Hollywood looks at itself, and it's difficult to evaluate that gauge using a different set of cultural standards. Let's not forget, *Titanic* may have won the O-word award, but *Raise the Titanic* won a BAFTA! Anyway, given who votes in Hollywood (I read Dominick Dunne complaining he had to watch a bunch of videos in order to cast his ballot, so people who don't make movies are voting on movies they never see in a theatre!) we shouldn't really care. Atkinson is excellent at identifying the basic things Hollywood looks for in a winner – which he characterises as films that are "artistically conservative, morally liberal". But so many of his judgements seem strange. Is *Shawshank* really atypical of Stephen King's work? Is *Silence of the Lambs* really an out-and-out horror movie? Is 'Leanesque' really the highest compliment one can bestow on a film?

Finally my own volume in the PE series, *Sergio Leone*. Not wishing to step on the toes of Christopher Frayling's excellent biography (see my review in CT22), my take on Leone indulges in a digression about his place within the context of the American western film. But it also spends a lot of time on *Once Upon a Time in America*, particularly on the dream v reality issues of exactly how the story takes place and also the two rape scenes, which have been the subject of much contentious revisionism. I'm not going to review my own book here. Really. But you should buy it, of course.

Michael Carlson

MADE MEN AND TASTY GEEZERS

THE BRITISH VERSUS THE AMERICAN CRIME FILM

Mike Paterson

United States	United Kingdom
They've got:	*We've got:*
Sgt. Bilko	Private Walker
Blue Velvet	*The Blue Lamp*
Bonnie & Clyde	Flanders & Swan
Gangsters	Spivs
Steve Buschemi	Rhys Ifans
Philip Marlowe	Miss Marple
Robert De Niro	Bob Hoskins
FBI	MFI
Goodfellas	*The League of Gentlemen*
Film Noir	Film Four
Al Capone	Piggy Malone

When a hillbilly kid named Elvis Aaron Presley first sang *Heartbreak Hotel* in 1956, it was the rock and roll equivalent of the revolutionary shot heard around the world. A truly indigenous American art form became a global behemoth. Then four kids from Liverpool took this sound, filtered it through their own experiences and influences and sold it back bigger, bolder and arguably better. As Elvis blended bluegrass, gospel and the blues through an alchemical mutation so did Lennon and McCartney further reinvent this new blend into one of their own. Within a few years one country's invention had been co-opted by another. Which is better – American or British rock & roll? The crime film is the rock & roll of cinema; simple stories about the sordid side of life told with primal energy and with Magnums instead of Gibsons.

History

The global power-shift during the twentieth century focused America into sharp relief. The most influential art form was the new media of film (and later, television) and the US dominated it not just in terms of volume of product but also subject matter. Whatever they took from other sources they homogenised. We're all American now. While Britain developed a film industry borne from a rich theatrical tradition and music-hall mass culture,

America had little in the way of precedent other than frontier stories and the mix of the migrant culture. Hollywood, being at the Westward boundary remote from the gentility of East Coast society, wasn't restricted by literary snobbism when producing commercial product. For Britain the class system asphyxiated the content of melodrama leaving a rarefied atmosphere of drawing-room whodunits and public school espionage. Until the Second World War only Alfred Hitchcock, with his impish sense of the perverse, could get under the radar of moral distaste in Britain. Drawing on the literary tradition of John Buchan and Conan Doyle, the British crime film of the twenties and thirties was a more artificial representation of criminal activity than its American counterpart.

The true underworld of British crime has barely had its surface scratched. Other than *Small Faces* (1995), the world of the Glasgow razor gangs, a major problem associated with the slum tenement living of the twenties to the sixties, has never been filmed. *No Mean City* is a pulp novel screaming to be translated to celluloid. Literature took the lead where film flinched. Even *The 39 Steps* (1935), one of the greatest British spy films of the pre-war era, depicted a landscape of wily foreigners and stereotypical locals utterly remote from the reality of violence. Somehow actors such as Leslie Howard and David Niven would have been unconvincing with a chib in one hand and a woodbine in the other. Even when film began to reflect the trend of gangsterism in London, it was already a third-hand copy of what was in itself an American cinematic archetype. The London underworld of the sixties, while using a unique argot of criminal slang, took its lead from the behaviour, stance and style of the Chicago bootlegger and their onscreen heroic rendering. The classic David Bailey image of the Krays in their sharp-suited swagger is a lobby-card carbon of George Raft at his coin-tossing finest. Life imitates art imitates life.

The American criminal is a different and unique breed. Born from the struggle of the migrant experience and raised in the poverty of the eastern city slums, what set them apart was their alternative aspiration to the American dream. The slums of New York and Chicago were breeding grounds for survivalists and proto-capitalists. With the introduction of prohibition in the 1930s, the previously small-time protection racketeers suddenly became leaders of their own underworld industry. Combined with the explosion of art and culture of the jazz age, this new found criminal prosperity produced a model of brutal style tailor-made for the visual flash required in the cinema. Add the American constitutional right to bear arms and the British petty crook pales by comparison. The macho mobster is not the only image of the criminal in American cinema though. Hitchcock, as ever the fly in the ointment, gave us some unexpected exceptions to the clichéd rule. *Rope*'s (1948) Leopold and Loeb are the Crane Brothers of strangulation, and Caldicott and Charters (*The Lady Vanishes*, 1938) witness events with the detachment of Wodehousian buffers. Hitchcock could disengage from the production line of studio émigrés who assimilated into American society by idealising it. Not until the seventies, with the rise of the movie brats, did American directors personalise their films to the same degree.

merica throughout the history of cinema has been the progenitor of the images of crime film. The rest merely imitate. The American experience in the history of the twentieth century was quickly assimilated into the themes of fiction. The Depression ushered in the racketeers, prosperity brought forth the private detective, and media scrutiny and an insatiable public appetite for sleaze overturned the stone to reveal the bugs festering underneath American society. Serial killers, the human-trophy hunters of our age, are the new anti-heroes and a specific product of an affluent society with mental health issues and too much leisure time. The devil will make work for idle hands to do. *10 Rillington Place* (1971) portrays a serial killer in action within a very British setting quite at odds with the more southern gothic of films at the margin of B movie exploitation of the US genre. American director Richard Fleischer (a dabbler in noir with *Narrow Margin*) successfully shows the drab psychosis of Richard Attenborough's John Christie within the context of post-war, ration-depressed London. The Grand Guignol of Jack the Ripper has given way to a more mundane, domestic horror. Later Thomas Harris would tie the loose ends of camp bloodletting, police procedure and pantomime villainy into an intelligent package to create the last great crime character of the cinema century in Hannibal Lecter. In the film adaptations of his books it could be said that the subconscious suggestion behind the portrayal of the genius sadist by skilled British character actors (Brian Cox and Anthony Hopkins) is in the tradition of suspicion of the alien 'other'.

Evil comes from elsewhere; it's the whining foreign accent of Peter Lorre, the Mafia, Colombian drug barons. When *Henry Portrait of a Serial Killer* (1990) shows the sickness as home-grown and cancerous it is a shocking jolt of reality within the usual stylised comic strip entertainment of teen-camp slasher movies. Henry is the American relative of *Rillington's* Christie; a loner, a sociopath, uneducated, unable to gain emotional attention other than through violence. This is more documentary than entertainment and is all the more unsettling for it. We prefer our truth with a Top 40 soundtrack. Comfort us.

Thematically, the US crime film differed from the British one; there is an arc of rise and fall of the lone anti-hero in many classic gangster movies of the early 1930s – *Little Caesar, White Heat, Public Enemy, Scarface* – that mirrors the larger canvas of storytelling of the time. Crime brings out the cynicism, sarcasm and bite of the American character, elements normally suppressed within the sentiment-heavy cinema of the time. The Hays Office in America was also a filter for the morally unacceptable, but such was the power of performance of people such as Edward G. Robinson, Cagney or Paul Muni that, despite the dilution of the message, the impact was still felt. Howard Hawks was forced to insert scenes in *Scarface* to correct the perception of an anti-Italian depiction in the main characters and to bludgeon the point of punishment and redemption so that no idea of crime paying could remain.

In Britain the tone of the crime film was of the aberrant thug fighting the system, a small man in an enclosed world – Pinky in *Brighton Rock* (1947), Jack Carter in *Get*

Carter (1971), Harold Shand in *The Long Good Friday* (1981): this was more indicative of the lack of organised crime in the UK compared to the American model. There was also the moral guardian British Board of Film Censors to ensure that our screens remained free of odious working class criminals setting a bad example. In the thirties there was a fear that the popularity of American films that made heroes of the gang bosses would result in British equivalents. Films at this time had to be submitted in pre-production stage to the BBFC for approval which, in the moral climate of the age, meant many films dealing with the subject of gangsters in a London setting were suppressed before filming began. The remove of violence in an American context was obviously more acceptable than in a British one. Such intriguing projects as *Soho Racket* and Edgar Wallace's *When the Gangs Came to London* never had their potential realised and were lost to history. However, after the war the slate was wiped clean. A nation that had experienced the true horror of violence could now stomach some reality in their melodrama. And with the added element of the American B movie bringing its romantic influence, the British crime film was now out on parole. With immediate recidivist tendencies, two films quickly set the tone for a new breed of post-war crime film in Britain; *Brighton Rock* and *No Orchids for Miss Blandish* (1948). Again coming from the literary (and pulp) tradition, the added element of violence in a realistic context upset sensibilities. The Evening Standard called *No Orchids* "a disgrace to the British Film Industry" with its "thoroughly un-British" gangster style. *The Blue Lamp* (1950) followed in their wake, introducing cinema audiences to new experiences with its police murders, knifings and use of the word 'tart'. Shocking.

Other than *Night and the City* (1950), a Hollywood production with American stars filmed and set in London, noir bypassed Britain on its journey from France to America. The 1950s and 1960s were largely a time of Bulldog Drummond and The Saint until the first dribbles of baby boom began to influence popular culture. We had no Mitchum, Bogart or Gloria Grahame. Only Stanley Baker, and later Michael Caine and Sean Connery, could be said to have the same blue collar authenticity. In Britain there were no working class heroes, only slapstick buffoons like Arthur Askey and Norman Wisdom. Even the sexpots were bottle-blond, seaside postcard versions. The power shift began as noir was exposed to the harsh light of the 1960s. Kitchen sink dramas transposed from theatre to cinema brought more realism and a working class voice. The relaxation of censorship saw the depiction of more sex and violence. Crime film was the ideal arena for all of these elements. London became the centre of a cultural explosion and could be exploited as a setting within which to frame stories. Two European art-house directors, Antonioni and Polanski, used it to best effect with *Blowup* (1966) and *Repulsion* (1965), both of which stretched the boundaries of the genre and showed up the more lame attempts of home-grown film makers to step into the world of swinging London.

Just as the movie brats were beginning to temporarily take over Hollywood in the late sixties and early seventies, Britain began to produce some crime films which set a standard for style. The Great Train Robbery, the Moors Murders and Reg and Ron Kray's mini reign of terror left a distasteful stain on the decade of peace and love and, like the Vietnam war and Civil Rights Movement in America, this wound of pessimism bled into a new decade. After the bright pinnacle of caper movies that was *The Italian Job* (1969) – a film of sadism, sarcasm, style and dark humour that characterises British culture at its best – a wave of films were appearing that showed the flipside to the bright entertainments that preceded them. *Get Carter* (1971) is Mike Hodges' masterpiece of economy that, like *Point Blank* (1967) and *Dirty Harry* (1971), is a classic thriller of lone revenge but given a British setting (drab, post-war, corrupt, sordid), a cast (crime novel loner and street-real hardmen) and a script (viciously hilarious) that turned it into pure gold. Films such as *Performance, Villain, The Squeeze, The Offence* and ultimately, *The Long Good Friday* were far more reflections of Britain at the time than stylistic references to American cinema.

Language

The shared language and cultural diversity of vocabulary is a signifier in the division between US and UK film. Although it was Hitchcock who gave us the first successful crime film with sound with the British film *Blackmail* in 1929, it was the tommy gun rattle and the snap of wise-guy dialogue of America's mobster movies that caught the global attention. The memorable sounds of crime film have largely been in an American accent. From "Mother of Mercy! Is this the end of Rico?" to "You find me funny? Funny how?" (or anything said by Joe Pesci), the quick-fire of dialogue is best delivered in an Italian-American/New Joisey-ese. Only recently, in the age of sampling, have we discovered the true worth of the home-grown version. Savour the thrill of "Just apply a little... pressure" said by a classically-trained actor (James Fox) or the authentic delivery of Johnny Shannon ("You know, I don't think I'm going to let you stay in the film business") in *Performance*, Bob Hoskins in *The Long Good Friday* or Michael Caine in *Get Carter* ("Piss-holes in the snow") to *The Sweeney's* incomparable "Alright, Tinkerbell. You're nicked."

And, as the urban hoodlum graduates from bootleg liquor to street-corner heroin, so does the lexicon of crime shift. It's no surprise that a playwright of the stature of David Mamet, a man skilled in the nuances of language, returns so often to the crime genre to ply his trade. The intonation, emphasis and articulation of the word 'fuck' is an essay in itself. Is there a word in any other language that conveys similar threat? Joe Pesci's "Fucking degenerate!" in *Casino* is a verbal weapon, and Ray Winstone's "This facking tool" in *Scum* is an unforgettable warning of brutal violence. Same words from two utterly different cultures but with the same effect. Add the seemingly wholesome and innocent word "mother" in front of it and we have a whole new world of street slang as popularised by Tarantino and borne from blaxploitation. This injection of vocal taboos has been in tandem with a relaxation of the depiction of violence in modern cinema and the rise of the influence of street culture.

Since the sixties both American and

British cinema have broken down the barriers of acceptability with debatable results. Sometimes less is more. Even in America there are still some things that are beyond the pale, but in Britain considered fair game for dramatic realism. Paul McGuigan's *Gangster No. 1* (2000), in its retro flip of criminal underworld style, has the word 'cunt' spat out with a viciousness and regularity that acts as a short-hand for the base brutality of the characters. The verbal dexterity of the characters in Guy Ritchie's films is more of a nod to the literary Picaresque that goes back to Dickens as well as the heritage of the golden age of television writing of the seventies. Regan, Carter, Arthur Daley and their ilk were mouthpieces for the ambitions of a plethora of talented writers who were influenced by the greats of American pulp and frustrated by a lack of opportunity in a rapidly dying film industry in Britain. This was the era of people like John McKenzie, who rose to prominence with some of the greatest television dramas of the genre but never found a consistent voice with cinema as they did with television. McKenzie was responsible for dramas such as *Just Another Saturday* and *Elephant's Graveyard* which had a filmic quality and authentic street voice but, other than *The Long Good Friday* has never properly reached the same heights in cinema. Possibly this is an indicator of the power status of British film. In film there is more to lose. A *Revolution* can bring down a film company (Goldcrest) and, ultimately, a film industry.

Style

The photogenic landscapes of America have become icons of the crime genre.

Where else could car chases take place and look as good other than the hills of San Francisco (compare Steve McQueen arcing over Fillmore Street to John Thaw skidding into cardboard boxes in a Docklands alley)? Is there anywhere as neon-soaked as Times Square or downtown LA? Grifters can grift anywhere but Art Deco race tracks or cross-state railcars give it that extra edge. America will always have the edge because of its sheer scale; could *Thunderbolt and Lightfoot* have been as glorious without the Panavision vistas of the Midwest? Compare the small-scale drab motorway psychodrama of *Butterfly Kiss* to Sailor and Lula in *Wild at Heart* or *Badlands'* dirt-track road trip. America has a larger canvas onto which stories can be painted. They set the style template and the world struggles to follow. The Manhattan skyscraper and LA future-urban landscape have been globally cloned. Every modern city from every transit lounge is a homogenised sprawl. A crime story filmed in Toronto, Sydney or Tokyo is a carbon copy (several generations faded) of Americana. So many of these films are puppy-love valentines to noir classics or Scorsese heroism. Exemplifying this trend is Danny Cannon's *Young Americans* (1993); a young British director lights Soho to look like Brooklyn, casts Harvey Keitel to echo Scorsese films, fills the soundtrack with contemporary music to add further cultural resonance and has hip mockneys behave like New York gangsters. While it has a flash confidence it has no originality and absolutely nothing to say other than "hire me, Hollywood". Shamefully it seems that British film makers emerging today have learned little from their 1960s and 1970s counterparts other than an occasional stylistic nod. While we have an embarrassment of riches in acting talent, the writers and directors with clout are not around to use it. They've all gone to LA.

As in football where talent emerges in the lower divisions and is immediately bought by the cash-rich clubs, British talent so often ends up in America. Production restrictions, even within the indie system, preclude a UK-based director becoming an auteur (only Ken Loach could be said to have total control of his work but only because his work is outside of the commercial loop). Most of the British directors that could be called auteurs – having enough of a recognisably unique style that each film they make has their own stamp on it – still have to be filmmakers for hire and are employed within the American studio system. They are still pressured to maintain a bias towards the globally commercial market. Stephen Frears, a director of films with intelligence and without compromise, is possibly the most consistently excellent British director working today. Yet his film work has mostly been with Hollywood studios or the larger independents – *The Grifters, Dangerous Liaisons, High Fidelity* – with British projects being funded by television (*Gumshoe* is a glorious parody of Bogart private eye flicks and *The Hit* (1984) one of the artistic successes of the short-lived British film industry of that era). Frears is a director who can combine social comment – *Bloody Kids* is a stylistic forerunner of the music video visual with an anti-Thatcher, punk-ethic anger – with humour and visual panache. *The Hit* is a prototype of the Brit-flicks of today; style in spades, a dou-

ble-act of exciting young actor (Tim Roth at the beginning of his career) playing off cool legend (Terence Stamp), sardonic humour, sudden violence and very sharp suits. While aware of the American cultural inspiration it doesn't bow down to its imperialist master and remains very much a British film. He has the skill to switch between styles; *The Grifters* is a very American and very stylised modern noir which uses its location and cast (particularly Angelica Huston) to link back to a literary and cinematic ideal.

This begs the question, what constitutes an American or British film? If the elements that make up a production are a combination of the talents of people from a variety of nationalities, what dominant factor determines its race? Despite being run by second generation Austro-Hungarian-German Jews, the American movie studios were as apple pie as they come in the 1930s and 1940s. Genre-defining American films such as *Point Blank* and *Bullitt* were directed by Englishmen, but their generic themes had the stamp of Americana imposed by the charisma of their stars and the individual settings. The rise of Film Four has allowed a small indigenous identity to flourish again in Britain; from *Mona Lisa* and *Stormy Monday* in the eighties to *Shallow Grave, I.D.* and *Face* in the 1990s, British production companies have created a body of work to compete with the proliferation of US small budget crime films within the last ten years, but no one person has emerged who can match the mavericks of American cinema. John Dahl in the early nineties was a one-man industry of noir resurrection with gems like *The Last Seduction* and *Red Rock West*. Abel Ferrara (*Bad*

Lieutenant, King of New York) continues to keep cinema dangerous, and the Coen brothers are the human lightning rods of the genre. We can do small scale though. Britain will never produce something as glossily epic as *Heat* or *Goodfellas* but there is no reason to believe that the low-key smartness of a *Things to Do in Denver When You're Dead* or *One False Move* is beyond us.

In today's lottery culture, however, it seems that the loudest and cockiest survive. The post-Tarantino generation of music video and ad directors are the ones in control now. You can cast Ray Winstone as a bull-headed criminal till Tuesday, but without a good script and restrained direction he's going to be wasted every time. There are a few exceptions that get under the wire – *Sexy Beast, Gangster No. 1, Croupier* – but for every *Snatch* there are a host of clueless imitators. How many more films of heists gone horribly wrong starring a selection of overacting, shooter-toting TV stars do we have to sit through before the lottery money dries up? Unlike in the States where the best work in crime is being done on television – *The Sopranos, Homicide, NYPD Blue* – we cancel *Cops* in favour of ratings-safe, soap-star detectives. British film needs to exploit better source material; translating the verve and style of David Peace's *Nineteen Seventy Four* from print to celluloid could give us a British *LA Confidential*. In America *The Sopranos* is indicative of how things are changing in the crime genre. The Godfather image of the Mafia is being replaced by nostalgia and pastiche. The codes of brotherhood have given way to existential angst. In a new criminal underworld of massive numbers, central American drug cartels are the new ganglords of America, former Soviet states the armoury. The housing projects of Washington DC, Chicago and East LA are run with AK 47s, firepower that Cagney could only dream of. The Sharks and The Jets this ain't.

Mike Paterson

United Kingdom *We've got:*	United States *They've got:*
The Lavender Hill Mob	The Dead End Kids
Alfred Hitchcock	Brian De Palma
Peeping Tom	*Raising Cain*
James Bond	Derek Flint
Get Carter	*Bring Me the Head of Alfredo Garcia*
Malcolm McDowell	Brian Dennehey
The Long Good Friday	St Valentine's Day massacre
Murder on the Orient Express	*Throw Momma from the Train*
H. E Bates	Norman Bates
The Singing Detective	*Cop Rock*
"Evenin' all"	"Let's be careful out there"
shooters	pieces
blags	bank-jobs
"Cheers, George"	"Boat drinks"

Contemporary North American Directors edited by Allon, Cullen & Patterson

Wallflower, £17.99, 1 903364 09 4

reviewed by Barry Forshaw

Many are the guidebooks to film directors, and wide indeed is the range of their usefulness. Some are little more than shopping lists, fine for simply checking off the movies of a favourite director as you catch them. But others quickly become essential items in any film lover's library. Actually, for the practised consumer of such books, it's a matter of seconds to check out the usefulness of a particular guide. Looking at Wallflower's comprehensive critical guide, it's instructive to turn to a reliable professional such as Walter Hill. Talking about his fascination with outsiders and outlaws in the second film *The Driver*, the guide reminds us that he previously scripted Sam Peckinpah's similar *The Getaway*, but points out that *The Driver* is more pared-down and existential in tone. And after a sharp and perceptive journey through his hit-and-miss career (ignoring his contribution to Ridley Scott's *Alien*), it brings us up to date with the disastrously received SF movie *Supernova*, from which Hill withdrew his name. Similarly, Tim Burton is intelligently handled, with *Batman* being described as blending Gothic horror interiors and exteriors with science fiction spectacle, while *Batman Returns* is identified as a much darker film in tone, with the grotesque Penguin emerging as a mutated orphan from the sewers to pollute his way through the film, while Batman, dressed in metallic body armour, struggles against Catwoman. The guide is even is up-to-date enough to discuss Burton's current work on the remake of *Planet of the Apes*. In other words, the entries are concise, pithy and on the nose. While one may frequently quarrel with the judgements on many directors here (and surely that is true of any halfway decent guide such as this), there is no quarrelling with the inclusiveness and intelligence that the book has to offer. Put it on your shelf – you can guarantee you'll be reaching for it very often.

Hannibal (Director: Ridley Scott)

reviewed by Paul McAuley

Let's get this straight from the start: *Hannibal* is not so much a sequel to the *Silence of the Lambs* as the third part in a franchise which began with *Manhunter*, an adaptation of Thomas Harris' novel *Red Dragon* originally lensed by Michael Mann (now slated for a remake with a cameo performance from the actor who has made the part of Thomas Harris' most famous creation his own – Sir Anthony Hopkins). Like all third acts in a movie franchise, *Hannibal* suffers from the usual problems of overcoming familiarity, of both teasing and fulfilling audience expectations, and of reaching a satisfying conclusion yet leaving the door ajar for another episode. That it succeeds far better than, say, *Aliens 3* or *Jaws 3(-D)* is due to solid performances from the two principals, Ridley Scott's operatic *Grand Guignol*, and a script that efficiently, although at times rather drastically, simplifies Harris's original novel.

As with the novel, the film opens with Clarice Starling's fall from grace with the FBI, some years after her triumph of catching Jame Gumb in *The Silence of the Lambs*. Julianne Moore, grainily luminous and very slightly detached, plays Starling as world-weary, quietly desperate and boxed in by the kind of masculine prejudice exemplified by the justice department's Paul Krendler (a petulant Ray Liotta). Moore shows only flashes of the confrontational grit Jodie Foster foregrounded in the original role, but of course this isn't Starling's movie: it's

Hannibal Lecter's. Lecter is about to take up the prestigious position of curator of the Palazzo Capponi in Florence when his assumed identity of the scholarly Dr Fell is penetrated by Rinaldo Pazzi, an Italian policeman with an expensive young wife. Pazzi, a sympathetic performance by Giancarlo Giannini, betrays Lecter to rich psychopath Mason Verger (Gary Oldman unrecognisable under prosthetics), a horribly mutilated victim of Lecter. Verger plans to capture Lecter and feed him alive to specially bred wild pigs; Clarice Starling, about to be drummed out of the FBI after a controversial shoot-out with a gang of drug-dealers, is drawn into Verger's spider-web as bait when Lecter sends her his condolences.

This time around, Lecter is portrayed not as Hannibal the Cannibal, a coldly calculating monster, but as a kind of Byronic anti-hero, playing Scarlatti while mooning over Starling's photograph in a scene straight out of *Phantom of the Opera* (he borrows the Phantom's wide-brimmed hat, too) – amoral rather than evil, killing only 'the free-range rude' and those who disturb his attempt to build a sanctuary where he can quietly enjoy his ultra-refined tastes. The attempt to kidnap Lecter in Florence goes horribly wrong. Pazzi suffers a very public and apt dispatch, and Lecter returns to America, where he schemes to rid himself of Mason's attentions while wooing Starling. Despite his imposing bulk, Hopkins infuses his role with a feline and almost gleeful menace, and allows a lovely wounded light into his gaze when he looks down upon a sleeping Starling after he breaks into her apartment. Lecter is no longer Starling's seductive, Mephistophelean tutor, but an unrequited suitor. Thereafter, the plot is hustled along with the efficient dispatch of a public execution. After a cat-and-mouse game with Starling in an indoor fairground, using mobile phones and sound cues in a scene reminiscent of *The Conversation*, Lecter is captured by Verger's henchmen (does he allow himself to be captured? it isn't made clear, but we must assume that he does), turns the tables on the gloating Verger with Starling's help, and offers up Krendler as a bonding feast and a final test of Starling's rectitude in a scene involving an aminatronic double and CGI that's immediately repulsive and then, as the camera lingers too long, rather silly – gasps were quickly followed by giggles in the preview screening. The pianissimo ending, famously embargoed by the studio, trails threads of story that could be gathered up in another episode.

With pin-sharp editing and some splendidly atmospheric lighting (most especially the blues and greys of the Florentine scenes), *Hannibal* moves along nicely enough. But although the disparate settings are cleverly linked, and there are some unexpected shocks (most particularly a surveillance camera sequence showing Lecter attacking a nurse in the psychiatric hospital where he was once incarcerated, something we've only heard about in the previous two films), the film lacks both the coherence and the relentless suspense of either *Red Dragon* or *The Silence of the Lambs*. Despite slasher film excesses – bloody bowels splashing on wet cobbles, pigs ripping off a man's face, gourmet brain surgery – this is at heart an opulently romantic film. And without the grounding of the Biblical sense of evil that permeates Harris' writing, Lecter, with his trademark lines (ta-ta, goody-goody, okey-dokey) threatens to become just another franchise villain, along the lines of Freddie Kreuger or even, God help us, Chuckie.

Paul McAuley's latest novel is The Secret of Life *(HarperCollins)*

CRIME ON TV

THE USA VERSUS THE UK

Charles Waring

Introduction

I think it's fair to say that the majority of British people regard British television as the best in the world. Some might say that this perspective is prompted by arrogance and patriotic bias but there's plenty of evidence to suggest that in terms of quality and content, British TV is second to none – except, however, when it comes to police drama. Even the most cynically jingoistic of Britain's tabloid TV critics is likely to concede that American shows like *Hill Street Blues, NYPD Blue, Homicide: Life on the Street* and *The Sopranos* are not only slick, superior pieces of television storytelling but are innovative and challenging too. When it comes to crime, most contemporary UK shows just seem mundane. And if they're not mundane, they lack credibility. Maybe the American way of life is so different, so much bigger, bolder and even

badder, that its TV cop shows possess a glamour that verges on the exotic compared with the depiction of police in boring, all too familiar Britain. Also, I believe that American cop shows with their frequent depiction of violent crime do truly reflect American society.

Mercifully, in real life we British are not yet habituated to murder on a daily basis, but you wouldn't think that watching some of our home-made cop shows – *The Bill* and *The Cops* reflect with a fair degree of accuracy the nature of British police work, but many (*Inspector Morse, The Ruth Rendell Mysteries, Frost* and in particular, *Midsomer Murders*) are absurdly unrealistic. The huge pile of corpses on these programmes would suggest that our idyllic rural villages are dangerous places to live – far more dangerous, in fact, than a crack house defended by AK47s in an American ghetto. But many people (including, believe it or not, many Americans) are fond of these cosy, slow-paced British detective dramas despite the fact that artifice outweighs authenticity. They may be a tad far-fetched but some viewers fervently believe that these British-made police programmes truly represent high quality entertainment (many of them are exported successfully all over the globe).

So, who's best at making TV cop shows, the USA or UK? In order to determine whether it's the Yanks or the Brits who have produced the best fictional crime entertainment on TV, let's compare and contrast a varied selection of British and American cop shows from the past five decades.

Round One: The 1950s –
Dixon of Dock Green v Dragnet

Dixon of Dock Green proved to be one of the first successful British television programmes depicting police work when it aired in May 1955. But from the off, there was an air of unreality about the show. For starters, the programme's eponymous protagonist, the amiable beat copper, George Dixon, was already known to British cinema goers – many had witnessed the same character (played by the same actor) blown away by a juvenile Dirk Bogarde as a callous cop killer in the famous 1950 movie, *The Blue Lamp*. So, by the time the BBC series was transmitted, Dixon had been pushing up the daisies for five years! But miraculously, the show's creator and writer, Ted Willis (a man who initially wondered if he had enough material to flesh out a meagre half-dozen episodes) resurrected him. Incredibly, though, the

show would eventually run to a staggering 367 episodes. Indeed, the most miraculous thing about *Dixon of Dock Green* was the show's longevity – it survived for a phenomenal twenty-one years, soldiering on right up to that scorching summer of 1976. What was even more remarkable was the man who played Dixon, the former music hall comedian and radio star Jack Warner, was at retirement age when the series began. Warner (1894-1980) finally hung up his boots at the ripe old age of eighty-two, by which time he had been promoted to desk sergeant, leaving most of the 'action' scenes to his more athletic son-in-law, Detective Sergeant Andy Crawford.

Affable, avuncular PC George Dixon was a community policeman long before politically correct terminology was coined. Every show would begin in exactly the same fashion: a head and shoulders shot of PC Dixon saluting the audience, followed by his signature catchphrase, "Evenin' all", and an outline of that episode's story. But there was no rough stuff in Dock Green. Violent criminals didn't exist in that part of the East End. Of course, it's possible to perceive that Dixon's original violent demise in *The Blue Lamp* had exerted a chastening effect on Warner and his perception of his role – the TV incarnation of George Dixon rarely experienced any kind of violence. Mostly, the series concentrated on domestic situations and generally humdrum police matters. Dixon was coshed in one episode, and I believe a young lad got murdered as well, but that was as about as violent as it got in over two decades. When the show began, it probably reflected the public perception of the police – courteous, helpful and like white knights to the rescue. But by the early 1960s and the advent of *Z Cars*, where the police were depicted as all too human with human failings, it appeared that the series had patently lost touch with reality. But *Z Cars* didn't kill off *Dixon of Dock Green*, and the show was still around (though on its last legs, certainly) when *The Sweeney* screeched onto British small screens – older viewers liked the cosiness of Dixon, who seemed like a real person. His friendly, reassuring face would tell you that all was well with the world and that we could all sleep safely in our beds at night. Indeed, at the conclusion of every show, George did just that, imparting some kind of morality tale and telling the viewers how everything had worked out in the end and resolved itself peacefully.

In many ways, the American TV cop show, *Dragnet*, while appearing radically different, shared the same values as *Dixon of Dock Green* – it often focused on routine police matters and aimed to minimise sensationalist content. Indeed, the show's creator, Jack Webb, had to adhere to NBC's rather draconian edict that there were to be "no blondes, shots, blood or thrills". Not much fun to be had there, then! Indeed, you'd think that no cop show on earth could survive without those four essentials. But that was not a problem for Webb, who shared NBC's philosophy – apparently he didn't want *Dragnet* to show scenes that he couldn't watch with his young children and even instituted what seems now a ridiculous dictum: bullets could be fired from guns, but they had to be rationed to one every four episodes! Contrary to what you might imagine, *Dragnet* was not a boring show – from the

public's perspective, Webb injected a real frisson of excitement into the show by giving it an authentic documentary feel using gritty narratives and members of the public as extras. The central character, the anal-retentive Sgt Joe Friday (played by Webb himself) spoke in a monotonous, expressionless voice: like Dixon, he had a memorable catchphrase – "Just the facts, ma'am". Also like Dixon, there was nothing glamorous about Friday: he was diligent, conscientious and just a little pedantic about dates and times. Unlike Dixon, though, his obsession with the numbing minutiae of police work kept him a bachelor.

Like George Dixon, *Dragnet* came into being before it hit the television screen – conceived, produced and directed by Webb, the series was first broadcast on the radio in 1949. Its ratings as a radio show were so high that the transition to a television format occurred within a two-year period. The show began in the winter of 1951 and ran until the spring of 1959. It was resurrected in 1967 (as *Dragnet 67*) with Harry Morgan as a new officer, Officer Bill Gannon. That incarnation ran for four seasons before expiring. In 1987, a Hollywood movie spoof starring Dan Ackroyd surfaced, resulting in a new TV version from 1989.

If you put Jack Warner in a boxing ring with Joe Friday, it's hard to tell who would win. Both shows, of course, espoused nonviolence, so a bout of fisticuffs between these two unlikely antagonists is out of the question. Dixon would rather pump up his bike tyres than use a pump-action shotgun, though admittedly, Friday could bore a person to death by firing off a few rounds of tight-arsed staccato dialogue. Both shows accurately reflected both the culture and era they belonged to and at their peak were genuinely entertaining. For me, though, *Dragnet* had more edge and excitement and for that reason, I declare it to be the outright winner of this first cop-show showdown!

Round Two: The 1960s – Z Cars v The FBI

In 1962, the BBC launched a twenty-five-minute police show that would radically change the nation's perception of the police. It was called *Z Cars* and reflected a country in transition after the austerity of the immediate post-war years. Cinema and theatregoers had already witnessed graphic depictions of northern working class culture in movies like *Saturday Night and Sunday Morning* and groundbreaking stage plays such as *Look Back in Anger*. Television's keenness to portray working class Britain manifested itself initially with the ITV soap opera, *Coronation Street*, in 1960. But *Coronation Street* was pretty tame stuff compared with what *Z Cars* had to offer. Prior to *Z Cars*, the British copper was either portrayed as an upper class, Oxbridge educated pipe-smoking detective or as a plodding beat bobby like good old George Dixon. It was a world where everyone knew his or her place in Britain's well-defined social hierarchy. But *Z Cars* illustrated a new Britain of teenagers and tower blocks.

The very first episode of *Z Cars* prompted a barrage of complaints from outraged viewers, many of whom were disturbed by the depiction of our nation's noble crime fighters as drunks, gamblers and even wife-beaters. Worst of all, the rough-speaking,

morally ambivalent cops who patrolled the fictional northern towns of Seaport and Newtown in their Ford Zephyrs possessed appalling table manners. They ate with their mouths open and spoke with their mouths full. It was more than cultured, middle class people could bear. The Chief Constable of the Lancashire police force (who had initially given a pledge of co-operation to the show) was incensed by *Z Cars* and attempted to pressurise the BBC into taking it off the air. When that failed, he pulled the plug on further co-operation. Additional complaints came from the Chairman of the Police Federation, who asserted that the image of Britain's police force would be irrevocably tarnished by such a programme. There were two characters in particular who caused offence – the plain speaking patrol car driver, PC 'Fancy' Smith, played by a young Brian Blessed, and the rotund, balding figure of Detective Inspector Barlow, played with great gusto by Stratford Johns. Barlow seemed the antichrist to Jack Warner's saintly George Dixon – he was moody, irascible and prone to supplementing a heated verbal discussion in the interrogation room with a few choice left hooks. He seemed more intimidating that the supposed villains. With bulging eyes and a profusely sweaty demeanour, Barlow always seemed on the verge of apoplexy. He was partnered by the more affable Detective Sergeant John Watt, who complimented Barlow's histrionics with a more gentle approach and who usually benefited as a result after the suspect had been softened up by Barlow's bullying tactics.

Other favourite characters who helped to bring *Z Cars* vividly to life included Bert

Lynch (who graduated from PC to Desk Sergeant), Jock Weir and David Graham, played by Colin Welland, who later went on to script *Chariots of Fire*. The programme was a triumph for its creator, Troy Kennedy Martin, who had originally devised the show after listening in to the police radio wavelength when recuperating from a bout of the mumps. Despite the show's immediate success (it had gained an incredible 14 million viewers by its eighth week), Martin quit the show after three months, claiming that the BBC were trying to tone down his original premise for the show. Despite Martin's absence, *Z Cars*, with Johnny Keating's infectious theme tune, moved from monochrome to colour and from twenty-five minutes to fifty minutes, continuing until 1978 and 667 episodes. Although *Dixon of Dock Green* wasn't killed off by the advent of Barlow and company, *Z Cars* seriously damaged its credibility. *Z Cars'* bold iconoclasm paved the way for gritty copshows like *The Sweeney* in the 1970s.

Around the same period that *Z Cars* made a profound impact on UK TV screens, American cop drama seemed to be in the doldrums. In 1961, the classic comedy, *Car 54, Where Are You?* made its debut and incensed American police chiefs, who believed that such a valiant, crime-fighting institution was being ridiculed. In 1965, however, while *Z Cars* was still in full-flow in the UK, ABC television unleashed on the American public what they regarded as a serious dramatic cop show. It was called *The FBI*. With a title like that, you could imagine square-jawed Feds sporting a crew cut and sunshades going head-to-head with Mafia types and master criminals. Unfortunately, though, Quinn Martin's programme lacked the kind of bite and verisimilitude that *Z Cars* so patently possessed. Starring the former *Sunset Strip* actor, Efram Zimbalist Jnr as the show's main character, Inspector Lew Erskine, *The FBI,* with its obsession with finding communist plots and political subversives who set out to destabilise the USA, came across as nothing more meaningful than a propaganda vehicle for the real Federal Bureau of Investigation, still run at that time by the notorious J. Edgar Hoover. Hoover, in fact, gave his full blessing to the show, which was no real surprise considering the show's whiter than white depiction of the bureau and its activities. As the show's material was purported to be based on authentic cases from the FBI files, Hoover's endorsement extended to consenting to ABC shooting some of the scenes at the FBI's Washington HQ. What confirmed that producer, Quinn Martin, was probably in cahoots with Hoover and the real FBI was the fact that it was customary for the programme to conclude by making an appeal to the viewers for information that would lead to the apprehension of some of the nefarious individuals on the bureau's infamous 'most wanted' list. Despite its manifold flaws, *The FBI* proved a success with the public and ran for nine seasons, from 1965 to 1974, totalling 238 one-hour episodes.

Almost all of the characters in *The FBI* were too good to be true – saintly, clean living, morally upright law enforcement officers who lacked any kind of human flaw and foible. In fact, they seemed more like automatons than flesh and blood human beings (the wooden acting of

Efrem Zimbalist Jnr didn't help matters either!). Consequently, *The FBI* stretched credibility too far and paled in comparison with a gritty, warts-and-all programme like *Z Cars*.

Round Three: The 1970s –
The Sweeney v Starsky and Hutch

Ask any male who was a teenager in the 1970s about the best police show on British TV and it's more than likely that they'll say without reservation, *The Sweeney*. Deriving its title from cockney rhyming slang for Flying Squad ('Sweeney Todd'), a division of the Metropolitan police force devoted to tracking down armed robbers, *The Sweeney* focused on the exploits of two uncompromising, foul-mouthed hard men. But they weren't villains: they were the police. The strong-armed, rough-tongued antics of the irascible Inspector Jack 'Guv' Regan (John Thaw) and his chirpy, Cockney sidekick, Detective Sergeant George Carter (Dennis Waterman) made a huge impact on the British public. Obsessed with blaggers, birds and booze, they drove like maniacs in a souped-up, shit brown, Ford Granada, striking terror into the heart of London's criminal underworld. They hit first then asked questions afterwards. When you heard Regan utter the immortal words, "Get yer trousers on, you're nicked", you knew that as a criminal, your days were over, sunshine. And if *The Sweeney* hadn't had their dinner, encounters with the dynamic duo could be even nastier! Whereas *Z Cars* bent the rulebook, *The Sweeney* dispensed with the rule book altogether.

Like *Z Cars* a decade earlier, The Sweeney broke the mould of British police shows, causing a public outcry in the process. Not only was *The Sweeney* regarded as gratuitously violent, but also its profane language shocked those of a nervous disposition, even though by today's standards, the use of words like sod, bloody, bastard and piss off seems pretty innocuous. Created by Ian Kennedy Martin for Euston Films with only a minuscule budget, *The Sweeney* screeched noisily onto our screens back in January 1975, enjoying a triumphant four seasons, concluding just after Christmas 1978. The series' success also resulted in a couple of spin-off movies. Like all great cop shows, *The Sweeney* also boasted an excellent theme tune by Harry South. The programme's enduring popularity has prompted recent repeats on Channel 5.

We had Regan and Carter clad in bad suits with flared trousers and kipper ties. The Americans had two, equally sartorially challenged plain clothes detectives in *Starsky and Hutch*. But they had a bit more style – for the most part they wore jeans and leather jackets, although fashion victim Dave Starsky was not averse to modelling a bit of dubious knitwear in the form of big white woolly cardigans. And they drove a flashier car than Regan and Carter – a conspicuous tomato red Ford Torino. Starsky and Hutch possessed the same gung-ho attitude as George and Jack but were a little more sophisticated – of course they beat up crooks, liked pulling the birds and downing the odd bottle of beer, but they didn't swear and never shouted (that was left to the pair's superior officer, the apoplectic Captain Dobey). Dave Starsky ate a lot (usually junk food, which littered the car's dashboard during stake-outs) and quiet Ken Hutchinson got to take heroin in one episode and slept with a hooker, but that was about as bad as it got. Regan and Carter were Neanderthals compared with Starsky and Hutch, whose buddy bonding would have caused the former to regard their American counterparts as a couple of 'gingers' (if my knowledge of rhyming slang is anything to go by!). Starsky and Hutch were good buddies first and cops second. They were also on friendly terms with Huggy Bear, a black ghetto dude of dubious morality. Certainly, Regan and Carter wouldn't have countenanced such a chummy, ambivalent liaison with a grass. They'd probably have nicked Huggy! Like *The Sweeney*, *Starsky and Hutch* ran for four years – from September 1975 to May 1979.

This particular duel is akin to fish'n'chips versus a Big Mac, or Newcastle Brown Ale taking on a bottle of Bud. It's a close call but for me, *The Sweeney* just edges it. From the second season on, mounting public criticism of the violence in *Starsky and Hutch* resulted in a perceptible dilution of that programme's original potency. *The Sweeney*, however, carried on at full throttle for its full duration and for that deserves the plaudits.

Round Four: The 1980s –
Hill Street Blues v The Bill

Devised by Steven Bochco and Michael Kozoll, the groundbreaking American cop show, *Hill Street Blues*, ushered in a new era for televised crime drama when it was broadcast on NBC in January 1981. And yet it was not a runaway success. In fact, in its first season, the show's audience ratings were disastrous – it languished in eighty-seventh place in a ranking of ninety-six prime-time shows. By American standards, it should have been pulled by the network, but positive reaction by the TV critics gave the show a stay of execution. It was the lowest rated show that NBC had ever recommissioned for a second series. But the company's faith in the show paid off: by the end of its second full season, *Hill Street Blues* had become a massive hit. *Hill Street Blues* depicted life inside a police station in a large, though unspecified, American city. The Hill Street station itself was located in a poverty-stricken, gang-torn inner city area and consequently witnessed many of the local inhabitants passing through its doors and into its cells in the course of a programme.

Hill Street Blues offered a realistic three-dimensional view of cop life as seen through the eyes of a large ensemble cast of regulars – the roving camera work gave the show a documentary feel while the complex and fragmented interweaving of several different strands of storyline (which often were ongoing) gave the narrative real depth and perspective. It was, in a sense, the first police soap opera. It didn't depict the police as heroic figures preoccupied with crime fighting twenty-four hours a day – rather it revealed them as all too human, with the fragile concerns, desires and problems that afflict all humanity. The cops on Hill Street were grappling with alcoholism, alimony and stressful personal problems in addition to fighting the city's criminals. At the centre of it all was the popular figure of Captain Frank Furillo (Daniel J. Travanti), a man who had his own fair share of personal battles but who managed to keep the station afloat during crises. *Hill Street Blues* seemed a reflection of life itself – it seamlessly melded moments of side splitting humour and genuine instances of tear-inducing pathos, as it illuminated both the absurdity and the beauty of the human condition in a superbly acted television spectacle. It was often compelling viewing. *Hill Street Blues* proved the blueprint for further successful Bochco created cop shows (all with theme tunes by Mike Post) – in the 1990s, Bochco masterminded both *NYPD Blue* and *Brooklyn South*. In all, one hundred and forty-five episodes of *Hill Street Blues* were made. The show ran for six years until 1987 on NBC. In Britain, the series was shown on Channel Four, garnering a devoted following.

Like *Hill Street Blues*, *The Bill* is centred on the activities of an inner city police station. It portrays the lives of all the police officers working in a fictitious district called Sun Hill, supposedly located in London's East End. Created by Geoff McQueen, *The Bill* was initially transmitted on ITV as an hour-long eleven-part series in October 1984 and instantly aroused the wrath of the Police Federation, who criticised the show for depicting racism in the police force. In 1988, the show was divided into two half-hour midweek slots though more recently, it has gone back to its original one-hour format, though continues to appear twice weekly. It is now widely viewed as an authentic delineation of the modern British police force. Like its predecessors, *Z Cars* and *The Sweeney*, *The Bill* aims to show the police as human beings, flaws and all – indeed, over the years, *The Bill* has had its fair share of unconscionable villains operating within the force itself: charismatic but corrupt figures like Frank Burnside (who

gained his own spin-off series), Ted Roach and, more recently, Don Beech, who left the series as a fugitive, jetting off to a tropical hideaway. There have been many faces that have come and gone over the show's eventful sixteen years but, like all good soap operas, the show has preserved continuity by maintaining a core of regulars – familiar faces like Sun Hill's head-honcho Chief Superintendent Charles Brownlow, the compassionate WPC June Ackland, and the irritating but affable hypochondriac PC Reg Hollis. Initially, the show concentrated exclusively on the characters' station activities, though in more recent years the viewer has seen into the sometimes messy private lives of Sun Hill's finest. Although *The Bill* has now been running for sixteen years, superb scriptwriting and an excellent ensemble of actors have resulted in a show that almost always makes for arresting viewing.

Absolutely no contest: it's got to be *Hill Street Blues*. Despite *The Bill's* consistency and good form for nigh on two decades, it has never got remotely near to producing some of those transcendent, my life-is-better-for-having-watched-this kind of television moments. And to my mind, *Hill Street Blues* delivered a fair few life-affirming epiphanies during its seven-year run.

Round Five: The 1990s – NYPD Blue v The Cops

In September 1993, the pilot episode to a new Steven Bochco police show was transmitted on America's ABC network. The show was called *NYPD Blue* and, although it became an immediate hit with the critics and the public, the show also ignited great controversy – America's TV watchdogs and moral guardians vociferously voiced their indignation at the show's adult content (sex, language and violence). But the show rode out the storm, and from its second season onwards garnered awards like they were gong out of fashion. Like its inspiration, *Hill Street Blues*, *NYPD Blue* is more of a soap opera than a police procedural, focusing on both the professional and personal lives of a detective squad based in the Big Apple's Fifteenth Precinct. With an expansive cast headed by ex-Vietnam veteran and Chicago-native Dennis Franz as the irascible detective, Andy Sipowicz, *NYPD Blue* has successfully married action, pathos and offbeat humour into an engrossing one-hour drama that is still running eight seasons and several Emmy Awards later. Despite the fact that the show has availed itself of good scriptwriters, it is Franz's charismatic presence which accounts for the show's success – although Franz has played many cop roles during his thespian career (including roles as two separate characters in *Hill Street Blues* – firstly as the nefarious 'Bad' Sal Benedetto and later as Norman Buntz), he made Andy Sipowicz a complex, multi-dimensional figure who arouses in the viewer both positive and negative feelings. Sipowicz is no angel – he's a bilious, deeply flawed man laden with prejudices and repressed feelings simmering under the surface. He can be an ogre, but he's also a sensitive, honest and deeply compassionate man who's been to hell and back already in the show's short life – he's both lost and gained a son, got shot, succumbed to alcoholism, fallen for a district attorney and lost a couple of partners

(Kelly played by David Caruso and Bobby Simone acted by Jimmy Smits). You name it; Sipowicz has been there, done it and got the T-Shirt.

Despite enforced changes to the cast over the years, regulars Franz, James McDaniel, Nicholas Turturro and Gordon Clapp have held *NYPD Blue* together. Although the show anchors itself around these stalwarts, the addition of new faces have undoubtedly added a freshness and zest to the show which looks far from jaded after almost one hundred and fifty episodes.

BBC 2's *The Cops* (recently profiled in *CT 3:2*) also depicts the professional and off-duty lives of policemen and women. Created by Tony Garnett, *The Cops* aired in 1998 – it too, stoked up a fierce controversy and made lurid tabloid newspaper headlines. The offended mostly included senior ranking British police officers who were appalled by the programme's depiction of this nation's law enforcers (images of drug-taking cops proved particularly offensive in some quarters). With its unknown actors, uncensored language, wobbly hand-held camera work, truncated editing and realistic locations, many viewers mistook *The Cops* for a gritty fly-on-the-wall documentary. In fact, Stanton police station, which overlooks the crime-infested Skeetsmoor estate, was pure fiction, but like all good fiction, it probed the nature of reality, presenting a candid portrait of modern British police work. It made for uncomfortable viewing – but it was also compelling and innovative.

NYPD Blue wins by a New York mile. *The Cops* and *NYPD Blue* are both, in their own way, excellent shows. However, I believe the former is too harsh and almost misanthropic in its depiction of humanity – almost all the characters in *The Cops* have no redeeming features and consequently you don't truly care what happens to them. The opposite is true of *NYPD Blue*: its characters are people that you can identify with and relate to.

And the Winner Is...

As contests go, this was a close one, perhaps even closer than I'd originally imagined – the USA just shaded it by three rounds to two. But in the 1960s and 1970s, Uncle Sam possessed nothing that could match the raw energy of classic Brit-cop classics like *Z Cars* and *The Sweeney*. In the 1980s and 1990s, however, it's been a different story, with woeful, formulaic British shows floundering in the wake of benchmark Bochco productions like *Hill Street Blues* and *NYPD Blue*. And then, more recently, there's been David Chase's superlative *The Sopranos*, which makes all British crime dramas look tenth-rate. In my view, the Americans have the edge when it comes to police and detective drama. Mind you, considering the enormous production budgets that fund shows like *NYPD Blue* and *The Sopranos*, it's no wonder that American police drama outshines its somewhat impoverished British counterpart. Even so, I suppose the consistently high quality of primetime American cop shows (especially those attached with Steven Bochco's name) represents something of an inexplicable and perplexing paradox when you consider the Godawful state of US television in general.

Ultimately, I suppose, it all comes down to personal taste and whether you prefer *Poirot* to *Columbo*, *Softly Softly* to *Hawaii 5-0* or *Second Sight* to *The Sopranos*, there's a wealth of crime fodder on both satellite and terrestrial TV at the moment to cater for all criminal tendencies. In that respect, TV crime has never been so healthy.

Sources

The Boxtree Encyclopedia of TV Detectives by Geoff Tibballs (Boxtree, 1992)

www.thesweeney.com

www.thebill.com

www.spe.sony.com/tv/shows/sgn/sh (Starsky and Hutch)

www.net-hlp.com/hsb (Hill Street Blues)

www.stwing.upenn.edu/~sepinwal/nypd (NYPD Blue)

Charles Waring

CT'S MUSICAL MUG SHOTS

QUINCY JONES

PORTRAIT OF AN AMERICAN LEGEND

Charles Waring

With a musical career that now spans some six decades, Quincy Jones is undoubtedly a living legend. However, due to his Grammy-winning association with Michael Jackson's Thriller album, most people seem oblivious to the extraordinary range of Jones' talent and tend to think of his career only in terms of being an accomplished record producer. But he's much more than that – he's a trumpet player, a bandleader, a Grammy-winning recording artist in his own right (he's enjoyed four number one singles in the US r'n'b chart), a musical arranger, a film composer, a record label boss, a television executive, a publishing magnate and, more recently, he's been a media entrepreneur. He's rich, he's famous and he lives in Hollywood. In fact, in 1996, Quincy Jones was voted by People magazine as one of the fifty most beautiful people in the world!

Some have knocked him for that and been critical of his achievements – maybe that's because success and all its desirable accoutrements seemed to come to him so easily. But the fact is that some commentators have conveniently forgotten that Jones was a ghetto kid who probably struggled twice as hard as any white person to reach the top of his profession. Through a mixture of perseverance, hard work and yes, even luck, Jones boldly went [sic] where no African-American had been before, breaking down racial barriers and proving himself an inspirational figure to those aiming to follow in his footsteps. By anyone's standards, Quincy Jones's achievements are phenomenal, though CT is focusing its attention on the maestro's adventures in Hollywood and, in particular, his contribution to the crime thriller soundtrack.

This is the story of the dude they simply call 'Q'.

From ghetto dreams to the Hollywood screen

Quincy Delight Jones was born on the 14th March 1933, a native of Chicago, the fabled Windy City and a place that ol' blue eyes, himself, Frank Sinatra, once declared was "my kinda town". But there was nothing glamorous about Jones' formative years in the big Illinois metropolis with the dramatic skyscraper skyline. He spent the first ten years of his life as an impoverished inhabitant of the city's deprived Southside ghetto area before his family moved west to Bremerton, a small town on the outskirts of Seattle on America's Pacific coast. Jones was interested in music from an early age and cut his musical teeth as a twelve-year-old singing in a gospel quartet

before taking up the trumpet in junior high school. Among his childhood friends was a visually impaired musical prodigy called Ray Charles Robinson, who later, with his name shortened to Ray Charles, became a soul music superstar. Jones actually played trumpet in a group he and Charles formed together as teenagers before winning a scholarship to study music at Boston's famous Schillinger House Academy (later, in 1954, it became the world renowned Berklee School of Music).

As a teenager, Jones was smitten by Hollywood movies and, in particular, the music that accompanied them. He confessed to spending many hours after school in movie houses – but he wasn't there solely to seek entertainment. He was studying the cinematic art form with a keen and probing intelligence, assimilating images, sounds and analysing the symbiotic meshing of film and music. Jones was nourishing a ghetto dream that he would one day score a motion picture: "I always wanted to get into films. By the time I was fifteen I'd read the back off Frank Skinner's book on film music, *Underscore*." The odds were against him but Jones was out to prove his worth. After his formal musical education finished in Boston, Jones, still a teenager, joined the famous jazz vibraphone player Lionel Hampton and his big band. Although a novice, Jones learned much by playing trumpet alongside seasoned veterans like fellow horn man, Clark Terry. Travelling on the road with the Hampton entourage for three years (1950-1953) was where Jones' musical education began in earnest, accruing experience and knowledge that would assist in propelling him into the big time. In Hampton's band,

Jones discovered he had a facility for arranging and honed his skills by swatting up on orchestration from textbooks. His diligence and enthusiasm paid off. After leaving Hampton's band, he began working as a freelance music arranger and news of his talent soon spread, resulting in recording sessions with people like the legendary bandleader, Count Basie, and the jazz singer, Dinah Washington. From 1956, Jones began cutting his own adroitly arranged big band jazz albums, making an immediate impact on both the critics and the public with long players like *This Is How I Feel About Jazz* and *Go West Man*. Also, in 1956, recognition of Jones' talent resulted in him being recruited by the legendary puff-cheeked bebop trumpeter, Dizzy Gillespie, not only to play in but also direct the latter's big band on an extensive globe-trotting tour. It was, in fact, a historic venture – the tour was funded and sponsored by the US State Department and went to Europe, the Middle East and South America.

Stimulated by the experience of working abroad, Jones went back to Europe shortly after the tour ended to live in Paris. That was 1957. His primary aim was to expand his musical knowledge by enrolling as a pupil of the famous French composer and teacher, Nadia Boulanger, who had previously been tutor to the great American composer, Aaron Copland. Jones studied composition and orchestration with Boulanger and also became a pupil of Olivier Messaien (who was once tutored by Paul Dukas, composer of *The Sorcerer's Apprentice*). During the same period, Jones took up the post of head of A&R (Artist and Repertoire) at a French record label called Barclay Disques. In 1959, Jones signed on to become the musical director of Harold Arlen and Johnny Mercer's blues opera, *Free And Easy*, for a tour of Europe, featuring an all-star big band. Unfortunately, the show proved a dismal failure and lost a prodigious amount of money. For Jones it was particularly catastrophic from a financial perspective, leaving him with a substantial amount of debts. The band that he had assembled and which he was responsible for lacked the funds to get back home to America, so they toured Europe attempting to recoup some of their losses. Jones was profoundly depressed by the experience and later confessed that it was the only time in his life that he seriously contemplated suicide. Ultimately, he was forced to sell the rights of his own nascent publishing catalogue to raise the money for everyone to travel back to the States. It brought home to him the precarious nature of the music business. Fortunately, though, better times lay ahead.

A year later, in 1961, Jones was back in business – he was back in the States, ensconced as the A&R person for Barclay's American division, Mercury Records, in New York. Significantly, it was also the year that witnessed his first film score. But it was no Hollywood blockbuster and represented a somewhat low-key entrance into the movie world. The film was called *Pojken i Tradet* (*The Boy in the Tree*), a small budget Swedish picture shot in black and white by director Arne Sucksdorff and which Jones once described as being "too weird to get released here [in the USA]". Few people saw the film and it was another three years before Jones got another shot at a soundtrack. Meanwhile, Jones' meteoric career at Mercury Records was about to make history – in 1964, he was promoted to the role of Vice-President of the company, which represented an unprecedented feat for an African-American at that time. As well as making his own albums, Jones was also cutting records with greats like Frank Sinatra and Ella Fitzgerald. One of his pop prodigies during his tenure at Mercury turned out to be the teenaged singing sensation, Lesley Gore, whose record *It's My Party* was one of several pop smashes he produced in the early part of the 1960s. With hit records to his name and his stock sky high, Quincy Jones finally got his big Hollywood break in 1964 when the film director, Sidney Lumet, hired him to score his controversial movie, *The Pawnbroker*. *The Pawnbroker* starred a dynamic Rod Steiger in the lead role as Sol Nazerman, an embittered Jewish refugee from Nazi Germany eking a life as a pawnbroker in a New York ghetto. Apart from the syrupy and rather inappropriate theme song sung by jazz diva, Sarah Vaughan, Jones created a febrile, jazz-inflected score that seemed perfectly in sync with the movie's psychological drama and Lumet's use of harrowing concentration camp flashback sequences. The success of *The Pawnbroker* prompted Jones to quit his lucrative position at Mercury Records and concentrate all his energies on film scoring. It was a gamble, though, that almost didn't pay off, as the composer related in the US magazine, *Urban Network*, a couple of years ago: "I assumed after that first picture that the jobs would come rolling in. But they didn't. My agent didn't want me to do B films, so I waited."

Jones waited, in fact, for almost two years before his next movie assignment came in. That was the film *Mirage*, a tense thriller about an amnesiac man (Gregory Peck) attempting to piece his past together. Legend has it that when some of the film's executives learned that Jones was black, he was close to being fired. However, fellow composer, Henry Mancini (responsible for *Touch of Evil, Breakfast at Tiffany's, The Pink Panther* and countless other movies) interceded on his behalf and Jones was retained to score the film. That was in 1966, a year that witnessed the rise of Quincy Jones' reputation as a capable and accomplished movie scorer, especially with soundtracks like *Walk Don't Run*, a film that turned out to be Cary Grant's cinematic swan song. Indeed, Quincy Jones was a new breed of Hollywood composer. In the 1950s, the innovative jazz-tinged film scores of Alex North and Elmer Bernstein brought a new musical language to movie soundtracks. In the 1960s, the symphonic romantic score, which had dominated Hollywood movies from the 1930s onwards, now seemed irrelevant when compared with the hip new polyglot musical currency introduced by composers like Jones and Lalo Schifrin. The following year proved to be even more significant for Jones. He supplied the memorable theme tune to TV's wheelchair-bound detective, *Ironside* (played by Raymond Burr), the Oscar-nominated incidental music to Richard Brooks's chiller-thriller *In Cold Blood* (based on Truman Capote's classic book) and another Sidney Lumet opus, *The Deadly Affair*, featuring an international cast headed by James Mason. This film, in particular, illustrated the further evolution of Jones' exciting cinematic style – he expanded his musical vocabulary and orchestral palette by assimilating the undulating bossa nova rhythms of Brazilian music, producing a spellbinding and distinctive Latin American flavoured score.

But undoubtedly the most important movie music written by Jones in 1967 was for the quintuple Oscar-winning film, *In the Heat of the Night*. This groundbreaking movie was directed by Norman Jewison and starred the black actor, Sidney Poitier, as a big city homicide detective, Virgil Tibbs, who is falsely accused of murder in a racially segregated backwoods town in America's Deep South. After establishing his innocence, Tibbs assists the town's white, bigoted Sheriff (played magnificently by Rod Steiger) to solve the case. Deemed controversial for its trenchant examination of America's race relations, *In the Heat of the Night* not only catapulted its African-American lead actor, Sidney Poitier, to superstar status, but also enhanced Hollywood's perception of Jones – though, ironically, Jones' evocative score, featuring the bluesy title song sung by his old pal, Ray Charles, failed to secure an Oscar nomination. It was, however, nominated for a Grammy (an award handed out by America's music industry). But what really mattered was that Quincy Jones had risen in the Hollywood pecking order, graduating almost overnight to tinsel town's coveted A list of composers and going some way to fulfilling his boyhood dream of writing music for the movies. Significantly, *In the Heat of the Night* cemented a strong creative bond between actor Poitier and Jones. This wasn't surprising as they shared something in common: they had risen from humble origins and were now

in an exalted position compared with the majority of America's black population. The fact that there weren't many black faces in Hollywood at this time no doubt encouraged the pair to join forces on several film projects over the years, including the sequel to *In the Heat of the Night*, 1970's *They Call Me Mister Tibbs*, directed by Gordon Douglas from a script by the screenwriter of *The Thomas Crown Affair* and *Bullitt*, Alan Trustman. Jones also accompanied Poitier on *The Slender Thread* (1965), *For Love of Ivy* (1968), *The Lost Man* (1969) and *Brother John* (1971).

Many other film projects followed in the late sixties, varying from comedies like *Enter Laughing*, spy movies such as *Dandy in Aspic* (a UK film starring Laurence Harvey, Tom Courtenay and the comedian Peter Cook), a western (*MacKenna's Gold*) and an adventure romp (*The Hell With Heroes*) to adult comedy dramas like *Bob & Carol & Ted & Alice*. When Jones scored the British caper movie, *The Italian Job*, about a bullion heist and starring Michael Caine, he provided further evidence that as a composer he possessed both versatility and a cosmopolitan eclecticism. However, despite his chameleon-like ability to deliver any style of music with consummate fluency and ease, the detective drama, *In the Heat of the Night* and 1968's robbery flick, *The Split,* had vividly demonstrated that what Jones excelled at was scoring crime movies – his dramatic, jazz-tinged musical style boasting funky bass lines, tense percussion patterns and exciting brass parts was particularly adept at accompanying action scenes. In fact, Jones was originally hired to provide the soundtrack to *Bullitt* in 1968 but had to withdraw from the project because of ill health (the score was handed to Jones' buddy and former big band member, Lalo Schifrin). By the early 1970s, Jones found himself scoring several crime thrillers, beginning with *They Call Me Mister Tibbs*. The thrillers that followed included two heist movies: *$ (Dollars)* with Warren Beatty and Goldie Hawn, and *The Anderson Tapes* starring Sean Connery with a young Christopher Walken. In 1972, Jones composed the score to Sam Peckinpah's adaptation of Jim Thompson's classic novel, *The Getaway*, starring Steve McQueen as the criminal mastermind, Doc McCoy. He also scored the soundtrack to a film version (directed by Peter Yates) of Richard Stark's novel *The Hot Rock*, starring Robert Redford in 1972.

After scoring up to eight movies in a year at the tail end of the 1960s and racking up over thirty-nine movies in an intense eight-year period (1965-1973), the mid 1970s witnessed Jones cutting back on his movie work and directing his energies on making his own albums. However, health reasons also prompted the curtailing of Jones's Hollywood activities – in 1974, he suffered two potentially fatal aneurisms to the brain (caused by a cerebral tumour), which resulted in him being unable to play the trumpet (although, in truth, Jones had not been an active musician since the 1950s). Despite this bout of ill health, Jones slowed down only fractionally – although his movie writing was occasional, he did, however, write many TV themes in the 1970s, including most famously the music to Alex Haley's epic drama *Roots* in 1977. Other memorable TV music by Jones includes the themes to the US shows *The Bill Cosby Show* and *Sanford*

& Son. In Britain, Jones is best known for his role as a record producer. His reputation for bringing a glossy sophistication to pop production began on his own pop-orientated records in the 1970s. He pioneered a sleek, urbane sound that found its quintessence in the albums he produced for Michael Jackson. This unlikely liaison proved a profitable one, beginning in 1979 with *Off the Wall* and reaching its apogee with 1982's multimillion selling *Thriller* album, the best-selling record of all time. But in the 1980s, Jones was contemplating challenging new horizons and sought to diversify his interests – he formed his own record label, Qwest, and also got involved in movie production. He was a co-producer of Steven Spielberg's film *The Color Purple* in 1985 (he also contributed the soundtrack) and in the latter part of that decade moved into television production, being responsible for the hugely successful US TV sitcom *Fresh Prince of Bel-Air*, which launched Will Smith's acting career. In the 1990s, Jones' career took another unforeseen twist when he entered the world of publishing, launching the glossy hip-hop magazine *Vibe* (it also spawned a successful television spin-off).

Now, at sixty-eight years old, Quincy Jones, the undisputed doyen of African-American music, can afford to take it easy, though it's doubtful if he will. He's got nothing else to prove: he's been there, done it and got the T-shirt too. And for his enviable list of achievements and the fact that his music has covered and celebrated the whole gamut of African-American music from blues through to jazz, soul, funk and hip-hop, everyone from jazz legends to pop stars and even gangster rappers, respect him. And we at CT do too. All hail the mighty Q!

The Film Music of Quincy Jones on CD

The Reel Quincy Jones: Hip-O Records, HIPD-40168

Despite Quincy Jones' renown as a movie composer, compilations of his motion picture scores have been few and far between since the advent of the compact disc back in 1983. Without doubt, the best one currently available is this exciting assemblage of the man's movie and TV themes put together by a specialist American label (though you can find it in the larger British record stores). It features some of Jones' best Hollywood screen work, including two contrasting cues from *The Pawnbroker*, namely *Rack 'Em Up* and *Harlem Drive*. There are several selections culled from crime thrillers that Jones scored – the propulsive *Money Runner* from the caper flick, *$ (Dollars)*; *Shoot to Kill*, a dramatic cue with shades of Bernard Herrmann taken from *Mirage*; the funky main theme from *They Call Me Mister Tibbs*; and

the deeply atmospheric *Peep-Freak Patrol Car* extracted from *In the Heat of the Night*. The theme from *The Anderson Tapes* with its percolating percussion also makes a welcome appearance. Jones' versatility is evidenced by the rich symphonic textures of *Canon Del Oro* taken from the only western he scored, *MacKenna's Gold*. There's also a classical pastiche that quotes from the *Hallelujah Chorus* from Handel's *Messiah* for the main title from the wife swapping comedy, *Bob & Carol & Ted & Alice*. Further illustrations of Jones' compositional skill are provided by tasty morsels taken from *The Color Purple*, *The Lost Man* and 1978's black version of *The Wizard of Oz* (*The Wiz*) starring Diana Ross and Michael Jackson. Jones was also adept at scoring for the small screen, as the themes from *The Bill Cosby Show* and *Sanford &*

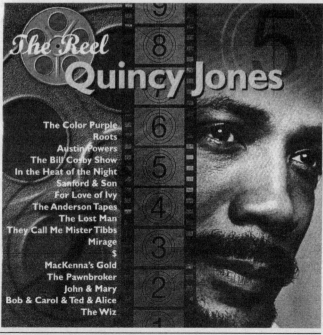

excellent annotations (with a liner note by film director Norman Jewison) and superb artwork. It also functions as a CD Rom that contains the original movie trailer to *In the Heat of the Night*. Although both films featured the exploits of the Philadelphia homicide detective, Virgil Tibbs (Sidney Poitier), Jones' respective scores for the two films are remarkably different from one another – *In the Heat of the Night* with its bluesy, almost countrified feel seems deeply redolent of America's sultry Deep South, while the music for *They Call Me Mister Tibbs* is sharper and more sophisticated, reflecting that particular film's big city scenario. The fact that Jones can convey atmosphere, action and character so compellingly with this music testifies to his extraordinary gifts as a composer.

Son vividly demonstrate. An added bonus is the inclusion of Jones' Latin-flavoured evergreen, *Soul Bossa Nova*, a track that seems to epitomise the swinging sixties and which, appropriately enough, recently featured in the spoof spy film, *Austin Powers: International Man of Mystery*. A highly recommended introduction.

In the Heat of the Night/They Call Me Mister Tibbs: Ryko, RCD 10712

If *The Reel Quincy Jones* whets your appetite and tempts you to delve further into Q's soundtrack back catalogue, then this single disc double feature comprising 1967's *In the Heat of the Night* and its 1970 sequel, *They Call Me Mister Tibbs*, is an essential purchase. It's an excellent, value-for-money package that as well as boasting snippets of film dialogue in between the music has

Also available:
The Pawnbroker/The Deadly Affair:
   Verve, 531 233-2
The Italian Job: MCA, 60074/112488-2

Charles Waring

TRIPLE THREAT

Paul McAuley

Only rarely are movie sequels either critically or commercially more successful than their originals. Usually, as the Roman numerals mount up on the route to straight-to-video-hell, original ideas are diluted, stars on their way up are replaced by stars on their way down, and budgets are pruned to the bone. The movie version of *The Silence of the Lambs* was one of the few exceptions to this rule, and its box office success, five Oscars and mountain of critical plaudits have overshadowed Dr Hannibal Lecter's first celluloid outing in *Manhunter* (adapted from Thomas Harris' second novel, *The Red Dragon*) ever since. But Michael Mann's movie, recently reissued by Anchor Bay in a 'limited edition' DVD box set (limited in the Franklin Mint sense: the edition size is a respectable 100,000), is no cheap quickie. There are three solid central performances, Mann's trademark glossily rapt attention to detail, and a sharp, fast-paced script that cleaves closely to the core of Harris's bestseller.

Retired agent Will Graham (William Petersen), physically and mentally injured after he captured Dr Hannibal Lecktor [sic], is recruited by former boss Jack Crawford (Dennis Farina) to track down the Tooth Fairy (Ted Noonan), a psychopath who murders an entire family each full moon. Dogged by odious tabloid reporter Freddie Lounds (Stephen Long), Graham, who works by intuition and empathy, visits Lecktor (Brian Cox) to renew his sense of the psychopathic mindset, but Lecktor, eager for revenge, begins a deadly cat-and-mouse game by sending Graham's home address to the Tooth Fairy. Although Mann foregrounds state of the art forensic techniques, most notably in a bravura sequence as FBI agents race to analyse a note found in Lecktor's cell, Graham's pursuit of the Tooth Fairy is subtler and more cerebral than the usual police procedural. The Tooth Fairy, given a fine mix of arrogance and anguish by Noonan, is a true monster, engaged in a great work of 'becoming' inspired by William Blake's watercolour 'The Great Red Dragon and the Woman Clothed in the Sun', yet still possessed by the vestiges of ordinary human impulses. Diverted from the next family he has targeted by a brief romance with a blind woman, Reba (Joan Allen), he sees possible redemption in her unexpected affection ("You look so good in the sun", he tells her, after their tryst), but in the end his frail hope of becoming something other than what he is can't withstand an instant of jealous rage.

Petersen brings a quiet intensity to his part, most notably in the scene where, running two home movies in parallel, he at last realises how the Tooth Fairy has chosen his victims, while Brian Cox is sardonically playful as Lecktor, a devilish mentor who taunts Graham as he is drawn deeper and deeper into the psychological universe of the Tooth Fairy. Although Cox can be an intimidatingly physical actor, Mann shoots him mostly in repose in a sterile white cell; his commanding gaze and nimble delivery intimates a quick, clever mind that in the end has trapped itself. This is a movie whose plot turns upon seeing – Graham finally understands the Tooth Fairy by seeing the same home movies that he saw, a nice doubling of the psychopath's voyeurism; the Tooth Fairy, obsessed with mirrors, needs to see himself in the context of an ordinary family, even if he has to kill them to stage his tableaux. Cinematographer Dante Spinotti lights key scenes of ordinary intimacy with sharp blue tones, as if menaced by the killer's moon, while Mann's framing of Graham and his family against a sunny ocean skyline is echoed both by a long shot of the Tooth Fairy and Reba embracing against a red dawn, and by a huge poster of a sunrise in the Tooth Fairy's lair: this is no ordinary, earthly sunrise – it's on Mars, neatly implying the distance between the Tooth Fairy's mind and those of ordinary people.

Manhunter is presented in a crisp widescreen (2.35:1) transfer of the American theatrical release, with a Dolby Surround 5.1 audiotrack, two short featurettes on its making, a muddled theatrical trailer, and a limited number of talent biographies; the keepcase contains twenty-four pages of photographs and other material in a miniature folder. A second disc contains the problematical 'director's cut', a slightly extended version produced for cable TV with grainier visuals than the theatrical release. Most of the four minutes of additional material underlines speculation about the Tooth Fairy's motivation, although a slight expansion of a scene in which Graham reluctantly explains what happened to Lecktor's victims usefully rectifies a fluffed bit of dubbing in the theatrical version, and there's also an unconvincing scene where, in the aftermath, Graham visits the family who would have been next on the Tooth Fairy's list. In neither version is a key fragment of dialogue quoted by Andy Black in his booklet notes, in which Graham defines his feelings towards the Tooth Fairy and shows that his resolve has not been weakened by his empathy: "My heart bleeds for him as a kid. Someone took a kid and manufactured a monster. At the same time, as an adult he's irredeemable. He butchers whole families to pursue trivial fantasies. As an adult someone should blast the sick fuck out of his socks." This speech was in the British theatrical release, although that is shorter than the US theatrical release. Perhaps the meticulous Michael Mann could at some stage sort out a final version; meanwhile, the Anchor Bay package, despite a mostly redundant second disc, is a fine presentation of an undeservedly neglected movie.

As in Harris' novel, the movie version of *The Silence of the Lambs* parallels and deepens the themes of its prequel, most notably in the mentor-pupil relationships between Graham/Lecktor and Starling/Lecter. In contrast to Michael Mann's more clinical approach, Demme amplifies the gothic undertone of Harris' novel, especially in his depiction of Hannibal Lecter's incarceration in what is little more than a dank medieval dungeon, in the limited autumnal palette of the cinematography, and in Anthony Hopkins feline portrayal of Lecter as a man who revels in the lofty isolation of his superior intellect. Lecter may be fallen, but he is not downcast; at times Hopkins allows an impish glee into his gaze, and his delivery switches fluidly from that of sober mentor to arch seducer. Elsewhere, the emphasis is on bureaucratic rather than forensic procedures, with Jack Crawford (Scott Glenn) as a dour, fastidious foil to trainee FBI agent Clarice Starling's (Jodie Foster) sometimes naive but vividly gritty determination. "You don't want Hannibal Lecter in your head", Crawford warns Starling before sending her off to her first fateful interview with the ex-psychiatrist serial killer, but that's just what Starling must do to win Lecter's help in chasing down the serial killer nicknamed Buffalo Bill (Ted Levine). Buffalo Bill, a rather more straightforward monster than the Tooth Fairy, skins his victims ("He's making a girl suit out of real girls", Lecter taunts Starling), and keeps them alive for a few days before he kills them. He has just kidnapped a US Senator's daughter; as the clock ticks, Lecter manipulates both Starling and the venal director of the institution where he's incarcerated, and Demme economically escalates the tension with a famously misleading intercutting of scenes before the climactic encounter between Starling and Buffalo Bill.

In both *Manhunter* and *The Silence of the Lambs*, Lecktor/Lecter is the apex of a triangular relationship between himself, a serial killer and the killer's nemesis. Both Graham and Starling need to learn from Lecktor/Lecter (Starling is the more willing and apt pupil), and he knows both the Tooth Fairy and Buffalo Bill – although only the Tooth Fairy asks him for enlightenment. A lector is, in certain universities, a lecturer – a teacher. More than that, Hannibal Lecter, with his emphasis on deduction from first principles, and his keen eye and nose for the telling detail, often reminds one of the famous consulting detective patiently explaining his reasoning to his sidekick. He is as much a detective as the FBI agents who need his help. The best DVD version of *The Silence of the Lambs* is available as part of the Criterion Collection series, with a sharp digital transfer from the 35mm interpositive preserving the original 1.85:1 aspect. The disc also contains with deleted scenes, storyboards, excerpts from the FBI crime classification manual and statements from convicted serial killers, and a somewhat fragmentary round-robin conversation about the making of the movie, the motivation of its main characters and its veracity, by director Jonathan Demme, stars Jodie Foster and Anthony Hopkins, screenwriter Ted Tally, and FBI Agent John Douglas.

Se7en, directed by David Fincher from an original script by Andrew Kevin Walker, at first appears to be a conventional odd couple police procedural, but quickly deepens into an unforgiving portrayal of a world in which evil is just beneath the surface. As in *Manhunter* and *The Silence of the Lambs*, the only way to solve a series of murders is to risk entry into the mindset of the killer. The story is framed by the troubled relationship between two mismatched cops: William Somerset (Morgan Freeman), patient, meticulous, experienced and deeply weary; and his replacement, David Mills (Brad Pitt), impetuous, somewhat naive, and quick to anger. Somerset, due to retire in only a few days, is unwillingly drawn into helping Mills investigate a series of inventively gruesome murders by serial killer John Doe (Kevin Spacey), based on Thomas Aquinas' seven deadly sins (Gluttony, Greed, Sloth, Lust, Pride, Envy, Wrath). With the help of Mills's wife, Tracy (Gwyneth Paltrow), the two men develop a grudging mutual respect as they realise they can both learn from each other, but in the end neither can escape John Doe's spider web. The unnamed city in which *Se7en* is set – dark and teeming and perpetually drenched by rain – is as important a character as any of the actors; Andrew Kevin Walker, who was working in Tower Records in New York when he wrote the script, calls this his 'love letter' to that city. Like *Taxi Driver*'s Travis Bickle, John Doe is an everyman figure disgusted by the human degradation routinely observed on his city's streets; like *Manhunter*'s Tooth Fairy, Doe draws on a classic work to justify his murders.

For what is ostensibly a variation on the well-trodden police procedural form, there's very little explicit violence or gore: a brief shoot-out and chase when Somerset and Mills discover John Doe's lair; just a single onscreen murder. Instead of overt violence, Fincher conveys a gothic atmosphere of squalor and spent violence by lighting, set decoration and claustrophobically low camera angles rather than close-ups of corpses and bloody flesh wounds. As always, horror is most effective when it is merely suggested; we don't need to see what's in the famous box that's delivered near the end of the movie to share Somerset's disgust and despair, to know what he means when he cries out that John Doe "has the upper hand now". The movie is presented here in a seemingly flawless and brilliantly clear anamorphic letterboxed version that, struck from the original negative and preserving the original 2.40:1 aspect, reveals a plethora of details previous hidden in the murky depths of the shadowy sets, with options of Dolby EX 5.1 or DTS ES Discreet 6.1 soundtracks from a near field mix specifically created for the DVD. Unlike the original one-disc release, the New Line Platinum version contains a host of extras. The two DVDs are presented in a keepcase with the appearance of one of John Doe's notebooks. The first contains the movie and four audio commentaries (Fincher, Pitt and Morgan discussing production of the film and its themes; a discussion of the story hosted by Richard Dyer (author of the BFI Modern Classics Series' volume on the movie) with Fincher, Andrew Kevin Walker, editor Richard Francis-Bruce and President of Production Michael De Luca; discussion of the design and cinematography; and discussion of the film's music and sound effects). The second disc contains extensive supplemental material, including the theatrical trailer and electronic press kit, filmographies of the cast and director, and a selection of deleted scenes, extended takes (most notably deleted material from the opening, showing Detective Somerset (Morgan Freeman) viewing the rural house to which he intends to retire, and from which he takes a cabbage rose cut from wallpaper, seen at the released opening when he is preparing to leave for work) and alternate endings. In addition, there is a selection of production design and still photographs with commentaries, a featurette on the making of John Doe's notebooks, and an interesting look at the preparations for the *Se7en* DVD. There's also DVD-ROM content (not seen by this reviewer), exploring the John Doe web site, fan sites, and a reading list and exploration of the seven deadly sins. I doubt that anyone is going to look at everything this DVD set contains, but no matter. The package complements the work of a director known for his fanatical attention to detail, and sets a benchmark standard for DVD release.

Manhunter: 1986, Anchor Bay DV11692, $39.98, theatrical version 121 mins, director's cut 124 mins, region one
The Silence of the Lambs: 1990, The Criterion Collection CC1530D, $35.99, 118 mins, region one
Se7en: 1995, New Line Platinum Series N4997, $29.95, 125 mins, region one

---

CT RECOMMENDS THE LATEST DVDS

Barry Forshaw

Just five minutes into the new DVD issue of *Charade* (Laureate), and you find yourself rehearsing that time-honoured phrase: they don't make them like this any more. And they really don't. What a package! At the time, the film was a considerable box-office success, but there were dissenting voices – those who described the film as a Hitchcock pastiche without the master's dash. There is an element of truth in that, but it has to be said that Hitchcock himself had stopped making thrillers as stylish, witty and exciting as this by this time in his career (later Hitchcock films such as *Torn Curtain* don't begin to match Stanley Donen's homage to the Master). But look at the ingredients. Donen, director of such great musicals as *Seven Brides for Seven Brothers* and *Singin' in the Rain* shows himself equally adept at this kind of sophisticated thriller, while the cast includes not only the inestimable Cary Grant and Audrey Hepburn, but such future stars as James Coburn and Walter Matthau (not to mention George Kennedy as a particularly nasty steel-clawed villain). Then, of course, there is Henry Mancini's memorable score, Maurice Binder's stunning title sequence... need I go on? A new DVD company, Laureate, is responsible for the packaging and extras. It's the brainchild of the multitalented Ken Barnes, and he's done a splendid job here, although a certain grain is evident in certain scenes (right at the start, in fact, which is a shame). Nevertheless, unmissable.

As yet another TV showing of Patrick McGoohan's cult series The Prisoner begins (shortly after a deluxe DVD boxed set of the entire series appeared), appetites whetted by the appearance of McGoohan's earlier series in which he played resourceful secret agent John Drake were keener than ever. And with Danger Man Volume Two (Carlton), we finally are able to sample again these sharp and stylish half-hour thrillers which clearly acted as a prototype for the later show. But why was there such a long gap between the first volume (which included episodes one to four) and this one? Possibly a rethink on the part of Carlton DVD: and, if so, the results of that rethink are more than welcome. The earlier DVD featured only four half-hour episodes, and volume two boasts double that number (episodes five to twelve). Carlton's new generosity is particularly cherishable, given the handsome offerings available here, some of which point forward to the glories that were to come in later series and, of course, in The Prisoner. A good example is the episode Position of Trust, which is marvellously played (all of the episodes feature the cream of the British acting profession) and tautly directed, with the excellent Donald Pleasence as an Anglo-Indian clerk caught in the crossfire of one of Drake's stings against a vicious enemy. Interestingly, this one raises issues of the morality of Drake's behaviour, which is to become a major theme of the (far superior) hour-long episodes which followed. But until they appear on DVD, McGoohan aficionados have plenty of cause to celebrate the second volume. Roll on, volume three... and roll on the DVD issue of the hour-long Danger Man episodes.

Looking at the astonishingly elaborate job video company Hong Kong Legends have done on their newly restored DVD of Bruce Lee's Fist of Fury, it's a testimony to the late Lee's grace and power that his celebrity was largely created in this country via poor quality, panned and scanned versions of his best films. Such was Lee's charisma, he created his legion of fans despite the substandard presentation of his work. But in the twenty-first century, DVD buyers demand something more than the shoddy video presentation of the past, and after the similarly splendid restoration job on another early Lee classic The Big Boss, Fist of Fury truly is, for once, a Special Collectors' Edition as the box reads. Apart from the digitally re-mastered and restored transfer, this DVD is anamorphically enhanced for widescreen TVs (the extra visual elements producing a far sharper picture), contains an informed audio commentary, a production photo portfolio, and a rare interview gallery. Most welcome of all, though, it restores all the censor cuts that a cautious BBFC insisted on fourteen years ago, and is truly an exemplar of what this astonishing new medium can do. Don't look for subtle characterisation here: it's not to be found. But the martial arts sequences still take the breath away.

A PERSONAL VIEW

Mark Timlin:

The creator of Nick Sharman (and crime reviewer for The Independent on Sunday) *gives CT the unvarnished truth (if he can just remember what happened last night)…*
(and check out www.nicksharman.co.uk)

I know I keep coming back to this, but are crime shows on British TV getting worse? As I write this (April 1 2001 – and that's no joke), the latest candidate for a series on BBC1 is *NCS: Manhunt*. The NCS or National Crime Squad is the British equivalent of the FBI, but you'll find no Mulder or Scully in this mob. Instead we have David Suchet, who seems to have lost most of his little grey cells along with his Poirot moustache; Keith Barron as the big boss, who seems curiously detached from the proceedings throughout, as if he had been peeking ahead at the script and didn't like what he saw – and who could blame him – or possibly he'd been sampling the office bottle, which of course turned up pretty early in the proceedings. No cliché left unturned here. And once again he could hardly be blamed for that

either; Samantha Bond as a cool blonde DS with the weight of the world on her shoulders; a young black woman whose only role was to tinker with a laptop computer, get things wrong and make up the ethnic numbers. The rest of the squad, and there were loads of them (it was a bit difficult to tell as it seemed there was a power failure at the NSC HQ, and everything was shot in a sort of twilight zone), were a bunch of ex-soapies and actors I vaguely remember from a commercial or two. Nothing wrong there, actors have to pay the rent same as the rest of us. But just a word about the ethnic mix in Brit TV crime. In fact, only about five per cent of the police are made up from minorities, and if you ever watch a true crime show featuring a British squad of detectives, it's invariably filled with overweight males, aged forty plus. But not on TV, oh no. The perfect squad is as follows: one middle-aged white man in charge, always with a back story (think Ken Stott in *The Vice*); one thirty something black male detective with family problems; one feisty young white woman with a penchant for short skirts; one Chinese; one Indian; and a bunch of nameless young kids. Check out *The Bill*, *The Knock* and many more too numerous to list here. Anyway, back to *NCS: Manhunt*. For the first ten minutes or so, Baron bleated on about the squad being 'the best'. He never bloody stopped. That is until the villain of the piece, Ricky Valesi (played by an old stalwart of Brit TV, Kenneth Cranham – you might not know the name, but you'd know the face) made total idiots of them.

This is the story: Valesi was an armed robber serving life who got transferred to a mental facility, then into a halfway house from where he escaped. During his sentence he's had a relationship by letter with the female DC who had nicked him in the first place. She was played by Phyllis Logan whom you might remember as the lady of the manor in *Lovejoy* who had a did they, didn't they? will they, won't they? relationship with Ian McShane. Now I've always had a soft spot for Phyllis, who was the only reason to watch *Lovejoy* as he constantly tried to get into her pants. And who could blame him? And she always looked especially fetching in jodhpurs. She's a bit worn around the edges now, but is still extremely sexy, and comes across as one of those women who you knew you had no chance with when in her prime, but might be desperate enough now to give you a go. Back to the show: Phyllis is now an embittered uniformed inspector put out to grass at Clerkenwell nick who's having a relationship with the superintendent there. She's on the gin, and her big turn-on is, as she explains to Suchet and the blonde DS, "I like to be tied up and beaten. Everybody likes something." Fair enough Phyllis. Things are looking up. Let's hear more. And we will, but wait up. Meanwhile, Phyllis' elderly mum has been kidnapped and beaten by Valesi, who filmed the scene on his video. And pretty graphic it was too, with urine dripping off her chair. The first mystery is why? The second is where is Valesi keeping mum hidden? And the third, does anyone anywhere believe this tripe?

So starts a manhunt that defies description. First off, a couple of cars are spotted round mum's council estate. A red Cavalier and a blue Range Rover. Valesi demands a ransom, communicating by mobile phone whilst on the move. Cue: a massive screen in the NSC HQ, which at least adds a bit of brightness to the scene, and a breathless chase along motorways and A-roads which culminates in some poor Asian bloke being nicked. Yes, you guessed it. He was driving a red Cavalier and talking on a mobile. Some good shots of a pair of plain clothes police bikers speeding along the M5 or whatever though. It was almost enough to stop you changing the channel. And please tell me why, when the cops go into darkened houses, don't they ever turn on the lights? Don't they know that at shoulder height, usually to the right, is a switch that might help them see? But oh no. It's an excuse to get out the prop torches and fan a bit of smoke about to get that exciting (yawn) *X-Files* atmosphere. Now they've lost him, Valesi demands that Phyllis delivers the dosh. She's wired for sound, with a microphone on her jacket (more of that later) and a tracking device in her bra. A very low-cut black one, which shows off her ample charms a treat, as they'd say in the *Sun*. I'm glad the NSC colour codes their undercover underwear: if Phyllis had been wearing a white blouse, she'd've looked a bit tarty, as my old mum would say, with her undies showing through. More of the black bra later too.

Off she goes, but Valesi is smarter. First of all he makes her take off her jacket, cleverly losing the microphone. And I know what you're going to ask: did she ditch the bra too? No such luck, my smutty friend. Also the bad guy, single-handedly manages to wreck two or three police cars and get clean away with Phyllis as his prisoner, leaving the best looking like the worst. Anyway, for some unknown reason Valesi is a bit of a potholer (no jokes please) and whisks Phyllis off to Wales and into a cave where the only entrance is a small tunnel twelve inches by fifteen. The squad turn up armed to the teeth, but the only casualty is one of the cops who gets shot in the arse. Does this beggar belief or what? When the forces of law and order finally get into the cave, of course the birds have flown – in fact to do over a building society nearby, where it appears from the CCTV footage that Phyllis is a willing accomplice. At this point I must confess my brain began to hurt. And finally, in a twist that defies belief, Valesi and Phyllis book into a motel under his name. Now, I ask you. After fooling the cops for two hours telly time and God knows how long in real time, they use his own name. So the cops come in armed to the teeth again

(personally I wouldn't have trusted any of them with a water pistol) and there's a shoot-out. During which Phyllis grabs a pistol and joins in the fun. Valesi is hit three or four times and Phyllis finishes him off with one between the eyes. The denouement is that she's charged with murder and the NSC heads home. In a postscript, just to add to the confusion, the bra appears again over Phyllis' heaving breasts as we have a flashback to Valesi giving her a good beating back at the cave. Of course she bleats: "He only did it because he loved me." Women! What are they like? Unbelievable? I'll say so. And by the time you read this it'll probably have gone to a series. Who commissions this stuff? Who writes it? Not that it's the worst crime show on TV. I think *Midsomer Murders* takes that prize. And they bloody well took *Sharman* off.

Timlin's Top Tips

Forty Words For Sorrow by Giles Blunt (HarperCollins)

Icarus by Russell Andrews (Little, Brown)

The Falls by Ian Rankin (Orion)

Mystic River by Dennis Lehane (Bantam)

Six Days by Brendan Dubois (Little, Brown)

Hard Landing by Lynne Heitman (Little, Brown)

Outcast by Jose Latour (HarperCollins)

Tell No One by Harlen Coben (Orion)

THE VERDICT

Icarus by Russell Andrews
Little, Brown, £9.99, 0 316 8574 8
Thriller addicts (and which of us aren't these days?) quickly learn to identify the various styles used by top practitioners: floridly written, penetrating psychological studies and pared-down, kinetic action epics being the two principal prototypes. With *Icarus*, Russell Andrews has subtly created a new genre. His previous novel *Gideon* marked him out as a

writer of sharply individual style, and his quirky, idiosyncratic use of language is further developed in the new book. Jack Keller is opening a new restaurant when a bungled burglary leaves his wife dead and Jack bleeding from bullet wounds. Andrews takes us through his slow and painful process of recovery (and is particularly good on the transformation from self-lacerating victim to functioning human being). This transformation is effected by Kid, a young man who Jack once regarded as a surrogate son, and has now become a physiotherapist. But Kid is also found dead, and Jack finds it impossible to believe that it was suicide or accident. Those who've read Raymond Chandler (in which two seemingly unrelated plots invariably converge) will not be surprised to learn that the murder of Jack's wife was the engine for all that followed. If the considerable length of the novel is slightly more than Andrews' plot can bear, few readers will fail to be gripped throughout.

Eve Tan Gee

Blink by Andrea Badenoch
Macmillan, £10, 0 333 90218 1
It's 1962. As the Cuban Missile Crisis unfolds, twelve-year-old Kathleen starts putting childish things behind her. This is difficult in

a part of County Durham continually looking to the past, where keeping up appearances seems to mean everything. Then
Kathleen's Auntie Gloria is found drowned
in Jinny Hoolets, a stinking pond that apparently infects the entire pit village with its
gloom. As the repercussions are felt
throughout her unconventional family,
Kathleen suspects foul play. According to
villagers like Nana, Gloria's modern ways –
self-employment, love affairs, fashion sense
– mean that she brought it on herself.
Accompanied by Nosey, her faithful Jack
Russell terrier, Kathleen's investigations
bring matters to a head within a week.

If this sounds like a trip into Enid Blyton's
home terrain, then don't be fooled. Kathleen's life and her brief foray into detective
work make for a plausible read. And when
the time comes to rely on grown-up law
enforcers, this is precisely what Badenoch
does, blending realism with a grim tension.

Even the gothic Koninsky family, shunned
by the villagers for being almost as unre-
spectable as Kathleen's kin, can be understood against the peculiar historical
backdrop. This is the great strength of *Blink*:
the way it works as recent historical fiction,
richly conjuring up the texture of a society
entrenched in pre-war morality, where
everyone knew their lot in life and ambition
was 'not for the likes of us'. It's a timely
reminder that, outside London, the swinging sixties often took an extra decade or
two to even partially materialise.

Purists and trivia brains might quibble
over some of the details. For instance,
would TV-less children be referring to Petra
the Blue Peter dog at the outset of said
canine's broadcasting career? (Real obscurity
merchants might even allude to Valerie Sin-
gleton's spin doctoring of the moment
when the first Petra puppy expired within
weeks of being adopted: perhaps Kathleen
could investigate this mystery in a future
novel.) But this would be to miss the point.
Blink shows Badenoch using the crime genre
to recreate an authentic snapshot of particular moods and moments sometime last
century, bringing the narrow-minded and
nasty underbelly of provincial Britain to life.
From here it's twelve years and a two-hour
drive south to the adult world of David
Peace's *1974*.

Graham Barnfield

Black Cat by Martyn Bedford
Penguin, £5.99, 0 140 27289 5
Martyn Bedford has always done his best to
steer the psychological thriller down previously uncharted back streets. His previous
book, *The Houdini Girl*, combined magic
and murder to great effect and garnered

OUT ON THE MOORS,
THE HUNT HAS BEGUN...

MARTYN BEDFORD

BLACK
CAT.

rave reviews in the process. The follow-up, *Black Cat*, attempts to blend the same elements in a genre-splicing mix of psychic powers and big game hunting on remote moorland. Chloe is a dowser, Ethan is obsessed with finding the legendary black cat. Both are on the margins of society and both are drawn to each other as they join forces to lure the beast out of hiding.

Of course with Bedford it isn't as simple as that. Just when you think you know where he's taking you, he drops in references to UFOs, the Hound of the Baskervilles and the strange power of standing stones. The overall impression is of a haunted, magical landscape that somehow exists in a separate dimension to the outside world. It echoes nicely the main characters' dislocation from reality, and provides the perfect backdrop to their self-destructive relationship of obses-

sion and jealousy. But anyone looking for a linear narrative is going to be disappointed – at the end of the day, Bedford is more concerned with painting mind-pictures than in constructing an easily navigable thriller. Read it for the outstanding prose though; it often has the ring of poetry.

Mark Campbell

Purple Cane Road by James Lee Burke
Orion, £5.99, 0 75284 334 6
It only takes two pages to transport us back to pre Civil War times. In Dave Robichaux's Louisiana there are always dark secrets buried beneath the soft bayou mud. Letty Labiche murdered Vachel Carmouche, the state executioner and a sort of Fred Leuchter character who, Dave suspected, abused Letty and her twin sister Passion. Letty is due to be executed, and Governor Pugh, who could offer her a pardon or commutation, is, like just about everyone else in Louisiana, an old school friend of Dave's. The Labiche execution, however, soon drags Dave into a much deeper and darker sort of swamp; the unsolved murder of his mother, found face down in a puddle outside a honky-tonk.

What is it with detectives and their mothers? Ellroy, Michael Connelly's Harry Bosch, and now Dave, all with mothers on the fringes of respectable society, all murdered with impunity. The upside of Dave's own mother being involved is that for once Dave gets a little more physically involved in the investigation. Likewise, a parallel story involving Dave's daughter Alafair with a hitman also helps shake our hero out of his permanent mood of contemplation. This is good, because much of *Purple Cane Road*, like so many Robichaux books, involves a lot of Dave driving back and forth to New Orleans (is it really two and a half hours each way? That's five hours per jaunt!) while he mulls the evils of the world, which are not oft interred with his ancestors bones. Or else he mulls Vietnam, not oft ditto. Of course, in the *Tale of Two Cities* context of this novel, all that commuting may have more relevance.

Meanwhile, Alafair's maturity reminds us that Dave and Clete are getting old, though Passion Labiche (now is that a name that keys a character or what?) doesn't seem to notice or care that Clete is twice her age, overweight and alcoholic. And with murders to solve and prevent, Dave as usual patrols the bayous, coming down hard on the scourges of society, like hitting a child, drinking while driving, or speaking to women in politically incorrect terms. Someday someone will sit in the no-smoking section of a juke joint and blow smoke Dave's way and he'll blow them away!

As ever, Burke writes a dense gothic swamp to entangle his characters. I just wish they cut their way through it with more energy.

Michael Carlson

Crime Time Capsule Comments

Vic Buckner, Ingrid Yornstrand, Barry Forshaw

Build My Gallows High (Prion) is Geoffrey Homes' definitive novel of crime and obsessive love, memorably filmed by Jacques Tourneur with Robert Mitchum. It's often a disappointment to go back to original film noir source novels and discover they were mere blueprints for more atmospheric movies. But it's not the case here, and Homes' tale of retired private eye Red Bailey sinking into a morass of sexual betrayal is quite as riveting as the famous movie.

Still with crime, **Forty Words For Sorrow** (HarperCollins) is a powerful psychological thriller by Giles Blunt in which four teenagers go missing in a small town. The police are prepared to give up the investigation, and only detective John Cardinal is willing to risk his career to find the truth – while confronting the dark secret in his own past. Elegantly written and carefully structured.

Henning Mankell has achieved a considerable reputation as the prime exponent of the tough European police procedural, and the two new books, **The Fifth Woman** and **Sidetracked** (both Harvill), will consolidate his reputation in this country. All the police procedural aspects, are, of course handled with total aplomb, but it's the effortless creation of atmosphere that really distinguishes his writing. Inspector Kurt Wallander, too, is a solid protagonist, and the elegant prose effortlessly distinguishes the book from many entries in the genre.

Gareth Joseph's antihero in **Homegrown** (Headline) is a small-town criminal trying to stay out of trouble. Needless to say (we've all read versions of this tale before), his attempts to stay on the straight and narrow are doomed to failure. Familiar material, perhaps, but handled with some style by a accomplished writer.

As a piece of historical detection, Jane Stevenson's **London Bridges** (Vintage) is exemplary, but perhaps its real appeal lies in its picture of the old city, which is conjured with breathtaking skill. Witty and erudite, this is highly entertaining stuff.

Michel Spring is noted for utilising elements of her own experience, and apparently **In the Midnight Hour** (Orion) is in that tradition. She remains one of the most accomplished writers around, and this tale of dangerous family bonds is handled with considerable skill.

Christopher Brookmyre, Britain's Carl Hiaasen, demonstrates his customary sardonic wit in **Boiling a Frog** (Little, Brown), a sharp-edged tale that is as much a demolition of the Catholic Church as it is a witty and inventive thriller.

The central character in **People Die** (Flame) by Kevin Wignal is a professional cleaner, ie a hitman. After a slip, he finds himself the target. This is spare, evocative stuff and an inventive new spin on the hitman genre.

As Eurothrillers thrillers go, Juliet Hebden's is one of the most impressive series around. **Pel and the Butcher's Blade** (Constable Robinson) is well up to par: a torso is discovered that has Pel dealing with a gruesome murder with no clue to the victim's identity.

Leonardo Sciascia has been described as a master of sophisticated detective fiction, but his tales in **The Wine Dark Sea** (Granta) are essentially brief and haunting stories of human nature, written with a genuinely evocative and clear-eyed vision; the undercurrents of human behaviour have rarely been explored with such intelligence.

A Citizen of the Country (Arrow) by Sarah Smith has been described as an amalgam of Poe, Agatha Christie, *A Tale of Two Cities* and *Chinatown*, which is a shrewd estimate of its appeal. Highly entertaining, this is a rich and heady brew indeed.

Chris Mooney's **Deviant Ways** (Simon & Schuster) is an unnerving picture of human evil, in which a patient escapes from the FBI's top secret (and highly controversial) Behaviour Modification programme, with bloody results. Plausibility is a strong suit in this impressive piece.

The small-town setting may be familiar in Janie Bolitho's **Plotted in Cornwall** (Constable), but it has rarely been handled with such skill as in this sharply-written tale of grim family secrets.

Jeff Gulvin is noted for his immense knowledge of anti-terrorist and firearms squads, and that research pays off in **The Covenant** (Orion), a thriller that screws the tension up to maximum effect.

The classic detective story is in good hands with Elizabeth George's **A Traitor to Memory** (Hodder), an absorbing and polished piece of work from a writer whose skills rarely fail her.

The usual acute sense of place distinguishes this latest entry from Bill Pronzini, with the moody landscape mirroring the dark universe of the protagonists. Long acclaimed in the States, **Blue Lonseome** (Canongate) is a novel that may thoroughly establish Pronzini in the UK – a long overdue turn of events.

In **Death in the South of France** (Allison & Busby) by Jane Jakeman, a gruesome discovery in a boulevard on the French Riviera establishes a murder inquiry. A series of mutilated bodies begin to turn up on the seafront, and the newly arrived young magistrate Cecile Galant finds herself in charge of a murder investigation that soon has her out of her depth. Strongly written and powerfully plotted.

Laurie R. King has been likened to P. D. James, and the comparison is not fanciful. On a lonely island off the northwest coast of America, a young woman in working on

a ruined folly. A discovery in the foundations leads to danger. **Folly** (HarperCollins)
is as absorbing as all of King's work.

One of the supreme stylists in the English
language, **Loving Monsters** (Granta)
shows James Hamilton-Paterson at his penetrating best, with layer upon layer of human
psychology peeled way in his most acute
and richly-textured fashion.

Wit is the order of the day in **The Bur-
glar King** (Serpent's Tail) by Danny King,
with a bristlingly funny narrative dispatched
with real panache by a skilled writer.

The author Perri Shaughnessy is actually
a portmanteau name for two sisters, and
Move to Strike (Piatkus) is an adeptly written thriller with a skilfully handled ration of
legal detail; characterisation, too, is handled
with real style.

Her car breaks down on this road
Then she's arrested for murder . . .

BLOOD
JUNCTION
CAROLINE CARVER

Blood Junction by Caroline Carver
*Orion, £16.99 hb / £9.99 pb, 0 7528 3846 6/0
7528 3847 4*
The dust and heat of the Australian outback
feature strongly in *Blood Junction*, as do
Aboriginal dispossession, casual racism and
petty prejudice. India Kane goes to Cooinda
hoping to find her last remaining relative,
and gets much more than she bargained for.
Physically, she is the perfect heroine (tall,
long-legged, beautiful), but India is not an
easy woman to like, for she is also hard-
nosed, argumentative and waspish. She is
wary of allowing people to get close to her,
and the only person who really knows the
vulnerable, warm woman beneath the brash
exterior is her childhood friend, Lauren.
Despite her less attractive traits, India has a
redeeming feature: she is loyal to the point
of lunacy – in the direst circumstances,
where most would turn and flee, India is
determined to 'tough it out'. Which is just
as well, since on her arrival in Cooinda she is
first pursued by a lynch mob and then
arrested for a double murder. India finds
herself part of a dangerous investigation –
one that has already resulted in several
deaths – cut off from her friends and with
only one Aboriginal policeman who believes
in her innocence.

The sudden shift from India's point of
view to Mikey the Knife's in Chapter Ten is
disconcerting, and from here on in, we get
glimpses of insight into various characters'
thoughts. But this aside, *Blood Junction* is a
thriller that keeps the pages turning. The
developing relationship between India and
Polly, an Aboriginal girl, is engaging without being over-sentimental, and Carver
keeps up a cracking pace, with a high body
count and plenty of incident. India Kane is

gorgeous, fallible and flawed – in short an interesting series character.

Margaret Murphy

Adios Muchachos by Daniel Chavarría (translated by Carlos Lopez)
Akashic Books, $13.95, 1 888451 16 5
Following the success of *Outcast* by Jose Latour, Akashic presents the second in a line of Cuban noir, straight outta Havana. The first suspense novel in English translation by internationally acclaimed Uruguayan mystery writer Daniel Chavarría, *Adios Muchachos* is a dark, erotic, brutally funny romp through the sexual underworld and black market boardrooms of post-Cold War Cuba. Seen through Chavarría's compassionate but uncompromising eyes, present-day Havana is a crossroads for petty hustlers looking for an easy mark, two-time losers looking for a fresh start, and

"Daniel Chavarría has long been recognized as one of Latin America's finest writers. Now he's about a mess why ..." — Edgar Award-winning author Willard Roffer son

high-rolling international speculators looking to take advantage of them all.

The novel describes the ill-fated alliance between Alicia, a stunningly beautiful prostitute who openly displays her voluptuous wares on the city streets, and Victor King, a desperately ambitious Canadian businessman with an enormous appetite for kinky sex and buried treasure – and a striking resemblance to Mel Gibson. Following an early erotic entanglement of their own, Victor hires Alicia to lure a series of handsome lovers into the bedroom of his estate for the voyeuristic gratification of his mysterious wife, Elizabeth, who watches the action with her husband through a two-way mirror. After a sultry drunken dance results in the accidental death of Victor's wealthy Dutch business partner, Rieks Groote, Victor sees his ambitions for wealth suddenly go up in smoke and Alicia faces the end of her dreams of escaping her dreary, dead-end life on the island.

Hustlers all the way, the two quickly decide to turn disaster into opportunity, hiding the body in a freezer and hatching an elaborate kidnapping scheme that will allow them to steal millions of dollars from the Groote family and start a new life together off the island. Through a series of startling plot twists and slapstick misadventures, Victor and Alicia find themselves unwittingly manipulated and ultimately outmanoeuvred by a sympathetic fellow hustler. In the end, everything revolves around the secret ingredient to an old family recipe and a long-overdue nose job – and only one of the novel's characters is able to make off with the loot and bid adios to Cuba and the past.

Vic Buckner

Darkest Fear by Harlan Coben
New English Library, £6.99, 0 340 76763 4
With each new novel, Harlan Coben seems to find more hard edges for his sports agent-cum-detective, Myron Bolitar. Although the cracking remains wise to the point of adolescent yuk, the reliance on both the sideshow of female wrestlers and the deus ex preppie-killing machina that is Myron's roommate Win has been reduced. In the process, the secret agent background of the two men has virtually disappeared. What this does is to put the emphasis firmly on Myron himself. In *Darkest Fear* even Myron's business has disappeared into the background, though the story begins with Myron learning he is the real father of the child his former sweetheart had with his basketballing arch-enemy (who has figured in a previous book). From that point onwards, however, as Myron launches a search to find the missing bone-marrow donor who might save his son's life,

the real focus of the novel is Myron's own character. He is forced to confront his own romantic preconceptions, his own idealised morality, and, eventually, to face the idea of maturing.

Crack open another YooHoo bottle, because Coben somehow manages to do all this while still moving things along briskly through enough comedy and action to fill a couple of less polished books. Still, for all the glitz, Coben seems to be steadily approaching Ross MacDonald. He's far more focused on Bolitar's character than MacDonald ever was on Lew Archer's, which allowed Archer to be far more acute in his portrayal of other people and they way they moved through society. But in his ability to make the past (especially the familial past) come back to impact and haunt the present, Coben reminds me of MacDonald at his best. His next book will be outside the Bolitar series, and it will be fascinating to see what he does with the freedom this provides.

Michael Carlson

The Killing Kind by John Connolly
Hodder & Stoughton, £12.99, 0 340 77120 8
In this exceptional novel, the discovery of a mass grave in northern Maine answers a question raised in the postgraduate thesis of Grace Peltier, former lover of private investigator, Charlie 'Bird' Parker, and now a murder victim: "What became of the families who, almost forty years ago, sold everything they owned, followed the charismatic Reverend Faulkner into the wilderness, then disappeared?" Grace Peltier was descended from one of the families that followed Reverend Faulkner into the wilderness. Initially, she believed that Faulkner disappeared along with his disciples, but as it becomes

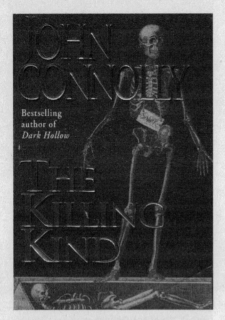

obvious that he is still alive, it also becomes obvious that he will stop at nothing to prevent anyone from discovering the true purpose of the religious organisation called The Fellowship. *The Killing Kind* is a worthy successor to Connelly's first two novels. It is equally compelling, not merely because the themes he has chosen to explore are unusual, or because his characters and the situations in which they find themselves are emotionally complex, but because a core of compassion runs through his work which is, at all times, literate and beautifully constructed.

J. Wallis Martin

Crimewave 3: Burning Down the House / Crimewave 4: Mood Indigo
edited by Andy Cox
TTA Press, £5.99, 0 9526947 3 5/4 3
"Crimewave's mission is nothing less than the total re-creation of crime fiction. We don't do cosy, we don't do hardboiled, we don't do noir… what we do is something entirely different to whatever you've read before". I like a good manifesto and I like *Crimewave*. It sets about its business well, and in doing so showcases a lot of talented new writers. Both these editions are worth a look. Generally the standard is high, although the usual range of not-so-good to very good is in evidence. Writers include Chaz Benchley, John Moralee, Patricia Tyrrell, Brain Hodge, Sean Doolittle and Marion Arnott. There is a good spread of international writers here and my guess is that there are more than a few future 'names' featured. *Crimewave 4* is worth getting for Anthony Mann's *Shopping* alone. Overall *Crimewave's* policy of showcasing new writers – along with a few established names – doesn't mean that style and quality have been sacrificed. It's also worth saying that the way the magazine is produced is excellent. The illustrations and artwork are very good and these things count. There are also a few good reader offers. Both clock in at around 130 pages, which also makes them very good value. My advice: give them a try.

Peter Walker

Big Sky by Gareth Creer
Doubleday, £9.99, 0 385 60230 8
Gareth Creer's first novel, *Skin and Bone*, was an accomplished debut. Combining raw brutality with a sanguine, almost archaic, poeticism, the Salford-born author pumped new life into the jaded urban thriller. *Cradle to Grave* upped the ante, soaking the prose in an explosive mixture of broiling hedonism and domestic dysfunctionalism. With his third novel, *Big Sky*, Creer has done it again. The protagonist this time is Jimmy

Fred & Edie by Jill Dawson
Sceptre, £14.99

In his 1946 essay 'Decline of the English Murder', George Orwell listed nine cases epitomising what he called our Elizabethan period of murders, a golden age of English homicide from 1850 to 1925. They occurred in a society where respectability was the next best thing to God, and where adultery was the next best thing to murder. Jill Dawson's third novel, shortlisted for the Whitbread, deals with the most recent of these classic cases – the murder of Percy Thompson, for which his wife Edith and her lover Fred Bywaters were hanged in January 1923. Her narrative moves from arrest to execution, while Edith in her cell revisits in memory both her affair and the events leading up to the murder. Most of the material is in the form of fictionalised letters from

Mack, a mute wideboy who's had enough of his turf on the north-east coast of England and wants to seek anonymity in Spain. But somehow he's got to save Angela, the love of his life, from a fate worse than death. And the only way he can do it is by pulling off one last job. One last *big* job. Creer's prose is electric as well as eclectic. He pulls aphorisms from the ether and twists metaphors like a magician. The language is at times so dense and unconventional that you find yourself re-reading great chunks to fully appreciate the cadence. Mack is the perfect conduit for Creer's rule-bending narrative – a character who internalises his emotions, painstakingly describing his thoughts and feelings without recourse to speech. Without a doubt, *Big Sky* is literate British crime writing at its best.

Mark Campbell

Edith to Fred. But Dawson also draws on contemporary sources, especially extracts from newspapers busily conducting a trial by media, 1920s-style.

Mr and Mrs Thompson lived in suburban comfort in Ilford, Essex, and worked in the City – he was a bookkeeper, and she managed a wholesale milliner's. There were no children. In 1921, when Edith was twenty-seven, she met Bywaters, a good-looking ship's steward just short of his nineteenth birthday, who was a friend of Edith's young sister. Bywaters briefly became the Thompsons' lodger, and soon a volatile three-cornered relationship developed. Fred and Edith launched themselves into an affair. Percy refused to sanction a divorce. During Fred's voyages, Edith wrote him a stream of letters. In October 1922, as the Thompsons were returning from the theatre, Fred attacked his rival with a sheath knife. A few minutes later, Percy drowned in his own blood. Both Fred and Edith were charged with his murder.

So far so nasty. Soon it was even nastier. There has never been any doubt that Fred killed Percy. But was the crime premeditated? Did Edith urge her lover to attack his rival? The court case turned on Edith's love letters to Fred. (Most of his letters to her had not survived.) In a sense, the trial legitimised the public's prurient curiosity about the affair. Edith made matters worse by going on the witness stand herself. The defence had another problem. Not only did the letters reveal Edith as an enthusiastic adulteress, they also included sinister references to poisons and other matters which significantly supported the case for premeditation. Edith and her lawyers knew that these references related, at least in part, to illegal abortions. But explaining this to a 1922 jury, while the press bayed its outrage outside the Old Bailey, was unlikely to do the defendant anything but harm.

Both Edith and Fred went to the gallows. (Her executioner later committed suicide.) There is even a possibility that she was pregnant when she died. If this had been established, she would automatically have been reprieved. Part of her Home Office file is sealed until 2022. Jill Dawson uses this rich material to construct a powerful novel which throws a harsh light not so much on Edith Thompson as on the society which judged her and found her wanting. Everything from the prison routine to the underclothing has an air of authenticity. Here is a world that frowned on women going out to work and on women failing to produce children. It reserved far worse treatment for women who looked for love outside marriage or sought out desperate remedies to deal with unwanted pregnancies. Part of the book's strength lies in the fact that Dawson does not sanitise her protagonist. Edith loathed her husband and certainly fantasised about killing both him and herself. To a large extent her words and actions must have provided the trigger that pushed Fred into committing murder. Edith was inconsistent, too. It is difficult to read her letters – both real and fictional– without feeling that she played a dangerous game with the two men in her life, setting one against the other. Part of her clearly relished the villa in Ilford, the fur coat and the cups of tea at the Café Royal. Would she ever have given up the comforts of her life with Percy Thompson? But wanting to have one's cake and eat it too is not a capital crime. On one level, of course, the fictional Edith is inevitably a figure of fantasy, implausibly articulate and self-analytical. But that does not detract from Jill Dawson's achievement. Whether Edith Thompson was guilty or not, this excellent novel makes us realise, she was tried – and condemned – as much for adultery as for murder.

Andrew Taylor

The Blue Nowhere by Jeffrey Deaver
Hodder, £14.99, 0 340 7650 2
Some authors are content to plough the same furrow for most of their working lives, while others need the recharging of batteries that a totally fresh approach brings. Jeffrey Deaver is clearly in the latter camp, for despite the success of such Lincoln Rhyme books as *The Devil's Teardrop*, his new thriller moves off in a very surprising direction, with little of the Doyle-in-the-twentieth-century approach of its predecessors. He has pulled off the considerable coup of introducing two distinctive new heroes: Frank Bishop (a flawed but ruthlessly effective cop) and his reluctant associate, Wyatt Gillette, a highly talented young computer hacker released from prison to help Frank track down that most topical of modern criminals, the überhacker. The villain in this one is a kind of online Hannibal Lecter, a criminal genius (without the taste for fava beans) whose trawling off and on the net allows him to follow every move and detail of a victim's life before moving in for the kill. Recently, authors such as Patricia Cornwell have come adrift when trying to create a fresh formula for their books, but Deaver writes as if the prose in *The Blue Nowhere* had been his house-style all along. Working against the considerable disadvantage of an online villain (Deaver really has to work

hard to make him truly sinister), he has created a high-tech thriller that suggests he need never go back to his Lincoln Rhyme books. But he probably will...

Judith Gray

Flint by Paul Eddy
Headline, £10, 0 7472 7114 3
Paul Eddy knows all there is to know about espionage and terrorism. What he does not know is how to write a decent thriller. *Flint* is the sort of book in which the prose is nothing more than a glorified film script. Characterisation, motivation and exposition tend to be missing from film scripts – you just get dialogue and the odd line of description. The visuals are the film's *raison d'être*. But with *Flint* we don't have the luxury of a $50m budget or the talents of Hollywood's A list. We've just got the words. And sorry, but these words just ain't

enough. *Flint* is about a woman's quest for revenge against a man who violently assaulted her. Against that premise, we have a whole bunch of faceless men and woman – referred to only by their surnames, it's *that* sort of book – who work for a variety of faceless organisations. Eddy's narrative jumps uneasily between them all, never sure who it should be following. Flint herself – the best character in the book – barely gets a look-in. Instead the author focuses on Harry Cohen, the man sent to find her: a man who, it must be said, is the dictionary definition of banality. Don't get me wrong – there are moments of tension, even the odd moment of excitement. And if you can follow the complexities of the poorly explained plot you might actually understand what's going on. But for me, I found this particular thriller far from thrilling.

Mark Campbell

And a second view...

Lauded with praise by no less than Frederick Forsyth, *Flint* is a debut thriller of real achievement, with Paul Eddy immediately registering as an authoritative and skilful writer. His publishers invoke Clarice Starling and Kay Scarpetta to persuade us to read the book, but such comparisons are unnecessary (except perhaps as a marketing imperative): the eponymous Grace Flint is a strongly drawn heroine – a resourceful and quick-thinking undercover cop. During an operation to ensnare vicious money launderer Frank Harling, things go pear-shaped and Grace finds herself under attack by a dangerous psychotic, leaving her scarred. Fighting the trauma, Grace undergoes surgery to restore her former looks, but she is unable to dissuade her masters from their idea that her personality has been similarly mutilated. But her speciality has always been placing herself in the utmost danger, and she insists on being back in the firing line, tracking down the man who attempted to destroy her. But will she come apart, as her bosses in the force fear? Paul Eddy is fully aware that the very best thrillers establish an inexorable conflict in their protagonists, one that needs to be just as forcefully handled as the mechanics of the plot. And we are made to care quite as much about Grace's state of mind as we are about the tracking-down-a-monster narrative. Eddy has a particular gift for the truly arresting image

Vic Buckner

The Cold Six Thousand by James Ellroy
Century, £16.99, 0 712 68976 1
James Ellroy's last novel, *American Tabloid*, ended as JFK was assassinated in Dealey Plaza. This one begins just before, with Vegas cop Wayne Tedrow Jr heading for Dallas to assassinate an uppity black pimp who has pissed off the mob. Wayne finds himself in the middle of the assassination cover-up and Jack Ruby's killing of Lee Oswald, engineered by the characters returning from *Tabloid*: Ward Littel, the Jesuitical ex-FBI man, and Pete Bondurant, the all-purpose muscle with few scruples but with a passionate devotion to the anti-Castro cause. Ellroy picks up the story *in media res*, running on all cylinders, and doesn't lift the pedal from the metal until the final page, by which time both Martin Luther King and Bobby Kennedy are likewise dead, ostensibly by 'lone crazed assassins'. He pulls out all the stops, working in a manic, three-

beat prose that drives the story at a furious pace. Ellroy kicks ass. Ellroy takes no prisoners. Ellroy's talking just the facts, ma'am. It's simple / repetitive / pounding. It demands. It infuriates. It's loaded with personal jokes and ticks many readers won't get. It reads like Ellroy's first-draft of *Finnegans Wake*. But it works.

In *American Tabloid* Ellroy introduced a triumvirate of characters, but CIA man Kemper Boyd was caught scamming and killed. Tedrow, whose father is a power in Las Vegas and in racist circles, actually sends him to Dallas because he knows the hit on 'Bad Back Jack' is about to take place. But Tedrow's encounter with the fugitive pimp sets off a trail of tragic murder, which pulls Wayne Jr deeper and deeper into the conspiracies. He winds up refining heroin in Vietnam, ostensibly to be used only in the Negro areas of America, and winds up with his burgeoning personal race hatred placing him at the site of the King shooting, where Jimmy Ray pulls the trigger alright, crazed but by no means alone. For Ellroy, the links of the conspiracy revolve around the Mafia and money, and the personal greeds of his characters reflect in what becomes public policy. Littel, a study in contradictions, who funnels money to King's cause by ripping off the Mob, the drug-addled Howard Hughes and the FBI, eventually finds himself inextricably drawn into the assassination of his idol, RFK, a fate he finds himself unable to accept. Bondurant, the true believer in the anti-Commie cause, is likewise disillusioned. His fervour has been used to indulge in drug and gun smuggling, whose aims are building a haven for the Mob under the cover of Hughes' money in Vegas, and keeping dissent at bay. Substitute Nicaragua for Cuba,

and you have the story of Reagan, Bush, Ollie North and the whole of the 1980s drug plague. The only question is why anyone doubts that this is how power does business. Presiding over all this is J Edgar Hoover, who starts like an evil Buddha, but as the book pounds on morphs into a kind of campy light relief. You half expect to hear him say 'okey dokey'. And lurking in the background, brought to the fore by the Mormon / Hughes / Vegas link, is the creepoid shadow of Richard Milhous Nixon himself, who will presumably star in the third volume of this shadow history of our most turbulent times. Tricky Dick and the Demon Dog, together at last. I can't wait.

Michael Carlson

The Red Room by Nicci French
Michael Joseph, £16.99, 0 7181 4387 6
Many are the writers who tackle the field of the psychological thriller, but few create such a dark and compelling world as Nicci French. Her latest novel, *The Red Room*, inhabits the same sinister universe as such previous thrillers as *The Memory Game* and the book that many consider to be her finest to date, *Killing Me Softly*. French is concerned with the unstable surface of reality and the malign undercurrents of human behaviour forever threatening to disrupt the tenuous happiness of her characters. In this new book, her particular priority is the queasy attraction of the forbidden and the terrifying. Kit Quinn has a job that many would find too disturbing to tackle. Her beat is the world of crime scenes, hospitals for the criminally insane, the grimmer prisons. In her latest assignment, colleagues in the police ask for her help in what initially appears to be a straightforward murder

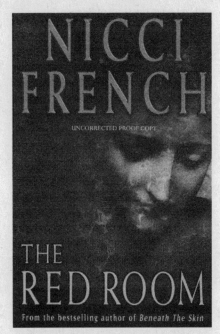

ary dangerous voyage to the centre of a mystery that is par for the course for the genre, but this is also a study of the troubled psyche of a damaged heroine, and her dark world view.

Brian Ritterspak

Of Tender Sin by David Goodis
Serpents Tail, £6.99, 1 85242 674 8
This would have been considered risqué when it was written nearly fifty years ago, during the boring Eisenhower years, but will it still appeal today? Serpents Tail have also published Goodis's *The Moon in the Gutter* and *The Blonde at the Street Corner*. Goodis's first crime novel – *Dark Passage* – was serialised in the Saturday Evening Post and made into a Bogart and Bacall film by Warner Brothers. At the end of his life he would sue the producers of the TV serial, *The Fugi-*

inquiry, in which a youthful runaway has been killed near a London canal. At first, the evidence points to the killer being a man who wounded the murdered young woman, but Kit has learned that the appearance of things in a deceptive world may not be trusted. As she descends deeper and deeper into a brutal underworld of lost and exploited youngsters, she finds herself as at risk as the young victims she is dealing with. What makes this more than a conventional thriller is the author's fastidious examination of her heroine's tortured psyche: Kate has suffered terrible wounds in a savage attack, and there is something unhealthy about her immersion in the kind of life that left her with terrible scars. French is particularly sharp on her efforts to push her life back into some kind of conventional order. *The Red Room* has the custom-

tive, for plagiarising it. After *Dark Passage* he became a screenwriter in Hollywood for a few years, before returning to his home town of Philadelphia to write novels. His work was kept alive by the French Serie Noir imprint in the 1960s and 1970s. He died in 1967 aged fifty.

The story takes second place to an introspective account of the psychological despair and decline of insurance clerk, Alvin Darby, down among the lowlifes on the streets of Philadelphia. "He tasted the mixture. The perfect blending had erased the individual flavour of snuff and aspirin and cola, to make the total a strange taste that couldn't be classified. He sipped the stuff and went on sipping it, and some minutes later he began to hear the liquid melody of a newly invented stringed instrument. The strings were made of velvet." Alvin's wanderings include philosophical exchanges with his co-worker Harry Clawson, with a 'heavy-set man' in a café, a cabbie, and street people like Woodrow and the thieves Rook and Chango. But his dialogue seems stilted and the action may seem bizarre, puzzling and incomplete to many. The world has moved on and there is a different madness now and the reading public knows other realist and 'absurd' writers. There are parallels with the work of Jim Thompson and Cornell Woolrich, but it definitely lacks the insight and black humour of the more socially aware, noir novels of Chester Himes and Charles Willeford. Carson McCullers was a precise contemporary of Goodis, having been born and died in the same years. Though not a crime writer, her introspective and many layered novels are finding new interest. Goodis will have a more limited appeal.

Martin Spellman

The Treatment by Mo Hayder
Bantam, £9.99, 0 5930 4542 4

Success was something of a double-edged sword for Mo Hayder with her début novel *Birdman*: the book enjoyed astonishing success, but called down a fearsome wrath on the author for unflinchingly entering the blood-boltered territory of Thomas Harris' Hannibal books. Part of the fuss was clearly to do with the fact that a woman writer had handled scenes of horror and violence so authoritatively, and there's little doubt that *The Treatment* will provoke a similar furore. Actually, it's a remarkably vivid and meticulously detailed shocker: less grimly compelling than its predecessor, perhaps, but still a world away from the cosy reassurance of most current crime fiction. In a shady south London residential street, a husband and wife are found tied up, the man near

death. Both have been beaten and are suffering from acute dehydration. DI Jack Cafferey of the Met's murder squad AMIP is told to investigate the disappearance of the couple's son, and as he uncovers a series of dark parallels with his own life, he finds it more and more difficult to make the tough decisions necessary to crack a scarifying case. As in *Birdman*, Cafferey is characterised with particular skill, and Hayder is able (for the most part) to make us forget the very familiar cloth he's cut from. The personal involvement of a copper in a grim case is an over-familiar theme, but it's rarely been dispatched with the panache and vividness on display here. Hayder will be able to shrug off the inevitable criticism when this one makes its mark – as it will.

Judith Gray

Hell's Kitchen by Chris Niles
Pan, £5.99, 0 330 48292 0
Gus and Susie Neidermeyer, a pair of innocent newly-weds newly arrived from Michigan, are excited about their move to the Big Apple and are hunting for their dream loft. Unfortunately for them, the sublet market can be lethal, as they discover when they unwittingly arrange to see a property owned by Cyrus Tower, millionaire playboy and deranged would-be serial killer. However, Cyrus's plans to achieve ultimate self-awareness and control of his life via serial murder are threatened by the arrival in New York of Marion Neidermeyer, a mother determined to find out what happened to her son with the help of Catrina Vermont, an ambitious television reporter. Also on the scene are Tye Fisher, a gorgeous young English ex-pat out on her ear after her lover's wife unexpectedly returns home and relying on her looks to land her a place to stay, and William Quinn, a would-be writer suffering serious block and severe housing problems. Together, they're on a collision course with Cyrus's grand plan for self-fulfilment.

Hell's Kitchen is a highly enjoyable black comedy about the perils of the Manhattan housing market, capturing the slightly deranged atmosphere of the Manhattan scene. The ensemble cast plays together well, and all the protagonists are well-rounded, interesting people, though sometimes the lack of a focus detracts from the flow of the book. Also, the climax comes rather rapidly, though it is extremely enjoyable getting there. Cyrus's thoroughly modern serial killer is a nice touch and something different from the usual crop of mini-van driving loners, mainly because of his earnest belief the rightness of his actions, based on a bargain-basement self-help manual. *Hell's Kitchen* is a thoroughly enjoyable read, but don't read it if you're thinking of moving house any time soon...

Dan Staines

Bodies of Evidence by Brian Innes
Readers Digest Association by arrangement with Amber Books, $24.95, 0 76241 029 5
This book is subtitled *The Fascinating World of Forensic Science and How It Helped Solve More Than 100 True Crimes*. And it is fascinating – I've spent the last twenty years reading true crime texts yet this still told me lots of things I didn't know. It's separated into seventeen chapters, such as 'Suicide or Murder', 'Mark of Death' and 'Hanging by a Hair'. Each chapter is richly illustrated with photographs of scientists at work, killers, corpses and their injuries. Author Brian Innes has spent many years writing true

crime manuals and it shows. He explores the science's roots – explaining that forensic merely means connected with the courtroom – and goes on to annotate the many roles of the forensic expert in today's laboratory. He also details how a body is cut up for autopsy, the rate at which bodies decompose, the life of the coffin fly and so on. There are numerous case studies in this large hardback book. This being Readers Digest, the layout is somewhat populist, with the cases being stamped 'Crime Solved'. But this doesn't detract from the sheer weight of facts in Brian Innes' text. Here you can learn about facial reconstruction, how to tell a male from a female skull, and about the origins of toxicology. Or read up on fibres or handwriting analysis and the part they've played in solving vicious deaths. The case files include infamous killers such as Ted Bundy, John Wayne Gacy and the Unabomber, but also less well-known ones like Karen and Michael Diehl. These parents from hell travelled through America on a

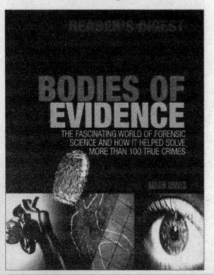

bus with their four natural children and thirteen adopted children. They regularly beat them with a wooden paddle in accordance with their Christian Fundamentalist beliefs. They handcuffed thirteen-year-old Andrew to his bed, naked, every night. They also whipped him. One day Karen 'tapped' him on the head with the paddle – her description. The abused child promptly went into cardiac arrest and soon died. Karen Diehl was charged with involuntary manslaughter and her husband was charged with first degree murder despite their defence asserting that the teenager had merely fallen twice. Although *Bodies of Evidence* is an American book, it is available online from amazon.co.uk for about £17. This volume provides both a first-class read and a true crime research tool. The numerous details about death also make it of interest to horror scribes.

Carol Anne Davis

Death in Holy Orders by P D James
0 571 20752 9
Despite challenges from Ruth Rendell and (more recently) Minette Walters, P D James' position as Britain's Queen of Crime remains largely unassailed. Although a certain reaction has set in to her reputation (and there are those who claim her poetry-loving copper Dalgleish doesn't correspond to any of his counterparts in the real world), her detractors can scarcely deny her astonishing literary gifts. More than any other writer, she has elevated the detective story into the realms of literature, with the psychology of the characters treated in the most complex and authoritative fashion. Her plots, too, are full of intriguing detail and studied with brilliantly observed character studies. Who

cares if Dalgleish belongs more in the pages of a book than poking around a graffiti-scrawled council estate? As a policeman, he is considerably more plausible than Doyle's Holmes, and that's never stopped us loving the Baker Street sleuth. *Death in Holy Orders* represents something of a challenge from James to her critics, taking on all the contentious elements and rigorously re-invigorating them. She had admitted that she was finding it increasingly difficult to find new plots for Dalgleish, and the locale here (a theological college on a lonely stretch of the East Anglian coast) turns out to be an inspired choice: we're presented with the enclosed setting so beloved of golden age detective writers, and James is able to incorporate her theological interests seamlessly into the plot – but never in any doctrinaire way; the non-believer is never uncomfortable. The body of a student at the college is found on the shore, suffocated by a fall of sand. Dalgleish is called upon to re-examine the verdict of accidental death (which the student's father would not accept). Having visited the College of St Anselm in his boyhood, he finds the investigation has a strong nostalgic aspect for him. But that is soon overtaken by the realisation that he has encountered the most horrific case of his career, and another visitor to the College dies a horrible death. As an exploration of evil – and as a piece of highly distinctive crime writing – this is James at her nonpareil best. Dalgleish, too, is rendered with new dimensions of psychological complexity.

Eve Tan Gee

The Earthquake Bird by Susanna Jones
Pan 0 333 48501
Where many a novelist is content these days

to merely sketch in a few rudimentary characteristics for their protagonists, it's refreshing to encounter a book as ambitious as Susanna Jones' remarkable thriller *The Earthquake Bird*, which has no truck with such cursoriness. The central character in Jones' novel, Lucy Fly, is not only realised with richness and subtlety, the reader is even allowed to change their mind about her as the revelations of the tale unfold – a rarity indeed these days. Not only that, Jones' book (her debut novel) is concisely written, making the amount she crams into this slim volume even more striking. Set in Japan, *The Earthquake Bird* begins with an earth tremor on its first page that echoes metaphorically through the book. Lucy is a young and insecure translator straining to survive in the bustling, impersonal city of Tokyo. She becomes the principal suspect in

THE
EARTHQUAKE
A Novel of Mystery   BIRD
SUSANNA JONES

a murder case when her best friend Lily is killed. Initially, her dealings with the police present her as vulnerable and ill at ease (she has a quirky way of talking about herself in the third person), but revelations about her past begin to pull the metaphorical rug from beneath the reader's feet. Jones' publishers invoke Iain Banks' *The Wasp Factory* in promoting the book, and the comparisons are not far-fetched. Like Banks' disturbing novel, the revelations here really do take the breath away (and it will take the most percipient of readers to anticipate them), but there's more on offer than complex storytelling. Principally, this is a study of the mysteries of human character, and the ambiguity with which Lucy is presented has all of the skill that distinguishes the brilliant novels of Iris Murdoch. Tokyo, too, is evoked with masses of intriguing detail, and acts as the perfect backdrop for the steadily unfolding narrative.

Vic Buckner

A Bicycle Built For Murder
by Kate Kingsbury
Berkley Prime Crime, $5.99, 0 425 17856 0
Although this book's title suggests that it is set in the 1920s, Elizabeth Hartleigh-Compton is in fact struggling to keep her English manor house running smoothly during WWII. She is hindered by the arrival of American GIs who wish to commandeer the house as headquarters while stationed in the village of Sitting Marsh. The Americans may bring nylons and cigarettes with them but they also bring problems, and when a local girl is murdered the villagers are eager to turn on the soldiers as scapegoats. Elizabeth is the only one prepared to look beyond local prejudice to discover the truth.

This is a new series by Kate Kingsbury, known for her mysteries set in the Edwardian Pennyfoot hotel. She has moved on several decades, but the hallmarks of previous series are still there – female heroine, romantic interest with an 'unsuitable' man, stereotypical village characters and baffled English constables. It is a book that is clearly written for an American market who may wish to think that the only things English people worried about during the war were the shortage of petrol and the fact that women had started to wear trousers. In fact despite Elizabeth's often expressed feminism and her interest in detective work "she often thought how wonderful it must have been to live in an age when women were cherished and pampered… she would never be seen in public without a decent frock and hat" (despite riding a motorbike!) The

FIRST IN A NEW SERIES

A BICYCLE BUILT FOR MURDER

A MANOR HOUSE MYSTERY

KATE KINGSBURY

characters and the plot are superficial, the evocation of wartime England sketchy and the murderer obvious. This is a book best described as a piece of popcorn reading for those times when one's brain doesn't want to work too hard!

Anne Curry

Hunting Humans by Elliot Leyton
Penguin Books, £4.99, 0 14 011687 7
Elliot Leyton is a Canadian anthropologist and considered to be one of the most widely consulted experts on serial killing. His works are apparently set books for murder detectives. But they are written in good English with no special knowledge required and will be of great interest to crime readers. In *Hunting Humans* he considers in detail the cases of four serial killers: Edmund Kemper, Ted Bundy, Albert De Salvo (The Boston Strangler) and David Berkovitz (The Son of Sam) plus two 'spree killers': Charles Starkweather and Mark Essex. He tries to answer why the US produces proportionately more of them than any other industrial nation. There have been about 100 serial killers in the USA since 1945, mostly in the 1970s and 1980s: fifty have been caught and twelve of those have attempted to provide some explanation of their actions. To say they are mentally ill, says Leyton, would be to "banish guilt beyond our responsibility". In fact they rarely display the cluster of readily identifiable clinical symptoms of mental illness. Contrary to current belief, Leyton is also sceptical of the claims of forensic psychology for its inability to predict an individual's potential for future violence or even diagnose a condition. Again, contrary to modern myth, he found that only a minority of them

had been abused in childhood but many were illegitimate, adopted or institutionalised in juvenile homes. It is in social conditions that the answer can be found rather than abuse, psychiatric or psychological explanations. "The major homicidal form of the modern era is the man who straddles the border between the upper working class and the lower middle class… More commonly, however, they punish those above them in the system – preying on unambiguously middle-class figures such as university women". He also questions society's priorities: "compare the tiny and short-term resources allocated to hunting multiple murderers with the huge sums allocated by the state for monitoring of political dissidents (the FBI ran 300 major operations in 1983, and its budget for undercover work alone in 1984 was $12.5 million). Nothing comparable is given to the police." Elliot Leyton's books, include *Men of Blood: Murder in Modern England*, also published by Penguin, examining why there are so comparatively few homicides in this country.

Martin Spellman

Bleak Midwinter by Peter Millar
Bloomsbury, £9.99, 0 7475 4835 8
Peter Millar's *Stealing Thunder* was a debut of considerable power and invention: a thriller much enriched by its carefully researched historical detail. The second novel is, of course, the post at which many a writer has fallen, but *Bleak Midwinter* is even more accomplished than its predecessor, with its scarifying picture of plague breaking out in Oxford. Two weeks before Christmas, Rajiv, a trainee doctor at an Oxford hospital, find himself dealing with a patient whose rare symptoms remind him of his native India and a disease he recog-

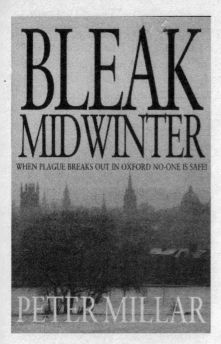

Deviant Ways by Chris Mooney
Simon & Schuster, £10, 0 743 2923 0

While Mooney's persuasive and edgy thriller may recycle familiar elements from the now overcrowded serial killer genre, it does so with imagination and invention. After all, there are now so many dogged cops with fragile private lives stalking (and being stalked by) grimly ingenious psychotics, it's impossible to avoid certain ideas popping up again and again. The real question remains: can an author make the material seem fresh? Largely speaking, Mooney pulls off the trick with real panache, and his troubled FBI profiler hero, Jack Casey, is a very plausible protagonist, even if his struggle with a life shattered by an earlier encounter with a psychopath is one we know well from many another thriller. His nemesis is The Sandman, a terrifyingly prescient madman who is slaughtering not just one individual at a time, but whole families and

nises as bubonic plague. Europe has been safe since the Black Death killed one third of the population centuries ago, but chaos may be about to reign once more. An American history student sneaks into the hospital to find out more about the patient, and soon a female reporter for a local newspaper is involved. The reader is quickly caught in a two-pronged attack by Millar: will it be possible to contain the secret as more and more people learn about it? And (more significantly) could the bacteria have been accidentally awakened from its dormant state? As before, Millar utilises the past in a particularly felicitous counterpoint to his modern narrative (the entire population of a small village died in the winter of 1348-49 and this is significant for the modern narrative), while his protagonists are a powerfully characterised group.

Ralph Travis

whole neighbourhoods. His method is explosives (shades of the Oklahoma bombings), and he knows quite as much about Jack Casey as he does about his well-researched victims – particularly how to really twist the knife in his FBI opposite number. Mooney kicks off with a joltingly orchestrated prelude, and the simmering threat of appalling violence keeps the reader transfixed throughout. Unless you've a serious case of serial killer fatigue, this is definitely one for the shopping list.

Judith Gray

Listen to the Silence by Marcia Muller
Women's Press, 0 7043 4672 9
Private eye Sharon McCone is taking a break to attend a wedding when a phone call tells her that her father has died. He has left instructions that she should clear out his

papers, and while doing so she is devastated to discover documents showing she was adopted as a baby. Unable to get answers from her adoptive mother, she decides that she will turn her detective skills to good use and track down her natural parents. The trail leads to an Indian reservation and Sharon discovers that the mystery of her birth is not the only secret there. She is advised to listen to the silences left when people are trying to keep secrets from others. Although the book is well written and anyone who has read previous Sharon McCone novels will be fascinated to see her discovering new aspects of her past, one should be aware that this is not a standard detective novel. It is more an exploration of Sharon's feelings as she comes to terms with the fact that everything about her childhood was founded on a lie which her parents maintained for years. She believes that only by finding her birth parents can she resolve her confusion, and, since this drives her actions in the book, helping to resolve the crimes on the reservation takes second place. Although the mystery is linked with her parents, the solution is revealed without Sharon's help as she stumbles into the middle of it by mistake. Readers expecting a typical Sharon McCone private eye novel will be disappointed, but readers wishing to know more about what makes McCone the person she is will be gripped by the story of her emotional journey chronicled in this book.

Anne Curry

The Skin Palace by Jack O'Connell
No Exit Press, £9.99, 1 901982 29 7
A welcome reprinting of the third novel by one of the most challenging crime writers around. After the immense promise of his

first novel, *Box Nine*, and a backslide of sorts in the less challenging *Wireless*, this was the book which demarcated the wide boundaries of O'Connell's writing. If it is not as successful as the brilliant *Word Made Flesh* that followed it, *The Skin Palace* merits consideration on its own terms. The key to the book is the business card of Jakob Kinsky, the son of one of the leading gangsters in Quinsigamond, O'Connell's meta-fictional Worcester, Massachusetts. Jakob wants to be a filmmaker, and his card reads 'Hyperreal noir for our entropic world'. As if to reinforce the point, O'Connell uses a quote from the master of entropy, Thomas Pynchon, to adorn one section of the book. It's as if O'Connell's aim is to find a stasis for all his gangsters, pornographers, artists, and moral crusaders, within his imaginary city's hermetically controlled environment. Para-

doxically, O'Connell's best writing is in the personal. Jakob and the other main character, Sylvie, are both searchers, and their mundane inner struggles are what keep the narrative moving as the bodies pile up in the outside world. In a sense, the difference between this book and *Word Made Flesh* is that in the latter O'Connell was able to bring the same sort of power to bear on the mechanics of the world itself. It's impossible to write about O'Connell without making comparisons, but I think the one that works best after four novels is to Don DeLillo, who also uses elements of genre fiction, and also seems to follow in some of Pynchon's fictional footsteps. I thought *Word Made Flesh* was one of the best American novels of the 1990s. If *The Skin Palace* isn't quite at that level, it's still interesting to see where O'Connell was going, and how he got there.

Michael Carlson

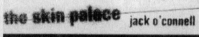

'Jack O'Connell is the future of the dark, literary suspense novel' – *James Ellroy*

Potshot by Robert B Parker
John Murray, £16.99, 0 7195 6284 8
I'm not sure why crime writers are so busy rewriting westerns these days – George Pelecanos did it after writing seven previous novels in two series. *Potshot* is the thirty-first novel featuring Boston private eye Spenser; but, just to keep busy, Robert Parker writes two other series at the same time. Spenser's previous, *Hugger Mugger*, saw him cracking wise in Georgia, where he dropped into the middle of a Tennessee Williams play. This time the setting is Californian desert, and Spenser re-enacts *The Magnificent Seven*. His seven includes long-term sidekick and straightman Hawk, and definitely un-straight man Tedy Sapp, the world's toughest gay bouncer who debuted in *Hugger Mugger*. Along with recurring Boston hitman Vinnie

A SPENSER NOVEL

ROBERT B. PARKER

POTSHOT

READ BY
JOE MANTEGNA

UNABRIDGED

daughter in *The Scarlet Letter*, in case you only read crime). We can only assume Spenser, Hawk, Susan, et al. actually age in dog years. It's all light-hearted violent fun. Spenser may occupy the hard-boiled end of the detective spectrum, but, for the second book in a row, the femme fatale walks at the end. Maybe as you get older you become more susceptible to their charms. Maybe that's why he seems irresistible. Spenser may seem to work a world away from the cozy English style, yet we've seen him out-quote English professors in Harvard Square, and in this book he quotes from, among others, Marvell, Frost and Wallace Stevens. Take that, Adam Dalgleish!

Michael Carlson

Eager to Please by Julie Parsons
Macmillan, £10, 0 333 72990 0
Many readers are admirers of the kind of crime narrative in which the central character is a police inspector or private detective. But the most cutting emotional insights are to be found in the crime novels in which the protagonists are ordinary people caught up in events that transform (or even destroy) their lives. And these books most closely rival serious literature in depth and psychological penetration. Minette Walters has made a speciality of this field, and it's hardly surprising that she is an enthusiastic backer of Julie Parsons, whose *Eager to Please* is one of the most astringent and involving entries in this field in many a year. Parsons has demonstrated her skills before in such powerfully-wrought books as *Mary, Mary* and *The Courtship Gift*, but the new book demonstrates that her writing has acquired a rich new dimension of complexity and authority. Her protagonist, Rachel Beckett,

Morris come three other blasts from the past, two of whom, appropriately enough for the story, are Bobby Horse and Chullo, Indian and Mexican LA gangsters. All these guys are drawn to Spenser because of his toughness, his adherence to the manly code, and his terrible sense of humour. A man's got to do what a man's got to do, even if, in Spenser's case, he must be seventy years old. I'm serious. Ageing characters are a problem exacerbated when the author reminds us of it, as Parker does when Spenser and Hawk actually reminisce about the Korean War. Yet given the way Spenser moves, and the way young women keep throwing themselves at him, it's hard to visualise a man much over, say, fifty-five. The only character who actually shows her age is Pearl the Wonder Dog, surrogate child for Spenser and Susan Silverman (Pearl was the name of Hester Prynne's illegitimate

has been in prison for twelve years for the murder of her husband Martin – and has spent the time protesting her innocence. The greatest torment for her has been the knowledge that another woman has raised her daughter Amy, and that (at the age of seventeen) Amy wants to cut all ties with her biological mother. When Rachel is freed, she has a single agenda: to revenge herself on her brother-in-law Daniel, who she claims fired the shot that killed her husband. As a picture of an obsessed heroine, *Eager to Please* would be hard to beat, particularly as Parsons cleverly balances the two fixed ideas in her heroine's mind: the resentment at having her much-loved child taken from her, and the sense of burning injustice at being in prison for a crime she didn't commit. Rachel is a complex and multifaceted character, and as the revelations of the plot continue to pull the ground from beneath the reader's feet, the pleasures of

the novel grow ever richer. The author is sharp, too, on the Dublin locales, which are atmospherically created, and the remorseless energy of the heroine (even though, at times, she's hard to like) makes this an exemplary thriller, delivered with real style.

Vic Buckner

Protect and Defend

by Richard North Patterson
Hutchinson, £16.99/£9.99, 0 09 179408 0
In his last two novels, Richard North Patterson has combined classic crime and suspense elements with politics. In *Dark Lady* it was the politics and corruption of city construction and drugs, and in *No Safe Place* it was potential presidential candidate Kerry Kilcannon, a lightly-disguised Bobby Kennedy clone, being stalked by a sniper motivated by the 'right to life' movement. The political elements of Kilcannon's story were far more

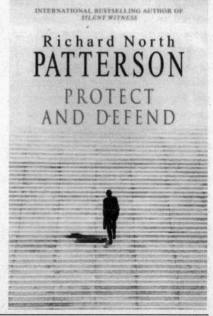

interesting than the stalking, and now Kilcannon is back, as President of the United States, in a novel that dispenses with a crime template and is what used to be called a political thriller, specifically in the tradition of *Advise and Consent*. And it holds up that tradition well. Kilcannon nominates Caroline Masters as Chief Justice of the Supreme Court, and the fight for her nomination soon becomes a political bloodbath. A high-profile appeal against a law prohibiting late-term abortions is filed by a lawyer who once clerked for Masters, and who remains her friend; the plaintiff is a fifteen year old carrying a hydrocephalic foetus, whose father is an anti-abortion leader. The two stories – Mary Ann Tierney's fight for an abortion and Kilcannon's fight to get Masters approved by the Senate – run side by side, and become more entwined as we learn most of the principles have secrets of their own, which they would prefer to remain secret. But the Christian right has its own file of dirt, and isn't above using it to smear. Patterson keeps this moving engrossingly; he's at his best when he can put words in the mouths of unappetising characters, and put his heroes on the spot. The legal story bogs down somewhat in appeal, and the political story stalls at just the point it needs most to speed up, but Patterson pulls it together nicely. Kilcannon's friend and possible presidential opponent, Chad Palmer, has the secret whose revelation leads to the key events of the finish. It requires a little bit of melodrama, but in the context of personal lives being torn apart for political purposes, it works. What is more strange is Patterson's own politics. Both Kilcannon and Palmer are what Americans call 'moderates', which basically means men of conscience and compassion devoid of politi-

cal philosophy. But the real heroes of this book are Robert Bork, the failed Supreme Court nominee, who insisted on principle that all law had to be made from the minds of eighteenth century men, and Clarence Thomas, the mediocrity whose nomination was opposed for all the wrong reasons and who has been proven a legal clown on the Court. Patterson's last two books were dedicated to George Bush père, and he seems to believe that a kinder, gentler right wing is the political ideal. This book was published before the Supreme Court's 5-4 vote to make Shrub Bush president, after the election tampered with and fixed by his brother. Even Chad Palmer and Kerry Kilcannon might have trouble with that one.

Michael Carlson

The Big Blowdown by George P Pelecanos

The
Big
Blowdown
George
P.
Pelecanos

Serpents Tail, 1 85242 738 8

Perhaps it's a cunning marketing ploy by Serpents Tail, but the copy I got had the last forty-odd pages at the beginning. Maybe they know too many hard-pressed reviewers tricks but they needn't have bothered – Pelecanos is very good and this is possibly his best. It's the first of the 'DC Quartet': the other three are *King Suckerman, The Sweet Forever* and *Shame the Devil* – in that order. Strangely, this is the last to be published. In chronicling DC's massive social change through the second half of the century, Pelecanos writes about the Washington that others don't, the other side of the tracks, the underbelly. Pelecanos says that *The Big Blowdown* especially is trying to give a voice to the Greek immigrants of his youth and to get away from the perception, the cliché, of the smiling Greek guy with the big moustache and so on. A lot of *The Big Blowdown* is based on real stories known to Pelecanos since he was a child. The whole first section through the war is his father's story. That all happened to him. This – and the rest of the book – is a completely authentic picture of a slice of American history as Pelecanos lived it. This is hard-boiled, thoughtful, working-class literature. The radical shift in culture after thirty years interested Pelecanos. In *The Big Blowdown,* blacks are basically invisible. In *King Suckerman*, young people are trying to check out each other's culture. In retrospect, of course, it didn't work. *King Suckerman* is the end of the party. *The Sweet Forever* is where you see that it didn't work, society hitting bottom. Then the final book in the quartet – *Shame the Devil* – is about real crimes, about some sort of ending to it all. To top it all, it is a cracking tale – of love, friendship, honour and redemp-tion. Those last forty pages – even at the start – blow you away. A true and lasting voice from another world made real and relevant by a great writer.

Peter Walker

Blue Lonesome by Bill Pronzini
Canongate Crime, £9.99, 1 84195 130 7
Bill Pronzini's first British publication is long overdue. Author of more than fifty novels, Pronzini deserves the exposure that the appearance of this excellent novel is likely to bring him. Jim Messenger is an ordinary guy bordering on the boring – indeed his college sweetheart wife left him after only seven months of marriage because the accountant was as staid as they come. Eating in the Harmony Cafe, alone and lonely, Jim notices a fellow diner who seems to him to bear the

BILL PRONZINI

BLUE LONESOME

same bitter marks of life's blows as he does. He begins to change his schedule to make sure that he regularly sees Ms Blue Lonesome, going back to the cafe most nights to eat at the same time as she does. After several months, over which time his fascination has grown to something deeper, Jim summons up the courage to approach Ms Blue. His attempt at conversation is forcefully, rudely, rebuffed. And then Ms Blue stops coming. Jim is disturbed, and perturbed by his own reaction to this stranger's disappearance. Initial investigations lead Jim to find out that Ms Blue had adopted a false name and then killed herself. Who was she? Why did she do such a thing? And why is this all so important to Jim? Pronzini's book is a perfectly formed, although never formulaic, tightly structured piece of work, which is also beautifully and clearly written. And jazz-loving Messenger is a sympathetic and quietly brave hero whose gentle existentialist crisis – or rather stutter – gives rise to an almost inevitable chain of events played out in a small, American backwater painted from the archetypal noir palette. The relationships in the book are drawn with perfection and the pacing is exquisite. Pronzini is a fine talent and this is a terrific novel.

Mark Thwaite

The Falls

Ian Rankin

The Falls by Ian Rankin
Orion, 0 75282 130 X
Success has a price, and the remarkable acclaim (both critical and commercial) that greeted the gritty Edinburgh-set crime novels of Ian Rankin has set the author a considerable problem. How does he maintain the freshness of detail and atmosphere that has made his books such riveting reading? And how does he keep his tough detective DI John Rebus from degenerating into a series of mannerisms? If Raymond Chandler grew tired of Philip Marlowe and Conan Doyle of Holmes, Rankin would have been in good company if he gave up on Rebus. Fortunately, his belief in the character clearly remains as powerful as ever, and *The Falls* is the most impressive Rebus novel in many a moon, in which the detective's personal problems – overused of late – are wisely sidelined in order to concentrate on a highly intriguing (and topical) plot. When a student vanishes in Edinburgh, there is pressure on Rebus to find her, particularly as she is the scion of a family of extremely rich bankers. Needless to say, this is more than just the case of a spoilt rich girl breaking out of the cage of family responsibilities, and a carved wooden doll in a coffin found in her home village leads Rebus to the Internet role-playing game that she

was involved in. And when DC Siobhan Clarke, a key member of Rebus' team, tackles the Virtual Quizmaster, Rankin finds himself struggling to save her from the same fate as the missing girl. Consummate plotting has always been Rankin's trademark, and that skill is put to maximum use here. The balance between developing the characterisation of the ill-assorted team of coppers that Rebus assembles and the labyrinthine twists of the plot is maintained with an iron hand, and Rankin's mordant eye remains as keen as ever.

Eve Tan Gee

The Watchman by Chris Ryan
Century, £15.99, 0 7126 8416 6
Readers of Chris Ryan thrillers know exactly what to expect: gritty, pared-down prose with regular doses of bone-crunching action and a hero not usually given to introspection. His books do not inhabit the same

Chris Ryan

atmospheric world as such thriller writers of the past as Graham Greene and Eric Ambler, and he lacks the political sophistication of such current writers as Gerald Seymour. But Ryan knows exactly what his readers want, and can always be counted upon to deliver a tough and fast-moving package. The theme here is a duel to the death between an SAS soldier and the man who trained him. Ryan's protagonist, Alex, has been recently commissioned from the ranks, and returns from a hostage rescue mission in Sierra Leone to find that someone has been gruesomely murdering MI5 officers, Hannibal Lecter-style (a skinning knife is involved). The security services believe that the killer is an insider, SAS-trained, and Alex is ordered to track him down. And as he gets closer and closer to the eponymous Watchman, the body count rises implacably. This one will glean no literary prizes, but bookshop tills throughout the country will be ringing just as merrily as they were for *The Hit List* and *Zero Option*.

Barry Forshaw

Holding the Zero by Gerald Seymour
Corgi, £5.99, 0 552 14666 8
Gerald Seymour has travelled to many a
war-torn battlefield in his former career as a
reporter for ITN – Cyprus, South Vietnam
and Pakistan to name but three. His bestselling debut novel *Harry's Game* capitalised
on his knowledge of terrorism in Northern
Ireland and since then his experiences in
various different arenas of war have
informed his writing. This authenticity has
lifted his books head and shoulders above
the crop of wannabe action thrillers, and his
latest novel, *Holding the Zero*, is no exception. The book concerns amateur marksman
Gus Peake who is drawn by a family debt
into a bloody war between Sadam Hussein
and Kurdish guerrillas. The guerrillas want
to reach their old city of Kirkuk, and it's
Gus's job to help them by picking off con-
cealed enemy targets. But despite his accuracy and efficiency, it's a war he's not properly equipped to fight, and with Iraqi sniper
Karim Aziz on his tail it looks as if the odds
are stacked well and truly against him.
Holding the Zero is a doorstop of a book,
jammed with convincing detail and believable characters. Seymour's skill in bringing
to life the complex manoeuvrings of two
rival factions should never be underestimat-
ed. And it's to his credit that he never forgets the human side of warfare either –
individual people with their own unique
agendas punctuate this fast-paced narrative.
Ultimately, though, it boils down to two
men – Peake and Aziz – in a cold-blooded
duel to the death. Memorable stuff.

Mark Campbell

HOLDING THE ZERO
SEYMOUR
From the bestselling author of *A LINE IN THE SAND*

In the Midnight Hour by Michelle Spring
Orion, £16.99, 0 75282 480 5
In the Midnight Hour opens with a brief
vignette: father and son, the one an explor-
er, the other still an infant, exploring
together the tempestuous cliffs and deserted sands of the Norfolk coast. Thrilling to
the mysterious pull of the faraway, beyond
the horizon. Barely two and a half pages
long, the prologue crackles with tension,
foreshadowing the terrible events that follow. The boy vanishes from the beach and,
twelve years later, his mother is convinced
that she has found him busking on the
streets of Cambridge. Laura Principal is
called in to discover the past of the boy, and
to protect Olivia Cable from this quiet and
troubled child who may or may not be her
son, Timmy. The themes of motherhood and
loss resonate throughout this novel. Laura is
a sympathetic and well-rounded character;
she has close friends, a family she loves – she

A LAURA PRINCIPAL INVESTIGATION

MICHELLE SPRING

IN THE MIDNIGHT HOUR

Laura Principal is Britain's hottest woman private eye.
Val McDermid

lives; her investigations may lay the ghost forever, or uncover new torments, more difficult to face than the original catastrophe.

Margaret Murphy

The Canary Thief by Kate Stacey
Piatkus, £8.99, 0 749932 04 X
In the sleepy suburban town of Righton, young runaway Jacob stumbles on a murdered prostitute. The police investigate, but draw a blank. Then another murder occurs – another prostitute – and this body too is discovered by Jacob. Now the police have something more concrete to work on, and it looks as if a secretive organisation of prostitutes is implicated in the crimes. Meanwhile the boy, now looking after the second prostitute's baby, is being held in the clutches of a decidedly sinister old lady and her villainous son. Kate Stacey's debut crime novel cannot decide whether it's Agatha Christie

The Canary Thief
A PITCH-BLACK CRIME DEBUT

KATE STACEY

even has a lover – and these aspects of her life are woven into the narrative, enriching the storyline and providing insights into Laura's present feelings and past experience. Laura is intrigued by the relationships within the Cable family: the proud and protective presence of Jack Cable's brother-in-law, Max, and the faint whiff of resentment from Jack's nephew, Robin. Timmy's older sister, Catherine, is angry and defensive; is she harbouring some guilty secret? She was playing on the cliffs the day her brother vanished. Does she know more about Timmy's disappearance than she is prepared to say? An unidentified sinister presence flits in the shadows, malevolent and destructive, determined not to allow the truth to be known. Gradually Laura is drawn into the tragedy that has blighted so many or Patricia Cornwall. She populates her fictional town with gossiping curtain-twitchers, cane-wielding headmasters and friendly café owners who give small boys free breakfasts. A product of the rose-tinted 1950s (the soundtrack to *Heartbeat* should accompany the book), it comes then as something of a surprise to discover her contemporary referencing of Darth Maul and Hannibal Lector. The characterisation is generally acceptable, although the supposed protagonist – black policeman Sebastian Lawson – is bland and incompetent to the point where it stretches credulity. At one point he forgets he has a prime suspect locked up in the police station's cells – doh! The titular character of Jacob comes across the strongest, and it seems that Stacey poured more energy into him than all the other characters combined. The plot, like the characterisation, is adequate, although at times I had trouble following the various twists. But what disappointed me most in this book was the unskilled writing. Clichéd, formulaic and naïve, Stacey's dialogue is patently unrealistic and her similes comically absurd (at one point, a billowing lace curtain is likened to a pit pony being released after months underground!). If Stacey can fine-tune her prose, her next book should prove more rewarding.

Mark Campbell

Death of a Pooh-Bah by Karen Sturges
Bantam Books, $5.99, 0 553 58131 7
Phoebe Mullins, the widow of a famous American conductor, has gone to Massachusetts to visit an estranged aunt. In view of her past stage experience, she is asked to help with the local dramatic society's production of Gilbert and Sullivan's operetta *The Mikado*. She soon discovers that the man playing Pooh-Bah (the Lord High Everything Else) is a perfect piece of casting – he is rude, lustful and pompous, and has managed to offend all of the rest of the cast members. It is no surprise when he is murdered and, no matter that it may be a case of the punishment fitting the crime, Phoebe decides to investigate, an act which puts her own life in danger. This novel is fascinating reading for people who are familiar with *The Mikado*. Those who are not will still find the book enjoyable but will miss out on some of the subtle in-jokes used by the author. Phoebe is an engaging older heroine who has to deal with difficult situations including the appearance of a young woman claiming to be her late husband's illegitimate daughter and a possible romance with

A Music Lover's Mystery
Death of a Pooh-Bah

"*Phoebe Mullins is a sleuth to cherish.*"
—Carolyn Hart

KAREN STURGES

one of the suspects. Because the character is so well written the book never descends into the type of bathos or schmaltz often seen in American novels and movies. Although this novel does not fit into the hard-boiled genre, the author has given Phoebe enough guts and self-confidence to keep our interest in her going until the final chapter. This is the second book in the 'Music Lover's Mystery' series, following *Death of a Baritone*, and I look forward to future novels by Karen Sturges with interest.

Anne Curry

Shirker by Chad Taylor
Canongate Crime, £5.99, 1 84195 119 6
Chad Taylor's third novel *Shirker*, set in present-day Auckland, attempts to combine supernatural thriller and whodunit with his undoubted skills as a writer. Sadly, for a number of reasons, Taylor just does not manage to pull it off. Ellerslie Penrose, a broker of some unspecified kind, is late for an important business meeting: the alleyway leading to the hotel where he is heading has been cordoned off and a crime seems to have occurred. Penrose notices a wallet on the ground, picks it up and moves to the police line. On showing it he is allowed through to a murder scene. The policeman has unwittingly presumed that Penrose has flashed ID and he finds himself discussing the gruesome spectacle in front of him with the investigating officer in charge, Tangiers. Capriciously Penrose keeps the wallet and finds himself drawn into an investigation of the murder of Tad Ash, an antiques dealer brutally killed in a glass recycling bin. Tad had found a diary, attempted to secure a publisher for it, and suffered the awful consequences. Penrose's

enquiries lead him to discover that the writer of the diary, born over a century ago in 1874, is still very much alive and fanatical about his privacy. Where Taylor's book fails is in its characterisation – we never feel that we get to know Penrose nor the novels' other supporting players. Despite the excellently written endpiece, where Penrose reprises his involvement in the bizarre affair, we don't ever really feel that close to him. Penrose's search for the villain of the piece doesn't seem to change him, and nor do we get a good insight into why the affair is obsessing him so much. Whilst the murderer is a constant presence in the book we do not get a full sense of his real motives. And the supernatural air that runs throughout the book, whilst on occasion adding tension, and sometimes confusion, bestows lit-

tle of substance to the plot. *Shirker* is a decently-paced, sometimes nicely-styled, well-constructed work, but not one that is ever demanding, invigorating or compelling enough to keep you up into the wee hours.

Mark Thwaite

Previous Convictions by Simon Temprell
Macmillan, £9.99, 0 333 90558 X
For years Jackie had been a housebound carer, until finally she fed arsenic to her mother and got rid of *that* nuisance. In her lonely TV-dominated existence, Jackie had developed a morbid crush on dashing Chip Freeman, star of Home Shopping Channel. Although she hadn't actually met Chip, he was her brother-in-law, married to Cherry, a dancer with The Next Generation back in the 1970s, but now an out-of-touch recluse. Cherry had always known what Jackie – and Chip's

adoring female audience – would now discover, that Chip was homosexual. Chip is outed when he acquires a handsome but gold-digging boyfriend Aidan, long-term boyfriend of the charming Edward, whose only consolation becomes his own long-unrequited love for his apparently heterosexual business partner Reuben. Jackie is so disconcerted by the news that she determines to slaughter Chip – practising first by murdering a loutish neighbour who drops in from time to time for mutually appreciated rough sex. Although she tries not to make a mistake, of course she does. Cherry, at this point, comes out of a twenty-five-year decline and picks up a toy boy. And Jackie, having got away with her murders so far, decides to do away with any other faggots who annoy. You'll have gathered that *Previous Convictions* is a comedy. It's dark, fairly outrageous, camp – and in its best moments, surprisingly tender – even if the author cannot resist ensuring that every single male character discovers that where sex is concerned, bum is best. Promoted as a camp crime shocker, its tender moments work best.

Russell James

Charles Willeford Titles from No Exit Press

The Woman Chaser
£6.99, 1 84243 001 7

Wild Wives/The High Priest of California
£7.99, 1 84243 003 3

Miami Blues
£6.99, 1 84243 009 2

New Hope for the Dead
£6.99, 1 84243 010 6
Comparisons are always misleading, but if

you haven't read Charles Willeford yet the best way of convincing you of what you're missing would be to have you imagine what it would be like if Jim Thompson had kept writing through the 1980s and produced Elmore Leonard novels. Willeford was both writers wrapped up in one. These reissues from No Exit Press cover both phases of Willeford's work, and neither should be missed. Though modern paperbacks can't recapitulate that wonderful sense of sleaze which the skinny original editions of Willeford's books, with their steamy covers, conveyed. *Wild Wives* and *The High Priest of California* are done up in Ace Double format, back to back, a rare reminder of the joys of getting two cheap thrills for the price of one. Willeford came late to pocket noir, but his vision was, if anything, even more bleak than Thompson's. Where Thompson's prose style is made by its subconscious associations, as what is below the surface fights its way to the top, Willeford's is consciously full of sarcasm and knowing innuendo. The selling of sex as a commodity, and commodity as motivation, is right there on the surface in all of Willeford's early pulp. *High Priest*'s Russell Haxby is a character right out of one of Philip K Dick's mainstream novels. Like Dick, Willeford sees right through the glitz and pretence of the fun in the sun, all the way down to the core of free market corruption that lies at the heart of the American Dream. It's still there when Willeford moves to Florida in his Hoke Moseley novels. These are the 1980s flip side of *Miami Vice*, Elmore Leonard without the glitz. *Miami Blues* remains the best known, because of George Armitage's decent film adaptation featuring a brilliant performance by Fred Ward as Hoke, missing dentures and all, but *New*

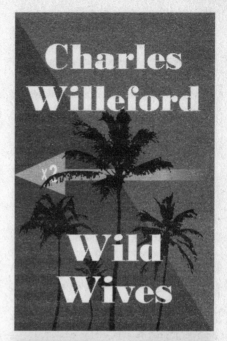

Hope for the Dead may be the best. It features a femme fatale who Hoke corrals mostly because of where she sticks her finger when they're having sex. It doesn't get much more manipulative, more down and dirty than that. And Hoke, for all his simplicity, turns out to be just as slick as Russell Haxby when it comes to getting the things he needs. Just who is seducing whom is the question Willeford always seems to be asking, and it's us, the readers, who are generally the ones really being seduced.

Michael Carlson

Winter Frost by R D Wingfield
Corgi, £5.99, 0 552 14778 8
Detective Inspector Jack Frost returns in this, the fifth book in R D Wingfield's excellent police procedural series. Here he's on the trail of a prostitute-killing serial killer and a murderous paedophile, all the while juggling Superintendent Mullett's whinging budget cuts and the various cock-ups of his incompetent Welsh sidekick 'Taffy' Morgan. Wingfield manages to pour so much into the frenetic narrative that the first 100 pages could have provided enough raw material for three novels from a lesser writer. But it's to his enormous credit that the action never seems contrived – humour and tragedy are uneasy bedfellows as Frost and his team cope with a seemingly endless stream of petty crimes and savage murders. The novel is littered with early morning post-mortems, gruesome 3am crime scenes and desolate wastelands. And all beautifully written. What impresses the reader most, though, is the sheer humanity of Frost. Here is a man who is sexist, racist and cynical in the extreme, and yet clearly on the side of good – just. Forget David Jason's cosy TV portrayal – this Frost is prone to lusting after sixteen year olds while berating people who feel the same about children only a few years younger. He's a man with shifting principles, irrational loyalties, guided by a sixth sense that invariably lets him down, stumbling blind in a world that clearly owes him no favours. He's a copper who has elevated straw-clutching to a high art. There's no logical trail of clues here – red herrings lie round every corner and the occasional step in the right direction is due to luck not design. Genuinely unputdownable, *Winter Frost* is probably the closest you'll ever get to life in the real police force. Infighting, corruption, office politics – it's almost scarier than the criminals they're after.

Mark Campbell

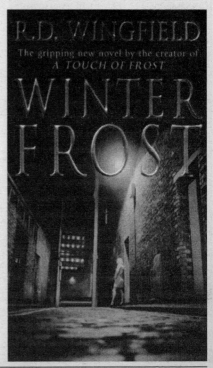

THE EARLY CELLULOID SLEUTHS

John Kennedy Melling

It wasn't many months after the first public showing of "movies" by the French Lumière Brothers that crime and detection appeared on the screens. As the nickname implies, the first films, all short and silent, were mainly movement – walls crashing down, trains rushing towards the terrified audiences, and horsemen led by Bronco Billy dashing across the screen – incidentally, do notice that horsemen riding westwards always go from audience right (or prompt side) to audience left – a fixed tradition.

Taking the first showings as 1898 we find George Meliès, former conjuror and inventor of cinematic spectacle, producing in 1899 a film 20 metres long, titled *Pickpocket et Policeman*, a comedic entrance for the drama, which seven years later was his 280 metres film *Incendaires* [sic]; another film had the strange title of *Le Crime de la rue du Cherche-midi a Quatorze Heures*! Charles Pathé engaged Ferdinand Zecca to produce *L'Histoire du'un Crime*. In 1908 Victorine Jasset produced *Les Aventures de Nick Carter*, a series of self-contained films. Years later Walter Pidgeon played Carter. In 1911 was first published the exploits of Fantomas in Feuilleton format, and just two years later Gaumont bought the film rights so in two years five books were filmed, including one, Le Mort Qui Tue which I bought in cartoon book form in Nice in 2000. Not to be outdone, Pathé produced Les Mystères de New York which was nothing else than the Pearl White serials, and in 1916 brought out another American serial Les Exploits d'Elaine, in which Craig Kennedy, Arthur B. Reeve's scientific detective, first appeared, proving a draw in subsequent American serials up to 1936.

It was America who first produced a Sherlock Holmes film – Sherlock Holmes Baffled in 1900 from American Mutoscope and Biograph Company – lasting 35 seconds – yes, seconds! (It was the original Mutoscope machine of flickering card pictures that coined the term "flicks" for films.) The Lone Wolf, Michael Lanyard, was first created by Louis Joseph Vance in 1914 in The Lone Wolf, and the first of a string of films featuring such heroes as Henry B. Walthall, Bert Lytell, from 1917 until the 1930s and 1940s when Francis Lederer, Warren William and Gerald Mohr donned the top hat and tails. Arsène Lupin, another gentleman-burglar, was created by Frenchman Maurice Leblanc in 1907 in a book with various titles including The Exploits of Arsène Lupin, but the first film came out in 1910 as Arsène Lupin vs Sherlock Holmes in one and two-reel series from Vitascope in Germany, six years before London films showed their 6,400 feet film Arsène Lupin. Arsène Lupin was a favourite on French television from 1971 till 1980, the latter year in which Fantomas had a brief television career. Germany produced the serials of English gentleman-detective Stuart Webbs; when the inventor Reicher

parted company with the producer Joe May, the latter created a new sleuth Joe Deebs. In Italy you didn't have film noir (taken from Serie Noire books) but the "yellow" films taken from the Romans Policiers published by Mondadori in yellow covers, starting in 1915.

Lady sleuths

The first lady detective was Ruth Roland in 1914-1915 in a series of shorts for Kalem. The list increases with the years until we get nine Torchy Blaine films from 1936 to 1939 mostly with wisecracking Glenda Farrell as Torchy. A shortlived series from Monogram was based on Kitty O'Day, three films in 1944 and 1945, with the last having a change of principals and cast names.

Husband and wife teams

Nick and Nora Charles in six MGM films between 1934 and 1947 with debonair William Powell (earlier one of the Philo Vance players) and Myrna Loy, once described by an American poet as brightening the way out of a grim Cotton Mather past. The Thin Man wasn't meant to be Powell, he was the missing inventor in Dashiell Hammet's only relevant title, The Thin Man. There were other teams. William Powell and Margaret Lindsay had starred in the 1933 aptly titled Private Detective. Joe and Garda Sloan in three MGM films in 1938 and 1939; Fast and Furious was Franchot Tone and Ann Sothern, Fast and Loose with Robert Montgomery and Rosalind Russell, and Fast Company with Melvyn Douglas and Florence Rice, all elegant, witty and sophisticated. England tried with Barry K. Barnes and Valerie Hobson, but the only two films were *This Man is News*, 1938, and *This Man in Paris*, the following year.

Two final thoughts

Two men can make a good sleuthing team as Jonathan Latimer proved with Bill Crane and his sidekick three of whose humorous books were filmed by Universal, *The Westland Case*, 1937 (*Headed for a Hearse*), *The Lady in the Morgue*, 1938, titled as the book, and *The Last Warning*, 1938, based on *The Dead Don't Care*, with Preston Foster and Frank Jenks. Hitchcock's British 1938 film *The Lady Vanishes* had the cricket devotees, Charters and Caldicott, portrayed by the new team of actors Basil Radford and Naunton Wayne, the well known cabaret artist. Radio and later films like *Crooks Tour* with glamorous Greta Gynti (a pun on the name Cooks' Tour) carried them on for years, not always as C and C. When I was Crime Book Reviewer for BBC Radio Essex, we all took part in Terry Wogan's *Save the Children* marathon. I wrote a parody of Charters and Caldicott which I broadcast with Barbara Miller and Michael Knowles, as a sign of respect. S. S. Van Dine and Monsignor Ronald Knox decreed the detective should not be the criminal. Private eye Dan Duryea was the villain in Paramount's 1949 *Manhandled* with Dorothy Lamour, based on L. S. Goldsmith's novel *The Man who Stole a Dream*. So there you are!

OBITUARY

Hélène de Monaghan

I have known Hélène for two decades, since a leading French newspaper in Belgium named her the best French writer for knowledge, elegance and accuracy. We corresponded and she agreed I should interview her for Jeff Myerson's lamented New York magazine *The Poisoned Pen*. Barbara Miller and I lunched with her and with her husband Patrice and daughter (the former child star in the classic Erich Rohmer 1970 film *Le Genou de Claire*) in their beautiful apartment in the prestigious Paris seventeenth *arrondissement*. Their daughter is now a barrister like her father and lives with her husband and children in a large chateau outside Paris. Hélène was a member of both the Paris and Casablanca Bars, wished to be an actress as a girl, wrote several plays which were performed in the Paris theatre and a string of crime and detective novels, mainly for Librairie des Champs-Élysées. She won the Prix de Roman d'Aventure in 1975. In 1997 she asked me to help her get published in England. I stayed with her and Patrice in 1999 to negotiate the contract and *Singleminded* was duly published by CT Publishing. Gwendoline Butler and I went for the day by Eurostar to lunch with them. Like her books she was witty, elegant, sophisticated, full of ingenious plots, and I was proud of her calling me 'her English family'.